Putting On the Ritz

ALSO BY
JOE KEENAN

Blue Heaven

Joe Keenan

PUTTING ON
THE RITZ

VIKING

VIKING
Published by the Penguin Group
Viking Penguin, a division of Penguin Books USA Inc.,
375 Hudson Street, New York, New York 10014, U.S.A.
Penguin Books Ltd, 27 Wrights Lane,
London W8 5TZ, England
Penguin Books Australia Ltd, Ringwood,
Victoria, Australia
Penguin Books Canada Ltd, 10 Alcorn Ave., Suite 300,
Toronto, Ontario, Canada M4V 3B2
Penguin Books (N.Z.) Ltd, 182–190 Wairau Road,
Auckland 10, New Zealand

Penguin Books Ltd, Registered Offices:
Harmondsworth, Middlesex, England

First published in 1991 by Viking Penguin,
a division of Penguin Books USA Inc.

3 5 7 9 8 6 4 2

Grateful acknowledgment is made for permission to reprint excerpts
from the following copyrighted works:
"They All Laughed" by George Gershwin and Ira Gershwin. © 1939, 1937 (renewed)
Chappell & Co. All rights reserved. Used by permission.
"Losing My Mind" by Stephen Sondheim. © 1971 Range Road Music Inc., Quartet Music
Inc. and Burthen Music Company, Inc.
"Let's Call the Whole Thing Off" by George Gershwin and Ira Gershwin. © 1936
Chappel & Co. (renewed). All rights reserved. Used by permission.
LIBRARY OF CONGRESS CATALOGING IN PUBLICATION DATA
Keenan, Joe.
Putting on the Ritz / Joe Keenan.
p.   cm.
ISBN 0-670-83877-2
I. Title.
PS3561.2363.P87   1991
813'.54—dc20   91–50161

Printed in the United States of America
Set in Bodoni

For
Geri Thoma

Acknowledgments

While I was writing this book a number of people were wonderfully helpful to me, offering advice, technical information, and much besides. I extend my sincere thanks to voice teacher extraordinaire Louise Warren Quinto; horticulturist Karen Fausch; crime adviser Walter Arsenault; computer mavens Eric Dehais, D. Fletcher, and Matthew Pimm; talk show survivor Charles Busch; Jordana Jakubovic and James Mc-Connell at the Rainbow Room; illustrator Daniel Torres; my editor, Ed Iwanicki; and, above all, Gerry Bernardi.

Putting On the Ritz

One

I've noticed over the years that Truly Bad Ideas, like flu strains named for Asian capitals, insidiously time their visits to occur during those periods when our defenses, reeling from some previous blow, are at their most tattered and flimsy. I see it all the time. Some friend or acquaintance who'd always seemed the very epitome of Reason will be jilted by his lover or passed over for a promotion, and the next time I see him he's talking about the marvelous career advice he's getting from his astrologer and would I like to buy some nutritional supplements? There are, of course, any number of crises capable of inducing this poignant tendency to grasp at straws. I can, however, say with some authority that few ordeals leave one half so limp and suggestible as the ordeal I had suffered a mere two weeks before my story begins. I refer to the spectacular and highly public demise of a musical play to which one has devoted the last three years of one's life.

The show, a cheeky satire of network television, was called *Here for the Season*. The book and lyrics were by me, and the music was by my longtime friend and collaborator, Claire Simmons.

Its failure, like that of most flops, was the end result of a whole series of dire miscalculations. If pressed, though, to name the one decision that really drove a stake through the thing's heart, it would be my agreement to accept as co-librettist our renowned director's twenty-four-year-old boyfriend.

Claire, whose radar at such times is more functional than my own, argued against it, but I felt that the script needed only minor changes and the youngster, who seemed amiable enough, was not seeking a dominant role so much as a ride on our coattails. This proved incorrect. We soon learned that our coauthor, far from being amiable, was a violently opinionated young man who, when contradicted, displayed a temper that called to mind Caligula with a toothache. To make matters worse, the director's only response to his paramour's screaming fits was to scream louder. If you want an idea of what our average rehearsal was like, rent a martial arts film and watch the last twenty minutes.

Chaos reigned. Actors quit and were replaced with inferior performers. Songs were cut, scenes came and went with dizzying speed, and the whole gossamer fabric of the show unraveled like a congressman's alibi.

The days following the show's closing, which coincided with its opening, were not happy ones. I soon discovered, as one does in these situations, that my friends, however sincerely fond of me, seemed to find my downfall a strangely agreeable spectacle. They phoned constantly, ostensibly to offer support but mainly to hear the grisly details and inform me of such venomous reviews as had escaped my attention. A typical call went like this:

CONCERNED FRIEND: (*cheerfully*) Hi, Philip! (*then, darkly*) How are you?
ME: I'm fine.
C. F.: I just want you to know I'm personally writing a letter to that Siswycz creep.
ME: *Siswycz?*
C. F.: Mark Siswycz. He reviews for *Avenue A*. You haven't seen it, then?
ME: I've never even heard of it.
C. F.: I guess they don't sell it up where you are. Well, I wouldn't worry—any critic *that* vicious must have problems of his own.
ME: I take it he didn't like us.
C. F.: Wait, I'll read it to you—

Now normally when my life begins to feel like an Edvard Munch painting sprung to life, I turn to my closest chums, Gilbert and Claire, and they rally round with inspirational slogans and cheap champagne. But, my little support system had, alas, broken down just when I needed it most.

Gilbert, to give him his due, spent the night after the closing with me, offering quiet sympathy while having pizzas delivered to the director's apartment. In the days since, however, he'd vanished from sight and was not returning calls. That left Claire.

Claire is normally one of those indomitable Mary Poppins sorts of women, who, faced with adversity, grit their teeth and think lovely thoughts. For a week or so after we closed she managed to put up a brave, sardonic front. But then the *Times* critic, trashing some other new musical, conceded that it at least lacked "the numbing incoherence" of *our* show, and Claire gave up, surrendering to that lush despair even the most stoic lady composer will feel when *The New York Times*, having buried her, returns a week later to dance on the grave.

Anyway, this should give you some idea of how pathetically susceptible I was on that fateful afternoon when Disaster, brilliantly disguised as Opportunity, first bade me come closer and listen awhile.

"Hi! 'S me!" chirped Gilbert into the phone.

His bubbly manner was miles away from the penitence I'd have expected from a friend who'd carelessly abandoned me to my burden of woe.

"Hi," I said in my most glacial tone.

"How goes it?" he asked. "Not picking at the scabs, I hope?"

"I'm fine," I said. "No thanks to you."

"Well, I like that!" came his miffed reply. "And here I am working day and night to rebuild your shattered reputation!"

"Oh?" I asked, hope and dread colliding within me. "How've you been doing that?"

"I got you a job!"

"A job?" I asked. If I'd had any sense, I'd have hung up right there and you'd be reading a pamphlet now, but, as I said, I was filled with the blind hope of the shattered and I pressed for details.

"This isn't anything illegal, is it?"

"Philip! You disappoint me. It's a *writing* job. Someone's doing a club act and needs the Cavanaugh touch to make it soar and glitter."

I asked if it was for pay, and he replied that, though fees had not been discussed, the performer was equipped to pay handsomely.

"Who is it?" I asked.

"I'll get to that. But first, what are you doing tonight?"

"Nothing, why?"

"Because we have to celebrate! My divorce came through!"

"*Great!*" I said, my anger entirely forgotten. "Already?"

"Yes! Isn't it grand? She's out of my life, Philly. Gone! Kaput! Extinguished!"

"Congratulations! That's wonderful!"

I should explain, I suppose, that though Gilbert is a contented—some would say devout—homosexual, a year ago he'd married a woman named Moira Finch. Romance was not the motivation. Both he and Moira had large, wealthy stepfamilies, well positioned to shower them with expensive gifts. Gilbert proposed a temporary merger, and Moira, whose scruples cannot be glimpsed without the aid of a particle accelerator, accepted.

Things came off rather less happily than expected, but come the finale the two were, in the eyes of New York State, if not the Lord, man and wife. They set up housekeeping and coexisted with increasingly strained civility for about six months. Then one night Gilbert ate some leftover Chinese food Moira had been saving for her lunch, prompting her to change the locks and file for divorce on a charge of mental cruelty. In the months since, Moira had been traveling and was now believed to be infesting the greater Los Angeles area.

"I'm so happy for you!" I said. "I thought she was holding things up, trying to get all this money you didn't have."

"She was. But now she's got her hooks into some rich sap and wants to haul him in but quick."

"Well, *that's* a break! God, the guy must really be loaded. I hope he's got a good lawyer."

"And a food taster. So, what say we put on our party frocks and celebrate? My treat, of course."

"You're on!" I said. "Thanks a bunch. This is just what I needed. Where do you want to go? There's this new place in Chelsea that's—"

"No, let's eat in. I want you to see my new place."

"New place?"

"Well, it's not mine really. It belongs to the fellow I work for. You'll be working for him, too."

"He's the one doing the club act?"

"No, that's somebody else. A woman. You'll be working for her, but you'll also be working for my boss, only she won't know it."

"*What?*"

"I'll explain tonight. Just come by around eight. I'll stuff you with champagne and caviar and give you the whole poop. You got a pen?"

I fetched one and scribbled down an address on Madison Avenue in the seventies. "This is your *boss's* place?" I asked.

"Right. Wait till you see it!"

"My God, Gilbert—are you telling me you have a *job?*"

"Yes! I'm a working boy again. It's great! I've been at it two weeks."

"Two *weeks?*"

I was frankly stunned. Gilbert and employment have never been on cordial terms. He tends to view jobs the way a rodeo artist views bulls; he's willing, when compelled, to take one on but neither desires nor expects to stay in the position for long.

"Yes, two weeks—you needn't make it sound so miraculous!" he added testily.

"What sort of job is it?" I asked.

"I'll tell you tonight."

"But—"

"*Tonight,*" he said, and rang off.

Annoyed as I was at him for leaving me so fogbound, I had to at least give him credit for taking my mind off my poor deceased musical. So mystifying were his statements that I could ponder little else for the remainder of the day. Apart from his fantastic assertion that he'd been cheerfully employed for weeks, there was this business about having found me a job, too. It worried me. Especially disquieting was his insistence on withholding details until I'd been stuffed with delicacies. A job that couldn't be offered without a side order of caviar was not, in all probability, a job I'd be wise to accept.

With these speculations fermenting in my mind, I donned the as-yet unpaid-for suit I'd purchased for my opening, strolled down to Ninety-sixth Street, and boarded a bus for that exotic faraway land known as the Upper East Side.

It was February and for the past two weeks the city had been pummeled by snow and bone-chilling winds, causing the homeless to flee into shelters and local news anchors to pantomime chilliness in well-heated studios. In the last two days, though, the winds had abated, temperatures had soared to record highs, and the sun had burst forth, inspiring an attendant sunniness in the normally funereal mood New Yorkers reserve for bad Februaries. Even now in early evening the breeze was mild and people wore light jackets and wide smiles. Stepping off the bus on the East Side, I decided to stroll down Fifth Avenue, where, I suspected, the cheeriness that prevailed on the West Side could only be heightened by the addition of twelve-room apartments and trust funds.

I sauntered downtown, exchanging little smiles with passersby, and arrived in due course at the Metropolitan Museum of Art. There was a party being held there that evening to celebrate some much heralded exhibition, and, as usual at such events, the limousines were thick and plentiful. But in the midst of their gleaming ranks there was now unfolding a scene of discord in sharp contrast with the avenue's springlike mood.

Two cars had apparently collided, and one, a stunning silver Rolls-Royce, its front headlight shattered, was now splayed across the avenue, blocking all traffic. Two liveried drivers were examining the damage, and standing next to one was a gaunt elderly woman in a pink gown, the elaborate bottom of which she'd swept off the wet pavement, exposing two unlovely gams. I couldn't hear what she was saying, as the waiting limos were starting to honk, but she seemed to be giving what-for to the other car's driver. Between the pink, upraised gown and the spindly legs, she looked something like an enraged flamingo.

The rear door of the other limo was now thrown open and a statuesque, raven-haired beauty leapt out and entered the fray. She had a loud, piercing voice, and so salty and direct was her mode of expression that the waiting partygoers told their drivers to lay off the horns and stop drowning out such first-rate entertainment. Rows of black limousine windows glided down and elegantly coiffed heads popped out like champagne corks. Bejeweled necks twisted and craned, seeking a better view of the festivities, and even those already ascending the grand stairs to the museum stopped in their tracks and gazed mesmerized at the battle.

Making a mental note to myself to check the columns tomorrow, I strolled on and soon reached the address Gilbert had given me. The lobby had burnished mahogany wainscoting and wallpaper that deep color I've always thought of as wealth green. I told the mummified doorman whom I wanted, and he directed me to the penthouse.

A dark paneled elevator with lovely inlaid designs brought me to the top floor, where there were only two apartments. I rang the appropriate bell and the door was at once flung open by Gilbert, who stood resplendent in a new silk suit. He smirked, curtsied, and yanked me in.

Interior design is not a topic on which I can discourse with anything approaching authority. My own apartment, though comfy by my standards, is not what you'd call "decorated" unless you consider the widespread use of milk crates to be motific. I do make the occasional stab at renovation, though this consists largely of turning over sofa cushions and realizing they looked better the other way. Given these circumstances, I'm inclined, perhaps, to be too easily impressed by such niceties as parquet floors, wall sconces, and armchairs without springs sticking out.

But *this* apartment, I could see, was of a richness calculated to dazzle eyes far more discerning than my own. Everything about it screamed (or, rather, murmured) of England and old money and high tea after the cricket match. I felt I'd stepped out of my own life and smack into the middle of *Brideshead Revisited*.

"Woof!" I said, or words to that effect.

"*We* like it," said Gilbert, yawning lightly, leaving me no option but to pull his hair.

"Ow!"

"Cut the Cecil Beaton routine," I said, "and tell me how you ever maneuvered yourself into this joint."

"That can wait. I have to show you the *rest!*"

Dropping all pretense of jadedness, he dragged me swiftly through eleven rooms, all done in the same Anglican Moneybags style.

There was chintz everywhere and huge fireplaces crowned with richly carved mantels and dark oil paintings. There were marble busts and heavy tables crowded with bibelots and photos in antique silver frames. Ancient editions of Shakespeare and Milton were tossed about like yesterday's newspapers, and thick brocaded draperies, covered with no doubt imported dust, framed each window. Gilbert babbled away, quoting prices on the more valuable tchotchkes, then saying "Think fast!" and tossing them to me.

"Don't do that! God, what a setup!"

"Twembly and Coleman!"

"Huh?"

"Ever-so-classy designers. Hand them a chicken coop and they'll make it look like Somerset Maugham lives there."

"You've actually moved in?" I said, wondering suddenly what had raised him to such opulence. It was not an apartment any young man of Gilbert's means was likely to attain *virgo intacta*.

"I *told* you—I just work here sometimes."

"And who's your boss?"

Gilbert smiled and leaned right into my face. "Tommy! *Parker!*" he said, then pulled back as though to avoid the flying spittle that would attend my screams of envy.

"Who's Tommy Parker?"

He heaved a sigh of exasperated disbelief. "Don't you know *anything?*"

"Well, pardon me for living, but I've never heard of him. Who is he?"

"He's *only* the editor of *Boulevardier!*"

He referred to the well-known men's fashion monthly. I'd heard of it, naturally, though I'd seldom given it more than a glance. I have nothing against fashion magazines per se, but I've never been able to see the point of spending money I don't have to look at men who won't sleep with me modeling clothing I can't afford.

"Sorry," I said, "but I'm not a subscriber."

"Obviously," he said, casting an eye at my suit. "Still, you *must* have heard of 'Nosy' Parker?"

This rang the vaguest of bells. "Gossip columnist?"

"Right," said Gilbert. "He wrote for *Boulevardier* for nine years before he was bumped up to editor. Anyway, Nosy Parker was *incredibly* famous."

"And you work for him?"

"Yes."

"But not at the magazine?"

"No, I work here."

"Oh. . . . Doing *what?*" I asked, and there must have been a certain something in my voice because Gilbert walloped me on the head with a chintz pillow.

"Fuck you! You're always making out I'm some kind of cheap gold digger who'll do anything to lead the high life. I truly resent that!"

"I'm sorry," I said.

"You should be!"

"I am. Where's the champagne?"

"Chilling. Anyway, the reason I work here is because the whole thing's an enormous secret. Tommy's putting his reporter's hat back on to do this major, *major* exposé, and I'm helping with the research and co-writing it."

"Exposé?" I asked, intrigued in spite of myself.

"Yes."

"Of who?"

"*Someone . . . very . . . big,*" said Gilbert, whose specialty is pointless suspense.

"*Who?*"

"I'm getting to it. Normally, of course, I'd never dream of co-writing anything since the results can be—well, I don't have to tell *you*, do I?"

"Champagne?"

"I'm getting it!"

He rose and I followed him down a richly paneled hall lined with little prints and paintings of hunting scenes.

"So," I said, "this Parker guy gives you the run of this place when he's not around?"

"Of course."

"And you're telling me there's *nothing* going on between you?"

He stopped short and exhaled wearily, as one mourning the death of tact. "My dear Philip, it is *extremely* unprofessional to sleep with one's coauthor."

"Ah. Struck out, then, huh?"

"I did *not* strike out! I've barely even tried. He's not the sort you can just pounce on. I'm laying the groundwork."

"And not much else, apparently."

We continued along the hall, snaking around corners as I goggled at the sheer vastness of the place.

"Anyway," he said, "the *important* thing is the story—whatever may happen between Tommy and me, it's something I really *have* to do. Even if it means putting aside the book for a while."

I let this pass without comment, even though such references normally provoked gales of satire from me. "The book" is Gilbert's novel, a steamy and provocative dissection of the urban scene. He's claimed to be working on it for five years now, but as for the actual manuscript, the yeti has been sited more often and reliably. He claims his zealous perfectionism has slowed his progress and seems to view it as a mark of precocity to have arrived so young at that state of tormented inertia it took lesser writers like Salinger and Capote years to achieve.

"I mean," he said, "I figure the book will always be there—"

"Indeed."

"But *this* story," he said, ignoring the dig, "is different. We have to strike while the iron is hot."

I followed him through a swinging door into the kitchen. I paused to take in its magnificence. Not even here, I saw, had stateliness surrendered an inch to modernity. Even the appliances were customized to appear generations, if not centuries, old.

"What are you goggling at?" asked Gilbert, fetching a stunning silver cooler from the cabinet that covered most of one wall.

"I've never seen a mahogany toaster."

"Actually, it's rosewood."

He hauled a magnum of Bollinger out of what looked like Oliver Cromwell's refrigerator, then reached into the freezer and pulled out two champagne flutes.

"Anyway," he said, filling the cooler with ice, "it's a wonderful opportunity! The minute I heard about it I thought, Philip *has* to be in on this. I owe it to him after all the grief I've inadvertently caused him."

"Very sweet of you. So, enough already. Who's this big exposé about?"

His eyebrows danced up and down a few times, and a grin spread across his face as he lovingly enunciated the name.

"Peter Champion!"

"Peter *Champion?*" I said, appropriately awestruck. "Wow! You're certainly gunning for the big game."

"Gunning?" He smiled, meticulously removing the foil from the champagne bottle. "Philip, my dear, we're going to *crucify* the fiend!"

"Well!" I said, impressed in spite of myself. Then I suddenly recalled his earlier statements and promptly broke into gooseflesh.

"Hang on a minute—you're expecting me to *help* you with this?"

"Absolutely," he grunted, pressing both his thumbs against the cork. "You're indispensable to the whole plan. Tommy and I will do the research and the writing. But *you*, Philly—*you* get the *fun* part!"

And with that the cork flew out, rocketing to the top shelf of the cabinet and severing the spout from a very pretty nineteenth-century Crown Derby teapot.

Two

"Philip, you baffle me," said Gilbert, standing on a chair and adroitly angling the teapot so that the missing spout could only be detected by someone standing on the rear burner of the stove. "How can you say you don't want to do something when I haven't even told you what it is yet?"

"I don't care what it is!" I said.

"Just *listen*, all right?"

He climbed down from the chair, then carefully returned it to the breakfast nook.

"You get so nervous over nothing! Just help yourself to that," he said, pointing to the cooler, "and I'll fetch the goodies." He rubbed his hands together greedily and bustled over to ye olde fridge.

"We have caviar and these yummy little puff things with crabmeat in them."

"Gilbert," I said firmly, "I will not be bought with caviar and crabmeat!"

He declined comment but couldn't resist rolling his eyes a bit. He knew better than anyone that my finances at the moment were such that I might be unduly swayed by pepperoni on a Triscuit.

"What are you balking at, anyway?" he said, poking among the fridge shelves, which were wooden. "I thought you couldn't *stand* Peter Champion!"

"Well, yes, but that doesn't mean I want to make a personal enemy out of him. He's a very rich, very powerful—"

"Scumbag!"

"Yes," I said, "which is all the less reason to fuck with him unless you really know what you're doing. Which, as a *rule*, Gilbert—"

"I don't?" he inquired snappishly. "Well, thanks for the vote of confidence!"

He took a plate of crab puffs from a low shelf and, conveying them to the counter, thrust them into Percy Bysshe Shelley's microwave. He jabbed a few buttons, then swiveled to face me.

"Why do you always assume that something's a god-awful mistake just because *I'm* involved in it?"

There was, of course, no really tactful reply to that sort of self-answering question. I shifted uncomfortably in my chair, pondering various evasions. But then, deciding I was at a perilous crossroads and plain speaking was best, I stared him directly in the eye and said that, while I had no desire to hurt his feelings or mar his delight over his new project, I felt nonetheless compelled to remind him that he was born under a malignant star, that everything he touched ended in sorrow and weeping, and that any person so bereft of reason as to assist him in one of his ventures should first consult a good dentist, as prolonged and intense gnashing of teeth might be confidently expected.

He stared at me for a long moment with a look of wounded astonishment.

"Is *that* what you think of me?" he asked.

"Yes."

"Well, it's not *true!*"

"It is."

"It *isn't!*"

"What about your wedding?" I asked.

"What about it?"

I reminded him that we had lived for months in stark, numbing terror and, in the end, barely escaped with our lives.

"You only remember the bad parts!" he said. "Besides—this is nothing *like* the business with Moira. Then I was young and all I wanted out of life was money."

"Whereas now you want money *and* glory."

"I want *respect*, Philip. Achievement! I want to do something I can be *proud* of."

He fetched a tin of beluga from the fridge and set to work, spooning it into a prechilled bowl.

"I doubt if you've noticed, Philip, being so wrapped up in yourself and all, but these past months I've been very depressed. It was Moira, of course, but it was more than that. I'd been looking back on my life, you know, taking stock, and I can't say I was impressed with what I saw."

"Oh?" I inquired delicately.

"Yes. What I mean is—what have I *accomplished* in my life?"

I feigned a coughing spell and was relieved to see from the speed with which he resumed that the question had been meant rhetorically.

"Yes, of course, I've been a great friend and delightful company and a wonderful lover and given all kinds of good advice. But I've never achieved anything. I've never *contributed*. So I started thinking that maybe I should take my writing skills and redirect them. Stop working on frivolous, commercial entertainment and try my hand at nonfiction. You know, something really timely that will change lives. Right wrongs. Make a *difference* in the world."

The microwave timer went off.

"Oh, good," said Gilbert, rushing to remove the plate. "Let's go to Tommy's office—there's a fainting couch and we can take turns being Lillie Langtry."

He put everything on a tray, lifted it, and, opening the kitchen door with a skilled bump of his fanny, led the way to a stately, book-lined chamber I'd merely glimpsed during the earlier tour.

It was a beautiful room, one that spoke seductively to my most shamelessly material dreams of Literature and genteel prosperity. There was a fireplace, a vast leather-topped desk, red walls dotted with Beerbohm caricatures, and floor-to-ceiling shelves bursting with beautifully bound volumes. The place exuded an urbanity that seemed almost transmissible, as if anyone who lingered long enough within its confines would find himself helplessly penning four-act comedies filled with roguish epigrams spoken by men named Cyril.

Gilbert plunked the tray on a venerable coffee table, then refilled our flutes while breathlessly describing his transformation from Jackie Collins Wannabe to Crusader for Truth.

"Of course, I had little real experience in journalism, so I decided

I'd better get some pronto. I set out to find a job at some good hard-hitting newspaper or magazine—"

"Like *Boulevardier?*"

"It's easy to condescend, Philip, but one has to start somewhere. I used to date this staff photographer at *Boulevardier*, so I had an in. He got me an interview and I landed a secretarial job. It didn't quite work out, though."

"What happened?" I asked.

"Well," he said, and frowned at the memory, "they *somehow* got it into their heads that I knew how to run this huge computer payroll program, when *I* never said anything of the kind. Still, I thought, How hard can it be? The next thing I knew it was Friday night and we were all on the phone, begging people not to cash these checks for forty thousand dollars the stupid computer gave them. And, of course," he added bitterly, "being the new boy, the whole fiasco was supposedly *my* fault."

"Gilbert," I said, "you actually told them you could manage the payroll for an entire *magazine?*"

"They leapt to conclusions!" he said, and it was clear from his look that, in his view, I was quite as mean and suspicious as the despots of the *Boulevardier* personnel department.

"Anyway," he continued, "Tommy Parker came down to sort it all out. And he was a *peach*, Philip. A real gentleman—and very easy on the eyes, too. We got to chatting, and I told him how wasted I was as a secretary when I was a terrific writer and should really be doing features. He said there was nothing at the magazine, but he had this *other* project he needed help with and did I have any background in journalism? So I told him about my years at the *Clarion*."

"The *Clarion?* That was our *high school* magazine."

"Yes. He seemed to assume it was something much bigger, and I didn't want to insult a potential employer by pointing out his mistakes. Anyway, he hired me to research and co-write the story. And this is it! An exposé of the biggest creep in town! Don't you even want to help, Philly?"

"Gilbert, it's nothing personal. I just have this premonition of—"

"Oh, you and your premonitions!" he snapped. "It's not as if we're going into this with our eyes closed, y'know. We're perfectly aware what a nasty, vengeful fuck Champion is. But who cares! Boyd Larkin's no slouch, either."

I inhaled sharply and my eyebrows took an express to the penthouse. "*Boyd Larkin's* behind this?"

"Well . . . in a sense," said Gilbert, spooning some caviar onto a toast point. "I mean, Larkin didn't *instigate* it. It was Tommy's idea. Still, Larkin does publish *Boulevardier,* so Tommy had to ask him for permission."

"And I'll bet he got it."

"Yes. Larkin adored the idea. In fact, he said it sounded too big to break in *Boulevardier*—he wants to make it a big cover story for *Choice.*"

At last things were beginning to make sense. This exposé was not, as Gilbert had painted it, the work of some righteous crusader determined to smite a towering symbol of Greed. It was merely the latest salvo in the ongoing war between Boyd Larkin and Peter Champion, the battling billionaires.

One of the problems of penning these little histories is you can never be certain what knowledge may safely be taken for granted and what requires explanation. You'll recall that earlier Gilbert dropped the name Tommy Parker, fully expecting me to say, "Oh, yes! Tommy Parker! I know just who you mean and I'm sick with envy that you work for him!" when, in fact, I hadn't a clue. I'm likewise tempted to assume that when I say "Larkin and Champion," my readers will exclaim in unison, "Oh, *they're* in this?" and I can get on with my story.

There are, however, people in this world who seldom pick up a newspaper, people who, when watching television, sneer in displeasure and change channels at the first glimpse of an anchorperson. While such willfully uninformed citizens are rare, emerging from seclusion only to serve on juries in trials of great national significance, they do exist. For their sake, if not your own, I will briefly outline the facts regarding those two colossi of New York society, Peter Champion and Boyd Larkin.

Champion is, of course, that fearless developer who has for the last decade devoted his every waking hour to giving us a bigger, bolder, and, on the whole, cheesier New York. His buildings, like his money, are plentiful and new, and while he is not an architect, he sees to it that each and every structure perfectly reflects the Champion style. This style combines flashiness with immensity of proportion to achieve a look that was most aptly described by the critic who referred to it as "Albert Speer Goes to Las Vegas."

Boyd Larkin shares three main attributes with Champion: he is rich, short, and addicted to publicity. There, however, comparisons end.

Champion is lean, forty-six, and a self-made billionaire. Larkin is stout, seventyish, and inherited his staggering pile from his father, a universally despised oilman. Champion's a human dynamo who personally oversees every aspect of his burgeoning empire. Larkin, by contrast, is content to let most of his wealth languish in sturdy investments, confining his personal attention to the publishing concern that represents the merest fraction of his net worth.

This company, Larkin Publications, came into being in the thirties when Boyd's father purchased all the magazines then owned by a rich Yankee named Miriam Gatch. Only a handful survive, *Boulevardier* among them, but Larkin started a dozen of his own. His personal pet and the flagship of the empire is *Choice*, the general-interest magazine he launched in the late forties. It was and remains a tastefully designed mélange of short stories, poems, cartoons, fashion spreads, profiles, travel pieces, and articles, all with a heavy—some would say pompous—emphasis on high culture and quality.

Choice was an immediate and roaring success and continued to prosper till the midsixties when its casual elitism proved anathema to the Woodstock generation. Though it's never quite regained its bygone luster or circulation, it remains a venerable, much quoted institution.

The rivalry between Larkin and Champion commenced when that Las Vegas crack about Champion's buildings appeared in *By Design*, a Larkin publication. Champion responded with an enraged letter, which Larkin published without comment, and there things might forever have rested. But then Champion built Champion Plaza, the opulent tower that serves as both his business headquarters and private residence. Larkin, on first glimpsing it, remarked, "If Joan Collins were a building, this is what she'd look like." This mot found its way into several columns, and from then on it was war.

Champion, who'd never before published so much as a flyer, decided to launch a "sophisticated" magazine that would compete directly with Larkin's *Choice*. He vowed, moreover, that within five years the publication would outstrip *Choice* both in circulation and revenue. He proceeded to launch *Estime,* a magazine whose "sophistication" derived from breathless reporting on the scandals and home furnishings of the celebrated, combined with cover profiles of Hollywood stars written in language Homer might have found a tad inflated. Needless to say, Champion achieved his goal, leaving *Choice* in the dust within a mere two years.

Larkin, though loath to admit it, must have been stung to the quick by Champion's triumph. This proposed exposé was clearly his long-anticipated counterpunch to his brash young adversary.

"Oh, *well!*" I said to Gilbert. "Here you are talking about this story like it's some grand, noble crusade when all it is is some goddamned plutocrat out to trash his business rival!"

Gilbert glared at me, his nostrils atremble with indignation. "*Really, Philip!* I fail to see how you can possibly put Boyd Larkin on the same level as Champion!"

Mulling it over a moment, I had to agree that, while there were many surface similarities, when it came to fundamental loathsomeness, Champion won the prize with points to spare.

"I mean," he continued, "I'm not saying that Larkin's Mother Teresa. He's a rich old glutton who throws himself balls to celebrate having his teeth cleaned. But who is he hurting? At least he's not running around building big ugly skyscrapers, turning Manhattan into his own personal theme park!"

"All right, so he's not as bad as Champion. He's still a horrible old fraud."

"What do you mean?" asked Gilbert.

"Well, he's *gay,* isn't he?"

"That's what one *hears,*" said Gilbert, shrugging and popping a toast point into his mouth.

"So why does he insist on playing Mr. Eligible Bachelor, 'dating' famous actresses and opera singers and letting the columnists gossip about wedding bells? I hate that! It's so creepy."

Gilbert sighed deeply and regarded me with profound impatience. "Philip—the man's pushing seventy. He grew up in a completely different world! Anyway, what are you mad about? That he hangs out with famous actresses? So would you if you knew any. Besides, it's not as if everyone doesn't know, anyway."

"Then why doesn't he just acknowledge it?" I asked. "The man's a fucking billionaire—he doesn't have to live by *anyone's* rules."

"Except *yours*, apparently. Look," he said, pouring me more champagne, "I don't see why you need to believe Boyd Larkin's a saint before you help him go after Peter Champion—Peter's the *real* criminal."

"Gilbert," I said, "I don't like him any better than you do, but it's no crime to erect ugly buildings."

"It is when you're bribing building inspectors!"

I goggled appropriately, and Gilbert smiled victoriously.

"He *bribed* building inspectors?"

"You've seen how fast those eyesores go up . . . haven't you ever wondered how he does it? According to Tommy he's violating *scads* of building codes and paying off crooked inspectors."

"Can he prove it?"

"Of course he can't," said Gilbert impatiently. "That's where *we* come in!"

I pointed out that investigative reporting was not exactly my forte, nor, despite years of experience rifling boyfriends' apartments for evidence of infidelity or concealed wealth, was it his.

"But *think* of it!" he cried with that passionate voice he usually reserved for loan requests. "Don't you see how *grand* it would be? To bring down the richest and sleaziest man in New York? To drag him kicking and screaming to justice? Do you know how *famous* you'd be?"

My expression was one of implacable resistance, but inwardly there was no denying the allure of his scenario. New York was filled with many communities, young and old, gay and straight, Jewish and Christian, black and white, rich and poor, all divided by wrangling and dissension, united only in their shared conviction that Peter Champion was the vilest thing to come along since spray cheese. If Champion were to suffer a humiliating plunge from his pinnacle, those who gave him the shove would enjoy waves of public respect and affection intoxicating to contemplate. Gilbert, encouraged by the dreamy look beginning to steal over me, hastened to paint still more glorious visions.

"Picture it, Philly," he said, an arm draped around my shoulder. "You'll walk into restaurants and people will nudge each other and whisper. 'Look!' they'll say. 'Isn't that the one who sent Peter Champion to jail? The bold young writer who fearlessly infiltrated his evil stronghold and obtained the crucial evidence that—' "

"Infiltrated?" I said.

"Yes. Hadn't I mentioned that?"

"No."

"I was getting there."

"*Infiltrate?*"

"Yes," he said, hastily ladling caviar onto a toast point for me. "I envy you. I really do. I'd give anything to do it myself, but I lack the right qualifications."

As far as I saw it, the only qualification needed was brazen stupidity, in which case his perceived shortage was wholly imagined. But I warily accepted the caviar and asked what he meant.

"I mean I'm not a songwriter. More crabmeat, perhaps?"

"What's songwriting got to do with it?" I asked.

"Champion's wife, Elsa, wants to make her nightclub debut, and she needs someone to write an act for her. *That's where you come in!* I think Tommy's already spoken to—Philip, that cushion's eighteenth-century crewelwork, so try not to spit champagne on it—already spoken to a friend of Elsa's who's helping her look for writers, so there should be no problem arranging a meeting. Frankly it may be hard to get the job. Face it, hon, after those reviews you're not a hot property. But the original songs were pretty good, so if you just play Elsa those, and—"

"*Back up, okay!*" I said, leaping to my feet. "This is going a little fast here! You expect me to work for Elsa *Champion?*"

"You have trouble with that?"

"Yes! I don't want to!"

"How can you *know* that?" he asked. "Have you ever met her?"

"No . . . but I've *heard* things."

"Like what?"

"Like she has to wear a wig because snakes won't hold a wave."

"Just *listen* to yourself!" said Gilbert, shaking his head with sad wonder. "Whatever happened to nerve? To intrepidness? Really, Philip, I knew you'd taken it hard about your show, but I'd no idea you'd been reduced to this timid husk of a man, too defeated and fearful to attempt even the simplest—"

This was a bit much.

"Fuck you, honey! You're not steamrolling me into this the way you did with your wedding! From what I can see we have a situation where *I* take all of the risks and you and this Parker clown get all the glory. *Maybe* this is something I could say yes to, but I'm not about to till I know a hell of a lot more than I do now."

I noted toward the end of my remarks that Gilbert had ceased regarding me with peeved impatience and was now staring over my shoulder with a sheepish grin.

"Hi, Tommy!" he said, delicately seating himself on the edge of the coffee table directly in front of the champagne and beluga.

I turned.

Standing in the doorway was a tall, fortyish man who looked something like what might have resulted had Leslie Howard given birth to Gary Cooper's love child. He wore a beautiful tuxedo with a richly brocaded cummerbund. His shoulders were pleasantly broad, his hips pleasantly slim. He had a long aristocratic neck, a lovely firm jawline, stunning cheekbones, and pale golden hair that fell onto his high forehead in little waves that twisted gracefully like the insides of seashells. His eyes, which were cornflower blue, took in the scene, and as they did, a smile of paralyzing suavity bloomed on his lips, a smile at once stern and amused, censorious and kind, accusing and forgiving.

Dear God, I thought—if I'm to have a prayer of keeping out of this, then *please* let the smile be a fluke. Let him be dreadful. Let him be bitchy in the worst sense, queeny and puffed up, inarticulate and charmless.

"Dull exhibit, was it?" asked Gilbert.

"Highly," he said in a pleasing, lightly clipped British accent. "Quite a curtain raiser we had, though. Miss Kitty Driscoll's driver cut off Horsey Kimball's vintage silver Rolls, cunningly smashing the left headlight. Horsey was so enraged she quite forgot herself and jumped out to give Kitty's driver what-for. Then Kitty, ever the soul of refinement, emerged from the backseat to air her views on the matter, and the gentle music of South Boston could be heard for miles."

"You're *kidding!*" said Gilbert turning to me and breathlessly explaining that Kitty was Elsa's baby sister. He then returned his rapt attention to Tommy. "Did you see it yourself?"

"I was just toddling up the steps when it happened, so I had a front-row seat. I could only assume this was some divine reward for good works done in a previous life. After all that, of course, a few walls of Flemish masterworks seemed rather a letdown, so I pleaded a migraine and left. It would be lovely, Gilbert, if instead of shielding my view of the caviar you offered me some. There's a good lad. And whom have we here?"

"Hello," I stammered. "I'm—"

"Of *course!*" he cried, smiting his forehead with one hand while extending the other toward me. "You must be Philip."

"Uh . . . yeah," I said, nodding stupidly as I felt his long graceful fingers twine around mine.

"I'm Tommy Parker. How thrilling to meet you after all the marvelous things I've heard about you from our friend, the champagne pirate. Here, let me tidge you up." He took my flute and began pouring.

"Maybe I can help Gilbert clear up some things about this . . . little project of ours." He grinned at me as if we now shared the most deliciously wicked of secrets.

"I just had a few questions," I said.

"What sort, dear boy?"

"Oh, you know, what I'll be doing, when I start. That kind of thing."

Three

All through the rest of that evening as we sat jovially con-
spiring, panicky messages kept flashing through my mind, like those
hurricane warnings that glide ominously across the bottom of your TV
screen even as the characters in the show you're watching chatter on
obliviously.

Stop it! I'd think. What am I doing? I'm not the one who does
this—*Gilbert* does this!

But, alarming as it seemed, there was no use denying that I had
appropriated the one horrible gift I'd always regarded as Gilbert's
exclusive property: I had fallen instantly and insanely in love with a
man I'd just met and about whom I knew virtually nothing, except
that he seemed as superbly unattainable as even the most stringent
masochist could require.

I tried for a while to tell myself it was just a passing infatuation.
But the longer I sat, listening to the words pour forth from him like
a river of butterscotch, the more I knew my feelings would not prove
fleeting. I loved Tommy Parker and I would go on loving him till I
either won him and possessed him long enough to grow weary of
perfection or, more probably, till I died of longing and frustration.

As for the Champion exposé, there was no point wondering anymore
if it was a good idea or a bad one. Tommy wanted my help and he
would get it. I could only be grateful he was merely trying to expose
a corrupt developer; he might instead have been determined to spring
some pal of his from a Bolivian jail, in which case the next morning

would have found me standing on an airstrip, fumbling with phrase books and plastic explosives.

Still, whether the champagne was to blame or the rising tide of my hormones, the Champion scheme was looking niftier every minute. Even my own proposed role as undercover songwriter had begun to seem less intimidating than enticing.

"Understand, Philip," said Tommy, "we are not expecting miracles of you. If there *is* evidence that Champion's been bribing inspectors, it's no doubt locked securely away, and you are not, I presume, a safecracker. Or are you?"

"No."

"I thought not, though there is no harm asking. All I request of you is that you place a few listening devices where they'll do the most good, after which I'll get some lovely rumors circulating about bribes and payoffs. Then we'll sit back and see what Peter and company have to say about it all in their more private moments."

While I had no desire to vex this flawless man by questioning the wisdom of his methods, I was moved to wonder aloud if certain government agencies, though fond of such tactics themselves, did not frown upon their use among private citizens.

"Goodness," he said gravely, "you may be right. Let's refrain, then, from telling them. Of course," he added, switching gears, "while you're there you need hardly confine your curiosity to high crimes and bribery. We'll want a spot of color for the piece, too, so any gossipy truffles you can dig up along the way will be most welcome."

"*Naturellement!*" I said, and blanched. The things that come out when we're trying to be suave.

"Marvelous!" he said, exposing two rows of perfect, gleaming teeth while placing a warm hand on my shoulder. He turned to Gilbert.

"Let's drink to Philip, shall we?"

"Oh, yeah, let's," said Gilbert, as though Tommy had suggested we pick up some chicks and take them bowling.

I immediately sensed that Gilbert, a skilled diagnostician in matters of the heart, had noted my strong attraction to Tommy and was, understandably enough, disgruntled. The issue of poaching had arisen, and I suspected that as far as Gilbert was concerned, there was no question of who was the poacher and who the poachee. A glance at him confirmed this. He was staring straight at me, nostrils flared, lips pursed, and chin elevated. It was the sort of look Julia Child might give you if she caught you sneaking out of her kitchen with a capon under each arm.

"To Philip," said Tommy, raising his glass.

"We know he won't disappoint us," intoned Gilbert, subtlety never having been his long suit.

We drained our glasses and Tommy cheerfully refilled them. He then extended the plate of crab puffs in my direction, posing a dilemma for me as I had, only moments ago, resolved to lose ten pounds by the end of the week. Helpless, though, to resist anything Tommy might offer, I took one. He then looked to Gilbert, who shook his head, patting his stomach in a gesture meant to convey that such sylphlike slimness as his own could not be maintained without the most rigorous self-denial. Gilbert then turned to me with a pitying smile. I smiled back and pointed discreetly to my chin to signal Gilbert that there was a bit of food on his own. There wasn't, in fact, though there was a pimple I'd noticed earlier, and I hoped that if he rubbed at it, the concealer would come off.

"I don't think you know, Philip," said Tommy, oblivious to this internecine ballet, "what an utter *godsend* you've been to us. For months now I've been trying to think of a way to get one of ours into the inner sanctum."

"You couldn't slip in a maid or something?" I asked.

"We *could* have, yes, but at the rate they fire people we doubted anyone would last long. Besides, we preferred it be someone they'd actually *talk* to, someone whom they might even take to their thorny bosoms."

I frowned. This seemed a daunting assignment.

"I don't think Peter Champion will take me to his bosom."

"Nor do I. But Elsa might. She's sticking her neck out with this act, and she's very skittish about it. She'll need a sensitive young man to hold her hand and say how magnificent she is."

"Well, that I could manage," I said, then confessed that, till Gilbert mentioned it, I'd had no idea she was even a singer.

"Oh, yes!" said Tommy. He flashed me a debonair smile, and I had to remind myself to breathe. "Not many know it, but Elsa was once *quite* the chanteuse. It was what she was doing back when she met Peter about twenty-five years ago. She had a lounge act."

"A *lounge* act?" hooted Gilbert, forgetting his animosity for a moment.

"Yes. Little Elsie Driscoll, the songbird of the Ramada Inn. She was quite determined to scale the heights."

"But she gave it up when she married Peter?" I asked.

"Actually, she didn't," said Tommy, pulling a cigarette case from his jacket.

Oh, God, I thought. He carries a cigarette case! If I lived to be a hundred I could never carry that off!

Spying a lighter on the coffee table, I sat forward and reached for it. Gilbert was closer, though, and he snatched it up and lit Tommy's cigarette, cupping his hand around my beloved's in a way that sent volts of jealousy sizzling through me.

"At least not at first," continued Tommy, exhaling elegantly. "Within days of the honeymoon she was back in harness, belting her little lungs out at a Revere Beach boîte called The Green Chapeau. But then she and Peter moved to New York, where Elsie's reputation had, alas, failed to precede her, and where, as you know, singers whose assets may be equally appreciated by the deaf are never in short supply. It was around this time that Peter's star was beginning its long, ghastly rise. Even then he was morbidly sensitive about his image and didn't much like having a wife who could regularly be glimpsed getting the bird at open mike nights. He suggested a hiatus, Elsie agreed, and good-bye, little dream, good-bye.

"Still, if the spark that burned within Elsie—now *Elsa*, if you please—was dimmed, it was by no means extinguished. Her friends say she was incapable of attending a musical without gazing wistfully at the stage and sighing about 'the old days.' A few years ago she resumed voice lessons and began making noises about a comeback.

"Of course, by *this* point," he added, grinning fiendishly, "she was no longer the same poor waif she was when she started out. Far from it. She was now rich, famous, and widely disliked—which meant her comeback's audience would include lots of dear 'friends' who'd spent their afternoons muttering dark prayers and lighting candles to the gods of False Pitch and Microphone Feedback. Elsa knew this and it scared the wits out of her. So she kept stalling.

"Then last month at Peter's big birthday gala, she led the assembled in 'Happy Birthday,' and someone—I believe it was Luli Carmody—told her how well she sang. Elsa, nine sheets to the wind, told her she was returning to the stage this spring. Luli told Liz Smith, who made a grand fuss about it in her next column. Elsa shyly confirmed the statement, Peter phoned the Rainbow Room, and here we all are!"

"But can she sing?" I asked.

"She can carry a tune," said Tommy. "How far she can carry it remains to be seen. And you, dear boy," he added with a gratifying touch of envy, "will see before any of us."

I bathed in his smile, thrilled beyond speech that this paragon, engaged in so exalted an endeavor, had seen fit to cast me in a pivotal role. At the same time, though, I couldn't help feeling there was something wrong with the picture and that the something was me.

Elsa, I pointed out, was a woman of staggering resources. If she was so nervous about her act, why would she hire a young writer—and one who'd just had a flop? Gilbert agreed that this did seem a problem, substantiating the point with quotes from two of the more negative reviews.

"Now, now," Tommy said firmly. "I will not brook self-doubts. For one thing," he said, casually squeezing my knee, "I've *heard* your songs and I think they're bloody marvelous!"

"Really?" I said, grateful that my suit bagged at the crotch. "You saw my show?"

"Alas, no. But Gilbert played me a tape, didn't you?"

"Yes," enthused Gilbert.

"*Wonder*fully funny and clever. Just the sort of thing our Elsa will scream for. And as for your reputation, dear, don't worry. Reports of your brilliance have already reached Elsa herself."

"Really? How did that happen?"

"I did a spot of proselytizing for you," smiled Tommy. "I became a Cavanaugh's Witness and buttonholed old Millie Pilchard."

"Who's Millie Pilchard?" I asked.

Gilbert sighed heavily and said she was *only* Horsey Kimball's sister. "You *have* heard of Horsey Kimball, haven't you?"

"Sure. Isn't she the one who organizes all those benefits for museums and libraries?"

"Yes. In fact, that was her tonight, defending her battered Rolls in front of the Met. Horsey is the dowager empress of the old guard. And her sister Millie's one of the few members of the ancien régime who'll give Elsa the time of day."

"Why? Does she like her?"

"Anything is possible, dear. One suspects, though, that the main reason is Millie's husband, who lived just long enough to squander her entire fortune. Now poor Millie's having a hard time maintaining the life-style to which centuries of inbreeding have accustomed her. Hence, a perfect symbiotic relationship. Elsa craves Millie's name and respectability, while Millie dotes on Elsa's sentimental—and highly pawnable—tokens of friendship."

"She *pawns* Elsa's presents?"

"That's the rumor. I can't verify it, so I content myself to repeat it. Anyway, I ran into Millie at a party last week. We'd only met once or twice, so I reintroduced myself and steered the conversation to the season's new musicals, and from there, straight to you—your brilliance, your burgeoning reputation, and the outrage the cognoscenti felt over the snide review some third-string Philistine at the *Times* gave your latest show. I told her *all* the leading lights who sing at Manhattan's chicest nightspots were lined up, begging you for material.

"Well! Her eyes glowed with avarice and she said, Goodness! it was all *too* perfect—her dear friend Elsa was planning *her* nightclub debut and needed material. She'd been asking around on Elsa's behalf, but ever since that Mr. Sondheim had been so terribly blunt she hadn't known *who* to turn to! She asked if I knew you and I said no, but I'd do my best to track you down for her. So," he concluded, handing me a card with a number on it, "here's your chance to make a greedy old woman very happy."

I rose and crossed to the phone on the desk as Tommy made for an armchair on the other side of the room, next to which was a second phone.

"Do you mind if I listen in?" he asked. "I adore eavesdropping."

"Feel free," I said, and began dialing.

"Remember," said Tommy, eyeing me sternly, "you're a *commodity*. Be aloof. Even a touch impudent. And, by the way—"

He held up a hand and I stopped dialing. He spoke in a hushed, conspiratorial whisper, which, while completely unnecessary, added an agreeable spice to the proceedings.

"You and I have *never* met! Elsa mustn't know you're friendly with anyone who works for Larkin. Not that I imagine Millie will tell Elsa I recommended you—she'll want to grab the credit for herself. But to be on the safe side, you don't know me."

I nodded and finished dialing. The line was answered by a machine with a standard "I'm not here" message, though from the slow, condescending tone in which Millie delivered it, one was led to assume most of her calls came from mentally challenged children of six, seeking loans.

"Hello!" I said after the beep, and then, remembering Tommy's advice, adopted a world-weary tone. "Hello. I'm calling for a Mrs. Poacher or something. My name is Phil Cavanaugh, and a friend of mine told me—"

I heard a click, and someone fumblingly picked up on the other end.

"*Hello?*" said a woman. It was the same voice as on the message but now sounded much more breathless and eager.

"*Hello!* Are you there, Mr. Cavanaugh?" In the background I could hear gales of canned laughter from a sitcom sound track.

"For God's sake, Helga, turn that thing down! Are you *there*, Mr. Cavanaugh?"

"Yes, I'm here."

"So good of you to call! My name is Mildred. Mildred *Pilchard?*" she asked hopefully.

"Yes?" I said coolly.

"Well . . . I have a close friend who's eager to meet you and see if you might do some writing for her. First, though, I want to tell you what a great admirer I am of your work!"

"Oh? You saw my show?"

"Oh, yes. I thought it was superb! So sophisticated!"

I directed an evil smile at Tommy. "Really? What song did you like best?" I asked.

"Oh, dear! They were all so delightful I couldn't possibly decide! Anyway, a close, close friend of mine is making her stage debut in two and a half months. You are familiar with the name Elsa Champion?"

"I've heard of her," I said blandly.

"Well, that's who it is. She has *the* most astonishing musical ability, which she has, naughty girl, kept secret far too long. She is going to be a very big star of the nightclub stage, and records, too, I shouldn't wonder, and I think it would be quite a feather in your cap to be associated with her so early in her career."

"I'm sure it would be," I drawled, "but the thing is, I'm very busy. As I was explaining to Rosie Clooney last week—"

"I need hardly mention, Mr. Cavanaugh, that Mrs. Champion is a very *generous* woman. I'm sure she would pay you handsomely for your services."

"Well . . ." I said, and paused.

It's strange, given that my finances were in their usual dire state, but until that moment I'd not even considered the financial opportunities inherent in my position—which is, I suppose, the most telling comment of all on the extent to which visions of Tommy Parker, lolling naked on a perfumed couch, had thus far dominated my thoughts. But now even such sweet visions as these were swept aside as my mind teemed with *Fantasia*-like images of dancing checkbooks pursued by Waterman pens.

Tommy, noting my sudden trance, began acting like a frenzied charades player, shaking his head vigorously while waving his hand in an airy gesture of dismissal. I nodded, embarrassed, and, taking his cue, spoke the most profoundly disingenuous sentence I have ever uttered.

"Mrs. Pilchard, I'm an artist—money isn't important to me."

There was dead silence for a moment, and I worried that Millie's effort to comprehend this sentiment had caused a cerebral hemorrhage or something, but then I heard a weak cough.

"I see. Of course. Quite. Let me assure you, though, that Mrs. Champion wants her nightclub act to be *very* artistic."

"Well, I don't knooow," I whined. "I've turned down so many people on the grounds that I don't write special material. And now if I do this, Liza will *hate* me, and—"

"Mr. Cavanaugh," she pleaded, "do at least come and meet Mrs.

Champion. I'm sure you'll be so charmed you'll be delighted to take the assignment."

I consented wearily. She said she'd be taking tea at Champion Plaza tomorrow at four, and we arranged to meet in front of Je Voudrais, a shoe store located in the lobby. I would be wearing a gray suit.

"Splendid! So delighted to hear from you, Mr. Cavanaugh. I just know we're going to be great friends! Good-bye now!" she said, and rang off.

For most of the conversation I'd had my eyes glued to Tommy, who smiled steadily at its progress. The smile now swelled into a wide grin of delight and approval that left me goofy with happiness.

"Why, Gilbert!" he cried as he rushed over and kissed my forehead, liquefying the bones in my legs. "You never told me what a consummate actor Philip was. A masterful job, Philip! We couldn't have chosen a more marvelous man to round out the team!"

Gilbert was smart enough to know any sniffiness would reflect more poorly on him than me, so he joined in, clapping me on the shoulder and offering compliments. But just as their praises were ringing agreeably in my ears, a dark thought struck.

"Wait a minute—Elsa wants brand-new songs, does she?"

"So I'm led to believe," said Tommy.

"New music as well as lyrics?"

"Ah. I see," said Tommy, quick to grasp the nature of my dilemma. "Here we've been promoting you as a solo act, whereas you require your collaborator to complete the package. What's she like, your partner? Would she be willing to help us?"

"*Claire?*" groaned Gilbert, slumping dramatically into a wing chair. "Never in a million years!"

And he was right. If you recall, earlier in the evening, before my objections had melted under the solvent of Tommy's charms, I told Gilbert he was born under an evil star and that only the more backward sort of cretin would hop onto any bandwagon that numbered him among its passengers. That I knew enough to say this was due partly to bitter experience, but due mainly to Claire, who has reinforced this conviction in every possible way short of embroidering it onto a sampler for me.

Not that Claire *dislikes* Gilbert. She's actually fond of him, in her way. But her experiences with him, particularly those involving his wedding, have left her with the firm belief that he's the nation's preeminent horse's ass and that she would sooner dance naked in an apiary than allow herself ever again to become embroiled in his affairs.

"Oh, dear," clucked Tommy, shaking his head. "Do you think Gilbert's right? Would Claire really refuse to write the act with you?"

"Well, yes, if she knew I was only there to gather material for some exposé."

"Oh, well," said Tommy, brightening, "there's no problem, then, is there? Don't tell her. I was going to request you keep mum about that aspect of things anyway."

"Oh?" I asked uneasily.

"Yes. Not much of a conspiracy if everyone and his composer knows about it. Much better to keep things between the three of us."

This didn't sit well with me. Claire is my most trusted confidante, a wise and loyal chum who's always there when you need her. The thought of bamboozling her, and at length, made me feel like something reptiles would shun. On the other hand, if I was honest with her, she'd advise me to go soak my head, in which case I'd be unable to write the act and would forfeit not only a much needed fee, but the good opinion of a man who had, albeit in the last forty-five minutes, come to mean everything to me.

These concerns must have been writ large on my face because Tommy frowned sexily and asked if I had a problem about withholding things from Claire.

"Well, I never like lying to my friends—"

"A commendable sentiment. Well, if you feel you can't assist us without betraying principles you hold dear, then of course you mustn't proceed a step further. And no hard feelings whatsoever."

"Of course not," said Gilbert fervently. "What an ass I was to even *suggest* you lie to Claire! I feel awful! Let's just forget about the whole silly—"

"Now, hold on!" I said, my head spinning. "Did I say I wanted out? I'm eager to help with this, and if it means telling a few white lies, I'll live with myself."

"Well," said Tommy, "if that's how you feel, we accept your decision with jubilation!"

It occurred to me that even if I did refrain from telling Claire my motive in seeking the job, there was no guarantee she'd go along. Her aversion to the Champions was as strong as the next girl's, and it would take much wheedling to make her agree even to meet Elsa. I voiced this concern, and Gilbert suggested that, as the meeting was tomorrow, I waste no time in running home to phone her.

"I'll get your coat," he said, and bolted from the room.

The thought of leaving Tommy in Gilbert's clutches affected my stomach like a handful of thumbtacks. It was some small consolation that while he fetched my coat I could cherish my first moment alone with my beloved.

"I'm so happy I've met you at last," he said. He took my hand as if to shake it, but then held it warmly in both of his own.

"Great meeting you, too!" I said, desperately trying to decide how best to handle the moment. I wanted to say something sophisticated yet genuine, flirtatious yet not crass or forward, something he'd remember that evening as he lay in bed and, remembering it, smile and reach under the blanket.

"Well," I began, "all I can say is—"

"Bundle up!" shrieked Gilbert, rushing in and hurling my coat at me.

"Yes, you'd better," said Tommy, releasing my hand. "It was starting to get chilly again."

Tommy led us out of the study and down the stately corridor to the foyer, burbling all the way about the laurels that awaited us on the grand day when we exposed Champion as the lowest of scoundrels.

"The doorman will get you a cab," offered Gilbert.

"Say!" I snapped my fingers. "Are you heading back to your place soon? I could wait and we'll share one."

"That *would* be nice, but I still have a few things to . . . finish up here," he said, freighting the words with as much sexual innuendo as could be achieved without actually miming orgasm.

Seeing a chance for a parting shot, I congratulated Gilbert again on his divorce, adding pointedly that I hoped he'd learned his lesson. I then turned to Tommy and asked if he'd heard the story of Gilbert's marriage.

"Keep warm!" said Gilbert, flinging the door open.

I promised Tommy that someday, when there was ample time, we'd have to tell him the whole story, as it was very amusing in a horrible sort of way. Tommy said certainly, then handed me a card, begging me to report to him the minute I returned from Elsa's. I promised I would, whereupon he flashed his dazzling smile and kissed me lightly on the cheek.

"Philip," he said, "there are glorious days ahead!"

I blushed crimson, which seems embarrassing in retrospect, though at the time seemed a happy alternative to swooning. I stood in the hall a moment after he'd closed the door, wondering if his kiss bespoke stirrings of affection. Deciding it had, I jumped up and down a few times and pressed the button for the elevator.

I glanced back at the door and, seized with an altogether natural desire, rushed back and pressed my ear to it. Gilbert and Tommy seemed still to be in the foyer, and I could just barely make out what they were saying. I was suddenly gripped by the dread certainty that I'd overhear something to shatter my hopes.

Gilbert said didn't it go well, and Tommy said yes, splendidly, and then, "You needn't work so late, dear. I'm sure there's nothing that can't wait till morning."

Gilbert said he had errands to run early and wanted his desk clean. Then Tommy said he'd be going out again soon, and Gilbert should lock up when he left.

Well! I thought, doing interpretive dances in the vestibule. So much for Gilbert's claims of romance in the offing! He's obviously no more than an employee! The merest lackey! I scurried back to the door and listened eagerly for some further reference to myself.

"Oh, by the way," Gilbert said.

"Yes?"

"You know that Crown Derby teapot?"

"Why? Did something happen to it?"

"Well," said Gilbert, "Philip was opening this bottle of champagne . . ."

Four

My elation over Tommy's affectionate gestures toward me and clear lack of passion for Gilbert was so great, not even an unjust reputation as a champagne klutz could begin to mar it. I emerged from the elevator with a sprightly hop, waved a gay farewell to the doorman, and literally danced into the night as though guided by some vivacious, if untalented, choreographer.

It's strange, isn't it, that while much is said about the glories of love, no one ever mentions its more odious side effects, chief among them this tendency it has of shattering inhibitions and seducing you into colorful behavior. Never mind that you've witnessed such behavior in others and found it revolting. Never mind your suspicion that you'll someday look back on your actions and groan like a hired mourner. You're in love, tra la, and you don't care. You go ebulliently on your way, grinning like a child and woofing at strangers' dogs, until some friend finally draws you aside and points out that, your apparent beliefs to the contrary, you are not Gene Kelly and none of this is charming.

On the evening in question, though, not even the bluntest friend could have induced me to put a sock in it. So joyous was the smile with which I greeted my fellow bus passengers that several changed seats, muttering darkly about the drug problem.

It was midnight when I reached home. Knowing Claire's the early-to-bed type, I wasted no time in phoning. By now, of course, I'd juggled my moral books with the skill of a Hollywood accountant, and my qualms had, like the profits of a hit film, entirely vanished.

I'd decided my deception—if you could really *call* it that—was, after all, merely temporary. The day would arrive when Champion would sit in the witness box, mumbling sweaty evasions, and I could then tell all to Claire, who would applaud my daring and regret that her own unreasonable prejudice toward Gilbert had kept me from taking her into my confidence.

Claire's machine answered, and I bellowed cheerfully into the receiver.

"Hello, love of my life! It's me! I know it's late, but pick up! Pick up, my angel, and I promise to reward you with—"

"All *right*," said Claire sleepily. "You needn't scream the place down. You know the machine's next to my bed."

"Sorry. Thought you might have the sound turned down."

"Would that I had. What are you, drunk or something?"

"Not immoderately, no. I bring you joyful tidings."

"They'd better be," she muttered. "What is it?"

"I've found us a job!" I said, and I could hear her suddenly sit up and rearrange the pillows.

"For pay?" she asked.

"Pay and plenty of it. It's not quite sewn up yet, but unless I miss my guess, we will be the creative team behind the long-awaited debut of—" And here I held the phone with my shoulder and made a drumroll on the table.

"*Who!*"

"Elsa *Cham*pion!"

It wasn't a nice thing to spring on a lady composer who'd only moments ago been asleep and dreaming of an Elsa-less future. I waited patiently for her to recover from the blow and frame a suitable reply.

"Gosh," she said at length, "couldn't you find someone *less* lovable to write for? I hear Leona Helmsley has a lovely contralto—"

"Now, now," I said lightly. "She's not the face in *my* locket, either, but a job's a job. And I need the money."

"So do I, pet, but I'm not sure I care to earn it working for people who make the Borgias look Amish. How'd this land in our laps, anyway?"

"Some friend of hers saw our show and recommended us."

"Well, *that* sounds probable," she said dryly. "Who's the friend? Someone we know?"

"No. Her name's Millie Pilchard."

"Hmm," said Claire, "where have I heard that name?"

"She's Horsey Kimball's sister."

"Ah," said Claire, and then, her voice full of wonder, "Horsey *Kimball's* sister is recommending *us*—to Elsa *Champion?*"

"Small world, *n'est-ce pas?*"

A brief silence ensued, and then Claire addressed me in that casual but steely tone I call her Scotland Yard voice.

"Philip," she asked, "would Gilbert happen to be involved in this?"

"No!" I said, unsettled as always by her keen powers of perception. "Why do you ask?"

"Because when something's wrong with the picture he usually is."

This line of thought clearly had to be nipped in the bud or all would be lost. I chastised her roundly, saying she had a low, suspicious mind that forever saw Gilberts lurking behind every shrub and lamppost. She was, I conceded, under no obligation to write songs for a woman who would, in a more perfect world, be hung by her feet in the town square and pelted with sequins, but she owed it to me to at least meet her before nixing the proposal. She whined a bit but in the end consented to take tea the next day at Champion Plaza.

This accomplished, I nestled into bed and commenced devising tender fantasies about Tommy and me and the life we'd someday lead. I saw us shuttling back and forth between New York and our little hideaway in the English countryside. My image of the English countryside was somewhat indistinct, deriving, as it did, solely from mystery novels, but it was nice to imagine the two of us passing romantic weekends there, cooking, making love, and explaining to the police why the vicar could not possibly have been a suicide.

The next morning I rose at ten and called Ma Pilchard to let her know she should expect an extra genius at tea. She seemed nonplussed at first, but when I inquired coolly if she hadn't noticed Claire's name in the playbill for our show, she came round.

"Oh, yes! Of *course!* Such a forgetful old woman I've become! Approaching senility, I shouldn't wonder!"

I passed the day going over our material, deciding what to play for Elsa. I then enjoyed a light lunch while perusing the gossip columns. With the exception of Daisy Winters, who is, I gather, one of Elsa's dearest cronies, the town dirtmeisters had a field day describing the previous night's showdown between "Empress Horsey Kimball" and Elsa's "feisty" younger sister, Kitty. While there was some variance of opinion as to whether Kitty had confined her remarks to the incompetence of Horsey's chauffeur or had gone on, as some maintained, to deliver a frank critique of the older woman's hair and facial features, all agreed that the incident would do little to advance Elsa's campaign to win a seat on the board of the Met.

I pondered the ramifications of this as I set about dressing for tea. I hoped Elsa's bad press hadn't left her in too vile a mood. It would be hard enough to win Claire over as it was, but if Elsa proved wounded and surly, there'd be no hope at all.

I walked the two blocks to Claire's and found her standing in the lobby, looking decidedly cross. I hailed a cab and we set off toward Broadway.

"I don't know why I let you talk me into this," she said, picking lint off the somewhat dowdy suit she reserves for our infrequent business meetings. "Elsa Champion's the last woman on earth I want to be identified with."

"It's a job, not a personal endorsement. Think what an advertisement it is for us."

"That's just what I am thinking," she said. "Cavanaugh and Simmons—toadies to the rich and untalented."

"Who says she's untalented?"

"Every instinct I possess."

"Look," I said, "if we give her good material, people will see it's good, whether she's up to it or not. And that might lead to more jobs."

"Well . . ." She sighed, sinking into her seat. "I suppose there's something in that."

"Look at the bright side," I said. "Our price will go up."

"Not to mention our blood pressure."

The cab turned onto West Fifty-seventh Street and moments later deposited us in front of that glittering cathedral of consumption, Champion Plaza.

"Good Christ," said Claire, gazing up at the sheer height of it. "Why is it every time I look at this place I expect to see flying monkeys circling the top?"

For those of you who've never made the pilgrimage, Champion

Plaza is an immense black-and-gold edifice that occupies an entire city block. It's topped by three towers of varying heights, meant to suggest the blocks that Olympic champions—*get it?*—stand on when receiving their medals.

The vast gold revolving doors lie at the end of a fifty-foot promenade, majestically landscaped and lined with gold street lamps outfitted with flame-shaped bulbs. If you make it past those without dying from laughter, you enter a five-story black marble atrium drenched in such *faux luxe* trappings as hanging gardens, an aviary, dancing fountains, and, dead center, between twin escalators, an immense bronze statue of the god Apollo trying to reach something on a high shelf. The strange thing about the place is that, vast and solid as it is, when you look at it from across the street it doesn't seem quite real. It looks like matte work or else some stunning but two-dimensional set built for the finale of Radio City Music Hall's *Salute to Mammon.*

The revolving doors spun dizzily as a mixture of wide-eyed tourists and affluent shoppers hurtled in and out of the lobby. Claire and I maneuvered through the crowd, passing two doormen dressed in uniforms that made them resemble generals in some fashion-conscious army.

We stood for a minute, ogling the array of larcenous boutiques and cafes that occupy the prize space on the ground floor. Above and in front of us three more floors throbbed with commerce, each tiered back from the one beneath so that all four could be taken in from ground level. Though the predominant color was black, each surface was so highly polished that wherever you looked you were blinded by glints of light bouncing off shop windows and the free-standing display cases that dotted each level. Classical music blared even louder than the deafening buzz of voices, strings, and French horns playing *molto vivace* as if to spur the clientele into greater frenzies of spending.

"Yeeks," said Claire. "It's like a great ugly pinball machine."

Mrs. Pilchard had suggested we meet in front of a shoe store called Je Voudrais. We located it and settled in to wait. Immediately a sixtyish woman in mink burst through the revolving door and barreled toward us, heels clicking on the marble.

"Mr. Cavanaugh?" she called, still several yards away. I waved and she raced the rest of the distance, her hand extended like a relay racer's.

"Gracious me, I'm not late, am I?" she said, shaking my hand. "I prize punctuality!"

She was a small, round, birdlike woman with large bespectacled eyes, a sharp little beak of a nose, and no chin whatsoever. Her manner as well was marked by a trend toward the avian. She chirped and twittered with incessant cheer even as her eyes darted nervously about as though searching for predators.

"So good of you to come on such short notice! And would this be Claire? Thrilling to meet you! I adore your music! So beautiful and so much, uh, variety!"

"Why, thank you," said Claire, shaking her hand. "Is there any particular style you like best?"

"Goodness, you mustn't ask! I know nothing about music! I mean, I know *quality*, of course, but the vocabulary, it quite eludes me! We'd best run along. Elsa hates to be kept waiting."

We took a crowded elevator to the forty-fifth floor, Mrs. Pilchard chattering all the way in a piercing whisper meant to insure that her fellow passengers would not entertain the slightest doubt as to her identity or the exalted circles in which she was accustomed to travel.

"Oh, dear, Claire—I haven't even introduced myself! I'm Mildred *Pilchard*."

"Yes, I know," said Claire.

"You probably haven't heard of me. I'm not one for the limelight. Unlike my sister, who quite delights in it. *Her*, I suspect, you would know. Hortense *Kimball?*"

"Oh, yes," said Claire. "She's quite well known."

"I should say so! Quite the dynamo is Hortense, or Horsey, as she's known, though I call her Hortense, being her sister. Such drive! I don't have half her energy, even though I'm *quite* a few years younger. Dreadful business, though, wasn't it, about her and Elsa Champion's sister?"

"Really?" said Claire. "I didn't hear."

"Best not to go into it now, as"—and here her whisper grew quite deafening—"*we'll be seeing Elsa in just a few minutes*. Poor dear Elsa! She's quite fond of her sister, but, oh, what a trial she can be! So headstrong! But such a beauty she gets away with it. As *I* did once upon a time, although," she added with a coquettish laugh, "you wouldn't think so to look at me now, would you!"

Barring the possibility of a midlife accident in which she'd lost her chin, there was no way one could imagine Mrs. Pilchard having begun life as a beauty. But we murmured dutiful not at alls as I glanced uncomfortably at our fellow riders, several of whom were rolling their eyes. One droll fellow had his hand cupped at the back of his neck and was fluffing imaginary curls.

The elevator reached forty-five and Mrs. Pilchard, smiling contentedly at a job well and subtly done, led us out.

We were in a red-lacquered reception area. On the wall facing us, the logo of Champion's magazine, *Estime*, stood out in gleaming brass letters. Ringing the other walls were framed covers featuring interchangeable celebrities. Mrs. Pilchard sailed proudly to the receptionist's desk.

"Mildred Pilchard and guests," she announced to a fetching young man, who greeted her warmly and buzzed us through a side door. We entered a hall, where a beefy, thuggish-looking fellow sat on a stool, reading a Tom Clancy novel. He nodded politely to Mrs. Pilchard, then gave the two of us a mistrustful once-over. He led the way through two more doors, unlocking each by punching numbers into numeric keypads on the wall. Claire and I hung back, making droll faces at each other, but furtively, as if we feared discovery would lead to locked rooms and ungentle strip searches.

The second door led to an elevator, which our silent Cerberus summoned with a magnetic card *and* a number code. We stepped into the marble-and-brass interior, and he pressed a button marked "P." The doors *whoosh*ed shut and a moment later *whoosh*ed open again. Mrs. Pilchard, waving a coy little good-bye to the guard, led the way out, and the elevator closed behind us.

We were now in a foyer, standing before two massive gold doors. They were decorated with a stunning bas-relief of the labors of Hercules, who, one couldn't help noting, bore an uncanny resemblance to Peter Champion. Mrs. Pilchard, smiling at our astonishment, pressed a bell on the wall.

Seconds later the doors began slowly swinging open, and I felt a sudden stab of dread. I couldn't overcome the feeling I was entering some pagan fortress where cannibal kings offered human sacrifices to petulant gods. But I thought of Tommy and how he was counting on me and resolved that, no matter what I encountered, I would be a model of composure.

A uniformed butler appeared and said Mrs. Champion was behind schedule, but would be with us momentarily. Then, taking our coats, he withdrew. Claire and I stood there, taking the place in, and then, at exactly the same moment, burst into helpless giggles.

"Gracious me!" said Mrs. Pilchard. "I've witnessed many reactions to this room, but I can't say I've ever seen *that one!*"

The room—if "room" begins to say it—was circular and of dimensions I had never seen in a private home, let alone an apartment. The walls and floor were of pink marble, and the room was ringed by Doric columns, between which stood ornate pedestals bearing what seemed authentically ancient statues of the Mount Olympus crowd. Between the vastness of the place and the marble, columns, and statues, the room resembled the departure lounge of some ancient Greek airport.

In the center of the room was a large fountain topped by a statue of Poseidon. Grouped around the fountain were chairs and sofas of widely divergent styles and periods, costliness being the only unifying element. Massive glass doors led onto a terrace with another, still grander fountain and a heliopad.

Mrs. Pilchard directed our attention to the wall next to the doors we'd entered through. Our eyes widened as we took in a floor-to-ceiling aquarium, in which were swimming, if I was not mistaken, three baby sharks. She then pointed overhead. We gazed up and discovered the ceiling had a vast domed skylight. It then occurred to us that what we were seeing wasn't a skylight at all, but instead a white plaster dome, rimmed at the base with projectors that, regardless of the actual weather outside, sent serene images of blue skies, drifting clouds, birds, and the occasional plane dancing overhead.

"Stunning, isn't it?" said Mrs. Pilchard with the hushed reverence of a tour guide at Lourdes. "So grand and yet so warm!"

On the wall facing the gold doors were two more doors leading to the rest of the apartment. These were now flung open and Elsa Champion burst fabulously into the room.

She was not, we were dismayed to note, alone. She was, in fact, flanked by a veritable court, a churning mass of humanity that danced attendance on her, obeying her every command and recording her every word and gesture. There were maids, stenographers, photographers, and assorted other retainers whose roles were less immediately discernible. Glued to her elbow was a small whippet of a man in a dark silk suit and sunglasses, wielding a tape recorder. He seemed familiar, but I couldn't quite place him.

"*Millie,* my angel!" bellowed Elsa, and the air filled with whirs and clicks. Two of the photographers raced to find new angles from which to record the scene, never once lowering their cameras from their eyes.

"So good to see you!" cried Elsa, dramatically hurling her arms open. "Today of all days!"

They embraced warmly as Elsa, much the taller, stooped and made kissing sounds in the area of Millie's face. She wore a flowing blue silk dress that set off her pale complexion and white heels of a height that would have given pause to even the most courageous transvestite.

"Elsa, dearest," simpered Millie, "how stunning you look! But whoever are all these people!"

"Can you forgive me! It completely slipped my mind when I talked to you, but *Estime* is doing a piece on me today."

"How marvelous!" declared Millie, overjoyed to have wandered unwittingly into Coverage. "What sort of piece?"

"Just a typical day in my life. Sorry to keep you waiting, but I was in the study, reading to blind children."

Elsa turned to the man wielding the tape recorder and introduced him to Millie as that "marvelous young writer," Hoot Mulvaney.

Claire and I regarded each other with raised eyebrows. Mulvaney was one of the more notorious "downtown" authors. He'd scored a great success with his first novel, a study of amoral, self-destructive clubgoers called *I Am a Nostril.* His second, third, and fourth novels about amoral, self-destructive clubgoers had met with rather less rapturous receptions, prompting him to try his hand at journalism. He was now making a very comfortable living writing cover profiles for *Estime.*

His eyes were, as I noted, not on exhibit, but his mouth had a sullen twist to it. It wasn't hard to guess why. A journalist, even a celebrity journalist, desires a certain measure of latitude in describing his subjects. When, however, that subject happens to be his publisher's wife, his leeway is at a minimum. He can say she is dazzling, or if he prefers, he can select an appropriate synonym. That is the extent of it.

Whatever his mood, he was at pains to be civil, and he smiled nicely at Millie and shook her hand. She pumped his energetically, saying she was a great admirer of his books. He asked which was her favorite, and she said she enjoyed them all equally.

"Now, Millie," said Elsa, "you *must* introduce me to your two young geniuses!"

Introductions were made, and we were photographed shaking hands with Elsa, who posed cocking her head with a "You don't say?" expression, though neither of us had uttered a word.

Face to face now with this legend, I had to admit that, as much as I instinctively disliked her, she was some package. Being Irish myself, I hope I won't offend my countrymen if I acknowledge that although we do produce many beautiful women, they tend as a rule to be somewhat Faustian in nature, enjoying themselves tremendously for a few years, then going straight to hell. Elsa, though, was an exception. She couldn't have been a day under forty-five, yet she remained a classic black Irish beauty with dark glossy hair, alabaster skin, enormous black eyes, and a pert nose, all perched above a body that put one in mind of early Jane Russell.

After the photos were taken, Elsa took Millie's hand and told her, in sepulchral tones, how wretched she felt over the recent skirmish between their sisters.

"You will tell Horsey how *ghastly* I feel?"

"Of course!" said Millie.

"You can also tell her I called Kitty this morning and let her know I was *ab*solutely furious!"

"You mustn't be too hard on her! Personally, I blame the press for making too much of it."

"You said it! Goddamn vultures!" remarked Elsa, serenely oblivious to the army of reporters hovering inches away from her. "They're nothing but a buncha *savages!*"

Claire shot me a panicked look, and it did not take a mind reader to guess what had triggered it.

It was the voice.

If Elsa's face represented the very best Ireland had to offer, the voice that issued from it had little of the music of Killarney. It was deep and rumbling, with a smoker's huskiness and a nasality that, though ever-present, became harrowing whenever she emphasized words with a flat *a*, such as "ghastly" or "savages." It reminded me of someone, though I couldn't, for a moment, think who. Then it hit me. She sounded exactly like Lucille Ball did at those moments when her sitcom character, faced with some painful situation, would burst into tears—which, if you'll recall, involved Miss Ball staring directly into the camera and screaming, "*Waaaaaaaaaaaah!*"

"Now, Elsa, my dear," said Millie in a lofty tone, "you must do as you always do in these situations—rise above it!"

"I'll try, Millie. But that Kitty—she just gets me so *maaad!*"

Elsa shook her head philosophically, then her eye caught Mr. Mulvaney, who was smiling. She informed him in the steeliest of tones that her remarks concerning her sister were *not* for the record; he was to rewind his tape and record over them. His mouth tightened for a second, then he complied with the crestfallen air of a python ordered to cough up the rabbit and apologize to it.

This matter attended to, Elsa turned and addressed the assembled. We would now, she informed us, adjourn to the "salon," where "this dy*nam*ic young songwriting team" would audition for her new act. She led us through double doors and down a wide hall, hung with enormous paintings of nudes and performers. So indescribably hideous were these canvases that I formed an instant suspicion and peered at the bottom of one. There, sure enough, was Elsa's own name, scrawled proudly in the corner. The artiste, meanwhile, swept along ahead of us, her retinue hanging on each word that fell from her lips.

"Picking the writers is *the* most crucial decision in putting an act together. There's lots of famous songwriters I could have approached, but me, I like to keep my nose to the ground, looking for the stars of tomorrow. Of course, it helps to have knowledgeable friends, and Millie here sees *everything* and always knows who the next—"

Claire and I brought up the rear, whispering furiously.

"Remind me to thank you for this. Something tells me I may forget."

"Look," I said, "the woman has lots of money—"

"*Really?* And what tipped you off?"

"A job's a job!"

"Philip," she hissed, "she *can't* sing!"

"How do you know that?" I said. "We haven't even heard her yet."

"Didn't you say she tried once and flopped?"

"That was twenty years ago!"

"That's my point," said Claire, her eyes on Elsa. "If she struck out when she was twenty years prettier than *that*, trust me, *she can't sing.*"

Elsa herded us into a large room obviously consecrated to Music. There were sofas facing a white grand piano on a platform and, in front of the picture window—you guessed it—a statue of Orpheus strumming his lyre. In one corner was a long table where two maids stood ready to serve a very high tea.

"Help yourselves to tea," said Elsa, then wafted over to where Claire and I stood cowering in the doorway.

"Philip, Claire—my schedule is *fran*tic today. Wouldn't you know, the Literacy League insisted on giving me this *plaque* on the same day I set aside for this article! We've got twenty minutes, so give me your two best numbers. You got anything real sophisticated? Cole Porter–type songs?"

I said yes, we had a few pieces with something of that flavor.

"Great! And how about a ballad? A real lump-in-the-throat kind of thing where I would maybe cry when I heard it?"

We nodded dumbly.

"*Fab*ulous!" she said, and then, turning to the horde, clapped her hands.

"Gather round everyone! Concert time!"

The horde grabbed sandwiches and made for the sofas. As we advanced toward the piano, all eyes were upon us.

When you write musicals, you are from time to time called upon to sing your material before assemblies of strangers, few of whom are either eager to hear or likely to enjoy it. These concerts tend, mercifully, to take place at night, with ample opportunity beforehand to drown the butterflies with some suitable beverage. It's not often you're asked to perform dead sober in the middle of the afternoon and less often still that you face your audience with the grim knowledge that if you lay an egg, you'll not only lose the man of your dreams, but will live to see the whole appalling episode described by your least favorite writer in the pages of your least favorite magazine. The unhappy concurrence of these factors reduced me to a state for which the term *stage fright* is altogether inadequate.

Claire took her seat and, looking up into my ashen face, said, "Start with 'Hard to Be Me.' "

I stared, aghast. The song was from an old show of ours and was sung by a spoiled, filthy rich socialite who's telling her maid how fortunate the servant is not to lead a life as glamorous and exhausting as her own.

"She'll never laugh!" I said. My teeth were sweating.

"She won't have a choice," Claire said calmly.

"I can't do it!" I said in a choked whisper.

"Sing out, Louise," replied Claire, and played me a fanfare.

I wiped my palms on my trousers and turned to face the audience. Elsa was leaning forward with an intense, critical gaze the photographers were capturing from several angles. I explained the premise, causing her to mug briefly, but then she resumed her Discerning Aesthete face and Claire struck up the intro.

I hammed it up dutifully, playing the grande dame determined to mine tragedy from her glittering existence.

> *Although you may think it's*
> *All trinkets*
> *And mink, it's*
> *Hard to be me!*

Whether because she liked it or feared being thought a spoilsport, Elsa began laughing. The others followed suit, and I finally began to breathe (always a help when you're singing) and hammed it up even more:

> *The staff that needs training,*
> *The mad entertaining,*
> *Night after night!*
> *And even complaining*

Is terribly draining—
If you're doing it right.

The song finished to a boisterous hand as Elsa mimed amusement like a silent film star. Our ballad was a song cut from our recent show, one of those time-honored smart-woman-botches-romance numbers called "Live and Learn." Though the content was familiar, it was one of Claire's loveliest melodies, especially the haunting progression under the long, slow finish, where the words are, "Live /And love /And lose /And learn."

There was silence when we finished, then Elsa stood and, brushing a photogenic tear from her eye, led the applause.

"Wonderful! The job is *yours!*" she boomed, rushing to the piano.

"Thank you, Mrs. Champion!" I said, my knees rubberized with relief.

"Please! It's *Elsa!* I can't wait to get started!" She turned to Mulvaney, who'd hastened to her side. "I'm *very* decisive. When I see real quality, I don't hesitate—I *grab* it!"

"Well—" said Claire, standing.

"No, don't get up!" cried Elsa, shoving her back onto the bench. "Play that ballad again! I want to learn it!"

I sat on the bench and began singing again as Elsa plopped down on Claire's other side and warbled along tentatively. The photographers clustered round to record the scene, and Mrs. Pilchard sent one sprawling as she elbowed her way to the foreground. She posed standing behind Elsa, swaying gently, her face aglow at the sweet tones emanating from her friend.

The tones were not, in fact, any too sweet. True, there was a smoky quality that seemed right for a cabaret diva, and the pitch was generally on target. But that flat, bleating sound, distressing enough in her speaking voice, became fairly bloodcurdling when applied to a sustained high note.

Claire smiled gamely for the photographers as she coached her illustrious pupil.

"Lovely, Elsa! But just half a tone higher there."

"Where? Go back, go back! . . . 'It end-ed the way it be-GAAAAN . . . !' "

"*Half* a tone."

We stumbled through to the end, Elsa prolonging the final notes in a manner that proved that, if nothing else, she had lungs. Her entourage, knowing on which side its bread was buttered, applauded madly as Elsa took coy little bows.

"Mildred, you darling," she gushed, "how can I repay you for bringing me these *fabu*lous people?"

"Hearing you sing is payment enough for me!" fibbed Millie.

The love feast was interrupted by the sound of a throat being cleared somewhere behind the throng. The crowd parted, and there stood an imposing woman in her fifties with short gray bangs and the convivial air of a reform school matron. She advanced toward Elsa and murmured, her tone heavy with significance, that Elsa's sister was on the phone.

"I'm running late," said Elsa. "Tell her I've left for the Literacy thing."

"I mentioned the ceremony," the woman said darkly, "and she said she planned to attend."

Elsa gave the woman a look you could store fur in and, saying she'd take the call in the study, departed with a purposeful stride. Her court, free now of its queen, made straight for the refreshments as wild whispers and strangled giggles filled the air. Claire took the opportunity to drag me behind the piano.

"So," she said, "how much are we asking for this?"

"You mean you'll do it?" I asked, completely nonplussed. I'd been prepared for a long, uphill battle.

"We haven't much of a choice, have we?"

"What do you mean?" I asked.

She jerked her head toward Hoot, who was spitting poison into a photographer's ear. "Philip, if there's one thing worse than people saying 'Oh, God, they're writing for Elsa *Champion!*' it's people saying 'Oh, God, they *auditioned* for Elsa Champion and couldn't get hired!' "

"But we *are* hired."

"Yes," said Claire. "But if we turn her down—after auditioning in the middle of her wretched article—what do you think she'll say about us then?"

I frowned. "Nothing terribly nice."

"Bingo, cookie. And she'll say it in a very popular magazine. *Which*, coming after a one-night flop, is all our reputation needs."

"I see your point," I said grimly, though I was, of course, delighted that fate had conspired to undo her objections.

"We're stuck, me boyo, so let's at least make it worth our while. I say we each get at least three thousand. Maybe even . . . cheese it," she murmured. "The velvet foghorn approaches."

Elsa walked over to us, and matron, apparently Elsa's personal secretary, followed two steps behind clutching a folder. Between the annoying interruption of her sister and the momentary absence of her recording angel, she seemed less effusive but said politely enough that she was glad we'd come and looked forward to starting work. She wanted Peter to meet us, too, and asked if we could attend a party the next evening in celebration of both Valentine's Day and the third anniversary of *Estime*. Being anxious to get off on the right foot, we said we'd be delighted.

She was about to go when Claire delicately broached the subject of our fee. Elsa, flustered to be faced with so vulgar an inquiry, let out a beleaguered sigh. The disquieting thought struck me that the money issue might put the kibosh on Claire's involvement before we even began. The Champions were widely regarded as the ne plus ultra in stinginess. Stories abounded of maids fired for shopping without coupons and of *Estime* T-shirts given as Christmas tips. They were especially notorious for their apparent delusion that they were some noble philanthropy to which merchants, caterers, and designers should happily donate goods and services. Claire, I knew, could scarcely bring herself to abet Elsa's career, let alone subsidize it.

"Well, of course, I want to pay what's *fair*—" began Elsa, but before she could offer us five bucks a song, plus concession rights at the concert, Hoot materialized, microphone poised, and Elsa leapt at the chance to repair her image as Queen of the *Nouvelle* Tightwads.

"I hate to haggle," she said, her voice a shade louder, "so what say ten thousand each?"

"Ten *thousand?*" I repeated, floored.

"Oh, make it fifteen!" said Elsa. She turned to Hoot. "I've *always* believed that people who work for me should be well rewarded." She then saw this could be interpreted several ways and rushed to add,

"I mean creativity should be rewarded. It's a *tragedy* how little artists make in this country. Why, just look at Philip's shoes!"

Everyone gazed down to check out the rip in the seam of my loafers, and Hoot scribbled a note. He then oozed off to the buffet, clearly burning to tell his cohorts about Elsa's Lady Bountiful routine. Elsa turned to go again, but the secretary cleared her throat and thrust some forms into her hand.

"What the hell are these?" asked Elsa. "Oh—right!"

She handed the forms to us. "You have to sign these first."

"What are they?" asked Claire.

"Confidentiality agreements. They say you'll respect Peter's and my privacy. You know—not to talk to reporters about us or write a book or help anyone who's out to trash us."

"Ah," I said.

"Peter's a *fiend* about having people sign it. Ever since that oily little deck hand from our boat told the press that big crock about Peter buying a woman for the zoning commissioner!"

"Oh, yes," said Claire. "I read about that."

"You didn't *believe* it, did you?" asked Elsa through narrowed eyes, and Claire replied diplomatically, if vaguely, that she certainly didn't credit everything she read in the papers.

"The woman was a *dancer*," fumed Elsa, "not a hooker, and Peter never gave her a dime. She was in *love* with that old man, though to hear the press tell it . . . well, never mind. We just don't want it to happen again. And with *you* two—well, if you're gonna capture my personality in song, you'll have to get to know me a bit, right? I'd hate to think anything I told you might find its way into some sleazy—"

"Mrs. Champion," said Claire, "I'm sure I speak for both of us when I say we wouldn't dream of betraying a single confidence."

"Good. This town's full of rats just dying to do us dirty, and if we can't trust our own people—!"

"Well, you can trust *us*," said Claire. "Right, Philip?"

"Oh, absolutely."

"*Fab*ulous," smiled Elsa. "But sign anyway."

Matron handed us a clipboard and pen. Claire looked it over to make sure it said no more than Elsa had indicated. Satisfied, she signed, then handed the clipboard and pen to me. At the moment she did, a photographer materialized in front of us.

"Hey, whazat?" he inquired. "A contract? Make a great shot for the spread!"

He raised his camera to his face.

"Hey, pal—*smile*, will ya?"

Five

As those who've crossed her can testify, the Wrath of Claire is a mighty and terrible thing, a great articulate wind that leaves its victims feeling much the way a cornfield does when the locusts have just departed. She could not, of course, unleash it in the presence of some dozen strangers, all equipped with recording devices, but as we wended our way out of Champion Plaza, I paled at the thought of what she might say once we had some privacy.

It was a considerable relief, as such, to discover that she did not hold me responsible for our having been cornered into the job. Not even Mrs. Pilchard had been forewarned of the media blitzkrieg, so how could I have known? Now that we were committed, it was, she felt, best to focus on the bright side. The money, for one thing, was a godsend. And if Elsa, as seemed all too probable, failed to enchant, we'd see to it that her material was such that no one could blame her failure on us.

Claire headed off to Bergdorf's to "take out a mortgage on a frock" for the *Estime* bash. The secretary had advised us the party would be black tie, so I made for the nearest tuxedo rental shop to have my measurements taken, then raced home to apprise Tommy of our success in winning the assignment.

When I got in, the phone was ringing, and positive it was Tommy, I snatched it up and uttered a breathless "Hello?"

"Are you having asthma again?" asked Gilbert.

I tensed. It occurred to me that I had, till this moment, given no thought at all as to how to handle relations with Gilbert now that we were obvious, if unacknowledged, rivals in love. On speedy reflection, I decided that as I clearly had the upper hand and to gloat would be unkind, I'd disregard the topic entirely and see how he chose to handle it.

"Hi, Gilbert," I said pleasantly. "I'm fine. I just got in."

"How did it go?"

I summarized the day's events, laying stress on our brilliance and composure. If he was feeling any of the envy I'd have expected, given his base, competitive nature, he concealed it well, offering congratulations and saying he'd known I'd come through.

"So Claire's in?" he asked.

"Unhappy, but in."

"You didn't tell her anything you shouldn't have, I hope?"

I replied coolly in the negative and asked how things were going with him.

"Swell! I'm off to Boston for a few days. Top-secret mission."

"Why Boston?" I asked.

"It's Peter and Elsa's hometown. The low-rent suburbs, anyway. I'll be interviewing old chums and combing newspaper morgues—you know, trying to discredit some of the tripe Peter and Elsa have dished up about their glorious youth."

He tried to sound eager, but I suspected he viewed the assignment without enthusiasm. Not only would it be tedious, but he'd be surrendering the field to me.

"Sounds fun!" I said.

"Should be. Tommy's putting me up at the Ritz! Which reminds me—how much is Elsa paying you two?"

"Fifteen grand," I said nonchalantly.

"Are you kidding! You're getting seventy-five *hundred* out of this deal!"

"Fifteen grand *each*."

"*What!*" he said apoplectically. "Well! I should hope you'll send some of that my way!"

"Why?" I asked bluntly. "Are you planning to write the material for me?"

He pointed out that had an agent arranged so lucrative a deal, I'd owe him ten percent. I pointed out that he was not my agent. I was, of course, grateful for his assistance, in recognition of which I would forget about the five hundred dollars he'd owed me for several years now. I knew that Gilbert, who views all his personal debts as having a six-month statute of limitations, had long since forgotten about it himself, but I would offer no more.

"Now if you'll excuse me," I said, "I have to call Tommy and tell him how it all went."

"Oh," he said.

His tone suddenly changed, though not in the way I'd expected it to, becoming tense or bitchy. It was suddenly gentle, even concerned.

"Uh . . . since you'll be seeing more of Tommy, Philip, there's something I think I really ought to mention."

"Yes?" I asked warily.

"Speaking as a friend," he began, "I'd be doing you a disservice if I didn't suggest you stop behaving with him the way you did last night."

"And what way was that?" I inquired.

"*Well!*" he said in that condescending "oh-dear-must-one-spell-it-out?" tone that precedes nine out of ten homicides. "It was *obvious*— if obvious isn't too mild a word—that you had quite a little crush on him. And as despicable as that was of you, coming right after I'd confided *my* feelings for him, I want you to know I don't blame you."

"Thank you."

"I mean that. Tommy's a very attractive man, and I'm sure you can't help nursing these unrealistic fantasies about him. But, please, for your *own* sake, try not to make such a spectacle of yourself!"

I counted to five and said that I'd not been aware of any point in the evening when my conduct in Tommy's presence had entered the realm of spectacle. Gilbert replied kindly that my obliviousness to my behavior went a long way toward explaining how I could have kept it up at such unseemly length. But just so I would know, my "mooning" over Tommy had been *the* most embarrassing exhibition he'd ever witnessed in his life.

"I mean, really!" he said with a light, musical laugh. "*Lunging* to light his cigarettes! And those longing glances you were giving him!"

"Longing glances?"

"Yes. I had a dog once that used to look at me that way whenever

I'd pick up a can opener. I know you didn't realize it, Philip, but it really was the most *ludicrous* display of—"

"Oh, *please!*" I said, having reached my breaking point. "I don't need lectures on ludicrous displays from *you*, Sister Honkey-Tonk!"

Gilbert's tone strained for blandness. "I can't imagine what you're suggesting."

"I'm sure! You and your smoldering gaze! All you needed was a garter belt and a lamppost!"

His reply was a sigh of boundless pity. "Oh, *dear*," he said. "I feared you'd be sensitive about this, though I had hoped you'd at least refrain from making hysterical accusations with no basis in fact."

"No basis?" I hooted. "Come off it! You told me yourself you were *dying* to jump his bones!"

"Which seems to have had little enough effect on you!" he snapped. "Nice behavior from my so-called best friend! If I didn't feel so *sorry* for you—"

From then on the conversation grew increasingly rancorous. He strongly suggested my giving up, as I hadn't the slightest hope of seducing a man of Tommy's exacting standards, besides which he'd met him first. I said that I refused to honor some debatable point of sexual sportsmanship if it meant handing over the love of my life to a youth who, if history was any indicator, would reward him with a six-week affair and the loss of several neckties. Gilbert replied that if I were so sure his romance with Tommy wouldn't last, why not let him get on with it and wait my turn? I countered that I didn't care to woo Gilbert's castoffs, then withdrew this, saying that on second thought, no one should curtail his dating pool as drastically as that.

"Philip! I'm only trying to save you from embarrassment and heartache! He doesn't feel a thing for you!"

"Like hell he doesn't! He said wonderful things about me!"

"Such delusions! I bleed for you, Philip!"

"You may yet!" I said, and, feeling this was as good a moment as any, slammed down the receiver.

I sat a moment, breathing heavily but smiling at having gotten the last word. The more I thought about it, though, the less I found to smile about.

However furious I was at Gilbert, however much it would have delighted me to tie him to a chair and have at his hair with garden shears, this did not alter the fact that he was my oldest and dearest friend. Our relationship, which began as a brief but memorable adolescent affair, had now spanned more than a dozen years. Other friends had come and gone, but we had stood by each other through fights and reconciliations, through poverty and boyfriends, through accomplishments and debacles.

But all the various bricks hurled at our friendship over the years were, I feared, paltry things indeed when compared to the approaching meteor that was Tommy Parker. It had been years since I'd wanted a man even half so badly, and it seemed monstrously unfair to me that Gilbert should want him, too. After all, I reasoned, if *I* won Tommy, Gilbert would soon recover and find someone else; his passions, while deeply felt, occurred on a more or less quarterly basis. For me, though, passion was a less frequent visitor. If Gilbert stole Tommy away from me, forgiveness would not come soon or easily. Things might never be the same between us again, and the thought that I might, in one calamity, lose both dream lover and best friend was painful to contemplate.

I fretted a while, then consoled myself with the thought that such concerns were decidedly premature. I'd only met Tommy last night, and then under the influence of good champagne. Who could say, despite the intensity of my feelings, that they might not yet prove ephemeral?

As if to disprove the likelihood of this, the phone rang, and on answering, I once again heard that exquisitely cultivated voice purring into my ear.

"Philip, O intrepid one! How are things behind enemy lines?"

"Hi!" I said, dissolving instantly into a puddle of longing. "How are you, Tommy?"

"A bit squeamish, I fear. I'm sitting in my office watching 'Live at Five,' which has seen fit to air some appalling footage of Dame Elsa accepting a plaque from the Literacy League. Why they should give Elsa a plaque I can't imagine, unless they view her as some hope-giving example, someone illiterates the world over can look to and think, Well, if *she* can read . . . ! Do these old eyes deceive me or is that Hoot Mulvaney slithering in the background?"

"No, that's him all right," I said. "Wait, I want to see this."

I rushed to my TV, grabbed the pliers on top, and turned it on. Elsa wobbled into view. She stood in a crowded ballroom, surrounded by microphone-wielding journalists to whom she was making some not very spontaneous remarks likening books to torches thrust into dark corners. Hoot could be seen lurking behind her.

"Dear me," said Tommy, "don't tell me *he's* pocketing a plaque as well? I suppose one could argue he encourages new readers by writing books full of easy words, but—"

"He's there doing a feature on Elsa for *Estime.* It's a day-in-the-life piece."

"I *see,*" he said. "A day in the life of the publisher's wife! One waits breathlessly to see if he'll be kind or not. Am I correct then in assuming your own audience with Miss Moffat here was viewed as fodder for this watershed in sycophancy?"

"Yes," I said. "Mulvaney was there when we arrived."

"*Really?* Before sunset? So much for my vampire theory. How did it go?"

I gave him a rundown, which he interrupted often with gratifying exclamations of delight.

"O *brave* Philip! What a job you've done! Of course, my expectations were high, but you have so far surpassed them that I'm left limp and speechless! Is there no end to your miracles?"

"Come on," I said, flushed with delight. "I got the job, that's all."

"Yes—and got it right in the pages of Peter's own magazine, which is too delicious for words. And to think I keep wondering where all the extraordinary men have gotten to, and here they are hanging about in my own study. What a shame you're spoken for!"

"Huh?" I blinked.

"Your boyfriend," said Tommy. "Jealous fellow? Gun collector?"

"*Gun* collector?"

"I trust Gilbert broke no confidence in mentioning him to me. You may offer the man my personal congratulations, and tell him that if he doesn't treat you right, guns or no guns, he'll have Mrs. Parker's little boy to answer to."

Inhaling deeply, I informed Tommy in the lightest tone I could muster that I did not, in fact, have a beau at the moment, armed or

otherwise. Gilbert had invented him in some odd, whimsical frame
of mind, not attributable, one hoped, to substance abuse.

"I doubt it," said Tommy. "Gilbert doesn't need drugs. His mind
teems with natural opiates. So, I can flirt with you then without undue
concern that I'll wake some night to discover an irate fellow with a
Winchester, requesting an audience?"

"Oh, absolutely."

"Happy to hear it. Tell me, are you free the night after tomorrow?"

"Yes," I said, my heart leaping. *A date? Already!*

"Wonderful. Come by around eight and I'll give you lessons in how
to be a proper mole. Be great fun. I'll outfit you with bugs and high-
tech gizmos, and before we're done you'll be the envy of Interpol."

So, it was less a date than a meeting. Still, I'd finally get to be
alone with him. And who could say what began in business might not
end in ecstasy? My heart aflutter with hope, I swore to be there on
the button, bade him adieu, and passed the afternoon in isometrics.

The next day I went to the library to peruse back issues of *Estime.*
My acquaintance with it had been confined to waiting rooms and
checkout lines, and as I'd soon be meeting the publisher and staff,
it seemed prudent to study a few recent samples. Flattery is among
us spies' more useful weapons, and this way I could equip myself to
make those fawning comments that do so much to break ice and lower
defenses.

I retired to an armchair with a stack representing a year's worth of
the slickly produced journal, the cover motto of which monthly promised its readers "A Peek at the Peak." I began by inspecting the
current issue.

The cover, like most of them, featured a glamour shot of a film
star, in this case Rebecca Mueller. She'd risen to fame last year in
Judy's Hammer, a hugely improbable thriller in which she played an
assault victim who lapses into a coma and awakens a year later,
transformed, as coma victims so often are, into a monosyllabic killing
machine. She was opening in a new film in which she portrayed not
a psychotic killer, but the *sister* of a psychotic killer, dispelling forever
any lingering doubts as to her versatility.

The article was composed by Hoot Mulvaney in rhapsody mode. Titled "Rebecca Mueller—From Star to Super Nova," it began:

The head swivels as the intense, glittering eyes circle the restaurant like a searchbeam, a beam that does more than illuminate—it scalds. Embarrassed, the diners blush and avert their gazes. Even here in the middle of Le Dôme, Rebecca craves, needs, *gets* privacy.

I repeat my question. She ponders it and a cloud darkens her face, a face that only a tiny mole near the mouth saves from unendurable perfection.

"Yes," she says in that gravelly purr that is sex made sound. "I suppose I did feel for a while that I had to put on, you know, an act. People are real threatened by intelligence, especially in models. So you let people assume you're not that bright, and before you know it you've got like this image."

But Rebecca's image will never be the same again. The cynics who tittered at her thoughtful work in such otherwise forgettable films as *Blood Picnic* and *Scuzzies III: The Showdown* will sing a different tune when they see her riveting portrayal of a terrorized geneticist in Sydney Graves's stylish new thriller, *Right Behind You. . . .*

I slogged through a bit more, then checked out the rest of the issue. The day-in-the-life story, apparently a regular feature, centered on an ultrachic restaurateur, among whose successes was Ici, where, coincidentally, tonight's party would be held. Another regular feature was called "*À Table.*" Printed in playscript form, it purported to capture the actual conversation spoken at a dinner attended by six or eight celebrated guests. The one I read, which was studded with bon mots and wry little aperçus, seemed about as improvised as a coronation, and I had to assume that either the transcripts were heavily edited or the guests had arrived bearing index cards and crib sheets.

I glanced at the remaining stories, all of which shared a high dirt quotient. There was an opera star going through an acrimonious divorce and another piece casting suspicion on the coroner's verdict in the death of a Nobel Prize–winning chemist. I sifted through a few back issues, scanning the tables of contents, and found more of the same.

It seemed that for all the magazine's much vaunted emphasis on Culture and Achievement, its strongest appeal was to the public's boundless appetite for scandal. Of course, not every article dragged someone through the mud; many pieces, like Rebecca's, were quite fawning. But when you started to examine who was flattered and who flattened, a curious trend emerged.

Celebrities with wide national popularity were given fulsome profiles heralding their latest projects, while less well known celebrities from the realms of high culture or business merited inclusion only if in the midst of some personal tragedy, the rule of thumb being the less famous the subject, the more sordid the tragedy. Thus a fading star, painter, conductor, or ballet dancer might win a feature by battling cancer or addiction, but truly minor celebrities—poets, scientists, and classical musicians—stood little chance of appearing unless involved in some grisly murder or suicide, preferably with occult overtones.

I was in the middle of a juicy account of a promising young cellist who'd died of autoerotic asphyxiation when, seeing that daylight was fading, I hastened off to fetch my rented tux and prepare for the night's festivities.

The party was held at Ici, downtown's latest restaurant-to-be-seen-in, and as our taxi crept down lower Broadway the limo traffic grew so thick, Claire and I decided to walk the last few blocks rather than sit, staring balefully at the meter.

We entered just behind an Oscar-nominated director, who strode regally past the maître d', a tall bland fellow with shoulder-length blond curls. We gave him our names, which he found at discomforting length on what appeared to be a supplemental list. We then checked our coats and headed for the main space, which was below street level and reached by means of a grand staircase.

Elsa had informed us that the party would celebrate not only *Estime*'s third anniversary, but Valentine's Day as well. It was clear to us from our first glance at the decor that when the Champions threw a party, they took pains to make sure their intended theme would be unambiguous to the meanest intelligence. I didn't know what the place looked like on a normal night, but on this one it was a vast, kitschy, red, white, and pink Temple of Love. Everything—and I mean everything—was heart-shaped. Tables, chairs, plates, centerpieces, floral arrangements, food displays, ashtrays, matchboxes, even the *bandbox*. The band, led by pricey society pianist Dick Brandy, played only songs with "Love" in the title. Diminutive cater waiters, dressed as cupids with white silk diapers and pasted-on wings, paraded about offering skewered hors d'oeuvres, carried not on trays but in quivers slung over their bare shoulders. Still more cupids floated overhead on shifting clouds suspended from wires. They lolled or sat on their fluffy perches, their expressions hovering between winsomeness and stark terror as they waved to the guests and sprinkled them with rose petals. Teams of actors and actresses portraying romantic couples from history strolled among the tables or performed tableaux vivants in various alcoves ringing the main floor. The alcoves were equipped with curtains that parted amid trumpet flourishes to reveal such celebrated lovebirds as Antony and Cleopatra or Bonaparte and Josephine, posing in overwrought clinches.

Champion had not, amid this orgy of sentiment, forgotten that he had a magazine to promote. Blowups of past *Estime* covers, squeezed into heart-shaped frames, dotted the walls while large banners celebrated "America's Three-Year Love Affair with *ESTIME*." And dead smack in the center of the room, perched on a dramatically spotlit pedestal, was a six-foot-high solid chocolate heart with the *Estime* logo boldly carved into both sides.

It was only eight-thirty, but the party was boiling along at full steam. The room swarmed with beautiful, stunningly dressed people, all laughing and chattering away with the furious happiness of the Arrived. Many were famous, and those who weren't devoted much energy to looking it. Claire and I stood as if paralyzed at the head of the stairs, ogling the spectacle. My emotions careened between pride at being included, shame at the shallowness that permitted the pride, and terror of not fitting in. Claire, who was gazing, appalled, at the cupids of the airborne division, seemed ready to announce a headache and bolt. But then Barbara Walters, whose path we were blocking, cleared her throat politely, and we said, "Oh, sorry," and started down the stairs.

Six

"Just remember," she said as we descended, "*you* got me into this, so if you abandon me to this crowd while you run off and chase your dream date—"

"Don't worry," I said. "We're Siamese twins, all right?"

"Thank you. Oh, look—there's Mr. Mulvaney. As he's the only one here we've met, I say we go feign our respects."

We approached Mulvaney, who was chatting with two fellows I deduced were writers, as they seemed enormously self-satisfied without being handsome. Mulvaney wore a shiny suit and that cocky air that is perhaps inevitable in a young man who's surrounded by film stars, all of whom have to be nice to him. We hovered, waiting to speak but not wanting to interrupt him in midkvetch.

"Do you be*lieve*," he fumed, "he would *dare* do that to me?"

"I hope you called him on it," said one companion.

"I *did!* I said, 'Where the fuck do you get off assigning that geek to review my book when you know I panned that turd collection he put out last winter! You can't find an author I haven't crucified?' "

"Well," drawled the other friend, "they *are* getting scarce."

"Hello, Mr. Mulvaney," said Claire. "So nice to see you again!"

"Hey!" said Hoot. "Nice to see you, too . . . uh . . . ?"

"Claire Simmons. And my partner, Philip Cavanaugh."

"Right!" he said, snapping his fingers. "Nice little songs."

He introduced us to his friends, Keith and Toby, both novelists we hadn't read but to whom we said, "Ah!" with that delighted surprise meant to suggest long and enthused fanhood.

"Philip and Claire," smirked Hoot, "are writing Elsa's night-club act."

"*Really?*" asked Toby, and a wry smile ricocheted among them. Apparently Hoot was already spreading the word about Elsa's golden larynx.

"Interesting voice Elsa has," said Hoot. "Sort of . . . *unique*, huh?" He addressed Claire. "You write music. How would *you* describe it?"

"Goodness!" Claire said sweetly. "I'm not sure I could. Fortunately, I don't have to. *You* will, though, won't you, Hoot, when you write your piece about her? I look forward to seeing how you manage it."

Atta girl, Claire! I thought. Go get 'em!

Hoot's friends pursed their lips at this reference to his status as bum kisser to the court, and Hoot, eyes flashing, seized the offensive by asking if we hadn't had a musical open recently.

"Yes," I said, my jaw clenching.

"I'd *love* to see it," said Hoot. "Can I get seats or is there a long wait?"

"The wait," said Claire with a carefree smile, "will be for the revival. We got dreadful reviews and closed opening night."

"Oh, too bad," said Hoot.

"Terrible production," I said, taking Claire's cheerful lead. "Sort of makes me envy you novelists!"

"Why's that?" asked Hoot.

"Well, nothing stands between you and your audience. No actors or directors interpreting what you've done. So when you get reviewed you know they're responding to *you* and just you. That must be nice."

"Sometimes," Toby said with a droll look toward Hoot.

"I would *love* a drink," said Claire, eager to quit while we were marginally ahead. "Lovely meeting you all!"

"Well," I said once we were a safe distance away, "we sure peed in his Cheerios."

"Yes," she agreed sourly. "*Such* fun. One drink, thank you to Elsa, and we're out of here, all right?"

Suddenly a wave of energetic applause swept through the room. We turned and saw that Elsa, clad in an opulent long-sleeved scarlet number, was majestically descending the stairs amid a fusillade of flashbulbs. At her side, his arm hooked affectionately through hers, was our host, Peter Champion.

Claire and I turned excitedly to each other and whispered the exact same words.

"He's so short!"

The babble of conversation subsided as the applause grew. The band launched into a soupy version of "Our Love Is Here to Stay," and the Champions, smiling benignly upon their crowd, made dignified, almost papal, waves.

They reached the floor, where they kissed to a chorus of ahhhhs and a fresh round of applause. They then proceeded in different directions, each accepting congratulations and hugs from their glittering guests. Claire and I, feeling that Elsa would not soon be available for thanking, made for the bar, elbowing our way through a crowd that included Bill Blass, last year's Tony-winning actress, and Dido and Aeneas. We ordered champagne, which was, needless to say, Dom Pérignon.

"Well," I said, "it probably wasn't very smart, talking to Hoot that way. When he writes his piece he'll probably have at us like a *ginsu* chef."

"I doubt it," said Claire. "After all, Elsa *hired* us. If he makes us look too bad, she looks bad for wanting us. And speak of the devil!"

I pivoted and saw Elsa swimming toward us through the crowd, hotly pursued by her leading apologist, the columnist Daisy Winters. I waved and she waved back and was soon upon us.

"Jameson, rocks," she croaked to the bartender, making it clear that thirst and not our smiling faces had drawn her so hastily to this corner of the room. Still, there we were, and she greeted us brightly with hugs and air kisses. Our eardrums were once more assaulted by the attack of the killer vowel, but we ignored it and said how thrilled we were to be there.

"Well, I'm *hap*py you could come!"

"Elsa dolling!" said Daisy, pushing her way through, notepad at the ready.

"Daisy!"

They embraced gingerly. Daisy was a woman in her fifties, dressed like an Egyptian priestess. She had high hair, long dangling earrings, and a pale moon-shaped face that was not, one suspected, first draft. For all her careful attention to beauty, she had a swaggering style and a rough Old New York way of speaking. She was like Nathan Detroit after a transsexual operation.

"Elsa," declared Daisy, "you are the epitome of tremendous. The cupids on the clouds are to die for!"

"Please!" said Elsa. "I don't even dare look up! I'm convinced one of 'em's gonna fall off on purpose, just so he can sue us!"

"You got an item for me?"

"Right here," said Elsa, gesturing to Claire and me. "These are the fan*tas*tic young songwriters who'll be helpin' me out with my act. Give 'em a mention, they deserve it."

Daisy dutifully sought our particulars and noted them down. Elsa then told us there were scads of people she wanted us to meet and dragged us to a heart-shaped table some yards away. Around it sat a bevy of local anchorpeople and other media sorts. My eyes widened to note that among them was Spark Chandler. Once a local investigative reporter, he was now the host of one of those afternoon talk shows that provide the unbashful a chance to air their more lurid personal confessions before inquisitive studio audiences.

Next to Spark, right in the heart's cleavage, sat a small woman whose dainty appearance seemed perfectly in keeping with the decor. She had bow lips, a snub nose, and round rosy cheeks, all framed by wispy blond curls. We soon saw, however, that her manner in addressing a nearby subordinate was anything but cherubic.

"I want it on my desk by noon *tomorrow*, or your butt's in the shredder! Why you thought you could come to a fucking party is more than I can imagine! Elsa, darling!"

She leapt to her feet as the subordinate skulked miserably away. Elsa introduced us. She was Joy Cudgel, the editor-in-chief of *Estime*.

"Nice meeting you," she said with a smile that, had it come and gone any faster, would have amounted to subliminal niceness. She then addressed Elsa as Daisy hung back, her pencil tumescing.

"Look at you! Younger every time I see you! I could spit!"

"Well, look who's talking," said Elsa. "I love your dress."

"Please!" said Joy. "It's ancient!"

She spoke at great speed, gesticulating violently with sharp jabs and slashes like someone giving instructions to a deaf assassin.

"Listen! Saw the photos for your piece! Priceless! That shot of you and the blind kids? It's an *essay* on caring! We're talking about a bigger print run, major campaign, newspapers, radio, the cover, you, everywhere! Buses, subways, complete saturation. What say we bump it back a month, closer to your opening? Better timing? Talk to me."

"I'll discuss it with Peter," said Elsa, a shade overwhelmed. "He always knows best."

Perhaps because Joy had cold-shouldered us, Elsa took the trouble to introduce us to Spark Chandler, who was, we blanched to learn, Joy's husband. Spark rose, his photogenic smile gleaming, and extended his hand munificently. Elsa gushed a bit about our work, and Spark made some obligatory remark about looking forward to hearing it.

"*Spark!*" cried Elsa, splaying her fingers across her bosom. "I saw your show today during my massage! My God! Where do you *find* these people!"

"Good researchers." He smiled. "Provocative, didn't you think?"

"Provocative isn't the word!"

Elsa turned to Claire, with an aghast, pop-eyed look. "*Handicapped hookers!* I mean, who would have dreamed? My masseuse was so *flabbergasted* she didn't know what she was doing! I kept saying, 'Stop, Juanita! You're hurting me!' "

"Handicapped *prostitutes?*" said Claire, clearly appalled. Spark gave her a condescending smile.

"I gather it seems a bit tawdry to you, Miss Simmons, but I believe there's no area of human experience so distasteful as to be unworthy of our attention. You can't understand what you refuse to examine."

"Precisely!" said Joy.

"On my show," he continued loftily, "we peer into life's dark corners and report what we find, regardless of whom it upsets. Who was it who said, 'I am human and nothing human is alien to me'?"

"A. C. Nielsen?" offered Claire.

"There!" said Elsa, laughing merrily. "Didn't I say they were delightful!"

The Chandlers did not seem in agreement with this assessment. Spark managed a thin smile, but Joy's face was that of a woman who regretted having left her guillotine at home.

Turning to Elsa, I saw that she'd suddenly stopped laughing and was staring over my shoulder with a rapt, horror-struck look. We all followed her gaze to the staircase. Descending now with a showgirl's regalness of bearing was Kitty, Elsa's baby sister.

She spotted Elsa immediately and broke into a big wicked smile. She waved daintily to us and began pushing her way through the crowd, oblivious, it seemed, to the stares that followed her progress.

As a gay man I don't often give much thought to bosoms, but it's always seemed to me that some women have what I can only call comedy breasts—tits so vast and bouncy and perfectly round that you can't stand before them without feeling you've been thrust into some low burlesque skit and should, by rights, be wearing a zany doctor's suit with a big, naughty stethoscope. Kitty had such breasts, and as she maneuvered toward us they jumped and strained at her low-cut gown with what seemed a will entirely their own. It was as if they were puppies and she was taking them for a walk.

Elsa looked wearily to Joy, who shook her head sympathetically. Spark, by contrast, perked right up, adjusting his tie and breaking into that inane grin with which heterosexual men since cave-dwelling days have greeted the Kittys of this world.

"Hi, sis! Howaya!" said Kitty, giving Elsa a big hug. "Some *crowd* you got here! Can't swing a cat without hittin' a movie star!"

"Why, Kitty!" said Elsa, like a maître d' greeting a bag lady with a gift certificate. "It's been ages!"

"Whose fault is that?" Kitty asked delicately.

Seeing her up close now, I was struck by her resemblance to Elsa. They might have been twins, except that Kitty was at least ten years younger. I realized suddenly that this, more than Kitty's gum-snapping demeanor, was the source of Elsa's profound aversion to her.

Elsa, though lovely taken alone, did not benefit at all from comparison with this younger version of herself. In fact, placed alongside each other, they seemed a textbook illustration of the gulf that separates beauty effortlessly possessed from beauty arduously preserved. Elsa, a profoundly vain woman, was aware of this and could not look at Kitty without a sororicidal gleam entering her eye.

"There's a bar right over there, dear," said Elsa, "and tons of food! All your favorite things! So, why don't you—"

"*Spaahk Chandler!*" squealed Kitty, leaning down to shake his hand. "Do you remember me? I remember *you!*"

"Of *course* I do! Peter's birthday! Good to see you again. You remember my wife . . . ?"

"No."

Introductions were remade, and Elsa graciously included Claire and me. Kitty gave us brisk handshakes, then proceeded to flirt brazenly with Spark, running her fingers all over his shirtfront as she heaped praise on his tireless efforts to enlighten the public.

If her critique lacked brilliance, it did provide an interesting window into Elsa's past and the distance the elder Driscoll had traveled. Elsa's working-class Boston accent, though clearly detectable, seemed the merest vestige when compared with Kitty's more robust version. The flat *a*'s were flatter still, the nasality more strident, and while, like Elsa, she tended to drop any *r* that didn't begin a word, Elsa had mastered a *faux* posh accent that made the dropped *r*'s sound like an Englishwoman's or, at any rate, a Kennedy's. Kitty, on the other hand, sounded like a sheep with a head cold.

"That show you did on sex toys that *break!* I said, Thank *Gawd* there's someone out there not afraid to discuss these things! Sure opened *my* eyes!"

"Kitty!" cried Elsa, laughing a shade maniacally. "You're too wicked! What am I going to do with her! Oh, look, it's Misha! I *must* say hello!"

Following Elsa's abrupt departure, Joy informed Spark there were advertisers present he simply had to meet. He tried to protest, but she literally dragged him away like an irate mother extracting her child from Toys-Я-Us. Kitty watched them retreat with a miffed, if not surprised, expression.

"Well, don't *she* light up a room?"

She asked if we'd been working long for Elsa and what we thought of her so far. We replied, rather uncomfortably, that she seemed a warm, lovely woman.

"Not to me, she's not! I em*barr*ass her."

"Oh, I'm sure that's not true," said Claire politely.

"Yeah?" Kitty said flatly. "What makes you sure?"

Claire frowned, embarrassed, and said Kitty was right, of course.
Elsa did seem embarrassed by her.

"She's always on my case about *improving* myself, sayin' I should
take more interest in culture. I tried to get a little culture the other
night, and let me tell you, it did *not* work out."

We said that yes, reports had reached us.

"Would you believe," she continued, "that she *begged* me not to
come to this? 'Dahling,' she said, 'you wouldn't *enjoy* yourself. These
aren't your sort of people.' What she meant, of course, is I was too
vulgar for 'em."

She jerked her head indignantly to where Joy stood nearby, hob-
nobbing with Judith Krantz. "Miss Fancy Editor over there ran a story
this month 'bout some musician who died hangin' himself *while he
jerked off!* And *I'm* vulgar!"

She gave a ladylike hiccup of disdain, then, deciding to rise above
it, thrust out her bosom as if lifting two suitcases and sailed off toward
the bar.

Left on our own, Claire and I drifted about, eyeballing the cherubs
and the celebs. We decided to get some food and ran into Millie,
who was pillaging the buffet.

"Hello!" she burbled, piling her plate high. "Lovely to see you
again! Such extravagant parties Peter throws! So glad I skipped lunch!
Try one of these! They're beggars' purses stuffed with truffled lobster
and quail meat!"

Claire noticed a jeweled butterfly broach on Millie's jacket and
said how pretty it was.

"Isn't it!" said Millie, grabbing some heart-shaped salmon canapés.
"It came just today. From Elsa. She saw it in the window of Cartier
and it reminded her of me, so she just walked right in and bought
it. So impulsive, our Elsa! Oh, look, here she is now!"

We turned. Elsa and Peter were standing a few feet away, peevishly
plucking rose petals from their drinks and glaring up at the chagrined
cupid who'd deposited them there.

"Elsa, love! Over here, my sweet!" sang Millie.

"Oh, *there* you are, Mill!" croaked Elsa, and they wandered over.
"Hi, darling! Oh, Peter, these are the writers I was telling you about.
Claire, Philip, this is my husband, Peter *Champ*ion."

He was, as I noted earlier, short, a fact that mightn't have struck me so had he not managed to conceal it so adroitly in photos and on television. Apart from that, he looked exactly as I'd expected. The skin was pasty and the brown, heavily lacquered hair so badly cut it resembled thatching on a cottage roof. The eyes were small and suspicious; the lips, even at rest, curled contemptuously; and the neck, had he ever possessed one, had long since retracted into his chest, like that of a cartoon character recently beaned by an anvil.

I said hello and extended my hand. He gave it a curt, manly shake, halfway to jujitsu, then performed a more delicate version with Claire.

"Terrific party," I said. "Thank you for having us."

"Please, it's I who am grateful to you for accepting on such short notice. I want you to know how pleased I am that Elsa has found such gifted collaborators to help with this show of hers. I'll rest easy knowing she's in capable hands."

The voice was flat with a raspy, adenoidal quality. Though he was reasonably articulate, he spoke with the careful, stilted cadences of one who can use words but doesn't really like them. It's that same manner you hear in locker room interviews.

"Elsa," he continued, "is the best, and she deserves the best, and I'm glad she got it."

Claire asked if he was familiar with our work, and he said no, he wasn't, but Elsa had praised it and that was good enough for him.

"There is no one, and I mean *no* one, in this town who knows more about songwriting than Elsa."

His estimate of Elsa's ranking among our city's musical scholars seemed unduly generous, but we thanked him for his praise and offered our own warm, if guarded, compliments on Elsa's "unique vocal quality."

"She's the best," he repeated, mantralike. "I think between the three of you, you're gonna bring back a whole era of New York night life. That bygone glamour and sophistication."

"Stop it," giggled Elsa. "You're embarrassing me!"

"Oh, I just know you'll make a tremendous success!" gushed Millie, a bit of quail meat flying out of her mouth. "How proud I feel to think it was me who brought you all together!"

I gestured to the wall where all the *Estime* covers hung and offered my congratulations on the magazine's success. Champion glowed and sailed into a set piece on the magazine's special place in his heart. He said that proud as he was of his glorious buildings, they were after all stationary things, viewed and enjoyed only by those fortunate enough to dwell in the cities that contained them. *Estime*, however, had enabled him to extend his influence to homes all over the country, and this meant a great deal to him. He could now, as never before, touch far-flung hearts and minds and share with the entire nation his great love of culture and quality.

"Real estate," he concluded loftily, "may be what I do, but *Estime* is what I am."

There was little arguing with this, so I just nodded in what I hoped looked like awed respect. He asked where Claire and I came from and was delighted to learn we hailed from working-class suburbs of Boston, much like the one in which he and Elsa had grown up. It increased his liking for us to find we'd emerged from the same lowly beginnings as he, only to arrive at this transcendent moment, standing between him and a buffet crowded with labor-intensive hors d'oeuvres.

Mrs. Pilchard suddenly inquired if Claire and I were an item. We said no rather firmly, and she said, in *that* case, that there was a *delightful*, well-to-do young man nearby whom Claire *had* to meet. Claire balked, but Elsa backed Millie and the pair of them dragged her away while shrieking the name "Rodney." I found myself suddenly alone with Champion.

"I'm glad for this opportunity, Philip," he said, his tone suddenly different, cooler. "Do you have a moment to speak privately?"

"Uh, sure," I replied, dread welling up within me.

"If you don't mind," he said, and, placing a hand on my shoulder, led me toward the kitchen. Glancing over my shoulder in an effort to alert Claire, I saw two sides of beef in tuxedos rise from the bar and begin following us. Both had eyebrows that met in the middle.

We entered the kitchen, where a cluster of giggling cupids paled at the sight of Champion and dispersed. We passed through a door into an alley and from there strolled out to the sidewalk. I heard the alley door open and shut again and knew the tuxedo-clad primates had followed us out.

"Excuse me, Philip," he rasped, "but it's impossible to talk pri-

vately at these parties. They're crowded and someone's always crowd-
ing me, wanting to talk to me or else eavesdropping. You're not cold,
are you?"

I was. It was mild for February, but not that mild. But I said no,
I was fine.

"Good. We'll just be a minute. We could use the manager's office,
but I like fresh air. All year round. Never catch cold, never get sick.
I have no time to."

We began walking down lower Broadway, away from the restaurant.
He draped an arm around my shoulder, a gesture I found ominous,
though under the circumstances there weren't many gestures I
wouldn't have found ominous.

"I suppose you must think I'm a very fortunate man," he said.

"Well," I said, and paused, caught between an impulse to ingratiate
myself and the fear of seeming a disingenuous sycophant. He seemed
the sort to both crave and mistrust flattery.

"Well," I said, "I think you're fortunate to be so good at what you
do. Not many people are."

This seemed the correct response. He smiled.

"You're right, Philip. I'm the best. And because of that I've acquired many things I'm very grateful for. But I've also acquired some
things I could do without."

"Like what?"

"Enemies, Philip," he said, gazing directly into my eyes.

We turned onto a dimly lit side street. I could hear the slow click
of his goons' shoes echoing behind us. It was all getting a little film
noir for my taste, but I resolved to betray no anxiety unless and until
he'd unmasked me, at which point I resolved to scream and make
like a gazelle.

"Enemies," he repeated. "All around me."

"Well, we all have those," I said breezily. "I've got my share!"

"Not like mine," he said, annoyed.

"No, I suppose not."

"Mine are very rich, Philip, and very resourceful. They hate me
for outdoing them, and because of that they'll stop at nothing to
discredit me, even destroy me if they can."

"Well, let 'em try," I said, adopting a tone of hero worship even as my stomach was imploding. "I'd say anyone who thinks he can get the better of *you* has made one big mistake!"

He smiled and seconded the opinion.

"So, you understand, then," he said evenly, "that's it's necessary for me to protect myself? To deal with such people however I see fit and show them no more mercy than they would show me?"

"Absolutely," I wheezed.

"I'm glad you understand."

He came to a halt, and the footfalls behind us fell silent as well.

"Now," he said, "let's talk about Gilbert Selwyn."

Seven

Once when I was seventeen I arrived late for a glee club practice and, taking my place in the back row, fumbled to find the *King and I* medley in my book bag. I held the bag up to peer inside, thus sending my books tumbling to the floor, among them a well-thumbed copy of an all-male pictorial essay titled "Ranger in Paradise." I leapt to retrieve it but was beaten to it by a vile little tenor named Eddy Farren, who snatched it up, screamed, "Look—a *homo* book!" and began waving it about in full view of the chorus and Sister Joselia, a stern dragoon of a nun whose nickname was The Mutilator. This incident, of course, has no bearing on my present story. I mention it only because it was among the scenes from my life that flashed before my eyes in the split second after I heard Peter Champion utter Gilbert's name.

I stared at him blankly, and he repeated the name.

"Gilbert *Selwyn?*" I asked in one of those moments that give life to the concept of bladder control.

"Selwyn." Champion nodded.

"Ah. What about him?"

It's not easy to make executive decisions when events are spiraling out of control all around you and there are two large men with shaving nicks on their foreheads loitering in the middle distance. But despite these impediments to concentration, I swiftly resolved to feign complete innocence as to the drift of Champion's questions. Clearly he knew I knew Gilbert and that Gilbert worked for Larkin—why else bring him up? Beyond that, however, who could say what he knew?

Best, I felt, not to regard a single bean as spilled until evidence of same had duly arisen.

"You still know Gilbert, then?" he asked.

"Uh, yes," I said.

Then, seized with one of those inspirations that occur all too rarely under pressure, I gave him a quizzical look and asked with unmistakable suggestiveness if he, too, uh . . . *knew* Gilbert.

He stared a moment, uncomprehending, then, catching my drift, flinched like a man spotting a bee in his soda can.

"No!" he exclaimed. "What do you think I am—some kind of fairy!"

"Gosh, no!" I said. "It's just you seemed so *interested* in Gilbert. He's really quite good-looking, and he's always gone for you wealthy guys—"

"Well, not this one!" snapped Champion. "I've never even met him!"

"Right."

"And I'm *straight*."

"Well, that's what I'd always *heard*—"

"I know nothing about him. That's why I'm asking you!"

"Of *course*."

I regarded him with mild confusion even as my heart sang with glee. The maneuver had worked! By calling his sexuality into question, not only had I unnerved him into admitting what he knew, I'd diverted suspicion from myself as well. After all, what could have led me to so provocative an assumption except a complete inability to imagine any *other* reason he could have for bringing Gilbert up?

"Christ," he muttered, still shaken. "I've been called a lot of things in my life, but never a fucking—"

Something stopped him, presumably the icy stare coming from my direction.

"*Not*, of course," he added lamely, "that I have anything against gay people, which I take it you're . . . one of."

"Yes."

"Yes, I thought so. So many of you creative people seem to be. And it doesn't bother me. Not a bit! In fact," he added with forced jocularity, "I kind of *prefer* it, seeing how much time you'll be spending with my wife!"

He paused and performed some strange nose-breathing exercise with the apparent purpose of regaining equilibrium and focus. Then he continued.

"I should explain, Philip, that when I hire someone, or when Elsa does, we run a background check. Standard procedure, you understand. Police records, former employers, various . . . other sources. We did this with you, and everything checked out fine. The only unusual thing was some newspaper stories from a year or so ago."

"Gilbert's wedding?"

"Exactly."

I should have seen it coming. The story of Gilbert and Moira's wedding had proved a godsend to the tabloids, most of which milked it for days. Many trumpeted details of the young bridegroom's gay past, as former lovers stampeded forth to sell their stories—the market value of which declined rapidly, Gilbert's ex-lovers being neither scarce nor shy.

"You were his best man, right?" asked Champion.

"Yes."

"Are you still friends with him?"

This was a hard one. He'd confessed to knowing nothing about Gilbert, and as distance seemed advisable, I decided to chance the lie.

"Not really, no. I mean, I see him around."

He frowned. "Yes. I didn't imagine you would be. Not after that, uh, unpleasantness."

"Well, you know how it is," I said. "People grow apart."

"I know all about it," he said, nodding paternally. "As we climb life's ladder there are certain friends who might weigh us down and who have to be . . . jettisoned."

"Right," I said, appalled at the sentiment.

"From what I read in those tabloids," he continued, "Gilbert wasn't too, uh, *discreet*, was he? Gays these days can be so—brazen. Strident. Obnoxious. People can behave how they choose, of course. But it's no way to get *ahead* in the world, is it?"

I was gripped by a strong desire to seize him by the tie and scream enlightenment into his face. But I realized that such an approach, while satisfying in the short run, could only undermine our more long-range goals, so I winked complicitously and nodded. He smiled to see we understood each other.

"I can see you're a shrewd young man, Philip. You were wise to drop him."

"It was time," I said with a Republican smile.

"Right. Now I want you to do me a favor."

"What?" I asked eagerly.

"Become his friend again."

We rounded the corner and headed back downtown. Champion explained that Gilbert had recently been hired as a personal assistant to Tommy Parker, managing editor of *Boulevardier* and a close associate of Boyd Larkin. Larkin was, of course, the publisher of *Choice* and a man who, deranged by envy, was single-mindedly devoted to Champion's destruction. Parker was gay, and Champion had reason to suspect Gilbert was his lover.

This little tidbit, of course, pierced my vitals like a heated stiletto, but I stared blandly and was soon relieved to find his suspicion was based upon a misreading of the facts.

Champion had several spies at *Boulevardier*. According to them, Gilbert was a shadowy figure of apparently minimal competence who, though fired shortly after landing a secretarial post, was immediately rehired by Parker and assigned to some nebulous "special project"— as obvious a euphemism for boy toy as they'd ever heard. This assumption was further borne out by Gilbert's behavior. He sometimes visited the office around lunch to "confer" with Parker behind closed doors. He had, in addition, been spotted entering and leaving Parker's apartment building.

Champion felt that if Gilbert was sleeping with Parker, then Parker, a known confidant of Larkin, might let slip certain professional secrets in the way that slightly older gentlemen—especially, one presumed, depraved gossipy homosexuals—do when trying to impress attractive bedmates some years their junior.

If I would renew my friendship with Gilbert, I might adroitly extract from him any secrets to which he'd been made privy. Champion would pay me handsomely for the information, which would then be incorporated into a scalding exposé on Boyd Larkin to be written by Hoot Mulvaney as a cover story for *Estime*.

By this point we had rounded two more corners and were back on Broadway, a short distance from Ici. Though my head swam at the notion of pretending to accept this offer, I had, of course, no choice but to do so. I thought it prudent to hem and haw a little first. I wanted to win his trust, and an ally too readily purchased might just as easily be recruited by the enemy.

"I don't know," I said, frowning at the sidewalk. "I mean, Gilbert used to be a really good friend."

"I appreciate loyalty in a man, Philip. I demand it myself. But there are times when loyalty can be misplaced."

"I know, but . . ."

He placed a hand on my shoulder. "I would consider it a personal favor."

I looked at him, doing my best to seem the awestruck youth, unable to believe so eminent a man should desire his aid and—dare he hope?—friendship.

"Well . . . ," I said, drowning in his charisma.

He smiled and, removing a checkbook and pen from his breast pocket, scrawled a check. He tore it off smartly and handed it over. It was made out to me in the sum of five thousand dollars.

I gaped at the check, then at Champion, who beamed with the smile of a man who never tires of seeing people dazzled by sums he considers chump change.

"We'll call that a consulting fee. There's more when you report back to me."

I pocketed the check and, my voice choked with pride, said I'd be honored to help him thwart any enemy who dared cross him.

He thanked me and turned toward the restaurant, clearly not a man to linger over finished business when there are still things to do and people to buy. As we reached the door he remembered something and turned to face me.

"By the way, Philip. One more thing."

"What, Mr. Champion?"

"Peter! We're friends now! Uh—about Elsa. She's a little high-strung sometimes. And her vocal range is narrower than some encourage her to believe. But—*I want her to have the career she's after.* And it all depends on this act."

"Right."

"If she flops, I'm holding you responsible."

"Check."

"Don't let us down," he said, and, patting me smartly on the cheek, entered the restaurant, followed by his protectors, who scuttled to close the gap between them and their ever-imperiled employer.

On reentering the party, I stood at the top of the stairs and searched for Claire. I spotted her near the band, still in the grip of Mrs. Pilchard's young bore. I was suddenly overcome by despair at the thought of keeping this twisty business a secret from her. With her keen powers of reasoning and perception, she was always the first person I approached when faced with any dilemma. Now, preparing to take on a colossus like Champion without recourse to her advice, I felt like Dr. Watson might feel racing off to do battle with Moriarty but forced to tell Holmes he's just running to the corner for cocaine.

I toyed briefly with the idea of telling her all. But then I considered the likelihood of her withdrawal from the act, not to mention the cold fury she'd feel at my having let her go *this* far uninformed, and I knew that honesty was no longer among my options.

I navigated through that sea of fame, eavesdropping briefly on a well-known married fashion designer who was trying to get Abelard's phone number out of him, and made my way over to Claire. She was listening to Rodney's heartbreaking lament on the difficulties he'd encountered trying to procure an acceptable polo pony, and she fell upon me as though I were a Saint Bernard. I dutifully dragged her to freedom and apologized for my disappearance, explaining that Champion had requested a tête-à-tête.

"Really? And what did he have to say?"

"Basically he said Elsa's no Maria Callas—"

"Now there's a bulletin."

"—and it's up to us to make her look good."

"Lovely!"

We were about to leave when we saw that the stairs were blocked by Peter, who was standing halfway up, holding a microphone and preparing to make a speech. Silence fell, and he launched into a grandiose set piece, very similar to the one he'd delivered by the buffet. He enumerated his achievements in language that made Ozymandias sound self-effacing, then spoke of *Estime* as his crowning accomplishment. It was, he asserted, foremost in his affections, and all those present had earned a small piece of his heart. In recognition of this, he pointed to the towering chocolate heart that dominated the center of the room and informed us it belonged to us all, and we were welcome to take a piece when we left. A platoon of cupids then paraded smartly around it, holding red velvet pillows on which rested sterling silver hammers and chisels.

After the speech had finished to wild applause and bravos, Claire and I waited a decent interval and crept out. My last image was of dozens of rich, opulently dressed men and women swarming madly about that enormous heart, shrieking with drunken laughter as they hacked away at it with their sharp, shiny chisels.

One result of my chat with Champion was that I realized, and not a moment too soon, how vigilant a watch he maintained over his enemies. If there were spies in position at Larkin's magazines and even outside Tommy's building, then surely *I*, a newcomer entrusted with a sensitive mission, could expect equal scrutiny. And since I could never know at any given moment whether I was being watched or not, my only safe course was to assume always that I was. The irony did not escape me that the only defense against Champion's paranoia was emulation.

On returning home, I changed, took a walk, and called Tommy from a pay phone. I gave him a rundown of the night's events, which he interrupted with frequent explosions of mirth.

"Dear me!" he cried. "So the special project I'm engaged in is Gilbert's pants, is it?"

"That's what he's heard."

"And this from my own staff? I'd give them all bonuses, but one so wants to discourage gossiping. So, now you're spying on *us*, then?"

"Yes. But we have to be careful about this. He obviously keeps a close watch on you people."

"No closer than we keep on him, dear."

"Yes, but if he's that suspicious, how long before he catches on to *me?* I'm so nervous I'm calling from a pay phone."

"How John le Carré of you. I wouldn't worry about the phones, love. There are ways to find out if a line is tapped. We check ours often and he's never even tried."

"Still," I said, beginning to feel a bit foolish, "he *has* used surveillance."

"Yes, that's more his style. Silly asses in trench coats, lurking about scribbling in notebooks."

"What if he trails me to our meeting tomorrow?"

"I doubt he would, but you have a point. There is a chance, so all right—let's play spies!"

He said we would switch the locale of our rendezvous to a "safe apartment," as his own was being watched. He asked if I had a bright scarf, and I said I had yellow one. He said I should leave my apartment at seven wearing the scarf, then walk to Broadway and Ninety-ninth and hail a cab downtown. I agreed, tingling pleasantly, and said I'd see him tomorrow.

The next evening I did precisely as instructed, reaching the corner a few minutes past seven and hailing the first cab I saw. As it approached, another cab cut in front of it in a terrifying squeal of tires. The interloping driver, strikingly handsome for a cabbie, leaned out the window.

"I think you're looking for me, Phil!"

We cruised sedately down Broadway for a few minutes, then the driver rocketed through a yellow light, careened toward West End, and zoomed madly around corners until we somehow wound up back at Ninety-ninth Street and Central Park West.

"Well," he said, turning around and flashing the smile of a man who enjoys his work, "I sure *hope* we were followed. Hate to waste all that!"

He drove me to an apartment tower in the East Fifties, a hideous modern job drenched in smoked glass. He instructed me to ask for apartment 12-F and to say my name was Harry Lime.

I did as I was bid and was soon standing before the indicated door. I stood a moment, anxiously arranging my hair and crunching on the breath mint, then rang the bell. The door was instantly flung open by Tommy, who was wearing a fedora and brandishing a pistol.

"No one followed you, did they?" he asked menacingly.

My reaction must have been something to behold because he immediately dropped the tough-guy tone and giggled apologetically.

"Oh, I *am* sorry, love. Just joshing—you know, playing up the atmosphere. Poor lamb, look at you! Come in and have a drink!"

I entered the foyer, which was unremarkable but for two early Picassos. Tommy pecked me casually on the cheek and took my coat.

"I'm on the phone, so I'll be another moment," he said, pointing me to the main room. "You can go in there and play."

His meaning, elusive at first, became clear the moment I entered the room, a long book-lined chamber filled to bursting with toys. Everywhere you looked there were gadgets and games, ranging from antique mechanical acrobats to the latest in high-tech diversions. The walls were lined with old, faded playing boards for all manner of arcane games, and there were display cases holding antique dolls and hand puppets. The whole place resembled some obscenely affluent toddler's private Fun Museum.

I approached one of the more modern diversions, an arcade-style video game emblazoned with the improbable legend "White House Ninja Bitch!" Curious, I turned it on and saw that it was one of those noisy, violent martial arts games lovingly reprogrammed so that the black leather-clad protagonist now bore the face of Nancy Reagan. She burst through a dungeon door, screaming, "Ayahhh!" and proceeded to kick the groins of several armed guards, all the while screaming her husband's campaign slogans. The volume alarmed me, so I flicked the off switch and fled to a display case containing two ancient dice and a wooden cup.

All at once a door leading to a kitchen burst open and a very short, round, elderly man bustled into the room. He wore a blousy white silk shirt, black velvet trousers, little brocaded slippers, and over the whole ensemble a frilly white apron. In his hand was a carefully balanced wooden spoon containing some pale yellow sauce from which wisps of steam arose.

"Well, hello!" he sang buoyantly. "You must be the new *spyyyy!* I'm Boyd Larkin! Taste this."

Eight

"Good?" he asked eagerly.

"Delicious!"

"Enough mustard?"

"Oh, yes."

"But not too much?"

"No. It's perfect."

"It needs something else."

"Like what?"

"I'm torn," he said, and scowled contemplatively. He tasted it again. "Lemon juice," he said decisively, and padded back into the kitchen.

My emotions were divided. On the one hand, I'd counted on having Tommy all to myself and was vexed to discover his boss would be present, much diminishing the likelihood of long, meaningful looks erupting into ardent embraces and lost shirt buttons. On the other hand, meeting my second billionaire in as many days seemed an intriguing way to pass an evening, especially when that billionaire was as fantastic a creature as Larkin was fast proving.

He soon returned, having removed the apron.

"How *won*derful to meet you at last!" he said, pumping my hand vigorously. "Tommy has been *trump*eting your praises, and I have been saying to him when do I get to *meet* this person?"

He had an odd manner of speaking. His voice was quite high pitched, and he spoke with a slow, deliberate singsong, often italicizing strange words until you wondered if he thought you were a foreigner with hearing problems. As for his general bearing, I had no idea how straight he behaved in public or in his business dealings, but here in his toy room the flaming was enough to make you gaze apprehensively at the sprinkler system.

"*So!*" he said, flapping his hands. "Champion's *parrrr-ty!* Tell me all about it!"

"Well! For a minute there I thought he was on to us."

"No, I meant the *food.*"

"Oh. Uh, it was good, I guess. Pretty fancy stuff, most of it. There were these little crepes stuffed with truffled lobster and quail meat."

"*Together?*" he said, and collapsed onto a chair, emitting a high, piercing laugh like a squeaky hinge.

"Oh, how *claaassy!*" he wheezed, clutching his sides. "And what was there to drink? Caviar frappes? Hee hee hee hee!"

I saw there would be no discussion of more pressing topics until he had quite recovered from Champion's hors d'oeuvres, so I stood, smiling stupidly, until his mirth subsided.

"Oh, my, my!" he said, coming out of it. "Where are my manners! Please sit down. Or *play* with something if you like," he added, giving me a Groucho leer that came and vanished so quickly I didn't know if I'd imagined it.

I told him I admired his collection, and he pointed out a few favorites, saying there was much more "at the house."

"You don't live here, then?"

"What, *this* place? This *lean-to?* You insult me, dear! No, this is just m'little hideaway. I only picked this *outhouse* of a building because it's owned by Mr. Champion, and I liked the idea of plotting against him right under his own leaky roof. What are you drinking? Martini all right?"

I said a martini would be great, and he clapped his hands delightedly.

"Oh, *good!* 'S nice to see a young person who still knows how to en*joy* himself. So *stuffy* they're gettin' these days, with their briefcases and health clubs and their French seltzer. Offer 'em a cocktail and they look at you like you suggested *ritual suicide.*"

He puttered over to a liquor cabinet and began removing the necessary accoutrements.

"Now, forget everything you've learned—*this* is how you make a martini."

I struck a suitably attentive pose, and as I watched this bizarre little gnome dancing around his funhouse, mixing and stirring and chattering away, I couldn't shake the agreeable feeling that I'd wandered into a mildly decadent update of *The Wind in the Willows* and he was Toad of Toad Hall.

"*Here!*" he said, finally handing me the drink, which sloshed around the rim of a crystal martini glass the size of a small birdbath. "Is that perfection or what?"

"It's great," I said, tasting it. "Strong!"

He replied with another of his evanescent leers and said, "That's the ideeeea!"

Tommy returned, and dinner was served by a pretty Filipino boy. The meal was delicious, though ruinously fattening with course after course swimming in rich cream sauces. I knew that a man of Larkin's age and weight would be under the most stringent orders to abstain from this sort of food, but he displayed neither concern nor restraint. He attacked every course with gluttonous gusto, greeting each new taste with sighs and moans the likes of which I'd not heard outside of an all-male video. After dessert—a staggeringly rich *crème brûlée*—port was served, and Larkin, who'd not spoken a word during the meal that wasn't about the meal, got down to business.

"So!" he said in that high little voice. "You are now writing *songs* for the divine Elsa?"

"Yes."

"What does she sing like?" he asked. "Is she bad? Is she *execrable?*"

"She's not very good."

"You're not just saying that to make me happy?"

"No. I mean, she can carry a tune, but the sound's none too pretty."

"*Well,*" he said dreamily, "maybe I'll hire people to go to her opening and run from the room screaming and jabbing ice picks through their eardrums. That oughta rattle her, huh?"

Tommy and I conceded that yes, it would almost certainly throw her timing off.

"So," said Boyd, changing the subject, "has Tommy here told you what we want you to do?"

"Vaguely," I said. "You want me to spy on them."

"Right. We want everything you can find. We'd love incriminating, but juicy will do."

"Well," I said, "I don't have much experience with this cloak-and-dagger stuff."

"Don't you worry, sugar," said Larkin, patting my hand and rising. "We have everything you need right here."

He bustled to the sideboard and removed a black box from a drawer. He returned and set it down on the table.

"New toys?" asked Tommy.

"Nifties!" said Larkin. He opened the box and removed a small velvet bag. He loosened the drawstrings and dumped its contents onto the table. Having expected some gleaming piece of high-tech wizardry, I was taken aback to see nothing more than a half-dozen lumps of gray, well-masticated chewing gum.

"Want a piece?" asked Larkin, thrusting one at me and bursting into giggles.

"Boyd!" said Tommy, impressed. "What a cunning notion!"

"Huh?" I said, completely at sea.

"They're *mic*rophones," said Boyd. "Little transmitting devices inside the gum."

"Oh," I said, feeling like a dolt for not having guessed. "They can hear through the gum?"

"They can hear through half a foot of con*crete*, hon."

"Oh, *I* get it!" I said. "You plant them under chairs and things, and if anyone finds them—"

"*Exactly*," said Larkin. "That's usually the problem with these thingies. They find 'em and right away they know—*someone's listening!* But *these* little honeys, if they find one, they throw it away and scream at the maid."

"Marvelous!" said Tommy. "Another innovation from our friend, Mr. Vladimir?"

"Who else!" said Larkin. He turned to me. "Glorious man. Used to work for the KGB, but he defected and now he free-lances. I don't know what I'd do without him. More port, please, Tommy?"

"Are we attempting to expire in our sleep, Boyd? I should think after a meal like that you might at least cut down on the—"

"Oh, you!" he said, snatching the bottle away. "You have no idea,

Philip, how cruel this man is to me. But such a face, I keep him around anyway." He leaned in toward me and spoke in a stage whisper. "Isn't he gorgeous?"

"Oh, yes," I said, willing myself not to blush.

"Look, I've made him blush!"

"I shouldn't wonder. Now you behave yourself with Philip."

"Goodness!" he said to me. "You see the way he leaps to your defense. It's love!"

"You must excuse Boyd, Philip. He enjoys nothing so much as playing matchmaker with his employees."

Larkin directed his leer toward Tommy. "If you've got the match, hon, I've got the cigar!"

"I shall pretend not to have heard that."

"He always does," said Larkin, sighing to me. He gave a philosophical shrug, then placed the gummy microphones back in the velvet bag and handed it to me.

"Here," he said. "They're coated with a special adhesive that's activated when you rub it where you're gonna put it. Just spread them around the house wherever you can, though try to get 'em in private places like the bedroom."

"How am I going to get into their bedroom?"

"Ask Elsa for a tour. She loves to show the dump off."

I took the bag and reminded Boyd that Champion now assumed I would be busily worming *their* secrets out of Gilbert. What sorts of things should I report to him?

Larkin grinned fiendishly. "Why, what he wants to *hear*, of course! Filth! Depravity! Boys and dogs and hamsters! He thinks the worst, so let's confirm his most *dire* suspicions!"

"But no *proof*, of course," said Tommy. "You *hear* the most lurid accounts, but you're having a devil of a time documenting them."

"*Exactly*," said Larkin. "We will make him *crazed!* Keep him thinkin' he's on the verge of burying me in scandal if he could just get a scrap of evidence—and by the time he realizes he ain't gettin' any, *we're* hangin' *him* out to dry! Oh, what fun! I do love a good dirty fight! Hee hee heeee! Here," he added, tossing me a pen. "It's a camera!"

Our meeting broke up soon after that. I expressed concern over the confidentiality agreement I'd signed, and Larkin pooh-poohed my fears, saying that if I uncovered any criminal behavior, I'd be legally *compelled* to break the agreement or face charges as an accessory. As I was donning my coat, he gave me one more James Bond gadget, a lucky rabbit's foot key chain in which were concealed twenty skeleton keys, suitable for unlocking file cabinets and desk drawers. He stressed that he didn't expect me to actually break into any offices but felt that I might conceivably find myself alone in one with time to kill, and good things come to those who prepare. He also gave me an envelope containing my first week's salary for my efforts. It was fifteen hundred dollars, paid in cash so as to thwart any efforts Champion might make to see if my bank balance was rising mysteriously.

I'd prayed that Tommy would leave with me, but Larkin, far from playing matchmaker, made him stay to discuss plans for a foreign edition of *Boulevardier*. Tommy, at least, seemed genuinely to regret having to stay and made me promise to call him as soon as I'd met again with Elsa.

That meeting took place six days later. I met Claire in the lobby of Champion Plaza, my fingers nervously caressing the five gummy mikes I'd brought in the hopes of secreting them in key spots around the Champion stronghold.

We went through the same security routine, which, of course, now presented new and terrifying dimensions, and were greeted at the door by Matron, who introduced herself to us as Miss Dunbar. She grimly escorted us to Elsa's "studio," a spartan high-ceilinged room with a vast window overlooking the park. Elsa, who was warbling Gershwin's "I Loves You, Porgy", motioned for us to sit.

Our seats afforded us a good view of Elsa's voice teacher. She was a tall, seventyish woman in a long black velvet dress and gold lamé turban who seemed born to lurk behind beaded curtains, clutching ornamental daggers. She made no acknowledgment of us but kept her large, heavily mascaraed eyes glued to her pupil. She was a skilled accompanist, though her style was a mite heavy-handed and ornate. From what we could hear of Elsa over the din, her head voice was pretty but very thin compared to her chest voice, which was of the robust, avalanche-inducing variety.

Claire leaned toward me and spoke out of the side of her mouth. "*This* is the diva responsible for Elsa's progress?"

"Some getup, huh? Good pianist, though—if a bit on the loud side."

"That, my dear, is the point," said Claire. "Fill the room with sound and Elsa might think she's making some of it."

"Oh, I see."

"That's also why there are no carpets or drapes. An asthmatic mouse would sound good in here."

Madame Fortissimo, miffed at the whispering, glared at us and we fell silent. At length Elsa finished and we gave her a polite hand. She bowed in mock grandeur, then turned to her teacher, devotion shining in her eyes.

"Was that better, signora?"

"*Sì, sì, cara!* Much better!"

"I was doing my mental imaging," Elsa declared proudly. "I could see birds soaring free over Catfish Row!"

"Yes, I could tell! Beautiful thoughts becoming beautiful sounds!"

Elsa beckoned us over and introduced us to teacher. She was Signora Lucrezia di Corteggiano, and she had been a great star at La Scala.

"Really?" asked Claire sweetly. "And when was that?"

"Years ago. Before you were born! Elsa, *tesoro mio*, I must fly! A rehearsal at the Met. Troyanos is doing *Rosenkavalier!*"

"Oh," cried Elsa, "I'd love to go! Such a voice she has!"

"She studied with me, you know. Years and years ago. Now, dear," she said, reaching into a bag beside her on the piano bench, "I've made you some more tapes."

"*Oh, thank* you," said Elsa, taking two cassettes from her. "They are *such* a help."

Noting our puzzled expressions, Elsa explained enthusiastically that the signora's technique involved listening to meditation tapes for half an hour before attempting to sing. They contained nature sounds plus a mix of spoken and subliminal messages that strengthened and relaxed the muscles necessary to sound production. They also worked to "cleanse the internal environment," preparing you to sing in a way so profound and mysterious, not even the signora could quite put it into words.

Claire and I greeted this tidbit with a superhuman show of tact, despite our shared instinct that if the tapes did in fact contain sub-liminal messages, they were probably confined to things like "Signora di Corteggiano's some brilliant teacher" and "I am not paying enough for my lessons." We said it sounded fascinating and hoped the signora would explain it all to us someday when she was not so pressed for time.

Elsa handed her Svengali a check, which the old dear pocketed with the swift discretion of a Times Square dope peddler. They kissed at three paces and the signora departed.

Elsa rang for coffee and we sat drinking it as she waxed idiotic about Signora di Corteggiano's methods and the self-confidence they imbued. Thanks to the signora, Elsa had overcome destructive habits and mastered a whole new approach to singing—and in a mere six years! After helping Claire collect the pieces of the saucer that plum-meted from her hand at this news, I changed the subject to the apartment. I said I found it dazzling and asked how large it was. Elsa, as Larkin had foretold, jumped at the bait and insisted on conducting a tour.

It was indeed one hell of a place. With its three levels and more than fifty rooms, it took us nearly an hour to get even a perfunctory look at it. There was parlor after parlor, all with arbitrarily assigned functions, such as the reading, sun, and sewing rooms. There were dining rooms of varying sizes, breakfast rooms, and a kitchen that could have housed the grandest of catering concerns. There were offices for both Elsa and Peter and a screening room that seated fifty. There was a gym, naturally, with a pool, weight room, tanning salon, and sauna. There were a dozen guest rooms, some with attached sitting rooms and even kitchens.

Last came the master bedchamber, a vast red planet of a room that was a cross between Command Central at NASA and an Arabian bordello. There was a working fountain, several chandeliers, and a vast raised bed that served as the control post for the floor-to-ceiling home entertainment system that covered the opposite wall. And, just in case it had escaped your attention that the occupants were people of means, the wall-to-wall carpet was mink.

I had tried throughout the tour to scout locations where microphones would do the most good. Champion's home office seemed a natural, of course, but we'd barely glanced in when Elsa whisked us away to the adjacent screening room. The smaller dining room, too, seemed a place where intimate conversations might occur. Here I had better luck, depositing one under the dining table while neither Elsa nor Claire was looking. I managed to conceal two more, one in the breakfast room and one under the bar in the main foyer Claire called the Air Zeus VIP Lounge. The master bedroom, though, seemed the ripest location, and I was determined to get one in there. This I accomplished by waiting till we'd just left it, then asking, with a certain subdued urgency, if there wasn't a bathroom close by.

"Oh, sure," said Elsa, pointing back into the bedroom. "The door next to the hologram of Peter."

I went in and proudly emerged a moment later, the mike duly deposited behind their very headboard. We all headed back down to the sunroom, where a table had been laid for lunch.

We sat down to diet portions of shrimp on beds of baby greens. Elsa complained bitterly about the new cook for a spell and then, some two hours after we'd arrived, finally broached the topic of the work we were there to do.

"Claire, dear, I was listening to the tape of your audition and you really do play marvelously. Would you consider accompanying me for the performances?"

"Certainly," said Claire, taken aback. "If you'd like."

"Oh, good. I was gonna ask the signora, but I think it'd make me nervous having her right there on stage with me. You don't mind?"

"No. Actually, it's convenient. It will save me having to copy out arrangements for whatever we write for you."

"Fan*tas*tic! I suppose I should give you a list of the songs I plan to sing."

Claire and I looked to each other.

"You've picked the songs already?" I asked, concerned.

"Of course. Is something wrong with that?"

"No, not necessarily," said Claire diplomatically. "It depends on how well the songs work together. Are they well sequenced? Is there something connecting them?"

"Well, of course there is," said Elsa. "They're all sung by me! What else does there have to be?"

"Well, that," I said, "depends on what kind of act you want to do. Is there a specific mood you want to capture? Is there a theme?"

"What do you mean, 'theme'?" she asked, flustered. "I thought I'd just sing a dozen or so favorite songs, plus something new and funny by you two, and then you'd write me some jokes to tell between numbers. Now you're saying I have it all wrong and everybody's going to laugh and say, 'Look at her! She doesn't even have a *theme!*' "

"No, not at all," I said. "We're just suggesting you try to make the whole thing cohere."

She regarded me with stunned horror. "But I don't *want* to make it *queer!*" she wailed. "The very idea!"

"No, co-*here*," said Claire, fast reaching the end of her rope. "Hold together. Anyway, it's entirely up to you to do whatever you like."

"Oh, I see," said Elsa, calming down some. "Well, what would *you* suggest?"

Claire said that there were all sorts of things people did to tie an evening together. The songs were often by the same composer or else treated the same topic, love being the most obvious and popular choice. Sometimes, she said, people chose and sequenced the songs so that they formed a sort of autobiography. At this Elsa perked up considerably, convinced that Claire was onto something hot.

"I *see*," she said. "You mean the theme could be *me?* Sort of my life story?"

"Well, yes," Claire replied evenly. "That's certainly an *option*."

"What a good idea!" said Elsa. "Well, I'd better start thinking of songs, then, because a lot of the ones I've been considering wouldn't be appropriate. I mean, I couldn't sing 'I Loves You, Porgy,' could I?"

I agreed that no, it didn't seem especially apt, and neither, for that matter, did "I Got Plenty o' Nuttin'."

"Oh, *you!*" said Elsa, braying cheerfully and slapping my hand. "Such a comedian! Well, I think we're off to a *grand* start! But if you're going to help me, you'll have to know all about me, won't you?"

We said that, yes, a little background would facilitate our efforts.

"Oh, dear," she said with a shy smile. "I've always found it so hard to talk about myself."

She sighed, speared a shrimp, and devoured it.

"But I'll try."

Nine

Some four hours later we emerged, limp and gasping, into the waning light of Fifty-seventh Street and staggered wordlessly toward the Oak Bar. We ordered whiskies, and our waiter, noting the crazed, haunted look in our eyes, fetched them with chivalrous haste. We raised our glasses in a listless toast and drained their contents, each giving a convulsive shudder that was half due to the whiskey and half to having just sat through the unexpurgated Gospel According to Elsa.

We had expected a standard rags-to-riches yarn, commencing with the usual humble origins and concluding with a choir-accompanied ascent to the pinnacles of wealth and closet space. What we got, however, was something else entirely—the unendurably poignant tale of a poor, misunderstood waif, ever searching for success and contentment but foiled at every turn by savage and powerful enemies who are unaccountably determined to destroy her.

At first we nodded sympathetically as she detailed her wretched teenage years. Her mother had died when she was only twelve, forcing her to spend her adolescence looking after Kitty, who was, in Elsa's account, a pernicious imp sorely in need of discipline, if not exorcism. We also managed to make suitable clucks as she described her early career attempts, which were foiled repeatedly by villains so fiendish and well coordinated in their efforts that the possibility of conspiracy could not be dismissed.

But then she reached what we'd assumed would be the happy ending, where she marries the dashing young businessman who promptly starts bringing the stuff home to her in baskets. To hear her tell it, though, this development, far from improving her lot, opened up whole new vistas of woe. It was at this point that Claire and I stopped clucking and began exchanging discreet glances of dismay. Here, we sensed, was trouble.

As she plowed on, detailing her travails from her twenties up to the present, the same chord was struck with a regularity Philip Glass might have found monotonous.

Elsa was a victim.

Of everything.

Her wealth, however sizable, was but slight consolation for the indignities to which life continually subjected her. These included, but were by no means confined to, a vulgar and ungrateful sister, lecherous and ignorant club owners and booking agents, a weight problem, untrustworthy servants, vicious journalists, duplicitous friends, larcenous contractors, condescending socialites, and a host of physical maladies, perpetually misdiagnosed as psychosomatic by obtuse and heartless physicians.

We were not, of course, to get the impression she was *ungrateful* for those blessings fate had sprinkled in among the afflictions. She was glad of her marriage, her beauty, wealth, homes, yacht, clothing, and jewelry. Still . . . as much as Peter adored her, he was often busy or away, and as for the perquisites of wealth, they soon grew stale and insipid—unlike its grievances, which seemed never to lose their savor.

It is never pleasant to sit and listen while a woman who ovulates Fabergé eggs bemoans her sorry plight. It's less pleasant still when you're expected to use this long and unseemly complaint as the basis for an evening's entertainment. Unwarranted bitterness is not an engaging emotion. It doesn't sing.

The problem for us was how to inform her that the persona she'd revealed to us was not one she'd be advised to share with the public at large, a problem complicated by her clear inability to see herself the same way we did. She saw herself as a scrappy survivor, buffeted by injustice but smiling through her tears. We saw her as a whining, ungrateful harpy.

The matter was far from resolved when at four o'clock her litany was interrupted by Dunbar's announcement that Elsa's masseuse had arrived. Elsa ushered us to the door, gushing all the way about how splendidly it had gone. She couldn't wait to get to her music books and select songs that suited this dramatic and moving new conception of the act. She trusted we would do the same and looked forward to hearing our ideas when we reconvened the following Wednesday.

"So," muttered Claire, taking a more restrained sip from her second drink, "any appropriate songs leap to mind? 'Melancholy Baby,' perhaps?"

" 'Glad to Be Unhappy'?"

" 'Someone to Walk over Me'?"

We continued in this vein for a bit, then Claire suggested we begin discussing our dilemma in earnest.

"The question," she said, "is how much of this nonsense can she get away with?"

"A woman with her looks, her husband, and her dough? I'd say two weepers are about all they'll stand for, and that's strictly for variety. If they think she *means* it . . . !"

"Exactly," said Claire. "They'll enjoy a good teary ballad or two, but if she prefaces it with any of that malarkey she gave us about how nobody knows the trouble she's seen, they'll laugh their heads off."

"So, how do we tell *her* that?"

"With infinite tact," said Claire, and fell silent.

We gazed thoughtfully out at the sidewalk. It was beginning to rain, and well-heeled shoppers were scampering down Central Park South.

"Well," said Claire at length, "she *did* talk about smiling through her tears. Maybe we can persuade her to play up the smiles and soft-pedal the tears."

"That's not bad," I said.

"Tell her to use her painful memories as subtext to give the up-tempo numbers an aching poignancy."

"Yick. You think she'll buy it?"

"She better," said Claire. "Because if she expects me to sit up there and accompany her while she hands a paying crowd *that* sobfest, I'm putting in for combat pay."

On my way home that evening I stopped at the local Red Apple to pick up some groceries and saw Gilbert strolling down the soft-drink aisle. I was still down in the dumps about our recent rift and was suddenly glad of Champion's demand that I speak to him, as it gave us both a good pretext for reopening diplomatic relations.

He was aloof at first, but when I apprised him of recent developments his fascination overcame the grudge.

"So, what's the deal?" he asked eagerly. "I feed you all this horrible dish about Boyd, then you run and spill it all to Petey?"

"Sort of. I got the impression from Boyd that he wants to make up the stories himself."

Gilbert snickered as he bent over the ice-cream bin, searching, as usual, for butter pecan.

"Well, good luck to him if he wants to invent anything juicier than the truth!"

"Oh?" I said, intrigued. "Why? What do you know?"

"I don't *know* anything," he said, "but, my dear, the *stories!*"

"From who? Tommy?" I asked.

"Hell no, not him. He's Mr. Discretion. But," he said as we steered toward the deli counter, "I have this friend who used to work on Larkin's yacht. *He* said that back when Boyd was 'dating' Dame Margaret Peasman, she went to his room once and found him in a deckhand sandwich!"

"No!"

"Yes! *That's* what decided him to buy her the diamond tiara that made all the columnists hear wedding bells. Oh, take a picture, it lasts longer," he said to the plump woman who stood nearby, staring at us in distaste.

"By the way," he added, returning to me, "is Champion *paying* you for this information *I'm* supposedly giving you?"

The suggestion was unmistakable and not without merit. He was my partner in this aspect of the operation, and offering him a share would do much to patch things up between us.

"Yes. Five grand to start. I've put aside half for you."

"Thanks, Philly!" he said, kissing me on the lips and sending the fat lady away in a frenzy of disgust.

"You're welcome!"

"I wasn't going to ask, you know."

" 'Course not."

"But it is decent of you."

"Well, I'm happy to do it."

An uncomfortable silence descended as we stood at the deli counter, struggling for some way to broach the topic of our recent discord.

"You know," I muttered, "about this fight over Tommy—"

"I'm really sick about it, Philly!"

"So am I."

"You're my oldest, *dearest* friend! I'd hate to lose you over something as silly as this."

"I feel the same way."

"I love you, Philly!"

"I love you, too, Gilbert. Uh, half pound of turkey, please."

The beefy counterman rolled his eyes and pulled the meat from the display.

"You know I'd never ever do anything to hurt you!"

"Well, same here."

Another silence fell as we each waited for the other to take the plunge into sexual martyrdom.

"But," I said finally, "you won't stop chasing Tommy?"

"No, I don't think so."

"I don't want to, either."

A third and still more tense silence ensued. Gilbert finally broke it by loudly declaring "So be it! But we won't let it come between us!"

"Right!" I said with more enthusiasm than I felt.

"Whoever wins, wins!"

"Pay at the front, Romeo."

"And no hard feelings!"

"Right," I said, wheeling my cart toward the meat aisle.

"Right!" he cried, following. "We can't help who he chooses! By the way, he wants to have dinner with us next Tuesday at eight."

"*Both* of us?"

"Yes. I was planning not to tell you, then say you had the flu, but those days are behind us!"

"Good."

"Fair play from here on in!"

"So," I said, pulling my appointment book from my bag. "Tommy's, Tuesday at eight?"

"Uh . . ."

He frowned guiltily as he examined some chicken breasts.

"Seven-thirty, actually. Oh, look, the boneless are on sale."

I phoned Champion the next morning and told him I'd renewed contact with Gilbert. Not only had I repaired the rift between us, but he'd been so glad of my forgiveness he'd invited me to dinner to meet his boyfriend, Tommy Parker.

Champion was pleased but had reservations about my meeting. Claire's and my affiliation with the Champions was now on the record, Daisy Winters having recently immortalized us in her column as "Elsa's Tin Pan Allies." Tommy would know better than to spill secrets to anyone employed by the enemy. Worse, he might warn Gilbert to keep mum as well.

I assured him that though Tommy might well be circumspect, Gilbert had great difficulty keeping confidences. In fact, the juicier the secret, the less he could resist divulging it. And lest either Gilbert or Tommy should assume I felt any allegiance to the Champions, I'd claim I'd barely met Peter and found Elsa demanding and insufferable. Champion gingerly conceded that such assertions about his wife would not unduly strain their credulity and would ease concern on Gilbert's part that any gossip he might share about Larkin would reach the wrong ears.

Claire and I spent Saturday digging through her music library search-ing for material for Elsa. We looked for songs that spoke of adversity and life's little setbacks but treated them with breezy stoicism or humor as opposed to Elsa's maudlin breast-beating. We had just drawn up a preliminary list that included "Who Cares?" "Pick Yourself Up," "They All Laughed," and Porter's "Down in the Depths (on the Ninetieth Floor)," when we were interrupted by the doorbell. Claire, pressing the intercom button, asked who was there and was greeted by the imperious, Italian-accented voice of Signora di Corteggiano demanding an immediate interview.

"Ah! How fortunate!" she said, sweeping in. "I am pleased to see you are both here!"

She was dressed in her usual dramatic fashion: a heavy blue velvet cape with a red silk lining, fastened at the throat by a silver clasp resembling two lions French-kissing.

"What can we do for you?" Claire asked warily.

"I have come to speak to you about Meesus Champion and this foolish thing she has been persuaded to do!"

"Foolish?"

"A most grievous mistake! To give a concert so soon into the instruction period—"

"But, signora," said Claire, "I heard Elsa say she'd been studying with you for six years!"

"*Sì*," said the signora, "but my technique, it takes at least seven, maybe eight years to master. And when I am working with a pupil who has for so many years tormented her vocal chords with inferior methods, why *then* . . . *!*" She sighed heavily and shrugged as if to say that under such trying circumstances, lessons might well continue indefinitely.

"I see," said Claire with a cool smile. "Elsa hasn't listened to enough tapes yet? Maybe you could speed things up by giving her all the messages right out loud instead of subliminally?"

The signora's eyes narrowed. "Young lady, do not mock what you cannot understand!"

She glowered in a manner that might have struck terror into the heart of some timid soprano who'd bounced a check but impressed Claire not at all. Seeing intimidation would not do the trick, the old diva tried a different tack.

"Signorina Simmons, I do not come here to quarrel." She smiled, exposing two rows of long, nicotine-stained teeth. "I am sure we all have Meesus Champion's best interests at heart. Do we not?"

"Sure," I said, "but what are you asking us to do?"

She proceeded to outline a suggestion as to how the matter might most tactfully be addressed. If Elsa could not be convinced that a debut was premature—and the signora had already exerted some effort in this line—she might yet be persuaded not to make it in so spectacular and *public* a fashion. If Elsa wished to perform, then let her, but at a *private* recital in her own home with, say, fifty or so close friends in attendance. Then, if that went well, she could at some future date (and the more future the better) contemplate riskier venues.

This plan had been put to Elsa, but she'd balked, feeling it was too late now. Her plans had been announced publicly, and if she were to scale back now, her enemies would have no end of fun mocking her retreat. But the signora hoped she might yet be persuaded, and we could greatly assist the cause by adding our voices to her own.

"I am sure you'll agree with me as to the wisdom of this approach, since your fee will, of course, be the same wherever the concert is held."

She apparently assumed the matter settled, for she stood and began donning her gloves.

"Not so fast, dearie," said Claire, and the signora, her nostrils flaring with indignation, resumed her seat.

"In the first place," Claire said, "Elsa's preparedness for exposure may be open to question, but ours is not. Putting the issue of money aside—assuming you're mentally equipped to do so—we agreed to write songs for an act to be presented at the Rainbow Room. Do you suppose we want to go through all the effort of writing material when it will only be heard once? And *then* by a claque of carefully selected bum kissers?

"Secondly, signora, for all your touching concern for your pupil, it's obvious your real fear is for your bank balance. You're scared that if Elsa lays an egg, she may know enough to hand some of the blame to you and your beautiful thoughts, and your long, lovely gravy train will grind to a halt—and about time if you ask me!"

"You hateful girl!" cried the signora, rising in fury. "How dare you speak so to me!"

"I have seen frauds in my day, signora, but you take the *tira mì su*. I've looked you up in the opera annuals, and as far as I can see, if you ever performed at La Scala, it was at a sing-along night."

"I have worked under several names!"

"I don't doubt it. And as for your vocal coaching, *cara*, you couldn't make a canary sing with six pounds of birdseed."

"You know nothing!" said the signora, hurriedly gathering her things. "My techniques are highly scientific!"

"Your techniques make Mary Baker Eddy look like a neurosurgeon. And now, if you've said all you intend to, may I suggest you leave? *We* have work to do."

The signora swept to the door and wheeled on us with a grand swirl of her cloak. "You will learn, impudent girl, what happens to those who earn the wrath of Lucrezia di Corteggiano!"

And with that she thrust out her bosom and opened her mouth wide, clearly gearing up for a supersonic high C that would pierce our eardrums and shatter Claire's china cabinet. She must not, however, have been thinking suitably lovely thoughts, because all that came out was an arthritic shriek that succeeded in shattering nothing except the nerves of the neighbor's Pekingese, who responded with a fusillade of furious, high-pitched yaps. Whereupon the signora, chagrined and coughing uncontrollably, opened the door and fled into the lobby.

Ten

That night Gilbert and I got together in an effort to live up to the queasy détente we'd established in the supermarket. We passed the evening pleasantly enough, eating Indian food, watching old movies, and dwelling upon the character flaws of mutual acquaintances. Our rivalry, though it hovered like a spectral presence, was ignored, except for one brief moment when I told Gilbert that Bill, an old flame of his, was back in town and what a great couple I always thought they'd made, and Gilbert said Bill had always been fond of me and would I like his phone number?

Tuesday we went to Tommy's for dinner. Tommy, acting more Peter O'Toole than ever, fanned the flames of our passion and rivalry. He met us with kisses and cocktails and seemed, throughout the evening, serenely unaware of the jealousy that simmered in our breasts.

Over a superb seafood dinner he filled us in on the progress thus far. The microphones I'd placed were transmitting away but had yet to yield much, as the Champions had spent the weekend on their yacht. He was confident, though, that matters would change once we leaked rumors that Peter was under investigation for substandard building practices and bribery.

After dinner Gilbert and I took turns reporting on our progress. Gilbert had a folder of clippings, photos, and notes from his research trip. He'd unearthed a few splendid nuggets, among them some taped reminiscences of Peter's childhood chums, one of whom bitterly recalled the day he gave Peter his rarest baseball card in exchange for what proved to be a terminally ill hamster. He also had photocopies from Peter's high school yearbooks, which curiously omitted all mention of the glorious sports career to which Peter often alluded. Best of all, though, was a photo from the infancy of Elsa's singing career. It showed her at some suburban Oktoberfest, crooning "Bei Mir Bist Du Schön" in a wig tastefully decorated with loops of the sponsoring company's braunschweiger.

Though Gilbert was rewarded with warm congratulations, I couldn't help feeling justified in my belief that his contributions possessed not a shred of the glamour attached to my own.

I modestly described the audacious brilliance I'd displayed in fielding Champion's inquisition about Gilbert, not to mention the intrepidity with which I deposited the chewing-gum mike behind his very headboard. Tommy showered me with kudos while Gilbert sat, writhing in envy. He congratulated me, too, of course, but with the bleak, upstaged air of an archaeologist who's just presented his few shards of Roman pottery, only to have Indiana Jones calmly produce the place mats from the Last Supper.

He maintained a glum silence during the cab ride home, claiming to have a sinus headache. As he departed the cab, tossing me a quarter of the fare, I detected on his face that strange constipated look that usually signals deep and cunning thought. But I was so much involved in committing Tommy's prettier compliments to memory that I shrugged it off and thought no more of it.

At our next meeting with Elsa, Claire and I arrived armed to the teeth with sunny, up-tempo tunes. We'd spent considerable time discussing strategy and felt confident that Elsa, if handled diplomatically, could be persuaded to approach her story in a lighter vein. Things did not, however, get off to an auspicious start.

No sooner had we begun than Dunbar entered in some agitation, with Kitty close on her heels. Dunbar explained acidly that she'd told Kitty Elsa was engaged but Kitty had insisted on interrupting.

"I'll see you out when you're through, Miss Driscoll," said Dunbar, and withdrew, her heels clicking like gunshots on the marble floor. Elsa directed a pained look at Claire and me and asked if we wouldn't mind waiting outside.

"Sit!" said Kitty, waving us down. "I want witnesses!"

"You seem perturbed, Kitty," said Elsa in that hypercultivated tone she tended to adopt in Kitty's presence. "Is something the matter?"

"You bet something's the mattah!" said Kitty.

She pointed an accusing finger toward the hall, where Dunbar stood, waiting to eject her. "I put in a call to Hitler's lovechild out there, to ask if she could arrange to have my allowance doubled—just for *one* month—and she said she had explicit orders not to increase it by one fuckin' dime!"

"I'm sure those weren't her words," said Elsa.

"Naturally I didn't believe my own *sister* could have ordered such a thing, so I came by to hear it from her own lips. *Well?*"

"Kitty," Elsa said calmly, "this is neither the time nor the place to—"

Kitty interrupted, addressing herself to me. "Look at what I'm wearing!" she said, throwing open her sable to reveal a fetching silk floral. "Completely out of style!"

"Looks nice to me," I said weakly.

"It is *completely* out of style! She's always on my case to find some rich husband like *she* did—not because she *cares* about me, mind you, but because she hates supporting me! Like she can't afford it or something! But how the hell am I s'posed to find a wealthy man when I'm walkin' around lookin' like a fuckin' dress museum?"

Elsa's reply was a derisive snort. "It takes more than *clothing* to attract a man, dear. It takes breeding—refinement!"

"*Refinement!*" shrieked Kitty. She turned to Claire. "*This* from a gal who got her start in *Frank and Bernie's Folies Bergères Revue!*"

"That's enough!" shouted Elsa.

"Sang 'La Vie en Rose' wearin' croissants on her tits! Don't think I've forgotten *that* one!"

"Dunbar!" screeched Elsa. "Will you kindly write my sister a check and show her out!"

"Grateful, I'm sure," sniffed Kitty. She then turned to Claire and me and waved a dainty farewell.

"Charmed to see you again," she said, and, pivoting toward the door, breezed regally past Dunbar, her fanny undulating like a lava lamp.

It was, of course, some time before our meeting got quite under way again, as Elsa felt the need to rehash a lifetime's worth of persecution at Kitty's hands. Eventually, though, she gazed at her watch and suggested we get back to business. Her mood seemed tired and defensive, but I attributed this to the residual effects of Kitty's unsoothing visit.

We outlined our thoughts, doing our best to steer her gently but firmly away from the "Marie Antoinette Sings Songs of Despair" approach she'd espoused at our previous meeting. Our success, however, was limited.

She agreed with us that "the real Elsa" was an optimistic survivor who could laugh at adversity and forge cheerfully ahead. She even seemed willing to go with some of our suggestions for songs, notably "They All Laughed." But she insisted on addressing the low spots in her life and giving them full dramatic and musical expression. After all, she argued, how could people know she was a survivor if they were not informed as to what she'd survived? How could she laugh in the face of unspecified sorrows? How could the audience appreciate her refusal to complain if they didn't know what ample justification she had for doing so? She'd be delighted to sing a few up-tempo numbers, but only on the heels of some "haunting and dramatic" songs, introduced with appropriate patter so that their full autobiographical significance was made clear.

Claire and I, with a delicacy that would have become a British bomb squad, suggested that regardless of what *we* knew to be the truth, many in Elsa's audience might be forgiven for feeling she was, all in all, rather *fortunate,* and these same people might tend to view a series of laments, however beautifully sung, as . . . unseemly. It was a good thing we weren't a British bomb squad, because if we had been, the next moment would have seen our earthly remains whipping through Piccadilly Circus in little gory bits.

"I *knew* it!" cried Elsa, leaping to her feet. "You're just like all the rest! 'Shut up, Elsa! Don't bother us! You have a big house and lots of money, so of course your life must be perfect!' "

"That's not what we said at all!" said Claire.

"It is! Don't deny it! Everyone else is entitled to talk about their problems and sing sad songs, but not me! I'm just supposed to smile and say how *haaappy* I am! I don't know why I expected you two to be any different. I should have known about you! I was warned!"

"You were *warned?*" I asked, getting dizzy.

"Yes! Signora di Corteggiano called me only yesterday to say she'd spoken to her psychic and *he* said I was in terrible danger—that a young homosexual and a plump girl had come into my life and they meant me great harm!"

"This," said Claire, flinging her hands up, "is more than I can deal with!" She stormed over to the piano and began stuffing her sheet music back in her bag.

"Elsa," I said as gently as possible, "are you in the habit of taking advice from your voice teacher's psychic?"

My tone seemed to calm her a bit. "No," she said, quieter. "In fact, until now, I never knew she had one. But I'm a great believer in the supernatural. When I was a little girl a terrible black crow came to sit on our porch and the very next day Kitty was born."

Dunbar suddenly materialized and announced that Millie Pilchard had arrived for their lunch date. Elsa asked that Millie be shown in, and a moment later she was upon us.

"Oh, look who's here!" twittered Millie. "So sorry to be early, dear, but I had a coffee date with Agatha Blore and I wasn't there half an hour before she remembered a previous engagement and had to dash. So forgetful, Agatha! I thought I'd pop round on the chance you'd be ready for me. But I see you're in the throes of creation! How proud I feel seeing the fruits of my handiwork! Everything going well, I hope?"

"Splendidly," croaked Elsa.

"Elsa, dear! Your eyes all puffy! I suppose you've been singing another of those haunting songs you cherish so. Such a moving actress, isn't she?" said Millie to Claire. "You must make her sing nothing but ballads."

"We were finishing up for today," said Elsa, a wary eye on Claire. "I'll just fix my face and call for the car."

"Excuse me," Claire said, returning from the piano, "but if we're to write three new songs for you, we really should discuss the contents. They'll take a while and we'll never finish on time if we don't start soon—that is, if you still want us to write them."

Elsa frowned, unsure whether or not we were fired, but unwilling at any rate to give us the sack in front of dear, helpful Millie.

"Well," she said, "I liked that one you sang for my audition, 'Hard to Be Me.' I *do* have a sense of humor about myself, regardless of what some people think, and I suppose that will help show it. I want some new lyrics, though, with, you know, things about me."

"Great!" I said with false heartiness. "We'll get right on that!"

Claire shot me a look that foretold of spirited discussions in the cab, then returned to the piano to finish gathering her things. Elsa, suddenly oblivious to my presence, took Millie's arm and began conversing in a low but audible whisper.

"So, tell me, hon—did you speak to Horsey? Can she make it to my opening?"

Mrs. Pilchard grimaced like a chicken doing Chekhov. "I did my best, dear, but you know Horsey—she's never gone in much for popular music, and she's so busy with her charities. So many benefits to organize, and she feels they really have to come first. Understand, please, that it's nothing personal, but—"

"Excuse me," I said, interrupting. It was a bit nervy of me, but an idea had occurred to me that, in addition to helping Elsa, might return us to her good graces. "I couldn't help overhearing that Millie's sister's too busy to come to your opening."

"*And?*" Elsa said frostily.

"Well, I just thought she might find time if you made it a benefit for her favorite charity."

Elsa stared at me as though I were suddenly bathed in a holy light. "What a fan*tas*tic suggestion!" she cried, hurling her arms around me.

She then fell upon Millie, asking which of Horsey's numerous causes was her particular pet. "Pet" proved an apt word, as, according to Millie, the charity closest to her sister's heart was Paws to Consider, a group that provided medical care and homes for stray cats. Though a board member in high standing of all the city's loftiest institutions, Horsey's flinty heart went out most to this small, underfunded organization. She'd contributed stacks to it and often spoke with asperity of the countless fools who saw fit to squander their money on less worthy causes.

Giving me and a bewildered Claire big kisses good-bye, Elsa grabbed Millie's arm and dashed off to Le Cirque to work out the details.

Elsa, when motivated, wastes little time. The very next day an item appeared in Daisy Winters's column announcing that tickets would soon go on sale for Elsa's long-awaited Rainbow Room debut and that the first performance would be a five-hundred-dollar-a-plate benefit for Paws to Consider, with National Chairwoman Horsey Kimball on hand as guest of honor.

This revised scheme called for certain adjustments. Elsa had planned to play her weeklong engagement in the Rainbow Room's cabaret, a cozy little room called Rainbow and Stars. This space was now deemed insufficiently grand for the proposed gala, so the opening performance was moved to the Rainbow Room itself, a far larger and more opulent venue able to accommodate more than twice as many guests. She would then play out the remainder of her engagement as planned in the more intimate room.

It was the opening, of course, that everyone, friend and foe alike, was determined to attend. There must, as such, have been lots of grumbling around town over the suddenly bloated ticket price. But so keen was the air of anticipation surrounding Elsa's premier, so cowed were the sycophants, and so hopeful the ill-wishers, that the tickets were snapped up completely within two days of being put on sale.

Over the next weeks Claire and I worked around the clock writing and rewriting the songs and patter to Elsa's maddeningly mercurial specifications. The rewrite on "Hard to Be Me" went over reasonably well, but the opening and closing numbers required endless revisions. No sooner would we settle on a concept and complete a first draft than Elsa would call to say that on reconsidering the matter, the song should *not* be about how singing was a joyful antidote to life's frustrations but instead about having the courage to make new beginnings. Then just when we were nearly finished with *that*, she'd call and say, "Forget all that new beginnings stuff and write me something really funny about how nervous I am to be doing this, something that will, you know, make them laugh, but really *sympathize.*" And, of course, when we finally completed this song and played it for her, she commended our efforts but said she'd changed her mind and was going back to the first song.

The finale, similarly, underwent numerous transformations. She originally requested a song about surviving and weathering life's little storms, then changed her mind, arguing that since she'd waited twenty years to do this, the song should logically be about not giving up on your dreams. One week later she called to say that on careful consideration she'd decided that since she'd not have dared even attempt the act without her husband's love and support, the song should by rights be an affectionate tribute to him, preferably titled, "I Owe It All to You." This approach, while not particularly fresh, seemed somewhat less hackneyed and easier to write than yet another "roll with the punches" or "hold onto your dream" song. It also, we realized, allowed her to tactfully acknowledge what would be transparent to everyone present—that her debut wouldn't be quite so glittering an event if she were not married to one of the richest men in the country.

As for her patter, she persisted in suggesting the most intolerably maudlin anecdotes. After she proposed that her story about how a vicious high school teacher had cruelly dismissed her from the cheerleading squad might make a suitable lead-in to "Am I Blue?" I took the bull by the horns and called Peter. He had charged us with making his wife look good, and if she was determined to thwart us, perhaps he could talk some sense into her. I'm not sure what he did, but the next time we met she showed a new willingness to keep the axe grinding to a minimum.

Gradually, in the course of discussions and debates so protracted as to make the Nuremberg war trials seem a mere coin toss, we settled on a program of songs. Following our opening "music helps me cope with life's traumas" number, titled "I Sing," she'd talk about how she'd started out as a singer, oh, so many years ago, before love and marriage pre-empted her career. She'd then sing a song about meeting Peter. No amount of pleading or ardently proffered alternatives could persuade her that this song should not be "Mad About the Boy," so "Mad About the Boy" it was. Then she'd describe her joy at winning him with "They All Laughed"—a title we hoped would not, given the way she sang "Mad About the Boy," prove unduly prophetic. After this she'd do "Easy Living," performing it as a sultry hymn to connubial bliss.

We couldn't talk her out of including some affecting treatment of her childhood, but we did at least persuade her to eschew chronology by saving it till fifth place (in lieu of *starting* with it, which would have been death). She would confide with a brave smile that she'd inherited her love of music from her mother, who'd died tragically young. This would lead into Rodgers and Hart's "Little Girl Blue," which she performed with such lachrymose intensity, we'd need nurses standing by to tend to those who'd bitten their tongues. She insisted upon following this with "Sophisticated Lady" to subtly indicate that the tragic tot of the previous number still dwelled within her.

After this, her third consecutive ballad, even Elsa agreed it was time for comic relief, so we put "Hard to Be Me" there. Elsa could delight the crowd with her self-spoofing references to her husband, her apartment, her glamorous friends, and her mad social whirl. This would be followed by "Get Happy," thus keeping the energy level high while giving Elsa a chance to show off her voice's most notable quality—volume. She could even do a few of those brisk, vampy dance steps that, though painfully simple, provoke frenzies of applause when executed by dignified nondancers over forty.

Then, for a change of pace, she'd wax philosophical—and show off her thin but pretty head voice—with Noel Coward's "I'll Follow My Secret Heart." She'd then coyly address the audience's curiosity as to what it was like being married to a man famed as a tough negotiator, confiding that he was just as stubborn at home in (what else?) "Let's Call the Whole Thing Off."

The next song, the penultimate, would be Sondheim's "Losing My Mind." There was no autobiographical logic in this, but the song, a perennial favorite with scenery-chewing chanteuses, was one Elsa had been wailing in private for years, and she was determined to use it here as one last, big, emote-to-the-rafters showstopper. She would then say good night and end with her affectionate tribute to Peter, "I Owe It All to You."

We finished and presented that number to her one Wednesday about two and a half weeks before her opening. She professed utter delight with it, then said she and Peter had planned a weekend cruise on their yacht with a few dear friends. She'd been considering taking it as an opportunity to preview the act for her inner circle, and now that the final song had turned out so wonderfully she'd decided to go ahead with it. Were we free to come? Claire, being Elsa's accompanist, surmised that attendance was not optional, and we said we'd be thrilled to join the party.

That evening I spoke to both Champion and Tommy. Champion called to say he hoped I'd been spending ample time with Gilbert and would have plenty of juicy stuff to report come the weekend. I hadn't, in fact, even phoned Gilbert in nearly a week, so preoccupied had I been with finishing the songs, but I assured him I'd been in close touch and had stories he'd have to wear sun block to listen to. I called Tommy to review the stories Boyd had devised about his shameful escapades. He glumly reported that plans to leak the bribery rumors had been postponed, as most of the chewing-gum bugs had been discovered by maids and removed, their last meager broadcasts consisting entirely of Spanish invective.

I told him about the cruise, and he became very excited. He said this was a *tremendous* break for us, as Champion often conducted business on the yacht, no doubt because of the seclusion and privacy it afforded. It was suspected that his most nefarious schemes were hatched within this seagoing sanctum, and a single well-placed device there might do more good than a hundred sprinkled about Champion Plaza.

I vowed to get my last microphone in place there and said I'd call him first thing Monday. He said I'd have to report to Boyd, as he was off to Europe for two weeks to see about launching foreign editions of *Boulevardier*. Nothing, however, could prevent his hastening back stateside to catch Elsa's debut.

Perhaps it was the thought of not seeing him for two weeks, but I was suddenly emboldened enough to stammer, "You know . . . when you get back I'd really enjoy seeing you and spending an evening that wasn't about Peter and Elsa. I'd love to cook you dinner or something."

I waited for what seemed about two operas but was in real time maybe a second and a half.

"You know, Philip, I should enjoy that very, very much."

I sat in lieu of fainting. Elsa's debut, I said, was on a Tuesday night. Was he free the Thursday after?

"Yes, I am. I shall be there at eight with flowers and a shy smile."

I hung up and promptly went into my Gene Kelly mode, dancing all over the sofa and coffee table. I then fluttered into my bedroom, opened my dresser, and began merrily packing for a voyage that, I little suspected, would be only marginally more festive than those of the *Titanic*, the *Lusitania*, and the *Marie Celeste*.

Eleven

Some years ago, after he'd completed his monumental Plaza, Peter Champion beheld what he had wrought, and discontent nibbled at his bosom. Yes, he thought approvingly, it was vast and hideous. Yes, it made Disney World look like something designed by Shakers. Yes, pigeons rounding the corner of Fifty-seventh Street were observed to rear up and fall, stunned, to the pavement. But—and here was the rub—could you plunk the whole thing down in the Hudson and sail it to Atlantic City? No, you could not. Champion, never a man to let discontent nibble for long, summoned the world's leading shipwrights to his side and outlined his vision of the ideal yacht. The shipwrights giggled a bit and built it.

The result, dubbed the *Champion Siren*, made its maiden voyage on an ocean of hype as journalists the world over derided its sybaritic excesses while lovingly cataloging the same. The coverage had been extensive, so as Claire and I sipped our cappuccino in the limo to the pier, we knew pretty well what to expect. We'd read about the disco, the cinema, the kennel, the patisserie, the beauty and barber salons, the pool (with sliding marble dance floor), the gymnasium (with trainers), the kitchen (with walk-in freezer), the grand salon (with orchestra on call), the sun deck (with formal English garden), and the chapel, where anyone inclined to offer thanks for the above could do so in pious luxury.

We'd also read quite a bit about the lavishly appointed suites, for these had come in for the most blistering denunciations. The complaints centered on Peter's apolitical fondness for controversial materials. Each suite was equipped with chinchilla comforters and tortoiseshell vanity sets, while ivory was the medium of choice for faucets, toilet paper holders, and sanitary napkin dispensers. Reports of these impolitic niceties spread quickly, the ivory sanitary napkin dispensers receiving particular attention, and friends of the concerned species sprang to action. Champion's crew often had to request Coast Guard protection from speedboats full of enraged environmentalists who chased the yacht, chanting through bullhorns and marring on-deck cocktail parties by pelting the guests with tampons.

Claire and I reached the pier early and were met by the first mate, a courteous young man with a pleasant cockney accent. He said we were first to arrive and, noting Claire's rapt gaze, offered to show us the formal garden. We climbed stairs to the sun deck and there it was—an incongruous expanse of grass, blossoms, shrubs, crumbling stone benches, and yew trees. There were brick paths winding lazily through it and, in the center, a lily-covered pool leading to a small gazebo where a statue of Cupid was laughing himself silly at the whole thing.

"Good Lord," said Claire. "It's only *March*. How do you keep it all from dying?"

"Well, usually," said the first mate, "it's enclosed by a greenhouse. But when the weather permits, the walls and ceiling retract. It's warmish this morning, so the captain gave orders to open her up— Mr. Champion likes it best that way."

"But the salt air?" I asked. "Do the plants like it?"

"Not much they don't!" He laughed. "We got horty-culturists cluckin' around 'em all the time, and we still wind up tearin' the whole lot up six, seven times a year and plantin' it all fresh. Trees are a pain, too. We had to replace the willows. Roots keep breaking through the ceiling of the wheelhouse."

"No!"

"Yes. Took weeks to fix, too, 'cause they got all tangled up with the wiring. Wasn't half strange sitting there with tree roots dangling overhead. Felt like a bloody badger."

He showed us to our adjoining suites on the B deck, Claire's the Minerva Suite and mine the Dionysus. They were sleek, color-coordinated chambers, all rounded corners, lacquered surfaces, and

posh art deco accents. I told Claire I needed to freshen up, then
locked my door and began perusing my notes on the seedy anecdotes
Larkin had cooked up to whet Champion's appetite. My studies were
soon interrupted by Elsa's voice blaring over the intercom.

"Philip? Are you there, *ma chérie?*"

I pressed a button marked "Speak." "Yes, I'm here,"

"C'mon up! We're all in the main salon. One flight up."

I ran next door to fetch Claire. As we were exiting her room we
bumped into Millie Pilchard, who was vacating the Terpsichore Suite.
She was wearing a nautically inspired blue-and-white dress that
seemed a mite *jeune fille* for one of her advancing years. Her manner
was as bubbly as ever.

"Ah, our two young songbirds! Such a glorious day! Did you see
the garden in all its glory! Spring on demand! Don't you adore it?"

"Nice to see you, Millie."

"I can't wait to hear your delightful songs! No, not the stairs, dears,
there's an elevator. Such a nice little party this will be. Did you hear
she's asked Hamilton Yearwood along?"

"Hamilton Yearwood?" I asked as the doors slid open.

"Yes. Charming man. Fabulously rich, you know, and quite the
catch since his wife passed away last year. Her heart, they claimed,
though I heard cirrhosis. Just between us, Elsa's *desperate* to set him
up with Kitty. Do her a world of good. Such exquisite manners! His,
I mean, not hers. He'd calm her down, I suspect, and give her a bit
of the polish she so desperately needs. He'd provide for her, too,
which would be *most* welcome," she confided, adding with breathtaking chutzpah, *"Kitty is rather a drain on Elsa."*

The elevator opened and we stepped into the lobby of the A deck
and from there through two grand doors into the main salon. It was
a long stylish room, done in white and pale gold tones. Inside it our
fellow voyagers, all richly and meticulously costumed, sat lounging
about, looking like the first reel of an Agatha Christie movie. Hoot
Mulvaney was there, slouching Europeanly behind designer shades.
Kitty stood at the window, gazing out at the water, and though I
couldn't see her face, her rump looked bored. Peter sat in one corner,
surveying *Estime* layouts with Joy Cudgel and America's father con-
fessor, Spark Chandler. Joy looked out of sorts, as if she'd woken up

ravenous only to have the maid say they were fresh out of babies. Elsa was playing backgammon with a spruce, sixtyish gent whom I took to be Hamilton Yearwood. He had a little white mustache and a jovial air, partly attributable, I suspected, to the martini he was sipping at only eleven in the morning.

Claire and I thanked Elsa for inviting us, and she introduced us to Hamilton, explaining that he was the only son of Harry Yearwood, the pickle magnate.

"Philip, is it?" asked Hamilton, lingering somewhat over the handshake.

"Yes, and this is Claire."

"I hear you write show tunes," he said with a slyness that spelled doom to Kitty's chances of hooking this new bachelor anytime soon. She lacked the proper bait.

"*Ham!*" brayed Elsa. "You are some *backgammon champ!* I wish I could finish losing to you, but I *must* see to lunch. Kitty, love!" she cooed across the room, and Kitty, rolling her eyes, strolled over like a waitress on break.

"Finish my game, would you? I am on the brink of di*sast*er, so see if you can't rescue our family's honor!"

Kitty, mumbling something about it being late in the day for *that*, plopped onto Elsa's chair and Elsa scurried away.

The boat began pulling away from the dock. Peter, Joy, and Spark were still in conference and Claire and I, having no inclination to make small chat with Hoot, went out to the deck. We traded limp wisecracks about the boat as we watched Manhattan recede, but my heart wasn't in it. I was nervously fingering my last gummy mike, praying I'd manage to plant it in Champion's office.

Hoot materialized at our side. He said he was finishing up the *Estime* piece on Elsa and, if Claire could spare me, he had a few questions about my background. As I'd suspected, this was a mere ploy to drag me to Champion's office, where I could give them the salacious lowdown on Boyd. He led me out through the salon into the A deck lobby, where Champion stood, a smug, crafty smile on his face.

Champion led us up the stairs to the wheelhouse deck, where there was a similar lobby. One door led to more guest suites and the wheelhouse, while another door, which bore an elaborate gold crest, was Champion's office.

Champion, consulting a card from his pocket, punched a code into one of those numeric keypad locks he seemed to favor so. Nine musical beeps, like those of a touch-tone phone, sounded. He smartly tapped in the final number, and all at once a deafening alarm bell sounded. I gasped, convinced for a horrified instant that the system was so sophisticated it had responded to my subversive brain waves. But then Champion said, "Oh, fuck!" and, consulting the card, keyed in the numbers again, even as two officers raced in from the wheelhouse to make sure the boat wasn't under under siege by tampon-wielding activists. Champion barked an apology at them, and we entered the office.

It would have been a spacious enough office on land, but here at sea it seemed especially grand and imposing. This was due mainly to the decorating scheme. While all the accoutrements, filing cabinets and such, were sleek and modern, the general theme was early *I, Claudius*, the most striking feature being a tiled floor with an elaborate mosaic of Romulus and Remus being suckled by the wolf. I had to wonder, given my host's penchant for mixing Roman and Hellenic motifs, if he didn't in fact view ancient Greece and Rome as contemporaneous sister cities, like Minneapolis and St. Paul.

There was a sitting area by the door, but the room was dominated by a gargantuan desk at the opposite end. It was white and shiny and curved protectively around the high-backed swivel throne behind it. Beyond this was a wide window overlooking the deck and the swimming pool. Champion pressed a dimmer panel by the door, and some lamps that looked like wedding presents from the Agamemnons flickered to life. He then pushed a button in a console on one wall, and heavy drapes slowly enshrouded the window, giving the place the sinister air of a star chamber.

As he seated himself behind the vast desk, I noticed a row of control buttons set into the middle of it. I was seized by sudden visions of trapdoors poised above piranha-filled tanks. Champion motioned for Hoot and me to take chairs, which were, in the classic mogul's maneuver, built low to the floor so we'd be made to feel like schoolchildren as Champion towered imperially above us. I smiled inwardly, knowing that this also placed my hands farther below desk level, enabling me to secrete the microphone under my chair with less chance of him noticing.

"A pleasure to have you aboard, Philip," he said.

"A pleasure to be here!" I enthused like a ten-year-old invited for a weekend at the BatCave. "This is one helluva boat!"

"There's not another like it in the world. Do you bowl? I just had an alley put in."

He said maybe we'd bowl a string later, then got down to business, asking if I'd had much contact with Gilbert. I said yes, I had. He'd been reticent at first, but I'd gotten him drunk and the stories had tumbled out.

"What did he say?" asked Hoot, swiveling his chair and leaning toward me with a rapacious smile.

"Hang on," said Champion, extending a hand toward the buttons on his desktop. "I'd like to record this for my personal records. Speak clearly, all right?" He pressed the button all the way to the right, then nodded for me to proceed.

I launched into my sordid anecdotes, sketching the details with lascivious glee. I told them Larkin was a depraved voyeur who in the summertime would hire as many as thirty male prostitutes to pair off and copulate all night on the grounds of his Connecticut estate while Larkin, dressed in a bird-watching ensemble, would creep through the shrubbery ogling them through binoculars. On his yacht, I said, he regularly threw orgies of a wantonness that would have raised eyebrows in downtown Gomorrah. For the most recent he'd had an enormous vending machine built and then stocked it with underage Moroccan boys.

Throughout this torrid recitation both Hoot's and Champion's smiles widened steadily. By the time I finished they looked like Christmas morning.

"Can you document any of this?" asked Hoot, so stirred he'd actually removed his sunglasses.

"Well, no," I said. "I mean, this is all coming from an old friend I haven't talked to for years. If I start asking him to *document* things, what's he going to think?"

"Philip has a point," said Champion. "We can't make Selwyn suspicious."

He turned to me. "He had no suspicions regarding your relationship with us?"

"No. I mean, naturally he wanted to hear dirt about you. Tit for tat, you know. I made up a lot of stuff about Elsa being cranky and screaming at the servants, and that seemed to satisfy him."

"You've done very well, Philip," said Champion, and I beamed boyishly. "But," he continued, "though this confirms our suspicions about Larkin's depravity, we'd like a little more concrete evidence."

Hoot said, "I know some guys who'd hire themselves out for one of these orgies if we paid 'em enough. They could wear a wire."

"Disguised as what?" snorted Champion. "A birthmark?"

Champion's eyes were on Hoot, and I took the opportunity to reach into my jacket and remove the bug. No sooner had I done so, though, than Champion stood up, giving him a much better view of my lap. I concealed the microphone in my fist and sat forward with my hands between my legs.

Champion smirked and said he had a means to garner far more evidence than any doped-up party boy could be relied upon to provide. He crossed to a marble-topped chest. He had his back to me now, but the minute I slipped my hand under my chair Hoot grabbed the arm of it and spun me toward him.

"You're *sure* he's been playing with jailbait? Because that's important. I mean, I write the guy's a closet case, it's like, big deal, that rumor's been around for years. But if he's diddling little boys, now *that's* a story!"

"Well, as I said, Hoot, I don't have any *proof.*"

"This should take care of *that!*" said Champion, returning to the desk. He sat on the edge of it, holding a velvet box in his outstretched palm.

"These little babies," he said, smiling, "should come in real handy for getting the goods on ol' Boydy-boy!" And with a nasal chuckle, he opened the box and dumped its contents onto the table.

I stared, appalled.

If there is one annoying flaw free-lance arms dealers tend as a group to display, it's that they are democratic to a fault. Though they facilitate warfare, selling the combatants all they require to rain destruction on each other, they remain, in spirit, above the fray, refusing to play favorites and offering their services to all solvent subscribers. Mr. Vladimir was no exception. Having devised a surefire crowd pleaser like the Chewing-gum Transmitting Device, he was not about to limit its market to just one vengeful billionaire. No, he got right on the phone, giving his sales pitch to vengeful billionaires all over town and probably sending them nice four-color brochures.

At any rate, word had reached Peter, who now stood grinning down at five of the little darlings. He outlined their benefits while I did my best to impersonate some poor rube who'd never seen a chewing-gum microphone in his life.

"Pretty fucking elegant!" smiled Hoot, inspecting one. "If old Boyd finds one, he thinks the maid or someone left it there."

Champion agreed this was a plausible scenario, saying he'd fired a maid for leaving gum under a dining room table only last week. He instructed me to take them and then do my best to gain access to Boyd Larkin's private lair, where I should deposit them under tables, chairs, and, most especially, beds.

He was interrupted in these instructions by a loud knock at the door. Elsa's voice cooed from without.

"Peter? Are you boys ready for lunch? I'm *fam*ished!"

Champion scowled. Gesturing to the microphones, he barked an order to me to take them. So sharp was his command that I forgot myself entirely and, extending my right hand—which already contained my *own* microphone—covered the lot of them, dropped mine into the pile, scooped them up, and thrust them into my pocket.

The door opened and Elsa thrust her head in. "What are you doing," she asked Peter, "boring 'em to tears with stories about your *deals?*"

She looked to Hoot and me. "I keep telling him people in the arts don't care about those things, but he thinks it's all *fas*cinating!"

"We weren't bored at all," said Hoot, winking at me conspiratorially.

"Well, the rest of us are sick of being *aband*oned so you all better come to lunch pronto!"

Champion gave her that wistful look that must often have crossed Bluebeard's face and said we had just finished. He rose stiffly and, pushing a button, ejected the tape from the recorder, which was also built into the desktop. He tossed the tape into a drawer and, ever the anal compulsive, removed a fresh tape from the same drawer, placed it in the machine, locked the drawer, and pocketed the key.

Elsa led the way down one flight to the dining room. I walked with Champion, smiling dumbly while suppressing a fierce desire to moan to heaven and rend my garments. It was bitterly clear that for all my swanking about, playing the dashing young master spy, I was in truth a disgrace to the profession. At a critical juncture, when cooler spies would have been planting bugs, snapping photos with their tie clip, and reading desktop documents upside down, I had fumbled pathetically. I'd mixed friendly bugs with enemy, thus botching the entire mission. How could I plant a microphone in Champion's office now with the odds six to one it would be one of his own? My heart sank when I thought of returning to Tommy and confessing that because *I* had failed, Champion's floating sanctum, the incubator for his vilest schemes, remained locked and inscrutable to us.

Such thoughts did little for my appetite, but I managed to profess pleasure on seeing the table fabulously set and our appetizers, fresh figs draped with gorgeous prosciutto, waiting at our places. Peter and Elsa sat at the ends of the table, and I took a seat between Kitty and Millie Pilchard.

Two waiters immediately entered with wine and began working their way down the table. I was relieved to see them, as I hoped that a good meal accompanied by sufficient wine would enable me to seek oblivion in an afternoon nap. As my waiter poured Millie's wine, I glanced up to where Claire sat opposite me, between Spark and Ham Yearwood. She was staring over my shoulder with a pale, astonished look. Turning to follow her gaze, I came face to face with my waiter, a swarthy Mediterranean fellow with black hair and an elegant mustache. The hair, however, was dyed, and the mustache was also a fake.

"Wine, m'sieur?" asked Gilbert.

Twelve

At moments such as these, when I am seized by the sudden conviction that I've just fallen face first onto a land mine, I find the only really therapeutic response is to jump three feet into the air, then stagger about shrieking inarticulately till I feel calmer. The last thing in the world I want to do is blandly pretend nothing's happened while fielding inquiries as to which comes first, the words or the music. But this, alas, I was compelled to do even as Gilbert made his way down the table, pouring wine with a bland insouciance that was, under the circumstances, utterly infuriating. My fellow diners—excepting, of course, Claire—seemed unaware of my dismay, so engrossed were they by the food, their hosts, and themselves. As for Claire, once the first shock had worn off, she betrayed no trace of the curious rage that must surely have boiled beneath her placid surface. She listened politely to the flood of anecdotes, offering those little exclamations and promptings upon which the self-flattering raconteur so relies. She did manage, though, when unobserved, to direct a few looks my way. These looks, though fleeting, were so pregnant with menace that I spent the entire meal gazing fretfully across at her like a Polynesian virgin contemplating a volcano.

As much as I dreaded the end of lunch and Claire's ensuing inquisition, I looked forward to holding one of my own. I burned to pull Gilbert aside and ask what precisely he hoped to achieve by infiltrating Champion's boat in this flimsiest of disguises. Why hadn't he *warned* me? How had he survived the background check? And *why*, having never visited the country or studied the language since high school, was he pretending to be a native of France?

"On-reee!" croaked Elsa to Gilbert in her own shaky attempt at bilingualism. *"Plus de* van, *s'il vous plaît."*

"Bien sûr," he murmured, refilling her glass, and I think one of Claire's menacing looks came right about then.

As the last of the honeydew sorbet was consumed, I was gripped by a desire to forestall the inevitable. If only I could steal away to some private nook, I could ponder the best way to frame my confession to Claire so as to minimize my treachery and the magnitude of her fury. Hoping to buy time, I turned to Ham Yearwood.

"Hamilton! How about some backgammon after lunch?"

"Well, wouldn't that be—"

"Philip!" said Claire, her tone sweetly admonitory. "You *know* I have those final chords to decide on, and I asked for your help!" She addressed Mr. Yearwood. "Can I steal Philip away, Ham? I require his ear."

Ham said fine, as long as she released me to his custody. We all rose, praising the meal, as Gilbert and his fellow waiter began clearing the table, Gilbert with a bland efficiency that made me want to hurl the centerpiece at him.

"Merci, Henri! You, too, Florindo!" said Elsa.

She then took Claire and me by the arms and led us down to the B deck. I begged their patience a moment and nipped into my room to shed the sport coat that held the five Champion bugs as well as the one from Boyd. I sensed that the forthcoming dialogue between Claire and me would not be anything either of my two employers ought really to hear. I emerged, and Elsa ushered us to a small, mercifully soundproofed music studio where we could work in privacy. I watched her depart as a convict watches the chaplain beat it out of the gas chamber, then turned to face Claire.

"This," she said rather slowly, "had better be good."

I toyed momentarily with the idea of insisting I hadn't a clue as to why Gilbert was pretending to be a waiter or, for that matter, a native of Paris. I sensed, though, from her steely gaze that she'd be no more willing to believe this than Sister Joselia had been to believe I'd found "Ranger in Paradise" on a playground bench and resolved to hide it before some impressionable underclassman could stumble on it and suffer psychological scars. It did, however, seem prudent to begin by flaunting what few scraps of innocence I could legitimately lay claim to.

"Claire, I had no idea Gilbert would be on this boat!"

This much she bought, as my surprise on first glimpsing him had been apparent. She'd seen subtler takes from Roger Rabbit.

"The question" said Claire, "is, *why* is he here? And don't tell me you don't know."

I frowned and said that while I could, of course, only speculate, my guess was that he was collecting material for the blistering exposé of Peter Champion he'd recently been engaged to coauthor.

"Exposé?" she asked, shutting her eyes and rubbing her temples gently.

"Yes."

"Of Peter Champion?"

"Yes," I said. "It's a magazine piece."

"And exactly when," she continued calmly, "did Gilbert tell you he was writing this piece?"

I coughed gently on the smoke that was issuing from her nostrils, then, adopting an injured tone, said I would confide nothing further until she promised not to yell at me. Which, in retrospect, was like trying to douse a brush fire with cognac.

"You fool!" she exploded. "You deceitful, pea-brained, backsliding ninny! You've known all along! That's why you cornered me into writing for these loathesome people—so you could help *Gilbert* with some ridiculous exposé!"

"It's not ridiculous at all!" I said.

"Oh, Philip!" she cried, kicking over several music stands. "How many times have I told you! When Gilbert tries to drag you into something you don't listen to him—you shoot him with a tranquilizer dart, after which you go home and rip your phone from the wall! You don't say yes! And if you *do* say yes, you don't involve *me* in it! And if you DO involve me in it, YOU DON'T REFRAIN FROM TELLING ME A SINGLE GODDAMNED THING ABOUT IT!"

I assumed a hunched, penitential posture on the piano bench and said how terribly sorry I was. I pleaded diminished responsibility for my actions, saying I'd fallen in love and that my passion had been so searing as to blind me to the moral niceties of the situation.

"Fallen in love?" she said, alarmed. "With *Gilbert?*"

"No. With Tommy Parker. He's the fellow Gilbert's writing with."

Feeling there was no longer much point in hoarding secrets, I spilled the whole story, keeping the emphasis on Tommy's sterling qualities and the moral turpitude on Champion's part that had prompted our efforts to begin with.

"Oh, lovely!" she snapped. "You want to prove the man's a criminal, so you immediately rush out and break every privacy law in the books! And this after you've signed—excuse me, after *we've* signed—a meticulously worded confidentiality agreement! Do you have any idea what sort of *lawyers* he's got? You're committing fraud against a man who has Satan on a retainer!"

"He can't sue me for planting bugs in his house! Not when he just asked me to plant bugs in Boyd Larkin's place!"

This stopped her. She gazed at me, uncomprehending. "What on earth has *he* got to do with it?"

"Tommy works for Boyd. He edits *Boulevardier*."

Her response was a prolonged, mirthless laugh. "Oh, *well!* How nice to see it's all so altruistic! Here you are going on about this great white knight who's some blend of Robin Hood and Eliot Ness, and all he really is is some lackey doing Boyd Larkin's dirty work for him!"

I rose from my seat, every trace of fear gone, and said that if she thought I was prepared to listen to her heap derision on a man I loved and whom she had not even met, she was very much mistaken.

"Oh, sit down, you jackass," she said wearily. "Christ, it *must* be love. You're talking like Greer Garson."

"He's a wonderful man. He's handsome and sensitive and dripping with charm."

"Obviously." She sighed. "And he works for that pillar of moderation, Boyd Larkin, on whom I take it you're *also* spying?"

"I'm only *pretending* to spy on Larkin. Champion asked me to because he knew I was friends with Gilbert, though he thinks I haven't been since Gilbert's wedding. Champion thinks Gilbert's having an affair with Tommy because his spies at *Boulevardier*, who know nothing about our exposé, think that's what Tommy and Gilbert are doing together. So Champion asked me to cozy up to Gilbert to get dirt about Larkin, because Champion's asked Hoot Mulvaney to write an exposé about *him*, only Champion has no idea Gilbert's also Henri the waiter, and neither did I till I saw him just now. I'm not sure why he's doing it, but I guess he wants to impress Tommy because he's in love with him, too, though so far neither of us has made much headway."

I suspected it was all getting a bit much for Claire, as she'd begun playing the piano with her forehead. I sat patiently and waited for the recital to end.

"Philip, you prince of buffoons," she said. "The night you told me about this job I *begged* you to tell me if Gilbert had the remotest connection to it. You did your damnedest to make me feel like the smallest, most paranoid hell-hag ever to mount a broomstick. And if that wasn't enough, you stood there and watched me sign an agreement that I wouldn't write about them *'or in any way assist anyone attempting to do so'!* How could you do this to me!"

I muttered something less than persuasive about love's power to lead us into desperate and unsavory measures. Claire just sat there, regarding me with a dull, wounded look that made me miss her earlier rage.

"Look at the position you've put me in," she said. "I can either blow the whistle and alert Champion, which is the last thing I want to do, or keep my mouth shut, in which case I'm practically an accomplice!"

"What will you do?" I asked uneasily.

"What the hell *can* I do!" she bellowed, and I realized I didn't miss the rage that much after all. "You've left me no choice at all, except to walk away!"

"When?" I asked, horrified. *"Now?"*

She snapped that her resignation could wait until we reached shore. She had no intention of being cooped up at sea while an enraged Elsa did her best to make a watery grave look inviting. The minute we docked, though, she was quitting.

"You can't!" I wailed. "What will you tell her?"

"Don't worry, Mata Hari—I won't finger you. I'll invent health reasons, or something. The songs are finished, and I'm sure she'll have no trouble finding another accompanist."

"You don't mean this, Claire. You're just mad at me!"

She replied that if this represented the level of deduction I'd brought to my investigation, they could start engraving my Pulitzer now. She then rose and, advising me that any future requests I cared to make of her, whether for melodies or bail, could be directed elsewhere, stormed out.

I sat awhile, shell-shocked, picking out mournful melodies on the keyboard. It was not long, though, before my grief turned to fury at Gilbert, whose impetuosity had caused the whole mess to begin with. I bolted from the studio and began searching for him.

I was keen to avoid my fellow passengers, who would only forestall my vengeance with chatter or board games. I crept stealthily past the main salon but, on peeking in, was alarmed to see Gilbert standing in the center of the room, giving a neck rub to Elsa as Millie sat nearby, leafing through the latest *Estime*. I dashed in and, struggling not to betray my anger, sat next to Millie, opposite Elsa.

"I *see*," Elsa was saying to Gilbert, "it's called a *montand*, is it? I'll remember because it's the same as the actor! Philip! Are you and Claire finished, then?"

"Looks that way," I said, my eyes boring into Gilbert's.

"Lovely! Not quite so hard, please, Henri. Oh, how rude of me. Philip, this is Henri, our new steward. Peter and I are going to France for Bastille Day, and Henri's helping me remember my French."

"Such marvelous slang he knows!" piped Millie.

"Philip," explained Elsa, "writes songs. That would be *chansons*, right?"

"*Oui.*"

"I'm going to be making my singing debut in a nightclub very soon. Now, what would the French for 'debut' be?"

"*Début*," said Gilbert.

"Of course! How silly of me!" laughed Elsa. "And 'club'? What would that be?"

Gilbert's eyes bulged briefly before he responded with casual authority. "*On dit ganouche.*"

"I see," said Elsa. "So a nightclub would be a *nuit ganouche?*"

"*Ganouche de nuit*," corrected Gilbert.

"I'll never get it."

Gilbert continued the lessons for some minutes, madly inventing nouns and verbs and idioms. Many of these were remarkably similar to their English equivalents, which delighted Elsa no end, though others had a deranged Gallic flavor utterly divorced from any etymological root one could imagine. What in heaven had suggested *vouplanger* to him as a plausible translation for the verb "to rehearse"?

The lesson was mercifully interrupted by Spark Chandler. He wandered in to announce that as a special treat for us all, he'd brought an advance video of a show that was to air next week. The segment, which was in Spark's own opinion among the most fascinating he'd ever produced, explored the shadowy world of the hermaphrodite. Elsa and Millie enthusiastically agreed that it sounded like must-see viewing. Elsa, rising, thanked Henri for the tutorial and asked if he wouldn't mind going to her suite and changing the flowers in the *salle de vivre*. I begged off on the screening, saying I had lyrics to polish. This earned me a disdainful glance from Spark, but I ignored it and, waving farewell, tore off after the rapidly retreating Henri.

Once out of sight, he commenced an energetic sprint, dashing round corners and up stairs. I lost him once or twice but eventually ran him to ground in Champion's floating garden, which, the temperature having plunged, was now glass enclosed. I stepped into its lush, verdant interior and called, "Hey, Gil-bare!" to where he crouched, seeking the inadequate protection of a gorse bush.

He stood and, assuming a dignified air, strolled out from behind the bush and took a seat on an ornate stone bench. I advanced to the spot and stood glowering down at him.

"Ooh," he said blandly. "How Robert Mitchum."

"You asshole," I hissed. "How could you do this without telling me!"

"Oh, right! As if you've consulted *me* about every move you've made for the last month. You might have warned me that you and Claire were coming on the boat! I'm not psychic, y'know!"

"Do you realize the trouble you've caused! Claire's quit the goddamned act!"

"Philip!" he said, leaping to his feet. "You didn't *tell* her about us, did you!"

"Of course I did! What was I going to say!"

"Great!" he snapped. "Now you've ruined everything!"

"*I've* ruined everything!"

"Do you think you might control yourself?" he asked, daintily wiping spittle from his cheeks.

"You idiot!" I screamed. "You were never supposed to do this!"

"Oh, *nooo!*" he said, and the bitter envy he'd suppressed for weeks now surged to the surface. "*I'm* not supposed to go spying! *I'm* supposed to sit around like Miss Moneypenny while you gallivant all over creation, planting bugs and infiltrating sanctums! *I'm* supposed to bat my eyes and coo with admiration while you swank around, puffing yourself up in front of Tommy, as if there's anything to it at all! I thought it was time I showed him you weren't the only one who could handle the cloak-and-dagger stuff!"

"He doesn't even know you're doing this?"

"No—and don't you go phoning him in Europe about it, either!"

"*You* might have spent some time overseas *yourself,* Mam'selle Berlitz, before trying to pull this off! Let's hope for your sake there's not a French dictionary on board!"

He said he'd investigated the matter and there was not.

I asked if it was *folie de grandeur* or mere imbecility that had led him to select an alias he was so staggeringly ill equipped to pull off. He replied coldly that he'd had no choice but to go Gallic, and a good thing it had been, too, as it had provided his ticket of entry.

He'd known when he resolved to infiltrate the yacht that his main obstacle would be the background check. He reasoned that as he couldn't invent an identity that would not, under scrutiny, be revealed as fictitious, his only hope was to appropriate someone else's. Toward this end he'd invited to dinner the one friend who possessed the most solid and illustrious background in food services, a veritable prince of cater waiters named Henri Foumier. He poured quantities of wine into Henri, and when the latter inevitably departed for the restroom, he reached into his coat and swiped his wallet.

It was then child's play to substitute his own photo for Henri's on the driver's license and apply for a job aboard the *Siren,* confident that his background check would turn up only the most impeccable credentials. He was at first informed the boat was already overstaffed, but the first mate, noting the name, asked if he spoke French. Elsa enjoyed honing her linguistic skills with the staff, and the only French-speaking steward, Jean-Louis, had recently resigned. Gilbert professed fluency, and the job was his.

"But, Gilbert! What made you think you could teach her French? *You don't speak it!*"

"Neither does she!"

I opined that a young man frantically engaged in devising a bizarre, hybrid language that could best be termed "Desperanto" was not in any position to carry out the demanding and sensitive work of the undercover operative.

"How do you even keep track of it?"

"I manage," said Gilbert indignantly.

"What's a *montand?*" I asked.

"Huh?"

"A *montand,*" I repeated savagely. "When I walked in she said, 'A *montand*—I'll remember that because it's the same as the actor.' What is it?"

He frowned. "Shit. I forget now. Oh, well." He shrugged. "No matter. She can never remember anything, either."

"You blithering dolt! Have you found out one single useful thing since you've been here?"

"Oh, no, you don't!" he said, standing precipitously. "You're not going to worm secrets out of me so you can call Tommy and claim them as your own! We'll both tell him what we've got when he gets back. Until then, *mon ami,* we're on our own. Now if you'll excuse me, I have *florets* to replace!"

"*Fleurs,* you idiot!"

"*Même chose,*" he sniffed, and, checking his mustache to make sure it was still in place, quit the greenhouse and traipsed off to his duties.

I began to follow, but realizing that this was the first privacy I'd been granted on this cruise of torment, I sat and breathed in the silent tranquillity of the garden. I ruminated upon my situation, and the more I ruminated the less I liked it.

I suspected Gilbert was bluffing when he referred to secrets uncovered in his brief tenure as steward and shipboard linguist. Peter was far too paranoid to give brand-new employees access to sensitive material. Gilbert, though, was very determined and willing to resort to any sordid means to get what he was after. Who could say what nuggets he might not unearth if he stayed long enough? By the time Tommy returned he might well have gathered an immense scented bouquet of damning documents—while I'd have nothing to offer except news of Claire's retreat and my own dismal failure in planting the bug in Peter's office.

Still, I reflected, all was not yet lost. I still had a night and a day left on board, and I also still had the key-filled rabbit's foot Boyd had given me. Peter's office might yet be plundered for such secrets as it would yield. A daring search in the dead of night, employing those tools—which Gilbert did not possess—and I might find more incriminating goodies in an hour than he could garner in weeks of unnerving and fruitless attempts.

The problem, of course, was getting into the office. The door was guarded by one of those infernal keypad locks, and as Champion himself had demonstrated, a single erroneous digit would provoke a nightmare of alarm bells and stampeding crew members. To one of my nervous imagination, such thoughts acted as a powerful deterrent. But as I sat watching seagulls crash into the greenhouse walls, a solution dawned on me.

Scurrying down to B deck, I ran to my room and grabbed my camera and Walkman. I strapped the Walkman to my belt, then went to look for Champion, finding him in the game room, where he sat eagerly arm-wrestling the captain of the boat. Introductions were made, and I explained to them that I'd been proudly snapping photos of the boat's many impressive features. Nothing, though, had impressed me nearly so much as that stunning Roman mosaic on the floor of his office. Might I take just one shot of it? Peter smiled magnanimously and led the way to the office.

It was, as I prayed, locked, and he opened it as before by punching the nine-number sequence onto the numeric keypad, once again consulting a card from his pocket. I wondered why he wouldn't have the code for his own office memorized and could only assume it was changed so often that even he couldn't keep track. The pad once more emitted its sequence of beeps, then a green light flashed briefly above it.

Champion admitted us and turned the lights up full to enhance the quality of my shot. I smiled gratefully and snapped away, catching different angles on the two wolf-suckled babes, while Champion proudly explained how the whole floor had been painstakingly removed from a seventeenth-century villa in Sardinia and reassembled here. I thanked him again, and he led me out, saying that if I gave the film to anyone on the crew, they'd have it developed in the boat's photo lab. This was a bit sticky, as I'd neglected to load the camera, but I promised I'd do so the moment the roll was finished.

He closed the office door and locked it, punching the same sequence into the keypad and causing a red light to flash briefly beneath it. I raced to my suite and, flinging the camera aside, rewound the tape on my Walkman and listened to the recording I'd made. The sequence of beeps when Champion had unlocked the door was faint but audible. I tried practicing it on my room phone but saw this was no good. Any sequence of two numbers would cause a line to ring elsewhere on the yacht and Joy Cudgel or someone would answer. I tried pushing buttons with the receiver depressed but found this merely rendered the beeps inaudible, which was no help at all.

It occurred to me there were several unoccupied suites on my deck. I ran into one and phoned my own room, then raced back and answered. I was now able to beep to my heart's content without disturbing anyone. Within minutes I'd worked out the numeric equivalents for Champion's office lock. I then scribbled them down and concealed the paper in my wallet.

Seconds after I hung up, the phone rang. The first mate informed me in his pleasant cockney that the cocktail hour had commenced in the main salon. I donned my suit and joined the party, which was in full swing.

Claire was playing the piano, which is what she always does at parties when there's no one she wants to talk to. I wasn't bursting with chat myself, but having no musical skills to fall back on, I sidled up to Joy, Peter, and Spark. Joy was happily vivisecting a gifted actress who'd won an Oscar once but had enjoyed no recent successes.

"Her agent," said Joy, "called me sniffing around for a *cover* story. Can you *believe* it? A *cover* story! What am I running here, *Lears?* A *feature* I could see—*ten years ago,* that is."

This prompted a general disquisition on lost celebrity, Joy chairing the panel with a lethal knowingness that wasn't, I supposed, very unusual in an editor of a celebrity-driven magazine. With happy assists from Peter and Spark, she took a meticulous inventory of those stars whose wide appeal had faded or seemed about to, gleefully exiling them to that purgatory of demicelebrity from which but few ever escape in the glorious reascension known as the comeback. Some of those banished, I noted, had only months ago graced the pages of her own publication, but this did not blunt the zeal with which Joy consigned them to fame's slag heap.

I was distracted from this compassionate discussion by the sudden sight of Gilbert gliding into the salon with a tray of hors d'oeuvres. Excusing myself, I scurried over to where he stood, proffering his tray to Elsa and Hoot.

"Phil!" said Hoot, friendlier in Elsa's presence. "How you doing? Get yourself a drink."

This seemed a good means to get rid of Gilbert, if only briefly, and I was about to request a Scotch when Florindo, the other waiter, materialized at my elbow and said, "Drink, Mr. Cavanaugh?"

Defeated, I ordered Scotch and he glided off to fetch it.

"Such lovely *morceaus!*" said Elsa, her fingers hovering indecisively over Gilbert's tray. "Henri . . . ?"

She pointed to a delicately browned scallop. "What would you call that in French?"

"We say toothpeek."

"No, under it."

Gilbert, ever cautious, looked to Hoot and said, *"Parlez-vous français, m'sieur?"*

"Uh, no."

"Ah, bon. C'est une, uh, moupé."

"Of course," said Hoot, eager to repair any damage to his cosmopolitan image that might have attended so shaming a confession, "my books have all been *published* in France."

"Really?" said Elsa, impressed. She turned to Gilbert. "Are Monsieur Mulvaney's *livres* very popular *au* France?"

"Monsieur Mulvaney?" asked Gilbert, politely baffled.

"Surely you've heard of him," said Elsa. "He writes those books about jaded young *ganouche* hoppers."

Gilbert said courteously that, though he'd been an *aveed redare* in his Parisian days, he had never encountered any of Monsieur Mulvaney's *livres*. He was sure, though, that they were *formidable*.

Millie drifted over and began sampling hors d'oeuvres so voraciously that Gilbert soon had to withdraw for a refill. On returning, he busied himself serving Spark and Joy, neither of whom were the sort to chat up the help, and Ham Yearwood, who seemed too busy ogling Florindo to pay any attention to him.

I eventually drifted to the piano, where Kitty moped glamorously, knocking back bourbons and casting a jaundiced eye to where Ham sat building bridges between the classes.

"Clap eyes on this one," she whispered, nodding toward Ham. "*This* is who my genius of a sister thinks I should marry!"

"Uh, you don't seem his type," I said, smiling sympathetically.

"His wife croaked last year. He grabbed an altar boy at the funeral mass and he ain't come up for air since!"

She held her empty glass out in front of her, waved it a bit, and called to Florindo. "Oh, *waiter*—if you have a *moment!*"

Eventually we streamed into dinner, where the conversation centered entirely around Elsa's forthcoming debut. Peter made a long, pompous toast, citing her years of diligent training, her stringent self-criticism, and irrepressible drive. He foresaw a lustrous future for her as she advanced in stages from local phenomenon to international stardom with sold-out engagements in all the glittering capitals of the world. Naturally, all present echoed this prophecy, offering our own shameless embellishments. Even Kitty joined in, saying she could just imagine how green those "skags from the old neighborhood" would be when they turned on their TVs and saw little Elsie Driscoll crooning away on the "Tonight Show." Spark made her promise to do a full hour on his show when she'd become a star, and Millie, true to form, rapturously anticipated her first command performance before the royal family.

Elsa ate it up, washing it down with glass after glass of Cristal. In the middle of dessert she picked up her full glass and tottered off to "prepare" for her concert, which, I supposed, involved listening to one of the signora's tapes and visualizing herself as a drunken lark. After dinner we filed into the salon and there she was, listening to her little Walkman with the serene smile of a woman who's marinated at length in champagne, compliments, and subliminal snake oil. We took our seats and she vamped over to the piano, waved Claire to the keys, then burst into her opening number and from there briskly on through about half of her act.

Perhaps it was the champagne or perhaps it was the warm sense of confidence our praise had instilled in her. But, whatever the reason, she wasn't awful. In fact, she was quite the least awful I'd ever heard her. The basic instrument, of course, was still reminiscent of a trumpet that had been dropped from a great height once too often. But the delivery was assured and winning, the break between the chest and head voices was a break, not a chasm, and if the acting on the ballads was still a mite overheated, she at least refrained from behaving like a woman who'd have to stand on tiptoes to glimpse hell.

The smoky, voluptuous world of the supper club is filled with women whose vocal abilities are nil but who manage, through style, charm, or sheer force of will to persuade audiences that they are great singers. Elsa's performance that night created the first dim twinkle of hope that she might yet number herself among their company.

It was unfortunate that her triumph had occurred on the one night when I was least capable of enjoying it. The boisterous calls of "Brava!" from that posh assemblage were barely audible over the alarm bells and stampeding footfalls that thundered in my head the more I reflected on the mission that lay before me.

After the finale everyone thronged to the piano, and there was much hugging and hyperbole. Elsa hoisted Claire off the bench and led a round of applause for us, extolling our brilliance and making much of how happy she felt to *finally* have an accompanist who understood her "rhythms."

"Now, Elsa," said Claire, "you can sing brilliantly with anyone accompanying you."

"You're too modest! I've had *scads* of people play for me, and do you know, none of them could ever follow me. You're an absolute treasure! I don't ever want to sing with anyone but you!"

Elsa, giddy with happiness, suggested a little moonlit dancing, and so buoyant was the party's mood that we all said, What fun, and headed up to the wheelhouse deck. Peter disappeared into his office, and soon festive lights flooded the deck. The marble dance floor closed over the pool, and the music of Benny Goodman filled the night air. It was nippy, but no one cared; the dancing would warm us. Florindo and Gilbert brought more champagne, and we all twirled away under the moonlight, on top of the pool, in the middle of the calm, twinkling ocean.

The hour grew late and people began trickling off to their suites. Claire was the first to beat a retreat, and I followed later, leaving only Joy, Spark, Elsa, and Ham. I looked in on Claire to mutter more mea culpas. She was curled up with a Jane Austen novel, which, luckily, was in paperback so it didn't hurt much when she hurled it at my forehead.

I returned to my suite and donned pajamas and a robe. I sat nervously going over the door combination and fingering my little burglar's kit until after two. By then it had been more than an hour since I'd heard any movement in the boat. Slipping the combination and the rabbit's foot into the pocket of my robe, I crept out of my suite and made a brief tour of the public rooms. I'd feared there might still be some late-night drinking going on or that Hoot, true to the heroes of his novels, might be coked up and on the deck, scanning the ocean for opportunities to yacht hop. Fortunately there was no one around. I climbed the stairs to the wheelhouse deck and found myself standing in dim light in the small foyer.

There were two doors. One led to a hall, off of which were the ritzy guest suites occupied by Ham and Kitty and, beyond those, the wheelhouse. The other door was Peter's office. I let my eyes adjust to the gloom, then reached into my robe for the combination. It was memorized by now, but, desiring to check it just once more, I turned to read it by the night-light over the door to the suites.

I unfolded the paper and stared down at the numbers and murmured them quietly to myself.

"Seven, three, four, seven, two, nine, six—"

"Pardon me, Mr. Cavanaugh," said a voice behind me.

Thirteen

"Florindo!"

"Evening, sir."

"You startled me!" I said, though he may have deduced this from the way I had spun, shrieked, and fallen, gasping, against the door.

"I'm sorry, Mr. Cavanaugh. I was just, uh, bringing a drink to Mr. Yearwood."

He was not, in fact, holding a glass, and the lack of it must suddenly have occurred to him. He winced gently and shifted his feet with the pained, hangdog air of a boy who never dreamed he'd moonlight as a courtesan, much less be caught at it.

"I see," I murmured, and then, trying for his sake to change the subject, said, "Well, I was just . . ."

I paused. I couldn't, of course, say what I was just. My previously displayed flair for improvisation under pressure abandoned me completely, and I blurted out the first thing that came to mind.

"I was just—having a drink with him myself."

This was regrettable. Florindo's expression changed, reflecting the abrupt plunge my stock had taken. I was no longer his illustrious employers' brilliant young guest. I was just the first shift.

"Oh, great," he muttered, not bothering to conceal his pique. "Thanks to you, this'll take all night!"

And shaking his head at the unfairness of it all, he pushed off to work.

Alone now and jumpier than ever, I unfolded the crumpled combination, read it one last time, and turned to face the lock. The fact had not escaped me that if I now failed and set off the alarm, it wouldn't matter a fig if I managed to return to my room undetected. There was now a witness who could place me at the crime scene. This knowledge was far from calming, and as I brought my finger to the pad it literally shook.

I began punching in the numbers. The tones, which before had seemed the gentlest of pings, now sounded like "The Anvil Chorus" in Dolby. I raced through the numbers, managing, in my jittery state, to hit the last one directly between the five and the six, jabbing my finger a mere centimeter away from discovery and incarceration. I shuddered briefly and pressed the five.

The little green light flashed exactly once. Respiration resumed and I slipped into the office, closing the door behind me.

The room was pitch dark. I located the dimmer panel by the door, pressed it, and lamps went on all over the room. The drapes were closed as before, and I prayed they were heavy enough to keep any light from passing through to the deck outside.

I removed the rabbit's foot from my robe and wondered which of several filing cabinets to plunder first. I decided to work around the office clockwise and advanced to a long, low cabinet on the wall in front of the desk. I pressed the base of the rabbit's foot. It swung open, revealing the keys, and I began trying different ones. It was tedious work, and I was starting to think I'd be best off scrubbing the whole key approach in favor of giving every drawer in the place a good firm yank when key number ten yielded results. My heart palpitating wildly, I slid open the drawer and peered in.

My emotions on viewing its contents were mixed. There was not, as I'd hoped, a file bulging with invoices for recently purchased congressmen, nor was there a folder labeled "Illegal Things I Have Done and Incriminating Details Thereof." There was, however, the most staggering collection of pornographic magazines I had ever encountered. Even Sister Joselia, beholding so vast a trove of prurience, would have staggered backward clutching her beads and made straight for the heavenly glee club.

I thumbed through them swiftly, noting to my amazement that though there were hundreds of entries, there was little in the way of thematic diversity. Not for Champion, it seemed, the more eclectic smut aficionado's fondness for variety and the fresh twist. Instead the magazines focused entirely on one narrow area of sexual congress: to wit, the humiliation of runty naked men by towering women with enormous breasts and free access to costume collections.

Among the roles enacted by these zaftig disciplinarians were such archetypes of the genre as the Governess, the School Marm, the Nurse, and, of course, the traditional Black Leather Whip Lady of Independent Means. At some point, though, the sedate appeal of nurses and academics must have faded for Peter, for as I rummaged further along, the career choices of the sultry martinets became increasingly exotic. Disgruntled lady physicists, jockeys, and federal judges pummeled naughty lab assistants, stable boys, and district attorneys. There was even a bosomy female astronaut who took time out from launching satellites to tie up a helmeted, but otherwise nude, cohort in a spread entitled "NASA-ty Lady."

My reaction, as I said, was mixed. On the one hand, it was dish of the first magnitude, offering, as only the best gossip does, titillation, amusement, and a new window into the soul of its subject. My heart sang when I thought of Tommy splitting his sides over it.

On the other hand, what real value had it beyond that of a spicy tidbit? For one thing, it couldn't readily be proved. And even if it could, what use was it in our efforts to expose Champion as financially corrupt? The man's carnal eccentricities, however risible, would be dismissed as irrelevant by any competent magistrate (with the possible exception of the tall, paddle-wielding justice pictured on the cover of "The Spanking Judge," who would, one sensed, view them as admissible).

I was nearing the end of the collection and noting a new trend toward the historical when my attention was seized by a muted bray of laughter from just outside the office.

I froze. I heard muffled voices and then the faint but dreadful sound of beeping as some unseen hand began unlocking the door. I stood transfixed for a few beeps before it occurred to me that inertia was not the canniest response to the situation. I pushed the file drawer shut and, racing to the door, jabbed the dimmer panel, plunging the office into blackness.

Finding a hiding place in a strange room within three seconds is never a simple task and more difficult still when you can't see your hand in front of your face. I had nothing to go on but a dim sense of the layout, and since the only thing I remembered at all was the desk, I now bounded in the blackness toward what I believed to be its general vicinity.

My sense of direction did not fail me. My sense of distance did. Either I'd grossly overestimated the length of the room, or the desk, eager to be helpful, had rushed across to meet me halfway. I slammed thighs first into the front of it and caromed across the top, landing on what I first assumed to be a chair. I soon dismissed this theory on the grounds that chairs, when struck, do not flinch violently and suggest you watch where you're going.

"*Gilbert?*" I whispered.

"*Philip!*" came the peevish reply. "Well, thanks a lot! You might have *said* it was you!"

This struck me as an unreasonable thing to have expected, but as the door was opening, I let it pass.

We heard two sets of footsteps, one *whooshy*, suggesting slippers, and the other a loud click, almost like tap shoes. The lights went on and there was Gilbert, hunched next to me on the floor, wearing the cheerless look of a burglar who's come to work expecting perfect tranquillity, only to find he's stumbled into some hot new after-hours spot.

The desk, at least, was plenty wide, and there was more than enough room for two of us to huddle under it. It was not, I feared, large enough so that Champion, if seated at it, would fail to detect the presence of two full-grown men cuddling his kneecaps. Still, we squeezed into opposite corners, leaving maximal leg room between us even as we leaned forward toward the opening, the better to catch any conversation between our visitors. They did indeed converse and, from their first words, so gripped us that we all but forgot the precariousness of our own position.

"Did anyone see you leave your room?" Champion asked.

"Nah," said Kitty. "The way they were guzzling tonight? We could ram an iceberg and they'd sleep through it. 'S just yoooou and me, Petey-poo!"

Petey-poo responded with low murmurs. I had no view of the action but would have wagered he had his face buried somewhere around her neck and was working his way south. Gilbert regarded me with a wild, delighted look, and I stared back with combined glee and relief. A man engaged in diddling his wife's sister was not likely to pause midway to catch up on his paperwork.

The dreamy murmurs were suddenly interrupted by the harsh crack of a slap.

"*Did I say you could do that!*" Kitty asked sharply.

"I'm sorry," gasped Champion.

"You're sorry, *what?*" asked Kitty.

"I'm sorry, ma'am."

"You've been a baaaad boy," said Kitty in an unconvincing show of menace. "And bad boys have to be taught a lesson!"

As I gazed across at Gilbert, who sat vibrating with half his bathrobe stuffed into his mouth, I found myself desperately wishing I'd had the foresight to bring my Walkman along so the exchange could be preserved for the archives. I rolled my eyes miserably toward the underside of the desk, and as I did I realized, with the force of divine revelation, that I was even now squatting directly under a built-in recorder, and that, furthermore, the button to activate it was only inches from my head. I leaned out a bit and, mouthing a silent prayer, raised my hand to the surface.

I felt along the row of buttons, and when I came to the last one, pushed it and quickly pulled my hand back under the desk. I pressed my ear to the underside of the desk, and the faintest of whirring sounds confirmed that my aim had been accomplished. Gilbert sat watching this with an air of terrified perplexity, obviously feeling that if you're going to wiggle your fingers over the top of it, there was little point in hiding behind a desk in the first place. I leaned in and mouthed the words *tape recorder,* and a look of awestruck envy came over him. We returned our attention to the dialogue, and it was clear inspiration had not struck a moment too soon.

"No, wait," Champion said earnestly.

"Uh-uh!" said Kitty. "Bend over and Mommy's gonna show you what happens to boys who—"

"*No!*" said Peter, and he seemed to mean it.

"Huh?"

He spoke in a tense whisper that combined anger and embarrassment.

"I said, 'Aphrodite'!"

"Oh, right," said Kitty apologetically. "Sorry, hon, I'm still kinda
blotto."

"Let me put the music on," said Champion, and we could hear
him pad over to the stereo and start fumbling through tapes.

"Speakin' of music," drawled Kitty, "wudja think of Elsie tonight?"

"She's getting better."

"Well," huffed Kitty, "she could *hahhdly* get worse!"

"Come on," he replied. "You should want her to succeed as much
as I do. Let her make a name for herself. Then she can spend the
next ten years touring with her pet fairy and that snotty cow of a piano
player."

"Oh, God, I hope so," said Kitty with that touching wistfulness of
hers. "You really think she could do it, hon? Get herself a big
international career and stay out of our hair forever?"

"She'll have a career all right. I don't care if I have to buy every
goddamn ticket myself!"

The room was suddenly full of low, pastoral music. There were pan
pipes and a harp and, unless I was much mistaken, bird sounds and
distant waterfalls. The lamps went out around the edges of the room.
It seemed that only the spotlight above the mosaic had been left on.
Kitty let the music create a mood for a moment, then spoke in that
stilted, husky tone favored by pagan vamps in fifties biblical spec-
taculars.

"Who goes there?" she asked haughtily.

The room was silent save for a little glissando from the harp. Kitty
spoke again.

"Who dares to spy upon me and defile my sacred temple? Come
forward now!"

We heard Champion take a few shuffling steps.

"*You!*" Kitty said grandly. "You have the nerve to spy upon the
goddess Aphrodite, you lousy shepherd! On your knees or I'll crush
you like the pathetic insect you ah!"

"Don't hurt me!" said Champion somewhat disingenuously.

"What was it you hoped to see, puny mortal? *These?!*" she inquired, and seconds later a filmy brassiere landed on the desk chair just beyond Gilbert, who was by this point dangerously close to swallowing his entire bathrobe.

"Feast your eyes, for they are the last sight ye shall evah behold!"

"Have mercy, Aphrodite! I came only to worship!"

"Yeah? Well, worship *this!*" she cried, and whap! came the sound of hand striking cheek.

"Take off your tunic," she said, "so that I may gaze upon your pathetic nakedness!"

There was a stage wait as Champion obliged, whereupon Aphrodite burst into contemptuous laughter.

"Ha ha ha! I see your pitiful member gorged with desire for what it cannot possess!"

"I beg of you!" cried Champion, whose histrionic abilities so far exceeded his partner's that it was like hearing Olivier play Lear with Vivian Vance as Cordelia. "Let me touch you but once!"

"*Nevah!* Bend over, lowly one!"

And from there on in, the blows fairly rained down on the poor shepherd's pathetic bottom. I was staring at the brassiere, wondering if now would be a good moment to throw it back over the desk, when an event occurred that relegated this to the bottom of the priority list.

The chamber drama of *The Spanking Goddess* was suddenly interrupted by a series of sharp knocks on the door.

"Peter!" said Elsa. "Peter, let me in there. I want to talk to you!"

The walloping noises ceased abruptly.

"Oh, shit!" said the deity, and Champion, who by the sound of his voice had been edging toward release, uttered the four words we'd least looked forward to hearing.

"Quick! Under the desk!"

I suppose he must have worried that the mood lighting might inflame suspicions because he scurried to the switch and turned the lights up full. At the exact moment he did so, the goddess of Love, clutching, as opposed to wearing, lavender silk panties, rounded the corner of the desk and dropped to a squatting position, thus bringing her face to within inches of where Gilbert and I sat staring out with pleading eyes, our index fingers pressed to our lips in a desperate attempt to preempt anything in the way of bloodcurdling shrieks. For a moment

I feared our efforts were in vain, as she opened her mouth in a manner that suggested Signora di Corteggiano attacking a china cupboard.

But at that precise instant Elsa called out Peter's name, louder than before, and Peter said, "Get down!" in a piercing whisper that blocked the scream as effectively as a hand clapped over her mouth. Kitty, her arms folded demurely over her boobs, pivoted smartly on her haunches, plopped her fanny to the floor, and backed in between us while mouthing the phrase *What the fuck are you doing here?* with such admirable precision that not even the least gifted lip-reader could have mistaken her drift. As the door was opening, it seemed inadvisable to explain, so we just smiled inanely, as if encouraging her to see the funny side. Kitty regarded us with frank disdain, then, arranging her nude bottom into a more comfortable position, settled back to wait with a ladylike dignity that was inspiring to witness. She might have lacked certain qualities, but aplomb was not among them.

"Peter!" said Elsa. "What are you doing in here at this hour?"

Peter, justifiably famed for his negotiating skills, seized the offensive. "Trying to get a little quiet. You were snoring again."

"Oh, dear," sighed Elsa. "Well, listen, I have to talk to you—about Kitty!"

"What about her?" asked Peter uneasily.

"Well," said Elsa, "I woke up a little while ago and wondered where you were. I assumed you were here, working as usual. But I was so excited about tonight I couldn't get back to sleep. So I decided to take a stroll on the deck. I passed Kitty's room and her light was on and the door was ajar, so I looked in. Only she wasn't there. Well, I'm no fool, you know, Peter. I knew just where she'd be!"

"Oh?" asked Peter, sounding once again like the nervous shepherd preparing to take his licks.

"Yes," said Elsa, "I knew she'd be with Ham Yearwood! And sure enough, I went by his cabin, and, my dear, you should *hear* the *sounds* coming from that room!"

"No kidding?"

Elsa gave a naughty giggle. "*Yes!* I could hear Ham clear as day! He kept moaning, 'Oh, *honey!*' and saying what a sweet *mouth* she had! I was blushing! I always suspected Kitty would be an absolute slut in bed, and now I know I was right!"

At this Kitty seemed ready to bolt out and enter the discussion, but Gilbert and I grabbed her arms and frantically shook our heads. She scowled furiously but settled back down. Perhaps it had occurred to her that a busty woman crouched under a desk in nothing but black stiletto heels was not in the best position to protest her virtue.

"Well," said Champion, eager to close this avenue of conjecture, "I'm, uh, happy they seem to have found each other."

"Oh, Petey," said Elsa, "do you really think he'd *marry* her? It would be so wonderful if he'd take her off our hands. I'm so sick of supporting that conceited leech!"

"Now, now," said Petey. "She's family, and God knows we have the money to—"

"Yes, I know, but how much nicer to have her out of our lives! You know, if she marries Ham, he'll probably make her spend winters down at his house in Key West. What could be nicer than Christmas without Kitty!"

"It's getting late, Elsa, and—"

"Why, Peter, look at you!" she said, and lapsed into screechingly coy baby talk. "Ooo! Did Mummy gettum all excited wif talk 'bout nasty ladies?"

"I'm not excited!" he said.

Good Lord, I thought—was his fondness for humiliation such that even this mortifying situation had its power to arouse?

"Dat's not what *I* see! Lookee, lookee! Da peter of da Peter is peeking out thwoo da bafwobe. It's saying, " 'Hu-wo, Mommy!' "

"Elsa!" said the Peter curtly. "I'm not in the mood, all right?"

A tense silence ensued.

There is an unwritten law of relationships, a law that all couples, gay or straight, ignore only at their peril: When one partner requests sexual attention and elects to do so in baby talk, the other partner, if disinclined, must make sure when refusing to employ the same dialect. To decline, as Peter did now, in a straightforward adult fashion is to add insult to injury and cause the loved one to retaliate by calling for an immediate and exhaustive dissection of the entire relationship with special emphasis on the issues of insensitivity and sexual unresponsiveness.

"What's wrong with you lately?" snapped Elsa.

"Honey," Peter whined, "do we have to go into this *now?*"

"Yes!" said Elsa, maturing rapidly. "You're *never* in the mood anymore! Even when your thing is up and pointing like a goddamned *bird* dog!"

"I'm sorry!"

"I *try* to please you," she said, suddenly close to tears. "I tie you up and pretend I'm Sandra Day O'Connor, which is pretty damned *accommodating*, if you ask me, but you still—"

"I don't want to talk about it!" said Champion.

"*Well, I do!*" said Elsa, and so grim and inflexible was her tone that even Champion thought it best to bow to the inevitable. He did, however, insist that further discussion wait until they'd reached the seclusion of their boudoir. Clearly he didn't want Elsa to vent her spleen in earshot of Kitty, which was a shame, as Kitty could have garnered many hints on how to imbue her next performance as a wrathful goddess with that authenticity it presently lacked. Elsa agreed to the change in location, and Champion hurried her out, turning the lights off behind him.

The three of us sat in the darkness, wondering how to begin. You couldn't blame us, really. Even Letitia Baldrige, had she been crouched under there with us, would have required time to devise a suitable opening.

Kitty finally broke the ice by asking again just what the fuck we were doing, eavesdropping on our betters.

Gilbert, mindful that he was still Henri, replied, "*Qu'est-ce que c'est* 'eezdrop'?"

I felt my way to a table lamp while Kitty, muttering curses, searched in the darkness for her brassiere. I turned on the lights just as she was petulantly inserting her arms through the straps. She then turned her back for Gilbert to assist with the hooks, which, after some understandable fumbling, he managed.

"Well, 'fess up," she demanded. "What were you doing in Peter's private office?"

This was a hard one. I'd realized earlier in the festivities that the question, already mouthed under the desk, would certainly recur. I'd meant to concoct some convincing reply, but so deeply engrossed had I become in the Champions' domestic drama that the matter had slipped my mind.

As it turned out, I didn't have to say anything at all. Gilbert fielded the question and with a glibness matched only by his utter disregard for my personal reputation said we'd come there with much the same errand in mind she had. I had, he explained, approached him that afternoon, requesting an assignation and saying I'd make it worth his while if our tryst could take place on our host's own desk. He obtained the combination by rifling Monsieur Champion's pockets when the latter was showering before dinner.

Kitty had no trouble believing this; a yen to make love on the desks of powerful businessmen must have seemed on the sedate side to a woman whose own love life combined elements of *The Story of O.* and *Bullfinch's Mythology*. That's not to say, though, that she was prepared to excuse trespassing.

"I'll warn you right now—Peter ain't gonna like it when he hears his desk is being used as some kinda Frenchy boy brothel!"

"Ah," I said, "but he's not going to find out, is he? Because if he does, I'll run straight to Elsa and tell her who's been defiling *your* temple."

She glowered briefly at this, but then she gave a resigned shrug and said that on mulling it over, discretion was perhaps the most prudent course for all concerned. She then addressed Henri with aristocratic hauteur.

"Gimmee a hand, will you? I had a pink satin peignoir when I came in, and Mr. Champion seems to have stashed it somewhere."

Gilbert and Kitty set about hunting behind the stereo and under chair cushions. When their backs were turned I took the opportunity to slip back to the desk, shut off the tape recorder, eject the tape, and slip it into my pocket. Gilbert found the balled-up peignoir under the sofa and gave it to Kitty, who thanked him and said that if we would be so good as to leave her in privacy, she wished to take advantage of the office bathroom's Jacuzzi, with which her own suite was, unaccountably, not equipped. Gilbert and I exited the office, closing the door behind us, and pressed the button for the elevator.

No sooner had we done so than a bedraggled Florindo emerged from the door to the connecting corridor. His eyes bulged wildly to see that I had apparently taken the money I'd earned from Ham Yearwood and used it to purchase Henri.

"*Slut!*" he said concisely, and swept past us and down the stairs.

Fourteen

I woke early the next morning and, after wondering for a bleary moment why I was in a strange bed and what romantic implications might attend this, remembered all. I crawled out of bed and fumbled under the mattress to make sure my precious cassette had not been purloined in the night. True, I might have surmised as much from a glance to the sitting room, where my wobbly barricade of chairs and toiletries remained untoppled before the locked door, but one could not be too cautious where Gilbert was concerned. And Gilbert was very concerned indeed.

The minute we left Florindo he'd made a vigorous attempt to induce me to surrender the tape to him for "safekeeping," employing every trick in the book from reason to tears to tickling. Naturally I remained unyielding in my refusal to let him lay so much as a finger on it. It was the fruit of *my* inspiration, not his, and I'd earned the right to present it to Tommy as a Cavanaugh exclusive. He threatened to call Tommy in France and say *he'd* made the tape and I'd pinched it. I replied that if he did so, I'd be compelled to clear up Tommy's profound misapprehension as to the extent of Gilbert's journalistic experience.

"What do you mean by that?"

"I have every article you wrote for the *Clarion* back in high school. How would you like it if I gave them to Tommy and told him they represented your *entire* output as a reporter?"

"You know, Philip," he said, "I'm beginning to see a new and reptilian side to your nature, and it saddens me deeply."

"Steal my thunder and I'll sadden you deeper."

He said that he failed to imagine why I thought showing his early work to Tommy constituted so dire a threat. As he recalled it, the pieces showed heaps of promise. I said they showed rather less promise when displayed in tandem with the sources from which they'd been plagiarized, and that seemed to settle the matter.

I tried to console him with the notion that I'd be leaving the boat tomorrow, whereas he had weeks still before Tommy's return to filch some trophy of his own. This did little to cheer him, and he hotly insisted I say nothing about "Henri" to Boyd or Tommy, as they'd frown on so rash a maneuver unless it had yielded results. I gave him my word that, unless he attempted to claim credit for my tape, I'd never mention "Henri" to either.

I showered, dressed, and was ambling off to breakfast when I saw Claire grimly emerging from the Minerva Suite.

"Sleep well?" I asked.

"Yes. The nightmares only come when I'm awake. Speaking of sleep, what were you and Clouseau up to last night?"

"Uhhh . . . what?" I parried.

"I came by to chat around two and you weren't in your room. What did you do? Don frogman gear and infiltrate passing submarines?"

I was tempted to offer some bland excuse and be spared another trenchant homily on the theme "Philip: Is There Hope?" But I'd resolved that my days of lying to Claire were finished, so I coughed lightly and said, "Actually, we were doing a little snooping in Champion's office."

She lowered her gaze and gently massaged the area between her eyes. "And here I was worried you'd done something reckless and stupid."

"Reckless, perhaps," I said suavely, "but productive."

I ushered her back into her suite, for mine contained five of Champion's bugs, and shut the door. I could see from her leery gaze that she was of two minds. She didn't want to encourage my endeavors by admitting curiosity, which I might construe as approval, but her feelings for Champion were such that if I'd dug up something truly greasy, she wanted the long version.

"Well?" she said.

I gave her a rundown of the night's events up until the point where

Champion and his mystery guest had interrupted my research. Then I nipped over to my suite and, returning with the Walkman and headphones, handed it over. I settled onto the bed to observe her reaction.

Her eyes grew large and she gave an astonished laugh as Kitty made her first threats in the unpersuasive tone of one who's toured too long in the role. Then her smile turned to a tight-lipped scowl from which I assumed she'd reached the part where Champion called her a "snotty cow." She listened to the remainder with reactions that ranged from disgust to hilarity, then, when it was finished, removed the earphones and eyed me with a strange blend of disapproval and pride.

"Well, *we've* been busy."

"All in a night's work." I yawned.

"And where, exactly," asked Claire, "did the goddess park her paddle when Elsa barged in?"

"She hid under the desk with us. It's fairly roomy."

"Hmm," she mused, trying to visualize it, "huddling naked under a desk with two young gay fellows? How like Deborah Kerr in *Tea and Sympathy.*"

She handed the tape back to me and could not suppress an evil smile. "This is a fairly nuclear tidbit."

"You don't know the half. They married so long ago they don't even have a prenuptial agreement. If Elsa gets wind of this, he'll be lucky to get away with his fillings."

"And what do you intend to do with it?"

I said I would convey it to my dream man, who'd know how best to maximize its potential. She frowned thoughtfully at this.

"You realize that if this tape becomes public, subpoenas will rain down on you like confetti and you'll wind up in the *Guinness Book of World Records* under 'Most Sued Homosexual'?"

"You always look on the dark side!" I exclaimed. "Peter's not the only one with flesh-eating lawyers. Larkin's got a pack, too. Besides, Peter will look silly suing me for electronic eavesdropping when he's hired me to do the same damn thing. He's no angel, either."

"He's an egomaniacal slug," said Claire with surprising venom. I could see suddenly how Peter's "snotty cow" remark had gotten under her skin. This, I felt, was an encouraging development.

If there's one thing that saves Claire's nature from intolerable loftiness, it's this sensitive, vain streak. She's easily wounded by criticism, and personal insults, especially concerning her weight, rankle for days. In extreme instances—and this, God willing, was one of them—a cutting remark will goad her to seek retribution. She knows it's silly and spiteful and immature, but she can't help feeling that if she could make the offender just the teeniest bit wretched, the sun would shine brighter and the breeze would once more blow clean and sweet.

"Egomaniacal slug," I said, "seems entirely too kind."

"I never thought I'd say this, but poor Elsa!"

"Yes," I agreed. "You begin to see the roots of her bitterness."

"Exactly."

"Here you are, this innocent Catholic girl. You spend your adolescence as an unpaid baby-sitter, and just when you think you've found a rich husband to release you from the drudgery, you find you're expected to spend your nights putting on fancy dress and beating him up. I mean, I'm sure it's great fun if you're into it, but if you're not, it must be worse than waitressing."

"That he of all people should call *anyone* snotty—!"

"He has no respect for us, Claire. You heard him calling me her 'pet fairy'! Think how lovely it would be if Elsa had her triumph and then Peter, instead of getting the adulterer's holiday he was counting on, gets hit with a humiliating divorce! Can you imagine what the tabloids would do with this tape? Big saucy headlines! 'Peter Slapped with Divorce!' 'Spankers Away!' "

She thought about it and her eyes glowed for a moment with a rapt, transported look. But then she shook her head.

"Just because we detest the man is no reason to descend to his level."

"We're not descending to his level. We're going lower. Imagine the *Post*, hon! Big red letters! 'Kitty Hits Bottom!' "

Her face once more took on that dreamy look, then she stared me in the eye and asked a short but thrilling question:

"How good are Larkin's lawyers?"

"The best!" I said, bouncing on the bed. "Absolute fiends!"

"Calm down," she said. "Don't start thinking I'm in cahoots with you, because—"

"Oh . . . absolutely not," I said. "But you *will* agree not to quit the act?"

"Well." She sighed. "I suppose Elsa will have enough rude shocks without me walking out on her."

She said she would stay on board but demanded one condition. I was not to present the tape to Tommy until she'd spoken with him and received his and Boyd's written assurance that I'd be legally indemnified by them.

"What do you mean, 'indemnified'?"

"I mean a legal statement saying you're in Larkin's employ and that should Champion sue you, which I can't imagine he won't, Larkin will provide you his best lawyers and foot the bill for everything, *including* fines and damages."

Naturally I didn't want to offend Tommy with demands for written guarantees of good faith, but the request could easily be laid to Claire's suspicious nature. I told Claire Tommy was coming to my place for dinner the Thursday after Elsa's debut. She could stop by around cocktail time and clear everything up to her satisfaction.

"Splendid."

She plucked the Walkman from my lap, fingered it lightly, and grinned for the first time in weeks.

"Then I say, if Peter likes being hit—let's hit him."

Given the preceding night's events, brunch held much fascination with the demeanors of the assembled suspects providing a study in contrasts.

Champion must have patched things up with Elsa, for she was in high spirits. She sipped her Bloody Marys ebulliently and kept trying to bring the topic around to her singing without seeming to try to. Champion himself, though, seemed sullen and kept stabbing his *frittata* as though it could feel pain.

Kitty pouted openly, drinking copiously and speaking only when the topic of Elsa's imminent stardom arose, and then she wondered aloud how the act might go over in Buenos Aires or Tokyo. Hoot, who was not, judging from his books, a morning person, sulked monosyllabically behind his shades. Other sulkers included Gilbert and Florindo. The former poured coffee with a sullen petulance that while not endearing, was at least authentically Gallic, and the latter, apart from sporting deep circles under his eyes, seemed to have developed a limp.

Joining Elsa on the Sunbeam Squad were the Chandlers, who happily stoked the furnace of their hostess's ambitions, and Millie, who was her usual twittery self. As for Ham, had he been rehearsing the role of Santa in a Christmas play, the director would have pulled him aside and said, "You've got the jolly part down perfect. You might even pull back."

We docked after brunch. Claire and I expressed humble gratitude to the Champions. Elsa, to our discomfort, grew misty and thanked us for all we'd done to help make her long-deferred dream come true. She hoped that as the debut loomed nearer we'd stick close by and offer the support she'd come to rely on so heavily. We stammered our guilty assurances that whenever she needed us, we'd be there.

As I mentioned earlier, one of the inconveniences of having a passel of high-tech bugs in your possession is that until you plant them elsewhere, they're perfectly content to eavesdrop on you. Obvious as this may seem, it's easy to forget about it, especially when your mind is on other matters. I completely forgot most of that Sunday, remembering only late in the evening as I was watching a cable TV commercial advising me that hordes of well-muscled, articulate men were eager to hear from me if only I would dial 550-BUMM. Cursing myself for the oversight, I switched off the set, proceeded to my records, and pulled out *I Had a Ball*, a show that possessed the distinction of being Buddy Hackett's sole Broadway musical. There, I thought, let him listen to that, and, putting in earplugs, went to bed.

The next morning a messenger arrived bearing an envelope with the *Choice* logo in the corner. The message within was succinct:

WHAT'S THE DISH? CALL PRONTO!
BOYD

There was, of course, dish galore, but the more I thought of it, the more I saw that serving it to Boyd was fraught with complications. For starters there was my vow to Claire. I'd sworn I wouldn't hand over my evidence without first demanding indemnification, a demand

I preferred to attribute to her. But how could I tell Boyd that Claire *knew* without telling him *how* she found out—in other words, by seeing "Henri," whom I'd promised *Gilbert* not to mention?

The real drawback of telling Boyd, though, was how hopelessly it would dilute the effect I hoped to have on Tommy. Boyd would call Tommy immediately with the juicy details, and by the time *I* got to see him my whole scoop would be yesterday's news. I supposed I could call Tommy myself before I sprang it on Boyd, but still, how ineffective compared to telling him face to face. What good was an aphrodisiac if you didn't administer it in person?

Plainly there was nothing to do for it but to stonewall the tape until Tommy's return. In the meanwhile I'd have to toss a bone to Boyd, especially as I'd failed to bug Peter's office, and I decided that a good, lurid report on Peter's taste in periodicals would appease him for now.

Heading out with a fistful of change, I located a pay phone on West End Avenue. It took ages to get through to him, but when he finally came on, his precise singsong was as coy and insinuating as ever.

"Well, *therrrre* you are! I have been holding my breath for *days* waiting to *hear* from you! How'd you like the boat? Isn't it *dire?*"

I got straight to the bad news about not planting the bug in the office and was relieved that his disappointment over my failure was largely mitigated by his delight over Champion's scheme to have me plant the same damn bugs Chez Larkin.

"But you *must* come plant them as soon as possible," he said, cackling with joy. "Just think of the fun I can have if Petey's bugging me but he doesn't know I know it! You have Gilbert call me and we'll work out a time when you can *infiltrate* me, okay?"

"I'll do that."

"So, is that *it?*" he said. "No dish at all?"

"Well," I said modestly, "I *did* manage to sneak into Peter's private office in the middle of the night."

"You clever boy!" he said. "Anything tasty?"

"You be the judge," I said, and began detailing my research into the Champion Smut Library. My task was rendered somewhat uncomfortable by the abrupt appearance at my left elbow of two young schoolgirls in plaid uniforms bearing the legend "Immaculate Heart of Mary." Eager to use the phone, the young ladies felt that hovering close by while scowling up at me would do much to inspire me to brevity.

"Well," I said, deciding to confine my vocabulary to such terms as would elude my audience, "he had this staggering collection of, uh, erotica. All S and M stuff and—"

"Speak *up*, dear," said Boyd. "Are we talking magazines?"

"Yes," I said. "Hundreds of 'em. The women were all these, uh, zaftig Amazons, but the men seemed pretty shrimpy. That's about it."

"*Details*, darlin', *details!* How many magazines? All hard-core or some soft-? Were they commercially produced or were there *private* photos?"

"Just magazines. More than a hundred, and all pretty—explicit. Hang on a sec."

I addressed the taller girl. "I'm going to be a while, so you may want to look for another phone."

"I can wait," snapped the little thug. She'd obviously gotten enough of my drift to convince her that here was an educational opportunity not to be forfeited.

"Philip, are you *there?*"

"Hi."

"What did the women *look* like? Were they *all* tall? How old were they? All white or black or a mix? Were they always doing the beating, or did the men do it sometimes? Were the men just beaten on the bottom or all over, and what'd the ladies use—whips or just fists or what? Was there bondage too and, if so, did they use handcuffs or ropes or studded leather, and did anyone pee on anyone?"

"Well, it was all pretty . . . eclectic," I said. "Some bondage and water sports. The main consistency was that the women were all towering, uh, dominatrixes."

"That's a hooker who gets paid to beat up twisted guys," explained the tall girl.

"I knew that!" said the other, offended.

"Can't you be a little *specific?*" Boyd said.

"Uh, there were lots of fantasy scenes with nurses and jockeys. A few of them had period dresses—"

"A period is—"

"I *know* what it is!" thundered the smaller girl, distressed by these persistent insinuations that she was born yesterday.

"Are you almost through, you sex maniac?"

"Do you *mind?*" I said.

"What is going on, Philip?"

"I'm sorry, but I'm at a pay phone and there are these two dreadful little girls, and—"

"WHO ARE YOU CALLING NAMES, YOU PERV?"

"Fuckhead!"

"Booger-eater!"

"Well!" said Boyd, blithely ignoring the scene on my end. "So Petey likes to have his bottom whacked! Isn't that *shabby!*"

"You bet! Look, I'm running out of change here, so—"

At this point the tall one spotted two chums heading our way and she beckoned them to come join the good fight.

"Melissa! Jenny! Come tell this big child molester to get off the phone!"

"Of course," Boyd continued obliviously, "the problem for us is how to *prove* it. Do you suppose he uses hookers?"

"Search me," I said.

"Look at him," explained the tall girl to the reinforcements. "He's talkin' about hookers with whips to some other pervert!"

"Ooh, *gross!*"

"Listen, Boyd, I really can't deal with this anymore, so—"

"All right!" he sighed. "I'll let you go, but do me a favor first and put one of the little dears on."

I protested, but he was insistent, so I told the ringleader my friend desired a word with her. Goaded by the rabble, she took the phone, elaborately wiping the receiver on her coat, and, raising it to her face, sneered, *"Yeah?"*

She listened a moment, then turned bright crimson and began shrieking uncontrollably. She dropped the phone and began kicking my shins while screaming for passing motorists to call the police, as she'd just been molested. The other three joined in the kick fest, screaming at ear-splitting pitch and whipping themselves into the sort of vindictive frenzy only Catholic schoolgirls can achieve.

They chased me for several blocks before I finally outran them and several other concerned citizens who joined briefly in the chase. I collapsed, spent, onto a bench in Riverside Park. When my nerves had partially recovered I found another phone, called Boyd, and asked what on earth he'd said to the little misery. He giggled and said he forgot.

Fifteen

Temperament—used here not to mean "mood" or "disposition," but rather "petulance in the artist"—is the one unavoidable hazard of life in the arts. It is the rabid dog in the manger of the theater, forever nipping at the heels of the susceptible. Even if you're nimble enough to avoid getting bitten yourself, you will, rest assured, deal frequently with those who've been well gnawed and are, in consequence, frothing with conceit and joys to be around. By the time Claire and I finished writing the act, we thought we'd seen the worst of Elsa's temperament. But as the opening drew nearer we discovered that her earlier tantrums, however memorable, were but the knuckle cracking that precedes the concerto. The silky confidence, displayed so briefly in her shipboard preview, evaporated the minute she set foot back in Manhattan and was replaced by an ever-mounting frenzy of dread.

There were numerous reasons for this, but I'd wager the main culprit was the explosion of media attention. With the show now just two weeks away, the Champion publicity golem, which had till now lumbered along at a sedate pace, began tearing wildly about, terrorizing the populace.

This was Peter's doing. He desired—for what selfless reasons we have seen—to make his wife a star. Up until now his suspicion that she was, in fact, strikingly devoid of talent had led him to soft-pedal the promotion, so that in the event of a complete rout, the embarrassment might be kept to a minimum. Elsa's startling display of competence at sea had allayed this concern, and Peter began publicizing the debut with his usual flair for bombast and flamboyance.

He took out two-page ads in every paper in town. They featured a bold line drawing of Elsa fellating a microphone, the words SOLD OUT splayed across her bosom, so that Peter was in effect blowing a hundred grand to tell the public that if it wanted to see his wife, it couldn't. He purchased the decaying Cheltenham Hotel, then called a press conference announcing his intention to restore it and install an opulent nightclub so that "top-name headliners," including his wife, would "finally have a New York showcase worthy of their talents," (a remark that must have delighted the Rainbow Room no end).

His PR people scheduled a whirlwind of interviews and personal appearances for Elsa, including public service announcements for Paws to Consider. In these Elsa was compelled to cuddle two terrified tabbies and hope her teariness would be attributed to compassion and not, more accurately, to allergies. The gossip columns seethed with updates on who'd be attending and what celeb had shelled out some obscene sum to obtain a ticket to the sold-out event.

Peter wasn't the only one beating the drums. Elsa's friends and sycophants, eager to show their loyalty and bask in reflected glory, rushed to add their voices to the oratorio of hype. The Tuesday after the cruise an item appeared in Daisy Winters's column:

Society songbird **Elsa Champion** played hooky from rehearsals last weekend to give her tonsils a little sea air aboard that swank dingy, the ***Champion Siren***. The air must've agreed with Elsa, 'cause she decided to give an impromptu sneak peek of her upcoming Rainbow Room gig to a few lucky guests and seagulls. Word has it she blew 'em away, and those doomsayers who've scooped up tix just to scoff will be paying 500 smackers to dine on crow à la Champion. Said lucky attendee **Millie Pilchard**, "We expected her to be *good*, of course, but, my dear, she was *breathtaking!* Elsa has a stunning voice and *true star quality*, and I think she's going to be bigger than **Lena Horne** or even **Liza Minnelli**, I shouldn't wonder." High praise, Millie!—but we know you can pull it off, Elsa, and here's one fan who'll be right there ringside rootin' for ya!

It did not escape Elsa that such efforts, however well intentioned, were creating expectations she might have some difficulty living up to. It surely occurred to her, too, that her charity ploy, while assuring Horsey's attendance, had also upped the ante considerably. An audience compelled to pay five hundred dollars a seat was bound to be more critical than one charged a more reasonable tariff. When you combined these factors with the wide lack of enthusiasm for the charity and the inevitable presence in the crowd of "friends" who'd spent the last few weeks sticking pins in their Elsa dolls, it was not hard to see why Elsa's feet were suddenly colder than a barefoot Eskimo's. Her terror grew daily, and the more it grew, the more temperamental she became.

The day the Millie item appeared, we'd been summoned to a rehearsal at the Parthenon, as Claire had taken to calling the apartment. We were ushered into the music room, where Elsa, wielding a copy of Daisy's column, was thrashing about like a maudlin tornado.

"How could you allow this?" she shrieked. "You fiend! You Judas! How could you let such a thing be printed?"

The target of her wrath was Carl Jamrose, the fortunate publicist Peter had appointed general of the campaign. Carl was a lanky man with a high crew cut resembling a wheat field and a pained smile so fixed and immutable you imagined him taking it out of a box every morning and spraying it with lacquer. Some dozen others stood by, dodging shrapnel.

"But, Elsa," he simpered, "*we* didn't arrange that! Daisy and Millie did that all on their own. Besides, you *hired* us to get nice things about you into print."

"I hired you to CONTROL my press! And what the hell's so *nice* about it? Now if I go out there and I'm anything less than fucking Lena Minnelli, they'll eat me alive!"

She flounced over to the sofa, where her eyes lit on some costume sketches that a short, impeccably dressed man was holding on his lap.

"What the hell is this?" she said, snatching them up. "Do you expect me to *wear* this?"

"Eet's what we deescussed," said the man I now recognized as the designer Jean-Louis Mallard. "Ze top vairy white, seemple and flowing, and hundairneath ze white slacks."

"When I said 'simple,' I didn't mean *this* simple. I'd look like a fucking male nurse in this! It's *wrong! C'est un* complete *Niçoise!*"

Mallard regarded her with that hostile confusion a genuine Frenchman is bound to feel when confronted with Gilbert's version of his language. He seemed on the verge of teaching her some slang of his own when something stopped him—presumably his realization that Elsa's debut gown would be the most photographed dress of the year, and if he wanted it to be one of his, tact was of the utmost.

"Elsa, darling, if eet does not please you, I will tra something else. Tell me what you weesh."

"I can't *possibly* think now! I'll call you tomorrow! Philip, Claire! Sit down, please! I'm not ready for you because I'm completely behind schedule! *Where the hell are the new ads!*"

She continued in this manner all that day and every day up till the opening, excoriating her arrangers, designers, band members, and the entire staff of the Rainbow Room, constantly demanding that anything that could be changed be changed and then changed back to the way it was.

Our own material was, mercifully, exempt from these demands, though this was not so much due to Elsa's unqualified admiration for our work as to her cold terror of learning anything new. She did, however, obsessively juggle and rearrange the songs. The running order was never the same two days in a row, and none of these altered sequences made any sense at all. We'd politely tell her so, leading her to rail against us, then apologize and tearfully beg us to stick around so she could scream at us some more later.

Such behavior, of course, endeared her to no one. Inevitably someone leaked word to a columnist and a maliciously accurate item appeared detailing Elsa's daily conniptions. The informer was never identified, so Elsa, who could hardly fire everyone, now augmented her standard tirades on incompetence with paranoid outbursts about traitors fomenting anti-Elsa cabals.

Paradoxically, the same hype machine that fueled her hysteria also provided our few interludes of calm. Carl Jamrose would appear at rehearsal with reporters from *People* or some local TV station, whereupon the atmosphere would undergo an abrupt transformation. Elsa, desperate to dispel rumors she was "difficult," would enact grotesque parodies of benevolence, affectionately hugging cohorts to whom she'd referred only moments before as "bloodsucking saboteurs."

Busy as Peter was cramming his wife down the maw of the public, he still found time to phone me daily to see when I planned to smuggle his bugs into Larkin's place. I informed him that to get into Larkin's, I'd need my pal Gilbert, who was not presently available—owing, as I did not explain, to the fact that he was even now sporting a French accent and prowling around Peter's own boat, riffling the waste-baskets. Eventually "Henri's" day off arrived, and Gilbert brought me round to Boyd's for tea.

The house was an imperial limestone palazzo off Fifth Avenue a few blocks up from Tommy's. We were shown in by Jailbait the butler and ushered to a large sitting room that had much of the stately coziness of Tommy's place but, on closer inspection, proved rather more eccentric. The mahogany walls featured all manner of stunning and intricate carvings of sunbursts and various flora, but also ominous mythological beasts and birds. Scattered among the sturdy antiques were more exotic pieces, including two ancient wooden chairs, towering and canopied, like thrones from some druidic temple.

The *objets* scattered about also showed a trend toward the bizarre, if not downright ghoulish. There were talismans, antique drug paraphernalia, and what looked to me like rusted instruments of torture. The combination of these touches amid so much chintz-covered furniture produced a sinister hominess, suggesting a collaboration between Mario Buatta and Charles Addams.

Eerier, though, than even the most macabre *tchotchke* was a photo in a silver frame. It showed a comely slip of a lad got up in Dionysian drag with a flowing tunic and laurel in his blond, wavy hair. Though the rest of the face was unrecognizable, the impudent smile was unquestionably Boyd's. It unnerved me to think this golden young man had matured into the corpulent sybarite who was even now padding into the room in his little brocaded slippers.

"Gil-bert!" sang Boyd. "So *glad* you could visit. And who is your charming friend here?" he added with a big wink to me.

:

Identities were established, and Boyd, who was clutching a large notepad, scribbled on it and held it up.

"YOU BRING THE BUGS, HON?" it read.

I nodded and pointed to my jacket pocket while inquiring as to the authenticity of a shrunken head.

"You bet it's real. I told that dealer, 'I'm havin' this checked, and if it's phony, I'll come back and shrink more than your head, honey!' "

He wheezed with laughter, then flashed the pad, on which he'd scrawled, "STICK ONE UNDER THE COFFEE TABLE!"

The inevitable trough of martinis appeared, and Boyd, after filling a stemmed tureen for each of us, announced he'd conduct a tour, as he could see how keen an appreciation I possessed for the finer things.

"Now, where *are* my glasses?" he asked. They were, in fact, right on his nose. "I am *forever* misplacing the damn things, and I'm blind as a bat without 'em! Oh, never mind. I oughta know where everything is by now, right?"

He led us from one strikingly appointed chamber to the next, describing their contents with a mix of pride and campy irreverence, all the while scribbling notes saying where he wanted the microphones. He also kept soliciting my impressions of my employers, the Champions. Peter had, you'll recall, instructed me to bad-mouth him and Elsa, the better to win Larkin's confidence. Elsa's winning ways of late had rendered the strategy a distinct pleasure, and I dished with abandon, detailing her rages at rehearsals and citing all the imaginative names the musicians had coined for her.

Before long, all six bugs were in place. One of these, of course, was Larkin's own, but he'd have no trouble ascertaining which. We settled back into the parlor for tea sandwiches and vitriol, after an hour of which we departed amid earnest pleas to visit again soon.

I was at last divested of all electronic eavesdroppers, so as we strolled up a twilit Fifth Avenue, Gilbert felt free once more to argue passionately in favor of my sharing credit with him for the Kitty tape.

"We were under that desk *together*, Philly! Granted, you pushed the button, but I was just as aware of that recorder as you were!"

"Is that why you looked so startled when I pointed it out?"

This stopped him, but just for a moment. "If I looked startled," he explained patiently, "it was because I had no idea *you* knew about it, too. In fact, I was *about* to press it myself when you beat me to it. And if I *had* pushed it first, I'd certainly share the credit with *you* instead of hogging it all to myself like some childish, self-centered—"

I said that if he devoted half as much energy to finding dirt of his own as he expended trying to give my credulity a hernia, he'd have bulging dossiers of scandal by the time Tommy returned. This assertion cheered him about as much as it was intended to, and we went our separate ways.

Claire and I didn't have fun that last week before the premiere, and neither did Elsa or Peter. Boyd, on the other hand, had himself a regular carnival. With the bugs now in place, Peter hung on every word Boyd uttered, and the wily old goat milked the situation for all the malicious fun it was worth.

The two men, both being potentates of publishing, traveled in much the same exalted circles and hobnobbed with many of the same industry leaders. Though these media muck-a-mucks publicly treated Peter with the deference due his wealth and influence, most privately regarded him with an energetic loathing to which Peter, being Peter, was largely oblivious.

But when Radio Larkin began its broadcast season, Boyd began inviting these luminaries to a series of dinner parties. There, encouraged by their host's superb wines and surgical tongue, they delivered themselves of the most devastatingly frank appraisals of Peter and Elsa's style, taste, and personal appearances. Galling as it must have been for Peter to plow through transcripts containing so many disagreeable observations, he didn't dare skip a word lest he miss some crucial nugget that would provide ammunition against the enemy he now more than ever wished to destroy. Alas, no such nuggets emerged.

More frustrating still for Peter was the lack of any statement proving Boyd enjoyed sexual relations with jailbait, or men at all, for that matter. Several times Boyd *seemed* to flirt with some young male member of his staff. The conversation between them would grow insinuating until the air was pregnant with innuendo. But then someone would come in or the phone would ring and the servant would be dismissed. The most maddening moment of all came when Boyd, broadcasting from the boudoir, coyly asked his strapping young masseur to fetch a new "toy" from under the bed. The masseur, crouching to remove the item, said, "Hey, someone left gum under your bed," and Boyd said, "Well, flush it down the toilet—then *hurry right back!*"

The Elsa publicity volcano continued to spew relentlessly, achieving its greatest eruptions on the Monday a week before her premiere. That day alone, features appeared in the *Times, Newsday,* and *W;* the *Estime* cover story hit the stands; and there were no fewer than three television appearances scheduled.

The first of these, as orchestrated by Mr. Jamrose, was a "surprise" visit to the set of Spark Chandler's talk show. Elsa, who would sing briefly, "asked" us to be in the audience for moral support, which I wouldn't have minded had the damned show not taped at ten A.M. This isn't an hour at which the average young, gay lyricist cares to find himself surrounded by hordes of voluble middle-aged women who've banded together to inspect some troubled specimen of humanity and shake the wretched thing down till it hasn't a secret left to call its own.

Claire and I shared a charming rush-hour subway to the studio. The doors weren't open yet, and the hall outside was swarming with Spark's loyal fans, including Millie Pilchard, who wouldn't have missed Elsa's appearance for the world.

"So exciting, isn't it! I've been telling everyone on line what a treat they're in for with Elsa coming on at the end!"

"But, Millie," said Claire, "isn't this all supposed to be 'unscheduled,' with Elsa claiming she was taping down the hall and just popping in for a surprise?"

"Yes. So lovely to be in the know, though, isn't it? Don't worry, I haven't told many people at all."

Elsa would not have to warble alone, as Spark's sole guest for the show was Frieda May Johnson, a once popular country singer. Her career and marriage had foundered, owing, she said, both to alcoholism and a debilitating lifelong addiction to promiscuous sex. She'd then found the Lord, who'd advised her, during apparently frequent debriefings, to write a book so that her recovery might serve as an example to others. The resulting memoir, which seemed pretty well soldered to Frieda May's hand, was now climbing the best-seller list.

Spark interviewed her briefly, lauding her courageousness in coming forward as an alcoholic, adulterous hussy. The singer was weirdly chipper about the whole thing, quipping that her nickname in Nashville had been "Tammy Why-not?" Eventually Spark opened the floor to his ladies, jogging athletically about the studio and asking his signature question, "What do *you* think?"

It was, according to my *Bartlett's*, a Madame de Staël who first remarked that to know all is to forgive all. Spark's ladies seemed to subscribe to de Staël's credo, being positively eager to forgive all if only they could know it first. There seemed no detail of the singer's life so intimate that one matron or another would not boldly demand the long skinny, and if Frieda May stinted on details, another would be in there like a shot with follow-ups. In fact, the only question in the whole hour that embarrassed anyone came from an elderly woman who'd apparently spoken to Millie and demanded to know when Elsa would be out.

Elsa finally did come out in the last minutes of the broadcast. Much was made of the surprise, with Spark expressing astonished delight and Elsa apologizing wildly for "barging in." She'd heard Frieda May was down the hall and simply *had* to come pay tribute to her very favorite country singer in the world. Spark suggested a duet. Elsa balked coyly, but the crowd loudly insisted till Elsa prettily capitulated, agreeing to one quick chorus of "Amazing Grace." Frieda May being country music's answer to the air raid siren, Elsa wasn't much worried about how she'd come off. She'd wagered, correctly, that it would be hard to tell where she began and Frieda May left off. After two blaring choruses Elsa scampered away, blowing kisses to one and all.

After the show Claire and I duly congratulated Spark and Elsa on how well it had gone. We then returned uptown to have lunch and inspect the *Estime* cover story.

For weeks we'd shared a subdued dread over how friend Hoot would elect to paint us. This dread was, we now discovered, amply justified.

Settling into a booth at Happy Burger, we inspected the cover photo. Elsa wore a red silk jumpsuit with pleated panels crisscrossing her chest, amply displaying her bosom, which, though freckled, had been airbrushed to snowy perfection. She'd been captured clapping her hands together, her head tilted back as though laughing at some delicious joke. ELSA CHASES HER RAINBOW! read the headline, and beneath it in smaller type, "The Champion of Chic Sings for Hoot Mulvaney."

Fingers atremble, we found the article and skimmed in search of our names.

"Oh, dear," said Claire. "Middle of page forty-six."

I found the spot and read:

Somewhere in the midst of this frantic roundelay of appointments, this mad pavane of pleasures and duties, mirth and mercy, Elsa finds time to interview two fledgling songwriters who hope against hope she'll hire them for her act. She greets the pair in that fabulous foyer, where they stand nervous, perspiring, clearly in awe of both their surroundings and hostess.

The same two writers, tunesmith Claire Simmons and Phil Cavanaugh, the word man, saw their first off-Broadway musical go down in flames less than a month earlier. Luckily for them, Elsa's pal Millie Pilchard, a keenly perceptive gadfly of the arts, caught the show in previews and, for all its flaws, saw something in it, a freshness and originality that eluded critics and public alike. That was enough for Elsa to give the fortunate novices this chance of chances.

"Where can you buy a gun in this neighborhood?" inquired Claire.

"Wait—it gets better."

Elsa, noting Cavanaugh's anxiety, lays a soothing hand on his shoulder and gives him that fireplace of a smile. He smiles back, shaky but calmer, and she leads us to an airy chamber where a gleaming white grand piano, once owned by Newport bandleader Binkie Stanhope, makes the whole room seem happily haunted by the ghosts of jazz babies past. Simmons, a motherly little woman, settles in at the keys. Cavanaugh sings "Hard to Be Me," the satiric complaint of a socialite who finds her schedule too, *too* punishing. Elsa, who can empathize, laughs her throaty laugh, a waterfall of honey and cinnamon sticks, then leads the generous applause. Cavanaugh finishes with a ballad called "Live and Learn." Despite Cavanaugh's bleating voice and zigzagging pitch, the song touches the spectators. Elsa leaps up and delivers her instant verdict—they're hired. The writers sag visibly, overwhelmed with joy.

Elsa joins them at the keys and flawlessly croons the ballad, her lush, warm vibrato caressing the words, adding nuances of feeling that elevate the workmanlike lyric into an achingly poetic (continued on page 87)

"Oh, dear—look at you," said Claire, pointing to a photo in the upper corner.

The photo showed the three of us on the piano bench. Elsa was laying siege to a high note, and I was trying so hard not to wince that I'd gone too far in the opposite direction, achieving a look of abject adoration best reserved for Nativity plays.

"What the hell were you thinking?"

"I was trying not to wince."

"You succeeded."

Claire, displaying that sensitivity to slights I have mentioned elsewhere, began muttering invective, comparing Hoot to various fauna ranging from reptiles, on the high end, to intestinal parasites.

" 'Motherly little woman' indeed! I've lost eleven pounds preparing for this miserable engagement!"

"And it shows! You look fabulous, really. Let Hoot do his worst," I said, reminding her that we'd already received extensive press, all of it far sweeter than this.

We had, too. The spotlight that shone mainly on Elsa and Peter burned brightly enough to illuminate us minions hovering in the background. As Elsa's songwriters we'd garnered a little nosegay of mentions, most of them highly complimentary. *New York* magazine even gave us a flattering profile in the "Brief Lives" column, with a headline that read BOUNCING BACK. We had, in a way, become marginal celebs.

I would be less than forthcoming if I didn't confess to finding this aspect of things hugely agreeable. In fact, so pleased was I by my newfound status that I soon became something of a pill. I began spending money rather freely on pricey clothes and swanky dinners. I casually rehearsed my Elsa stories and couldn't leave the house without praying I'd bump into some old writer acquaintance into whose face my new status could be rubbed like so much moisturizer. This prayer was answered once, and my, what a gay time I had, moaning disingenuously about what a circus it all was and wasn't it dumb what a *fuss* the media was making about it—though, thank heaven, the songs had turned out well, as so many people would hear them. My victim, Marlowe Heppenstall, a fellow lyricist of few recent accomplishments, soon remembered a dentist appointment, and I sauntered off, my face shining with that happy glow a writer can only acquire by bringing another writer to the brink of suicide.

Looking back on my behavior, the real wince prompter isn't how puffed up I became on such tenuous grounds, but the fierce hypocrisy it took for me to trade on the Champions' celebrity at all. I mean, there I was, working to bring Peter's kingdom crashing down around him, dishing his and Elsa's vulgarity to anyone who'd listen, yet all the while basking in their notoriety, wrapping my association with them around me like a tattered boa. How proud it made me that, while my friends could only loathe the Champions from a distance, I got to dislike them personally.

At the time, of course, I gave no thought to these little contradictions. I was too busy collecting my clippings, counting the hours till Tommy's return, and coping daily with the complexities of life in Elsa's court. The politics there, never a box lunch to begin with, grew more intricate and ticklish the closer we got to the big day.

The most odious development by far was the reascendance of Signora di Corteggiano.

For a while there, her influence had seemed to be in a virtual free-fall. Elsa had recognized Claire's superior skills not only as an accompanist, but as a vocal coach, too. Worse still for the signora, her dark, psychic warnings against our malign influence had succeeded only in making her look jealous, if not downright batty. Elsa had continued her lessons, but her panegyrics to the old girl's brilliance, once so frequent and vociferous, were discreetly abandoned.

But just as the lapsed Catholic will, in time of trial, return to the comforting arms of the church, so did the apostate Elsa, fearing hellish reviews, reembrace Corteggianoism with unprecedented fervor. She found its blend of flattery and mysticism a great solace, not to mention the convenient way in which it transferred the onus for success from her somewhat erratic vocal cords to her indisputably perfect soul. The old teacher became a constant oracular presence, her advice solicited on each and every detail of the production.

The signora, emboldened by this new deference displayed her, began adding tricks to her already bulging repertoire. Now, in addition to inspirational cassettes, she began supplying Elsa with a full line of homemade "folk remedies" geared to soothe and protect Elsa's golden larynx. There were medicinal teas, a throat spray in a Cartier atomizer, and an assortment of herbal lozenges lovingly wrapped in pink tissue. Their pleasant fruity taste and perfect uniformity of shape might, to a low, suspicious mind, have suggested commercial mass production, but Elsa devoutly accepted the signora's assertion that she made them from scratch, employing ancient recipes, hoarded and kept secret by the great divas of legend. As for the price of these nostrums, no one was talking, but you can bet it was hefty from the lengths to which the signora went to emphasize the scarcity of her ingredients.

"Forgive me, *cara*," she'd say, arriving at rehearsal late and breathless, "but I had to drive to a small convent in Pennsylvania, where I was told an aged sister from Firenze still grows the necessary herbs. A false lead, alas, but fear not—I'll find more before we run out!"

Our own relations with the old darling were as breezy as you'd expect, but, her first attempt to banish us having backfired so lamentably, she wasn't about to push her luck by trying again. She could not, of course, resist finding fault with our songs, but her insults, like her lozenges, came so prettily wrapped that it seemed churlish to cavil over the contents. "Ah, *perfetto!*" she would coo after Elsa had run through "Hard to Be Me." "Though, how I do wish the last word were not 'me'! The 'e' sound, you know—so very grating when sung on a high note. But we cannot expect our brilliant young lyricist to pay attention to such things when he is busy making his wonderful jokes! He has done his job—it is our job to keep it from sounding hideous. Such challenges you give us, Mr. Cavanaugh!"

Whenever the signora's toxic pleasantries or Elsa's extravagant mood swings dampened my spirits, I had only to think of Tommy's return to once more grin like a goof. Every evening, as soon as I got home, I'd dim the lights, play the tape, and imagine Tommy was beside me, writhing in mirth.

"Oh, Philip," my fantasy Tommy would say, "but it's *priceless!* How clever of you to get it! Let's have sex!"

But the more hours I spent constructing my dream castle, the more I began to perceive a critical flaw in its foundation, one that threatened to bring the whole edifice crashing down right in the middle of the housewarming. That flaw was my promise to Claire.

I had, you'll recall, vowed to tell Tommy nothing about the tape until he dined at my place two nights after Elsa's debut. Claire would swing by early and secure his written assurance that Larkin Publications would cover my legal expenses in the event of a lawsuit. It had seemed a simple enough promise when I made it, but now I had to wonder what effect it might have on my amorous designs. However much I blamed the request on Claire, it remained a singularly unromantic gesture and one bound to set the wrong tone for the whole evening. Nights begun in affidavits seldom end in bliss.

More distressing still was the Gilbert factor. Did I dare sit on my secret for three full days after Tommy's return, when Gilbert would surely see him at least once during the period? Could I really trust the young scoundrel, however cowed he was by my threats, not to blurt out the whole tale and claim *I'd* stolen the tape from *him?*

On reflection, I saw there was no option but to spring my secret on Tommy when he returned the evening before Elsa's opening. I'd phone and describe my scoop in such tantalizing terms, he'd fairly beg me to come by and end the suspense. Then, much later, as we lay in a tender postcoital embrace, I'd inform him that Claire—owing solely to Gilbert's blundering shenanigans—had learned all and had concerns for my welfare she wished to discuss with him. Would he be a dear and not let on to her I'd told him anything yet?

This seemed an acceptable strategy, allowing me to thwart Gilbert, display my implicit faith in Tommy, and mollify Claire all at once. No sooner had I settled on it, though, than I returned home to find a sweet phone message from Tommy saying he'd been detained in London and would, using Boyd's private jet, manage to arrive barely in time for Elsa's opening. He wished me fabulous success and could not wait to see me at the Rainbow Room.

I found this irksome. The Rainbow Room, though romantic enough as nightspots go, was not a place where people tended to get laid. But when I got tired of kicking furniture I began to see that the change in schedule was in some ways the best thing that could have happened.

After all, if Tommy flew in barely in time for the opening, there was no way poor uninvited Gilbert could gain access to him before I did. Besides, what riper time to play him the tape than right after the opening night party, when my glamour would have reached new and breathtaking heights?

There I'd be, resplendent in my tux, taking modest little bows and blowing kisses to Elsa even as I murmured witty asides to him about the miracles of espionage I'd achieved in his absence. Looking at me, Tommy would see in the same glittering instant Cavanaugh, the gifted songwriter; Cavanaugh, darling of the *beau monde;* and Cavanaugh, master spy—all rolled into one available package. How could so enticing a combination, abetted by ample quantities of champagne, fail to send affection soaring and zippers plummeting?

As I drifted to sleep the night before the opening, my fantasies seemed so real, my triumph so inevitable, that it was almost as though I'd ceased anticipating the event and had already begun to savor the memory. In the days that followed I often remembered a remark Claire once made to me after a failed audition.

"Philip," she said, "it's one thing to count your chickens before they're hatched, but do wait until the rooster's in the mood."

Sixteen

It is a very natural thing for performers to feel a few jitters in the hours preceding an opening night. Elsa's opening night jitters having kicked in ahead of schedule by some two weeks, we suspected the evening itself would find her a veritable Chernobyl of emotions. Peter, feeling that copious amounts of flattery might contain these emotions, ordered us of the inner circle to rally round the dressing room at four and bring trowels. We did as we were told, offering Elsa such slavish avowals of respect as would have embarrassed a dog, but by six P.M. the only victory we could claim was that she hadn't actually thrown up in an hour. Still, we kept gamely at it.

"You're an astonishing talent, Elsa," said Claire, whose shift it was. "I don't know if you've ever watched me when you sing a ballad, but often there are tears running down my face. Real tears, Elsa. Talk to me, dear. Am I bothering you? Do you want me to stop?"

"No."

Claire, casting a nervous glance around the room as though to assure herself this was not a court of law, resumed.

"You have this quality, Elsa, this strangely indefinable something. A sort of—"

"Magic?" offered Millie.

"Yes, a magic that only a handful of singers possess. And do you know something about these singers? They *all* get nervous before they perform. Every one of them. So you see, it's *normal* to feel the way you do. In fact, it's *good*. The adrenaline will *help* your performance."

"If being nervous will help my performance," snapped Elsa, "then why are you trying to talk me out of it?"

"Well," I said, jumping in, "there's such a thing as being *too* nervous."

"Well then," she replied triumphantly, "if I'm *too* nervous, it *isn't* normal and it's *not* all right, and it won't help my performance at all! I'll bomb and be disgraced, and everyone will laugh and make jokes about it for the rest of my life!"

Peter sighed. "Let me talk to her again."

He rose grimly and made his way through a thicket of floral tributes. These flowers had done little to hearten Elsa. To her, they'd struck a distinctly funereal chord, and she'd greeted each bouquet's arrival with a fresh outburst of tears. Claire happily relinquished the chief anesthetist's chair and joined Millie and me in the background.

"For cryin' out loud, Elsa!" said Peter. "Why are you so worried what these people are going to think of you? Who the hell are *they* that you, Elsa *Champion*, should give two shits about their opinion? They're just a lot of snobs who're all jealous—that's right, jealous—of you because you're rich and beautiful and married to me, and because you're going to be a very big—"

"Well, feast your eyes on this!" said Carl Jamrose, bustling in with the grandest bouquet yet. It was a lush four-foot-high arrangement that, in keeping with the trend toward ever more exotic and expensive blooms, resembled some set decoration from an old "Star Trek" episode.

"It's from Joy Cudgel and Spark Chandler," said Carl.

"How lovely," said Elsa, sobbing inconsolably.

Carl, interpreting this as sentiment, pressed on.

"Say! I got about half a dozen folks out here who'll name their first kid after you if you'll just let 'em come in here and get some film for the six o'clock news!"

Elsa lifted her face from her hankie and regarded him with that wide-eyed stare of terror caged bunnies give to men in lab coats.

"Actually, Carl," Claire said delicately, "Elsa's just the teensiest bit nervous now—"

"That'll play *great*," said Carl cheerfully. "The star-to-be having a few preshow butterflies! Channel two's all set up for a live remote. Why don't I just—"

Elsa shrieked and stamped her feet fiercely on the carpet.

"Get the hell out of here," thundered Champion. "Tell those vultures she can't talk now! She's meditating!"

"Right!" said Carl, and, nodding obsequiously, backed toward the door, colliding with Signora di Corteggiano, who'd just entered in a swirl of paisley scarves and packages.

"Watch where you're going, you oaf!" cried the signora. "Elsa, *carissima!* Forgive my tardiness!"

"Oh, signora!" wailed Elsa, wiping her eyes. "I've been waiting and waiting for you!"

"I am here now, *tesoro*, and I bring many powerful herbs! The woman who grew them, she was a witch to bargain with, but in the end I got what I desired. Millie, I will need to make a tea. Boil water. The flowers! They must go. She may inhale the pollen, which is an irritant to the throat."

"It *does* feel irritated," said Elsa. "Perhaps we should cancel?"

Champion asked Claire and me if we'd ditch the flowers and we agreed, thrilled at any excuse to depart that vale of tears.

"Do you think she'll be all right?" I asked Claire as we carried the last offending bouquets past the two tuxedoed pugilists Champion had charged with safeguarding Elsa's privacy.

"She'll be fine," Claire said wearily. "The signora will brew her a five-hundred-dollar mug of Red Zinger and she'll belt her lungs out. It's *us* who'll be basket cases before the night's over."

She checked her watch and frowned. "Damn. We have sound checks still to do, and I'm not dressed or made up. I'd better make tracks and see you upstairs."

She bustled off to the Pegasus Suite, which was being used as a dressing room for the band. The minute she was out of sight I patted my tux pocket for the fortieth time that day to confirm that my precious cassette was still in its place. I smiled rakishly, then checked my watch to see how many minutes I'd have to endure before being reunited with Tommy.

It was almost six-thirty. The guests would begin arriving around seven. There'd be cocktails and fevered speculations till eight, at which point Horsey Kimball would make some touching speech about the four-legged *misérables* we'd gathered to support, then introduce Elsa. Elsa would, God willing, perform for fifty minutes, then there'd be dinner, followed by dancing and commentary into the small hours.

I decided to head upstairs to the Promenade Bar to have a drink while I waited for the party to start. There were reporters lurking by the elevators, peering my way to monitor the dressing room front. I started down the hall, but then a door opened behind me and the press came rampaging straight toward me like panthers spotting a barbecue. Pinning myself against the wall, I saw that Peter had emerged from the dressing room and seemed, from his wary smile, to be in statement mode.

The first to reach him was a perky blonde with a cameraman in tow. The cameraman had an enormous light on his shoulder, and he switched it on, bathing Peter and the reporter in a harsh glare.

"Good evening, Mr. Champion," she said. "Could you tell us what's going through your mind tonight?"

"Happy to, Sheila," he said, putting on his TV voice, which is cheery but deliberately paced for purposes of vocabulary enhancement. "I'm feeling a sort of, uh, jubilant anticipation as I await—"

"Not yet, okay?" she said, listening to her earpiece. "I'm waiting for the anchor to . . . *Hello!* We're here *live* at the Rainbow Room, where Elsa Champion is scheduled to perform at a charity benefit that has to rank as the most eagerly awaited musical event since— well, since *what*, Peter?" She thrust the mike in his face.

"Since, I would say, uh, a Beatles reunion concert. Which, of course, never happened, and now never can owing to the unfortunate demise of, uh—"

"Any chance Elsa might let us in her dressing room here for a moment, just to wish her well?"

"I'm afraid that won't be possible, Sheila. My wife is a very disciplined, dedicated performer, and she requires absolute serenity and concentration to, uh, prime herself for the debilitating, or rather, exhausting—"

I sneaked behind the cameraman and took the elevator one flight up to the main floor. As I exited, the elevator across from mine opened and Daisy Winters swaggered out. She waved and I smiled, absurdly pleased that she knew who I was. She advanced on me with a rapacious smile and proffered a hand in greeting.

"Howdy, handsome. You must be plenty excited, huh?"

She'd been wedged into a scarlet-and-black beaded gown, and her hair was sculpted to an unprecedented height. Was the reason purely aesthetic, I wondered, or did she keep a typewriter in there?

"You seen Elsa?" she asked.

"I just left her."

"How's she doin'? Butterflies in her stomach?"

"Try bats."

"Poor baby," said Daisy. "I'll go hold her hand. Where is she?"

"Down one floor and hang a right to Center Suite B. It may be hard getting through, though. The signora just shooed us all out."

Daisy's response was a snort of raw contempt. *"Her! Two* mentions I gave that old windbag in one week. She thinks she's gonna play traffic cop with *me*, I'll have her head for a canapé."

Daisy called an elevator and marched into it like a bugle-beaded SWAT team. I wished her luck and sauntered happily toward the reception desk.

I spoke earlier of the terrible complacency to which I succumbed during this period. It probably reached its zenith in that hour before the show as I patrolled the Rainbow Room in my tux, taking in the sights and considering myself very much one of them. It's no surprise that my vanity should have peaked there, for the place is lovingly designed to leave its patrons fairly intoxicated with swank. Its grand, romantically lit halls and bars possess an elegant geometry all their own, and as I wandered through them now, I felt stylish and perfect and invincible.

I strolled into the Promenade Bar and waited by the door for the hostess. I surveyed the crowd, a mix of tired execs, trysting yuppies, and giddy tourists, all lapping up cocktails and basking in the glamour of their surroundings. After Peter's media blitz, I doubted any of them were unaware of the glittering affair due to begin soon just down the hall. I smiled to think that my tuxedo quietly announced my status as a participant and wondered if any of them recognized me from my picture in *New York.* A handsome couple in their middle years directed a smile toward me and beckoned me to their table. I grinned benignly, as one accustomed to these well-meaning intrusions, and trickled over.

"Yes?" I said accessibly.

"Is it all right with you if we change tables? That one by the window just became free and we'd rather sit there."

I corrected their misapprehension with what seemed an entirely forgivable acerbity, then headed to the bar and ordered a Campari and soda. As I sipped it I glanced toward the entrance and saw Carl Jamrose stagger in with the stunned, hunted air of an escaped convict negotiating a swamp. He drew up next to me and, leaning against the bar, waved limply to the bartender and whimpered for vodka.

I felt a stab of guilt. I realized I'd provided Daisy directions to Elsa without so much as a thought for the poor fellow whose duty it was to wield the whip and the chair. I inspected his face. His smile was, as ever, intact, but you could see where Daisy had scraped the plaque off.

"Seen Daisy, have you?" I said.

"Yes, just now."

"She get past you?"

"Yes, but the bodyguards blocked her way and I, uh—" He shuddered. "I instructed them to take her upstairs."

"Oh, brave Jamrose! Bet she didn't like that."

"No, she didn't."

"Hurled a few thunderbolts, did she?"

He nodded, shaken. "She said from here on in my clients can fuck dead babies in the window at Bloomie's—she *still* won't mention them."

I commiserated, assuring him that Elsa would smooth everything over. We nursed our drinks, girding ourselves for the rigors ahead, then made for the Rainbow Room, where guests would soon begin arriving.

In these last moments before blast-off the room was aswirl with carefully choreographed chaos. Elsa's band, in their Mallard-designed blue-and-gray outfits, were tuning their instruments. Waiters and captains, all tall, slim, and resplendent in their maroon rainbow-motif uniforms, bustled about, fussing over centerpieces and place settings. A flock of elaborately gowned middle-aged women, representatives of Paws to Consider, fluttered about clutching clipboards and anxiously checking place cards.

As I stood there surveying the room, a wide, idiotic grin bloomed on my face. From the circular dance floor with its parquet sunburst to the gently curved dining terraces to the tall windows whose lavender shirred curtains framed three hundred sixty degrees of twinkling skyline, the room epitomized that opulent, RKO Manhattan we young, glamour-starved queens scattered across the country always dreamed of and couldn't wait to grow up and run away to. What if we discovered on arriving that few such rooms had ever really existed and those that did had long since vanished? What if they'd been replaced by vast, noisy, strobe-lit migraine machines? There still remained, proudly, anachronistically, unaffordably, this last brave bastion of thirties splendor. The thought that I would sit here tonight and watch several hundred heartless socialites listen to my songs filled me with uncomplicated joy.

"I hope that canary you swallowed doesn't spoil your appetite."

"Hi, Claire! Didn't see you coming."

"Obviously. You're not squiffy already, are you?"

"No, the decor's just gone to my head. Have I mentioned how gorgeous you look tonight?"

She smiled an uncharacteristically demure smile. "Yes, but feel free to repeat yourself like crazy."

"You're stunning! I mean it—you look like some fifties society man-trap out to beef up her diamond collection."

She did, at that. Usually Claire's sensitive, pragmatic nature prevents her from attempting glamour. She fears that with her short legs and round, apple-cheeked face she'll miss the mark and look foolish for trying. But an event like this, she knew, demanded a certain minimum of oomph, and she'd risen to the challenge. She'd dropped some weight and persuaded Elsa not only to foot the bill for a décolleté gown of ice-blue satin, but to loan her an eye-popping necklace as well so all that cleavage wouldn't get lonely. She'd even cajoled a friend of hers who did makeup for Broadway shows into applying his artistry to her normally fresh-scrubbed features.

"You really do look terrific, hon!"

"Thanks." She blushed and looked to the door, where the first guests were beginning to arrive. "Here they come. Do you suppose there'll be any handsome straight men with big hearts, a love of music, and a healthy contempt for *nouvelle* society?"

"Plenty," I said, "but they'll all be bussing tables."

"You're probably right. Speaking of tables, have you found where they plunked us yet?"

We inspected various place cards and finally found our names at a table for four a few yards back from the reception desk and by the window. It wasn't one of the VIP tables that ringed the dance floor, but it wasn't nearly as far back as I'd supposed we'd be put. More surprising still, we were sitting with Kitty and her date, Ham Yearwood.

"Not bad seats for the hired help," I said.

"Yes," agreed Claire. "I suspect Elsa was nervous and wanted to make sure the faces close enough for her to see were friendly ones. Kitty may not be a cheerleader, but you and Ham are reliable support—so here we all are."

By now the guests were flooding in with a punctuality unusual for this type of bash. It was, I supposed, a sign of the rabid anticipation Elsa had inspired that no one wanted to miss a minute of bracing preshow speculation.

Claire's agreement called for her to play with the band before and during the show, then be relieved afterward. We kissed good luck and she shoved off to the ivories. I grabbed some champagne and commenced happily ogling the celebs while keeping an eye peeled for Tommy.

Daisy Winters, her jaw a bit set after her dressing room rout, was hard at work, foraging for items. I couldn't resist getting her version of events, so I tried intercepting her en route to Phil Donahue and Marlo.

"Hi! You manage to calm Elsa down?"

"Yes, she's much calmer," said Daisy without breaking her stride.

Peter had just come in and was chatting with Hoot and a few business types by the entrance. I went over to say hi, and as I hovered in the no-man's-land of the unintroduced, my eyes wandered to the long corridor outside. They were greeted by those of Horsey Kimball, who was navigating the hall like a disdainful galleon approaching some new and barbarous port. Her snowy hair was piled high, accentuating a long equine face with eyelids that drooped as though equipped with sash weights. Her gown suggested Elizabethan haute couture. It was a long, wide-skirted, green velvet number with satin ruffles surrounding the décolletage, puffed sleeves, and this vast, round piece spreading up from her shoulders and surrounding her head like a shrine. I remember thinking, Oh, well, if she's bored by the concert, she can probably pick up satellite channels.

Champion caught sight of her and seemed to do that nose-breathing thing he does when attempting to marshal his inner resources.

Peter did not, so far as I'd observed, share his wife's zeal for social climbing, feeling the whole concept rested on the preposterous assumption that there was any higher for him to go. He was, however, grimly aware that there were people who believed that in the skyscraper of New York society, his own quarters were adjacent to the laundry room, and that if these people ever held a rally, the lady now approaching would be there with pom-poms. But just as she was there only for her kitties, he had his Kitty to think of, too, not to mention his wife, and there was nothing to do but grin and get through.

Horsey swept up the stairs on her balding escort's arm and advanced on Champion with a ceremonious smile.

"Pita," she said grimly, "how lovely to see you."

"Pita" returned the sentiment and complimented her dress. Horsey introduced her escort, saying he was "of the Met" but declining to specify opera, museum, or insurance company. Peter introduced his colleagues, then Hoot, and finally me, explaining my role in the evening. Horsey granted me an exquisitely limp handshake and said, "How very proud and excited you must be. My sister has described Elsa's singing with even more than her customary effusiveness, so I can imagine what a treat lays in wait for us."

"Certainly a perfect setting for Elsa, huh?" remarked Hoot.

Horsey, as if alerted to her surroundings for the first time, turned and inspected the place through her great droopy eyes.

"Isn't it?" she said with masterful ambiguity. "So festive. I remember I was here before once when I was a mere teenager."

Given her archaic appearance and imperial demeanor, I was tempted to remark that when she was a mere teenager this place was probably a meadow, but I ignored this socially suicidal impulse. Champion made some barbed comment on how very *worthy* a cause it was all for, and Horsey regally ignored it.

"I'm delighted to find you in sympathy," she replied, surveying the crowd. "Ah, there's darling Mrs. Hemple. So helpful with the organizing. I must go thank her. I'm sure I'll see you all later."

With that Horsey hoisted her sails and navigated toward Mrs. Hemple. I smiled to note that as she did, Daisy Winters was heading straight for her port side like an invasion of pirates. I looked to Champion, who pulled a droll face at me in a show of solidarity between one son of the hoi polloi and another. I clapped his shoulder and went off in search of champagne.

I meandered through the throng, delightedly rubbing elbows with politicians and film stars, all the while watching the door for any sign of Boyd and Tommy. A few people, including some well-known closeted celebs, recognized me from the media blitz and introduced themselves, only to immediately commence pumping for dirt on Elsa. It would, I knew, be bad form to dish my employer, but I couldn't resist dropping a few wry hints about her terror of facing them. After a while I began to wonder myself how much Elsa's terror had abated under the signora's ministrations. I decided to pay a quick visit backstage to see.

I left the Rainbow Room and proceeded to the elevators. As I pressed the down button, the elevator in front of me opened, disgorging a Broadway director, three film stars, a fashion designer, several socialites, and a well-known East Side restaurateur named Agnes Fabrizio.

"Philip!"

"Aggie!"

My emotions on seeing her were mixed. On the one hand, I liked the old gal a lot. During the dark days of Gilbert's engagement to Moira Finch, she'd employed us and proved a genuine lifesaver. On the other hand, she was Gilbert's step-aunt and if she'd turned up in this unforeseen fashion, could Gilbert be far behind? A second glance confirmed that Gilbert was, in fact, about ten inches behind.

"*Hah!*" said Aggie with her signature firecracker laugh. "Look at his face, Gilbert. And me without a camera!"

"What the fuck are you doing here!" I sputtered.

"Aggie invited me," said Gilbert simply. "Is that Connie Chung?"

"I did *not* invite him. He invited *me* to scare up a few tickets—and if you think *that* was easy . . . ! But he promised me some swell gossip if I came through, and boy, did he deliver!"

"You *idiot!* What if Champion sees you?"

"We thought of that," said Aggie. "He's Henri's cousin. Let's go in, hon. I'm dying of thirst."

Gilbert smiled angelically and, taking his aunt by the arm of her scarlet-and-gold beaded jacket, steered her toward the Rainbow Room.

"*So,*" she said, her voice distressingly robust, "I *have* to meet the sister. Could you introduce us? Wait, of *course* you can't! Not after that business under the desk! Well, I'll meet her on my own, then, and you can introduce me to this marvelous beau of yours and Boyd Larkin. Who do you think Boyd will bring for a beard?"

Seventeen

The really galling thing was that I didn't see it coming. Which, of course, I should have. Hadn't I mere weeks ago sat, stunned and disbelieving, as Gilbert loomed into view in the dining room of the *Siren?* Did I not stumble over him that very evening in the seemingly impenetrable confines of Champion's office? After he'd repeatedly displayed this hideous gift for turning up, unbidden, in places to which he could not possibly have gained access, did I really suppose he'd be kept from entering the Rainbow Room by a mere *ticket shortage?* It was like thinking Hitler could have been barred from the Sudetenland through the judicious use of scarecrows.

I did not waste valuable time on these bitter reflections. They passed through my mind in the fleeting instant required to kick an elevator door and mutter the word *fuck* six or seven times. This had a calming effect and enabled me to ponder my dilemma.

It had been a nasty shock to find Aunt Aggie present and clutching a scorecard, but I decided, on reflection, that she was the least of my concerns. True, she was a boisterous old girl with a big appetite for other people's secrets, but we'd shared some doozies with her in the past and she'd always proved a model of discretion. The problem was Gilbert.

His intentions were obvious. He planned to monopolize Tommy to the greatest possible extent, stealing my thunder and telling him God knows what monstrous falsehoods concerning the events on board the *Siren.* The question was how, short of homicide, to prevent this?

I advanced now into the ballroom, and my first glimpse of him confirmed my suspicions. He and Aggie were dancing to a medley from—what else?—*Cats*, but even as he danced his neck craned this way and that, his beady eyes scouring the room for Tommy.

Oh, dear, I thought, has Claire seen him?

I looked to the piano, and sure enough, her expression contained more ashen horror than Andrew Lloyd Webber alone could account for. Her eyes caught mine. She jerked her head toward Gilbert on the dance floor and then back to me, raising her eyebrows in frenzied inquisition. *What*, she was asking, *is he doing here?* I pantomimed stunned incomprehension. She jerked her head back to Gilbert and his partner, then bugged her eyes even more wildly. *Is that his* aunt Aggie *he's dancing with?* I nodded. She then jerked her head to where Champion stood near the dance floor, chatting with Joy and Spark. *What's going to happen if they recognize him?* There was, of course, no way to pantomime "He'll claim to be Henri's cousin," without going for a "sounds like," which seemed unduly elaborate. I shrugged frantically, waved a hasty good-bye, and fled to the elevator bank, where I paced in nervous circles, pondering my next maneuver.

Clearly there'd be no keeping Gilbert from speaking to Tommy and telling whatever vile lies he wished. But, I reasoned, whoever hits first, hits best. I would reach Tommy before the performance and present my evidence, earning his stunned admiration. Then, my voice dripping with contempt, I would tell him how the deranged, mono-lingual Gilbert had posed as a French waiter, jeopardized our entire operation to no purpose, and then further imperiled our enterprise by showing up here under Champion's own nose. After that, Gilbert could say what he liked. Tommy, forewarned, would scorn his falsehoods and probably suggest he leave the party before he did any further damage.

There was only one flaw in this plan—how was I to play my tape for Tommy? I'd originally planned to present it to him at his apartment, where this would have posed no problem, but how could I play it for him *here?*

As I wrestled with this conundrum, an elevator opened and who should emerge but Tommy himself, his fabulously aristocratic features rendered still more paralyzingly sexy by a light coat of bronze.

"Philip!"

"There you are!"

"Well, hello, stranger!" bubbled Boyd, jauntily stepping out from behind Tommy. "You can talk to me, I'm not wired."

Both were with dates, and they introduced them to me. Tommy's was a woman named Amanda, the sixtyish editor-in-chief of *Choice*. Boyd's required no introduction—she was Dame Lottie Haverford, a world-renowned opera singer who was his latest media "romance." I suppose he brought the great diva in the hope that Elsa would spot her in the audience and be thoroughly unnerved.

"A pleasure to meet you, Mr. Cavanaugh. What an exciting night this must be for you!"

She was imposing up close but seemed chummy enough for a woman who could function as an air traffic controller without benefit of radio. But the sight of this famous diva put me in mind of a somewhat less legendary diva, the Signora di Corteggiano of the bogus inspirational tapes. If Elsa had not yet begun listening to a tape, might it not be possible to borrow her Walkman for, say, five minutes, play Tommy my treasure, then return the device to Elsa? I knew that if she went for it, found it missing, then learned I'd taken it, there'd be hell to pay, but given the stakes, I was willing to chance it.

I clasped my hands to my bosom in humble supplication and said I'd been lurking by the elevators in the hopes of having a private word with Tommy upon his arrival. I hoped they didn't find me rude, but it was, I assured them, a matter of great importance. Their eyebrows danced a bit, but they relinquished Tommy to me, saying we'd all catch up inside.

"Why, Philip!" said Tommy after they'd gone. "Such drama! Whatever's happened?"

"I can't say yet, but give me three minutes and I'll give you something that will knock your socks off."

"Don't be a tease, now. Tell me what it is."

"This," I said, flashing my cassette. "Pure dynamite! I have to go get a machine to play it for you, but I promise it'll be worth it!"

I was about to suggest he wait in the bar but realized that was no good. Gilbert would see Boyd come in and then hunt Tommy down in no time.

"Just come with me," I said, and yanked him into an elevator.

We went down a floor and I asked him to wait by the elevator, saying I'd be right back. He consented warily, and I dashed round the corner to Elsa's dressing room. Peter's Cro-Magnons were still standing guard, but they knew I was on the list and let me pass.

I hurried through the short inside hall into the suite, and there was Elsa, sitting in the middle of the room. She was fully costumed now in a gown that resembled Bob Mackie's interpretation of a vestal virgin. Her manner too was as different from my last glimpse of her as could have been imagined.

"Hello, Philip," she said with the unflappable serenity of a Buddhist on Valium.

"Hi! Gosh, you look wonderful!"

"I feel wonderful. The signora has hypnotized me."

"Ah."

"She did it with a ruby pendant. Now I'm here but I'm not here, and nothing can hurt me because I'm surrounded by light."

"Oh, good."

I smiled spiritually even as my eyes circled the room searching for the large Vuitton bag in which she'd carried her various supplies. I looked behind me and saw it on the floor in the little entry hall.

"Laaaaaaaaa," sang Elsa. "Can you hear how open my throat is?"

"Yes. It's miraculous. Can I use your bathroom?"

"Of course."

I ducked into the hall and, gingerly lifting the bag, dragged it into the john and commenced rifling through it. There was a hair dryer, an impressive-looking camera, and, at the bottom under some scarves, Elsa's slick, state-of-the-art Walkman, complete with headphones. I plucked it out, removed the cassette from my jacket, popped it in, then slipped the whole thing into my pocket. It was a sleek little machine and the bulge was barely discernible.

As I squatted to repack the bag I heard the dressing room door open. I froze.

"Here we are, darling! Just what the doctor ordered!"

Thank God—it was only Millie! I sighed with relief and slipped out of the john, shoving the Vuitton bag back where I found it. I emerged from the hall and greeted Millie, who held a bottle in one hand and clutched two champagne flutes in the other.

"Philip!" she twittered. "Just in time for a glass of bubbly!"

"Champagne?"

"You are an angel, Millie," Elsa said dreamily.

I frowned. I wasn't sure how shrewd it was of Elsa to go imbibing half an hour before showtime. But then I remembered how well she'd performed on the yacht when all but fermented and decided a glass or two couldn't hurt. As for me, though, I had better things to do than dawdle over drinks.

"No, thanks! I have to run."

"Be a dear, then," said Millie, "and hold the glasses while I pour."

Suppressing a groan of impatience, I took the flutes while Millie stripped the foil and, with a practiced hand, twisted the cage off. As she seized the cork and began yanking on it, she looked up at me with sudden vivacity.

"Oh, Philip! I just ran into a great fan of yours!"

"Oh?"

"Yes! A lovely man named Tommy Parker!"

And with that she gave a great yank, sending a geyser of Dom Pérignon cascading onto my tuxedo jacket and flooding the very pocket that contained the tape machine.

"Shit!" I said suavely, and, dropping one of the flutes to the carpet, ripped the machine from my pocket before it was hopelessly short-circuited and flung it to the dry safety of the sofa.

"Dreadfully sorry!" cried Millie. "Elsa, give me that towel there!"

Elsa languidly complied, and Millie put the bottle down and began rubbing at my pocket.

"Thank you, Elsa! Goodness! I'm glad at least I didn't get any on *you!*"

"You couldn't have," said Elsa matter-of-factly. "I'm surrounded by light."

"Are you really? Oh, dear, Philip, you're soaked. Anyway, this Mr. Parker was the gentleman who first told me about you and Claire. I mean," she added hastily, "about your musical. He told me I should go see it, which I did."

"Philip," asked Elsa, "was that my recorder you had in there?"

"No! It's mine! I brought it to tape the show! I hope you don't mind!"

"Not at all."

"Anyway, this Mr. Parker is quite an important man. He works for Mister—"

"Gotta run!" I said, and, giving Elsa a peck on the cheek, scrambled to the sofa, grabbed the recorder, and bolted from the room. Tommy, thank God, was still waiting in the foyer.

"Well," he said, pressing for the elevator, "guess who *I* just met?"

"I know. She told Elsa all about you, but I don't think it registered. Elsa's been hypnotized."

"If she were smarter," said Tommy, "she'd hypnotize the audience."

We returned to the main floor, where I took the recorder from my pocket and handed it to Tommy.

"This," I said with a debonair smirk, "is the gossip equivalent of the Dead Sea scrolls!"

Knowing Gilbert would be on the prowl, I suggested to Tommy we find a spot where he could listen undisturbed. Privacy would also, I knew, greatly enhance the odds of jubilant hugs and lingering kisses. I suggested the men's lounge, praying there'd be no attendant on hand to discourage clinches. We banged a right toward the Promenade Bar, then another right toward Rainbow and Stars, then trotted up the curved stairway toward the men's lounge. And there, just emerging from the lounge, was a depressingly familiar face.

"*There* you are, Tommy!" said Gilbert. "Boyd told me I'd find you with this one. How tanned you look. Has Philip been telling you about our triumph?"

It's an odd feeling to stand before a fellow you've loved like a brother half your life and be gripped by a keen desire to see his arms and legs tied to four strong horses. But as Gilbert stood there, grinning his insufferably cherubic grin, I couldn't imagine a single mode of demise so gruesome as to be worse than he deserved.

"Gilbert!" said Tommy, hugging him. "Leave it to you to crash the big event!"

"Wouldn't have missed it. Something the matter, Philly? You look nauseous."

"Not at all."

"So, Tommy! Has Philip been filling you in on my—I should, I suppose, really say *our*—exploits?"

"Not yet, no. He's kept me in the most intolerable suspense."

"Has he?" said Gilbert. "Well, step into my office and all will be revealed."

He motioned us into the poshly tiled confines of the men's lounge, where a thin, elderly attendant in a white jacket greeted us with a polite nod.

"Hello," said Gilbert in his debonair Tommy mode. "My associates and I need to discuss a matter of some delicacy. I trust we may rely on you to repeat nothing of what you hear?"

"Yes, sir. It's not like me to tell tales out of school."

"Capital," said Gilbert. "Tommy, you have the tape, I see. Excellent! What happened, dear, is this—"

"Perhaps *I* should explain, Gilbert," I said with commendable restraint for a man whose mind had become a charnel house. "You have this tendency to embroider."

"Could *someone* explain, and quickly?" said Tommy with a meaningful glance at his watch.

"Of course," said Gilbert. "The two of us were on board the *Siren* a few weeks ago—"

"*I'd* been invited—"

"And I was masquerading as a French waiter, which, if I do say so myself, was rather a—"

"Needless risk, and I told him so. Anyway, Saturday night I got into Peter's private office—"

"Some time after I'd already done so—"

"And I was looking things over when I heard Peter coming, so I hid under the desk, where Gilbert was already *cringing*—"

"Manning the controls of Peter's built-in taping system—"

"No, that was *me*, dear, so *I*—"

"So *we* recorded what happened, and *this*," he said, pointing to the Walkman, "was the result!"

Tommy eagerly placed the headphones on his head and pressed the play button. He frowned slightly and pushed the volume up as high as it would go. Gilbert and I held our breath as we watched his face, which, amazingly, betrayed no surprise whatsoever.

"What," he inquired at length, "is the significance of this?"

"Don't you recognize them? It's Peter and Kitty!"

"Peter and *Kitty?*" he asked, puzzled. "All *I* hear are crashing waves and some daft Italian woman whispering that I'm a seagull adrift over an ocean of melody. Doesn't sound a bit like Kitty. You look pale, Philip. Is something the matter?"

Eighteen

I clung for an instant to the pathetic hope that I'd somehow gotten hold of one of the signora's cassettes at a rehearsal, taken it home, and then brought it to the opening in lieu of the Kitty tape. But then I recalled listening to the sex tape just before placing it in my pocket and knew with crushing certainty that the machine in Tommy's hand was not the one I'd flung to the sofa when Millie bathed me in champagne. Clearly there had been two machines—this one, which Elsa had prepared for use, and a second one, stored as a backup in the Vuitton bag in the event of a malfunction. Some malignant god had contrived to place the first machine on the same sofa where I'd tossed the backup, and in my rush to escape, I'd snatched the wrong one, leaving behind my tinderbox of scandal.

The question, I knew, as I tore through the lobby, was this: Had the signora's hypnosis so quelled Elsa's anxieties that she'd seen no need of further therapy, or had she, proceeding on the theory that one can never have too much nirvana, decided to supplement the hypnosis with a soothing inspirational tape?

I careened from the elevator to the dressing room in such haste that I hardly noted the curious absence of Elsa's bodyguards. I burst into the room, Elsa's machine clutched in my outstretched hand like the baton in some infernal relay race. I pulled up short and, panting for breath, took in the scene.

It did not require a Holmesian acuity of perception to determine which scenario had prevailed. If the wires trailing from Elsa's ears to the recorder she clutched, white-knuckled, on her lap left any doubt, her facial expression removed it. It was that same helpless stare of horror you see on the faces of women in fifties science fiction movies, when they're about to be killed by some creature it's still too early in the movie to see.

"Shhh! Be very quiet, Philip!"

I started, amazed to see that Millie was still present and mysteriously unfazed by her friend's grotesque expression.

"Leave her be," said Millie, a finger to her lips. "She's meditating with the signora's tape. Look at her! Such fierce concentration!"

Ignoring Millie's plea for silence, I ran to Elsa's side and proffered my recorder.

"Oh, God, Elsa," I said, "I'm *really*, really sorry! I took your Walkman by mistake, so if you'll just give me mine back—"

I reached to take it, but Elsa shook her head madly and swiveled on her chair, hunching over to protect her bitter prize. She might not have been crazy about what she was listening to, but she was determined to hear every awful word of it.

"Elsa, please!" I implored. I got no further, though, before the door was flung open and Daisy Winters charged in like an affectionate terrorist.

"Elsa, sweetie! Don't you look just *marvelous!*" cried Daisy, who was in no position to be frank.

"Daisy!" said Millie.

"Forgive me for barging in, hon, but I was damned if I wasn't gonna get *something* for my readers about how you feel in these moments before you go on. You know, some real inside, heartfelt— are you all right?"

"She's meditating," explained Millie.

"I won't interrupt, then," said Daisy, pulling up a chair. "Just sum up your emotions for me in one word, okay?"

Even the most publicity-addicted of chanteuses finds there are moments in her life when she does not wish to open her heart to a gossip columnist. For Elsa, this was unquestionably such a moment. She gazed briefly at Daisy, winced, and then shut her eyes tightly as though willing her to vanish.

"She can't talk now, dear," said Millie. "She's in a trance, you know."

"A *trance*, huh?" said Daisy, who'd heard that one before.

"Yes. She's been hypnotized, and now she's listening to a meditation tape. She may not look it, but she feels *very* peaceful."

Daisy sardonically inquired when Elsa would be peaceful enough to chat, and I said she couldn't possibly do so until after the performance.

"Listen, snowflake," said Daisy. "I went through a lotta trouble to get in here. You think it was easy gettin' rid of those goons out there?"

"How'd you do it?" I asked.

"Had a waiter give 'em a note sayin' Peter needed 'em in the dining room pronto. When you've been around long as *I* have," she boasted, "you learn a few tricks about—"

Before she could share any pointers, the goons came galumphing down the hall outside, anxiously calling Elsa's name. Daisy, muttering "Shit!" made a beeline for the bathroom. As she reached for the knob, though, the guards entered and, immediately identifying her as the evil genius behind their fool's errand, grabbed her by the arms.

"Elsa, baby!" she screamed. "Tell them how you invited me in!"

"Elsa's meditating," I said butchly, "and this woman's bothering her!"

The guards, noting that Elsa indeed looked bothered, lifted the old gossipeuse two feet off the floor and bore her away amid threats, obscenities, and kicks to their shins.

"Millie," I said, "you'd better go unruffle her feathers."

"Yes, I'd better!" said Millie, terrified lest any of Daisy's wrath accrue to her. She flew out of the room, leaving me to the ruins of Elsa.

The earphones were still in place and she was slumped back on her chair, her long nails splayed across her eyes as her head rocked from side to side, a metronome of shock and denial. The machine was now unprotected on her lap. I reached out and switched it off.

"*Please*, Elsa. You really don't want to listen to that."

"Too late! I've heard it all!" she sobbed. "You hateful, hateful man! How could you bring such a thing to me! Tonight of all nights!"

"I'm sorry! I didn't bring it for *you*."

"Then who *did* you bring it for?"

I felt that, all things considered, this was not a good topic to get into, so I just begged her to calm down and seek therapy in one of the signora's real tapes. Her impulse, though, ran less toward Signora di Corteggiano than to Dom Pérignon. She reached for her glass, but her trembling fingers knocked it over, drenching her cosmetics and telegrams. She howled in anguish and, seizing the half-full bottle, raised it to her lips and drank greedily while clutching the recorder to her bosom.

It was this happy sight that greeted Peter as he sauntered in with a brash smile and a rectangular Tiffany box extended munificently in his hand.

"*Whoa*, baby!" He laughed, failing at first glance to gauge his wife's mood. "Take it easy!"

Elsa lowered the bottle slowly. She said nothing but instead fixed her husband with a small, indescribably bitter smile.

"What are you lookin' so mad about, huh? Wait, I know—it's Daisy, right? Barging in here like that! Well, don't you worry—I told the boys to see her straight back to her table, okay? And maybe this'll make you feel better."

He winked roguishly at me and extended the long rectangular box to Elsa, who, smiling more bitterly still, plucked it from his palm and smashed him across the nose with it.

"Hey!" howled Peter, staggering backward onto the sofa. "What the fuck is wrong with you!"

"Take it!" screamed Elsa.

It was now obvious that a full meltdown was in progress, and the containment dome was made of rather thin Styrofoam. She rose from her seat and viciously hurled the jewelry box at him, catching him smack on the jaw.

"*Take it! Give it to your slut!*"

"*What* slut?" asked Peter, managing unwisely to suggest a range of candidates.

"My *sister!* Your little *goddess! Your fucking Aphrodite!*"

Peter flinched violently and seemed about to speak when he became aware of my inopportune presence.

"What are *you* doing here! Get the fuck out—*now!*"

I said I'd be happy to go if I could just have my Walkman back. I grabbed for it, but Elsa clutched it to her bosom.

"You keep away from this! It's *mine!* It's my proof!"

"Proof of what?" snapped Peter.

"You didn't know about it, did you?" sneered Elsa. She jabbed a finger toward me. "*This* one made a tape of your disgusting games on the boat!"

"*What?*" said Peter, eyeing me with incredulous rage. "*You* did this to us? *You* got her in this state?"

"Not advertently, no."

He advanced toward me, then decided abruptly that my dismantling was not an immediate priority, besides which I was taller than he was. He wheeled on Elsa instead.

"Give me that tape!"

Elsa cried, "Never!" and Peter made a dive for it. She sidestepped him and he tripped over her chair, crashing into the dressing table. Elsa hurled an ashtray at him, shattering the mirror. Peter yelped in surprise and scrambled for cover under the table. Elsa seized the champagne bottle and, pausing only to drain its contents, began whumping him on his lower back with the empty bottle. Peter cursed imaginatively and tried to maneuver himself farther under the vanity.

"That's all my career was to you!" she screamed between blows. "Something to keep me busy so you could have your disgusting way with my filthy sister! I hate you! *I hate you!*"

"*Cara!*" said Signora di Corteggiano, sweeping in from the hall.

She gasped, and her horrified eyes drank in the scene. She could not guess what had happened, but one thing was clear: her pupil was no longer surrounded by light.

"*Signorrrrra!*" wailed Elsa.

She sobbed and extended her arms like a child wanting to be picked up. This gesture involved dropping both the bottle and the Walkman.

As Elsa lurched toward her guru, I nipped behind them and snatched up the machine. Peter, turning around under the dressing table, saw me do this and shrilly demanded that I hand it over. I disappointed him and bolted from the room as Elsa and Peter screamed for me to stop.

Charging down the hall, I ran past the guards, who were returning from escorting Daisy to her table.

"*Go to the dressing room! Peter needs you!*" I shouted, and the guards—who could, it seemed, fall for this ploy any number of times in succession—stampeded to the rescue, colliding with Elsa, who was on the way out. I ran toward the elevators as Elsa shrieked for the guards to stop me.

I jabbed a button and an elevator opened. I jumped in and pressed 65. Peering apprehensively through the closing doors, I saw Peter huffing his way toward me, the others right behind him. The doors shut and I heard the unmistakable *whump* of a homicidal billionaire hurling his body against them.

Reaching the main floor, I ran straight to the men's lounge, where I found Gilbert alone, save for the attendant, and looking miffed.

"Where's Tommy?" I gasped.

"Well, honestly, Philip! He couldn't wait here forever. He was being rude to his friends. Did you get the tape?"

"Yes!"

"Any trouble?"

"You might say."

I pulled him into a corner and informed him in low tones of the debacle that had just occurred.

"Oh, geez, Louise!" fumed Gilbert. "Leave it to you! What are you gonna do now?"

I said that if I could just get to the Rainbow Room unlynched, I could deliver the tape to Tommy. This posed no small problem, though, as Peter, Elsa, the signora, and the brothers Einstein would even now be combing the halls for me.

This assessment, however bleak, was soon proved the height of optimism. They were not combing the halls but were this moment piling into the men's lounge. Some benevolent stranger, I supposed, had observed my flight path and offered a helpful "He went thataway."

Champion led the pack, but Elsa, the signora, and the boys were right behind him. He glared menacingly and, wheezing from the chase, extended his hand and said, "Hand it over, you little shit."

Elsa elbowed him aside, insisting the cassette be delivered to no one but her. Meanwhile Gilbert and I closed ranks and backed away.

"I absolutely insist that you—" she began, then stopped, her jaw dropping low. "*Henri!* What are you doing here?"

"*Je ne suis pas Henri! Ee's ma koo-zan,*" said Gilbert, and, bowing politely, hightailed it through the door.

Champion rudely shoved his spouse aside and advanced grimly. I continued my retreat to the rear of the lounge until my back was literally against the wall.

The wall, however, was not smooth. There was something poking uncomfortably into my back. And unless I missed my guess, the protruding object was a doorknob. Wasting no speculation as to where the door might lead, I wheeled, plunged through it, and pushed it shut behind me, which took a certain effort, as Peter had shoved a few fingers through.

I found myself in a larger but more dimly lit space. The decor, with its accent on gray concrete slabs, meters, and toggle switches, suggested a generator room, and a lovelier generator room I'd never laid eyes on. There was a second door some yards away, and as Peter was now charging in from the men's room, screaming threats of castration, I thought I'd shove along and see where it led.

I sprinted through it, slamming it behind me, and found myself in a shabby corridor lined with small dressing rooms. I could hear music now and chatter and realized, with a thrill of relief, that I was getting close to the Rainbow Room itself. I wondered how this could be, as the men's room was one floor *above* the Rainbow Room. This mystery was soon solved.

The hall ended, breaking off in two directions. I turned right arbitrarily. I jogged a few steps, and suddenly the dining room came into view. I could see the reception desk and the tables near it, even Claire at the piano. I was, however, gazing *down* at them from some upper level. I trotted a few more steps and stopped short. I realized I was in the wing space just behind the grand staircase that led down to the stage, a staircase used exclusively by headlining performers and the Rockettes. I could, in short, enter the room, but in rather a splashier fashion than I cared to.

I suppose, in retrospect, that one bug-eyed young homosexual bounding down the grand staircase in a rumpled tux would not have aroused much comment. At the time, though, I felt shy, and this made me hesitate. And as the proverb states, He who hesitates is grabbed by the neck and shoved roughly against the nearest wall.

"Hand it over!" snarled Champion. I tried to twist away, but he gripped me firmly by the neck as his spare hand pawed at my pockets.

And came up empty.

"*Where is it?*" he hissed, doing disagreeable things to my Adam's apple. I shrugged madly, for I sincerely hadn't a clue. By now Elsa, the signora, and the goons had caught up and were standing by, awaiting developments.

I glanced helplessly to my right, where I could see the entrance to the dining room. Peter followed my gaze, so we were both watching when Gilbert jauntily entered the room, snapping his fingers in time to the music. He glanced over at Claire, and I waved from above to catch his attention. He saw us and waved cheerfully. Then, grinning, he produced the Walkman from his pocket, raised his thumb to his nose, wiggled his fingers, and sambaed off toward the dance floor.

This had a rather deflating effect on us. We all stood there feeling vexed, silly, and uncomfortably aware that we were visible to anyone who might gaze up from any of several tables. Champion stopped trying to make cider from my Adam's apple and told the goons to make themselves scarce. He asked what Gilbert planned to do with the tape. I said I wasn't sure, but I'd keep him posted.

Elsa had turned her attention away from us and was now gazing numbly out at the room. It had obviously crossed her mind that it contained everyone in the world who remotely mattered to her and that they'd each spent five hundred dollars to watch her perform a concert that should have begun several minutes ago. This thought affected her powerfully. She moaned and shook her head, her face a mask of pain and terror. If you'd handed her an asp, she'd have used it.

"Nooooooo," she sobbed, and, pitching forward, collapsed heavily into the signora's arms.

"She can't possibly go on," grunted the signora. "You must go immediately and make arrangements!"

A debate erupted as to how long the signora would need to bring her pupil to a state where singing was conceivable and what excuse might be given for the delay. So intent was our discussion that we quite overlooked our visibility to those spectators at or near the maître d's desk.

Horsey Kimball, a demon for punctuality, advanced now to this desk to ask an organizer when Peter would appear and give the signal to proceed. This put her in an excellent position to gaze up past the bandstand and note that Elsa and her husband, voice teacher, and songwriter were even now chatting in the wings. She smiled and gave us a regal wave of acknowledgment. Champion waved back, albeit more frantically, and violently mouthed, *Not yet!*

Horsey, nearsighted but vain about glasses, could not detect moving lips from this distance, let alone read them. She saw the wave, though, and, interpreting this as she chose, sailed out of our sight line and toward the stage. A moment later she tapped gently on the microphone. The music and conversation fell silent. Horsey's chairwoman voice, which has a quality I can only call chilly warmth, filled the room.

"Hello. Thank you all very much for coming. Kindly resume your seats now. We're ready to begin."

Nineteen

On hearing these words, Elsa slid, stricken, to the floor. From her throat came a soft, high-pitched sound like kittens drowning in a sack.

The signora crossed herself and sank creakily to her knees. She tore open her evening bag and fished out a hankie and a ruby pendant. With one hand she began making desperate repairs to her pupil's tear-ravaged makeup, even as the other swung the pendant before Elsa's bulging eyes.

"Listen to my voice! I will count backward from three!"

Meanwhile, on stage, Horsey continued, ignorant of the drama unfolding just yards away.

"I hope that I will not strain your patience if, before I introduce our star, I tell you all about the worthy cause to which she has generously donated her time and great talent. I shall try to be brief, as I've just glimpsed Elsa in the wings and she seemed very eager to get started."

Elsa let out a low, awful wail, as if she'd already died and commenced haunting the place. Peter and I rushed in and hoisted her to her feet, even as the signora kept up her fevered efforts at hypnosis.

"You are floating on a beautiful cloud of melody," said the signora.

"The hell I am," said Elsa.

It occurred to me that my presence was probably not much of a calming influence. Glancing behind me, I saw more stairs on the other side of the hall. I tiptoed down these and found myself in the front left corner of the dining room. My table was on the other side of the room, and I wended toward it as Horsey, in throbbing tones, recounted the history of her own dear Abercrombie, a half-blind tabby rescued from early death and obscurity by the vigilant folk of Paws to Consider.

Reaching my table, I was startled to find it empty. Claire, of course, was at the piano, but where the hell were Kitty and Ham Yearwood? Was Kitty, envious of the attention lavished on Elsa, boycotting the festivities? I hoped so, as Elsa would have enough trouble muddling through without Aphrodite yawning at her from ringside.

I took my seat. I tried to attend Horsey's remarks but heard little; I was too busy looking at Claire. Claire's view of the wings was the best in the house, and she kept stealing peeks at them through splayed fingers, like someone watching a film with lots of operating room footage.

Alas, unlike most speakers who promise brevity, Horsey kept her word, wrapping up the whole spiel in under three minutes.

"And now," she concluded grandly, "the moment we have all so breathlessly awaited." She squinted into the wings. "There's Elsa now, simply raring to go! Hello!" she called with a little wave. "Forgive me for keeping you waiting!"

She returned her gaze to the audience. "With no further preamble, then, I present to you the beautiful and very talented—Elsa Champion!"

The crowd erupted into thrilled applause. The band members raised their instruments and looked to Claire. Her lips moved briefly in what can only have been prayer, and bringing her hands to the keys, she gave them the downbeat, whereupon they burst into a lush, extravagant fanfare.

There was a long, intolerably suspenseful moment when it seemed Elsa would never appear at all. But then she suddenly materialized at the top of the stairs, entering in a wobbly burst of speed that suggested a brisk shove from behind. She gripped the balcony rail to keep from falling, then stood there, staring into the follow spot like a raccoon caught in the beams of an oncoming truck.

It was not a graceful entrance, but it had a certain drama to it, and the applause swelled thunderously. Elsa snapped out of her shock and attempted a smile. The result didn't resemble a real smile so much as cooperation with a dentist, but it was better than nothing. I detected movement on the opposite side of the room and saw that Peter had followed my escape route and taken his place at the ringside table he shared with Joy and Spark.

The band, which hadn't bargained on so protracted an entrance, ran out of music and had to start the fanfare over from the beginning. By now the crowd definitely sensed that all was not well with Elsa, though none could guess yet just how wrong things were. Heads converged all over the room as gossips rushed to whisper their appraisals. Others, feeling a benevolent impulse to calm Elsa's obvious nerves, began shouting "Elsa!" or "Brava!" and the applause grew heavier still.

Elsa, that awful smile frozen on her lips, began descending toward the stage with all the vivacity of a homeowner creeping downstairs in the dead of night to investigate noises in the kitchen. She took her time, casting several backward glances at the signora, who, I supposed, was still in the wings, swinging that pendant for all it was worth. The delay compelled the band to begin a third fanfare, which they played much slower, as nobody wanted a fourth. Eventually Elsa reached the microphone.

The audience, exhausted from applauding, fell silent, as did the band. Claire looked to Elsa, her eyes pleading for some assurance that if she played the intro to the opening song, Elsa would come in on cue and sing the damn thing. After a long, painful moment, Claire decided Elsa was as ready as she'd get and, with a quiet flourish, began the solo piano intro, cutting the rehearsal tempo in half.

You might, given our recent run of luck, be justified in supposing that Dame Fortune had turned utterly against us and resolved pitilessly to withhold all aid and succor. She had, however, vouchsafed us, amid this deluge of disaster, one droplet of hope.

"I Sing," the song we'd written for Elsa's opening, was a humorous ditty describing Elsa's love of music and the way she looked to it as a source of comfort whenever she was down at heart. It was possible the lyric would lead the spectators to suppose Elsa's shambles of an entrance had been an elaborate joke to set up the song. If so, they'd laugh all the harder, which might, God willing, give Elsa the confidence to slog through the rest of the set. As Claire finished the intro I mumbled a prayer that this scenario might come to pass.

The final chord hung interminably in the air. Just when I thought someone, most likely me, would scream from the suspense, Elsa opened her mouth and, in a voice like death, began to sing:

> *When my heart sinks low,*
> *When I'm in distress . . .*

The faintest ripple of amusement was heard, indicating that a few had already decided the horribly tense entrance was a put-on. Elsa, who'd never heard laughs so early with the number, gave a startled blink, then continued:

> *When I'm dealt a blow*
> *By the IRS . . .*

This got a solid response and a buzz of whispers even louder than the laugh.

> *Do I moan and mope?*
> *Do I lose all hope?*
> *Nope.*
> *For I've learned to cope. . . .*

Now the crowd was laughing and slapping the tables, amused and relieved that the stage fright had all been part of the act. Oh, that Elsa! they must have thought. She certainly knows how to get an audience's attention. The band joined the piano, and the tempo picked up. Even Elsa seemed a shade more assured.

> *When misfortune swoops,*
> *When my spirit droops*
> *When the gentleman cutting my hair says, "Oops!"*
> *Whatever the type*
> *Of nasty swipe*
> *That fate may bring.*
> *I count to ten*
> *And then*
> *I sing!*

Her volume had grown steadily through the end of the verse, and she finished, as rehearsed, with a droll flourish of her arms. The crowd applauded enthusiastically but briefly, not wanting to hold things up, and the band sailed into the chorus, a swingy tune with lots of rhymed references to Elsa's favorite composers. Elsa's relief at the reception was palpable, at least to me, and she attacked the song with the grateful energy of the reprieved. Though the preshow screamfest had taken its toll on her vocal chords, she seemed not to notice. Buoyed by the sight of so many approving smiles, she flounced her hips, snapped her fingers, and sang like a nightingale—a nightingale, perhaps, with a lifelong devotion to unfiltered cigarettes, but a nightingale nonetheless.

The applause at the finish was riotous. Elsa stood there, drinking it in, not making any of the demure pleas for silence customary on these occasions. I clapped along, loud as anyone, delighted and astonished that so inevitable a disaster had miraculously been averted. "Brava!" I shouted, and the cry rang through the room. "Brava!"

Then Kitty showed up.

She must have arrived during the opening and been asked to wait by the entrance till the song was finished. I spotted her as she stepped down from the reception area and was caught in the edge of the spot trained on the piano. She wore exceptionally high heels and a gaudy, low-cut, gold beaded dress slit to the earlobe. Ham was behind her in a tux with a red cummerbund.

As the applause swelled, a determinedly inconspicuous maître d' attempted to lead them to their table. He scurried along the edge of the dance floor, expecting Kitty and her escort to follow with the same self-effacing haste. Kitty had not, however, dressed in this fashion or arrived at this time in order to be inconspicuous. She sashayed onto the dance floor like a runway model, skillfully managing to suggest that the burgeoning applause was as much for her as for her sister. Having achieved a position visible to every table in the room, she stopped and shielded her eyes, suddenly blinded by the stage lights. Her dress twinkled so brightly you were tempted to scan the floor behind her for trailing extension cords.

She glanced behind her to Elsa and started, as though realizing just now, and to her boundless surprise, that there was a show in progress. She made a screamingly coy pantomime of guilt over her tardiness. Then, satisfied she'd done the polite thing, she made for her table, heading in the wrong direction even though the maître d' was plainly visible and beckoning to her frantically. She was thus compelled to cross the dance floor *again*, which she did with a comically sheepish air and sweet apologetic smiles to the ringside tables. Arriving finally at our table, which poor mortified Ham had long since reached, she turned for one last penitential bow to Elsa and, in doing so, caught sight of Peter. She waved to her naughty shepherd cheerfully and blew him a big kiss. Then she sat down.

Elsa's expression throughout this was indistinguishable from that she might have worn had the room been invaded by a tall, dark-hooded figure carrying a scythe. She stared, dead-eyed, first at Kitty and then turned her head slowly to Peter's table. Now the crowd, done with ogling Kitty, returned its attention to the stage and fell silent.

The silence lengthened uncomfortably, but Elsa just stood there with the air of a woman waiting for the chalk outline to be drawn. She swayed slightly, and I remembered the bottle of champagne she'd drained on an empty stomach. I realized with great trepidation that the program now called for her to deliver some lighthearted remarks about how she began a singing career years ago but gladly gave it up to wed her dear husband. She would then recapture the romantic bliss of this period by singing "Mad About the Boy."

Whether she forgot her speech or just refused to utter a word of it, we shall never know. All that's sure is that after an interminable silence, she blurted out some gracelessly improvised remark about being happy to be here and, omitting all reference to Peter, announced bluntly that she'd now sing a song by Noel Coward.

It was not, of course, a song that, given her druthers, she'd have chosen to sing at that particular moment of her life. The lyric, with its heavy emphasis on abject devotion, was bound to stick in her craw. Several times, in fact, it seemed literally to do so. You could see her giving herself psychological Heimlich maneuvers to dislodge the words from her throat, and when she reached the line "Lord knows I'm not a fool girl!" she couldn't bring herself to say "fool," so the line came out, "Lord knows I'm not a girl."

After a while, though, she seemed less shattered than angry. Maybe it was having to say the word *maaad* so often. Whatever the reason, the bloody rage she'd displayed back in the dressing room was soon rekindled. By the time she finished the song her eyes were blazing and she was practically snarling the words out.

The crowd greeted the song with baffled applause, clearly unable to decide what the hell had happened. Had Elsa gone bonkers, or was the approach a deliberate, if extreme, effort at dramatic interpretation?

As for Elsa, she seemed to find the anger bracing, or at any rate difficult to contain, for she attacked her next song, Gershwin's "They All Laughed," with the same vigorous contempt. Gone was the light-hearted spirit she'd brought to the lyric in rehearsal and in its place the most corrosive sarcasm:

> *The odds were a hundred to one against me!*
> *The world thought the heights were too* high *to climb!*
> *But people from Missouri never incensed me.*
> *Oh, I wasn't a bit concerned,*
> *For from history I had learned*
> *How many, many times* the worm had turned!

With each line she sang, it became clearer that Elsa's chances for salvation were now nil. She had wrestled with her demons, and her demons had mopped up the floor with her. Kitty's pert and ill-timed entrance had affected her as a full moon affects a werewolf, shattering her poise, leaving her beyond hope of containing her rampaging emotions. She snapped and howled, overwhelmed by bitterness and rage at her family's vile betrayal of her. She was off pitch, too.

> *They all said we'd never get together!*
> *Darling, let's take a bow!*
> *For* HO, HO HO!
> *Who's got the last laugh now!*

She belted herself hoarse on the big finish, spitting out the "Ha ha ha" and "He he he" with insane bile.

When she finished, there was a moment of stunned silence. Then the crowd broke into energetic applause, clapping louder than ever to drown out its own whispering. I don't suppose anyone had a clue what was going on, but no one could have doubted they were witnessing something extraordinary, something baffling and ugly and heartbreaking and altogether delicious.

"What the fuck is the matter with *her?*" whispered Kitty. I patted her hand and said we'd go into it later.

I peered across to Peter's table and saw that Spark and Joy, looking somewhat pale, were whispering rapidly into Peter's ear. Peter, reluctant to confide the real dish, was shaking his head and shrugging. Millie sat a few tables away, regarding the stage with ashen horror. I glanced back to Boyd's table, and also Gilbert and Aggie's, and found everyone joined at the forehead in ecstasies of gossip.

The remainder of the performance, though no less excruciating, did not lack for variety. Following the rabid sarcasm of "They All Laughed," Elsa decided to skip "Easy Living," going straight to her poignant "mama" monologue. She doubled its length, though, padding it out with rambling, macabre descriptions of her mother's last lingering illness, then throwing in scabrous, if cryptic, allusions to subsequent events Mama was "lucky she never lived to see."

She then literally cried her way through "Little Girl Blue," descending to depths of despair so profound she could not climb out of them for her next number, "Sophisticated Lady." The result was not only bathetic but disingenuous. It's stretching things to sing, "And when nobody is nigh, you cry," even as you sob your eyes out with everybody you know nigh as they can get.

I hoped her next song, "Hard to Be Me," with its breezy self-mockery would undo the damage, and indeed it might have, had she elected to sing it. But my preshow gift of the cassette had left her with an understandable impulse to expunge Cavanaugh from the repertoire, and she skipped right over it, informing a devastated Claire that her next number would be to "Get Happy."

She began with a big smile as though determined to take its message to heart. But her nerves made the pep talk sound desperate and maniacal, as though she were standing at the base of a tall building, serenading a jumper on a high ledge. To make matters worse, she applied the same manic spirit to Coward's gentle waltz, "I'll Follow My Secret Heart," belting it out in clarion tones more suited to "Gonna Build a Mountain." Anger returned, hotter than ever, with "Let's Call the Whole Thing Off," which in Elsa's rendition evoked Lizzie Borden crooning to her folks.

By now the audience's mood had changed. Their gossipy excitement had vanished, and they were rapt, hushed, almost reverently attentive. Their applause after the songs was scrupulously modulated; it would have been heartless to greet such efforts with silence, and crueler still to act as though you'd enjoyed them. Some might have felt a measure of guilt at seeing their most malicious fantasies so far exceeded. They could only stare with the mute wonder a group of hounds might feel if the fox they'd been chasing suddenly stopped in its tracks, rolled out a mat, and committed seppuku.

Her penultimate number was Sondheim's "Losing My Mind," the appalling aptness of which had struck me early in the performance. It struck Elsa too, now, and, moreover, it struck her funny. So funny, in fact, did she find it that she was unable to make it through the title line without breaking into hoarse hiccups of laughter.

Does no one knooow?
It's like I'm loo-hoo-hoo-hoo-zing my miiii-hi-hi-hi-hi-ind!

This left even the most coldhearted spectators squirming and averting their eyes. Elsa observed this, and by the end of the song the uncontrollable giggles had become equally uncontrollable weeping. She finished to thin, ceremonial applause and stood wiping her eyes and muttering "Thank you" in a barely audible voice.

It might have come as a relief to me that her next song would be her last, had the song not been Claire's and my "I Owe It All to You," a tender expression of gratitude to a loving mate. I writhed in anticipation of what dark miracles of reinterpretation she'd apply to it. My concern, though, was needless.

Claire played the song's gentle intro and Elsa stood, gazing out at all the people in her gilded world, her face drained of all expression. As soldiers maimed in battle are said to be initially oblivious to their wounds, so too did Elsa seem insensible to her surroundings. Her eyes were unfocused, her body limp. She seemed a sad, spectral presence, beyond embarrassment or emotion of any sort. The band finished the intro and she leaned, on cue, into the mike and began to sing, her exhausted voice like a rusty gate scraping across pavement. She did not reinterpret the words. She did not interpret them at all. She just croaked them directly at Peter with a numb absence of inflection that was more unsettling than the most extravagant rage.

She finished.

The band, wanting to assure the audience that the concert was finished, hurriedly struck up the exit music. The audience, dizzy with relief, applauded extravagantly, but Elsa was too out of it to bow. She just stood there, dazed, nodding at the crowd.

Some unspeakably cruel soul at the rear—opinion diverged as to who, and *no one* would own up to it—shouted, "Encore!" Elsa, snapping out of her catatonia, all but shrieked at the thought and, nodding one last time, fled the stage, disappearing behind the bandstand and into the kitchen.

Daisy Winters, displaying a devotion to her readers that many later derided as uncalled for, leapt to her feet and gave chase. Someone at a neighboring table had the good manners to trip her and send her sprawling into Diane Sawyer's place setting.

With the sacrifice cleared from the altar, the crowd lost any sense of restraint and the winds of gossip now blew through the room in great sibilant gusts. Amid the mounting babble, Horsey Kimball advanced to the microphone and, proving once again that old money, like helium, can rise above anything, made a bland statement, thanking Elsa for her "moving and dramatic performance" and announcing that dinner would be served shortly. The band, sans Claire, struck up some jaunty dance music, and the crowd, whose appetite was not for food, sprang up and began table-hopping.

I twisted about in my seat, taking it all in. Peter was making for the exit, hacking his way through a tangle of solicitous inquiries. Gilbert and Aggie were in midbeeline toward the table where Tommy and the two ladies sat observing Boyd, who was skillfully reenacting Kitty's entrance. Claire was heading straight toward me, looking about as sunny as you'd expect.

"Dear oh dear," said Ham, lighting Kitty's cigarette. "And to think I'd been telling everyone how *good* she was! What do you suppose made her such a wreck up there?"

"Who knows," said Kitty, taking a long, weary puff. "But just you wait . . . she'll find some way to blame the whole thing on me!"

Twenty

The next morning I was awakened shortly after nine by Gilbert's voice plaintively inquiring as to the whereabouts of my aspirin.

"Try the bathroom," I said in a tone such as Hamlet's father favored when posthumously strolling the battlements.

"They're not there."

"Try the shelf in the kitchen."

He rose from his crouching position, briefly gripped the arm of my sofa for support, and shuffled away. He returned shortly clutching a glass of water and seven Tylenol, which he consumed in one gulp.

"Oh, did you want some, too?" he asked. "Sorry. Soon as these kick in I'll run to the drugstore and get more."

"Thank you. What are you doing here?"

He said I'd invited him up for a nightcap. This stirred the dimmest of recollections.

"Yes, I guess I did. Then what happened?"

He replied that though the specific details seemed lost to history, the evidence strongly suggested I'd fallen asleep on the sofa without removing my tuxedo, while he had availed himself of my bed and a pair of cream silk pajamas with the tags still on.

I agreed this seemed likely, then asked if he wouldn't mind fetching me a glass of seltzer, as I felt peculiarly thirsty. When he'd gone I raised a hand and ran it gently across my skull. I found only hair there, squelching my theory that I was wearing a cast-iron bowler hat several sizes too small.

I had a sudden inkling that something of importance had transpired the previous evening. I couldn't think what, though. Rising a bit from my prone position, I applied what few soggy synapses I still possessed to reconstructing the night's events.

There was a blessed moment of confusion, and then, in a ghastly torrent, images of Elsa's performance flooded my mind. I groaned like the grave and fell backward, banging my head on the inadequately upholstered arm of the sofa. I lay there, whimpering with grief as I contemplated the yawning chasm that separated my expectations of the evening from its brutal reality. I had expected to emerge from the event hailed as the new, talented darling of the supper club set. And now, to the extent the public thought of me at all, I occupied a role roughly analogous to that of Yukio Mishima's sword maker.

Gilbert returned with my seltzer. I rose with some difficulty to a seated position and raised the glass to my lips. At that precise instant, my phone rang. The sound, which to my sensitive eardrums evoked Leontyne Price, Renata Tebaldi, and Dame Kiri Te Kanawa simultaneously spotting a mouse, caused me to flinch, dropping the glass of seltzer onto my chest. I swiveled madly, determined to lift the phone from its cradle before it could make that hideous noise again. I snatched it up, then, soaked and trembling, brought the receiver to my ear.

"Philip Cavanaugh?" asked an unduly robust female voice.

"Yes," I said.

"Please hold for Mr. Winthrop."

There followed a click and I was regaled with selections from *Hair*.

"Who's that?" asked Gilbert.

"I'm not sure. Some female yodeler just instructed me to hold for a Mr. Winthrop."

"Oh," said Gilbert, then added gravely, "I wouldn't."

"Huh?"

"Really, dear. After the kind of night you had, some bozo you've never heard has his secretary call and tell *you* to hold—do you think it's *good* news?"

I saw his reasoning and agreed that I was in no condition to be tangling with strange Winthrops. I handed him the phone and instructed him to hang up while the hanging was good. He was about to do so when a brusque voice issued from the receiver and he brought the damn thing to his ear.

"Hello?" he asked.

He listened a moment, then winked at me. "Yes"—he smiled— "this is Mr. Philip Cavanaugh. To whom am I speaking?"

"Uh, Gilbert—"

"*Reeeeally?*" He yawned, then covered the mouthpiece. "What'd I tell you—a fucking lawyer!"

"Hang up," I said, though not with any real hope.

"Oh, he said that, did he?" asked Gilbert. "Well, I'm afraid I can't help him, as the item you refer to is no longer in my possession."

He listened, then frowned. "No, actually, I wasn't aware of that." He covered the phone again. "Did you sign some kind of confidentiality agreement?"

I nodded.

"Well, *that* was silly," he said, and returned to Mr. Winthrop. "Ah, yes—it comes back to me now. Well, what of it? We all sign things from time to time and then think better of them. Probably wasn't legal anyway. . . . Well, go ahead, fuck-brain! See if I care! And you tell Mr. Champion for me that in the position *he's* in, he ought to be groveling on his knees and kissing my fanny instead of having stuffy old idiots like you phoning and threatening to sue me! If you call me again, it's harassment! Now buzz off, gramps!"

He slammed the receiver down. "You have to know how to talk to these people."

I thanked him for handling the matter so tactfully and suggested we let my machine answer any further calls. The wisdom of this policy was soon made manifest. In the next half hour alone we received high-strung messages from Peter, Millie, Daisy Winters, Mr. Winthrop, *Women's Wear Daily*, the *New York Post*, Hoot Mulvaney, Signora di Corteggiano, and Liz Smith.

The call I most dreaded, however, was Claire's. Of all the pictures in the gruesome slide carousel in my mind, none pained me more than my image of poor Claire, trapped and spotlit before the beau monde, trying to decide what facial expression was most appropriate to wear when providing musical accompaniment for a nervous breakdown.

I did my best in the madness that followed the performance to explain the events that led up to the debacle, stressing the pure flukiness of my mix-up with the cassettes. Nothing, however, could explain away my having brought the damned thing to begin with. It was obvious I'd fully intended to present the tape to Tommy without receiving any of the legal assurances I'd promised to let her secure. She was livid over this, but madder still at the destruction I'd stupidly wreaked on poor Elsa.

We did not see Elsa again that evening. She fled straight home, leaving Peter to trot out pathetic excuses for her behavior. It took him a while to think of something, but he eventually came up with nervous exhaustion combined with bizarre chemical reactions to non-prescription drugs. As for Claire, she left soon after dinner, having no stomach for the din of speculation or for the stream of prominent citizens who introduced themselves and used their deep concern over Elsa as a pretext to pump her for dish.

I received many a prying inquiry myself. Hoot Mulvaney was positively foaming to get the scoop, all the more so because Peter—who knew better than to confide his scandals to a journalist, whether in his employ or not—told him the same story he told everyone else. I stood firm in maintaining to Hoot, and to my glittering interrogators as well, that I hadn't a clue what had happened. I confess, though, that vanity and champagne led me to adopt the vague, knowing air of one who could, if he so chose, reveal all but was saving it for the book.

I steered clear of the Larkin contingent, there being too many in the room canny enough to wonder why Elsa's songwriter should, after so disastrous a debut, raise a glass with Peter's biggest enemy. Boyd was bursting to get home and listen to his tape, so he led his party away only an hour after dinner. I fell in behind them.

Peter and his goons stood by the door. They were obviously dying to fall upon us and wrestle back the damning evidence, but the sharp-eyed presence of several society reporters rendered such a move suicidal at best. He let us pass but fixed the lot of us with a look of scalding hatred that a nearby photographer captured and sold to several newspapers.

We dropped Boyd's and Tommy's dates off, then raced back to Tommy's place to listen to the tape. The spanking business had Boyd and Tommy literally on the floor, wild with laughter. And after sufficient champagne I began laughing, too. Their comments made it all

so wonderfully funny that after a while even Elsa's spectacular dis-
integration seemed not without its humorous aspects. I mean, not that
we didn't feel awful for her, because we did. We'd never have wished
a fate half so ghastly on her. Still, it was impossible not to giggle
when recalling her bloodthirsty interpretations of Ira Gershwin, or
Peter watching it all, drenched in perspiration. He'd planned to make
her a star, the better to clear the decks for hanky-panky, only to have
his low scheme explode in his face in the most spectacular fashion
imaginable. When the story came out, Elsa would enjoy universal
sympathy, and her humiliation would heal in time. The alimony,
though, would go on forever.

Gilbert, of course, claimed equal credit for the tape, and I went
along, knowing, as did Gilbert, that I'd seem hopelessly petty if I did
otherwise. At any rate, there were more than enough kudos to go
around. Both Tommy and Boyd were all over us with hugs and praise,
and the champagne flowed so freely that the tail end of the evening
remains no more than a pleasant blur.

What lay ahead, though, as morning crept by seemed equally blurry
and not nearly so pleasant. God alone knew how things could be
patched up with Claire. I'd placed her in dreadful positions before,
but last night's smash-up had been the frozen limit. Flowers would
not suffice, and claims that she would, in time, see the humor seemed
more likely to ignite than to dampen her wrath.

Around ten Gilbert crept forth into the world and returned with bagels,
Tylenol, and the daily papers. We spread the papers on the floor and
began warily searching for postmortems. I took the *Times* and Gilbert
scoured the *Post*. He found his first.

"Gawd, check *this:* 'Ms. Champion,' " he read, displaying a New
Yorker's uncanny ability to immediately find the most damning sentence in a review, " 'has a voice you could grate cheese with'!"

"How kind," I said. "Wait, here's the *Times* review."

"Read it out loud!" he said with unseemly eagerness.

The critic opened with one of those "I-anticipated-this-show-for-
a-long-time-and-really-*really*-wanted-to-like-it" paragraphs that are
always such a comfort to the condemned. Then, his benevolence
established, he let go with the flaming projectiles.

" 'I have no quibble with performers who, lacking great vocal ability, choose to stress acting over singing. Seldom, though, has this ploy been carried to such dubious lengths as it has been by Ms. Champion, whose interpretations go beyond mere overacting into shrill, self-indulgent hysterics. Working under the incompetent musical direction of Claire Simmons, she turns what might have been a festive hour of song into an embarrassing, ineptly performed psychodrama.' Shall I continue?"

"Please."

" 'The evening begins on a promising note, with Ms. Champion enacting a droll parody of stage fright before letting her real confidence shine through in a fine, brassy ditty called "I Sing." All too soon, though, her flair for histrionics becomes regrettably apparent.

" 'In approaching Coward's wry torch song, "Mad About the Boy," Ms. Champion has hit upon the dull notion that the word *mad* can be taken literally. This prompts her to begin the song in the manner of a dazed, overripe Ophelia, then build to an insane frenzy of anger that is as pointless as it is unconvincing.

" 'This trite technique of working against songs' intentions is employed repeatedly. Do we really need to be told that the cheery sentiments in standards like "Let's Call the Whole Thing Off" might mask genuine conflict and hostility? In more skilled hands these reversals might come off, but Ms. Champion's overwrought renditions make them seem mere dimestore ironies—though irony of any sort would be welcome in Philip Cavanaugh's leaden patter, which features rambling, lugubrious anecdotes more suited to a therapist's couch than to the stage of the Rainbow Room.' "

"You actually *wrote* those speeches?" asked Gilbert.

I said no, I didn't, Elsa improvised them, and Gilbert helpfully suggested I write a letter to the *Times* clarifying this.

The critic concluded by hoping Ms. Champion would try again in a less spectacular venue (though not, one sensed, any time soon), and that next time she'd choose collaborators better equipped to curb her excesses and emphasize her strengths.

"What strengths?" asked Gilbert.

The *Times* was, at least, the worst of the bunch. The tabloids had their fun detailing the dreadfulness, but none echoed the *Times'* altogether merciless assertion that Elsa's interpretations had been entirely premeditated. The others noted Peter's statement about nervous exhaustion and conceded that at times Elsa *did* seem somewhat out of control.

That was all, except for Daisy Winters, who agreed with the *Times* that Elsa knew what she was doing, but disagreed about the results. In Daisy's opinion it was "a knockout! The powerhouse debut of a female Pagliacci! Elsa is not only a fantastic singer, but a great singing actress who moved me to tears again and again! Producers take note—here's one gutsy lady who could put the Great White Way back on its feet and cheering! Brava for La Champion!"

Some of the reviews carried sidebars noting that Elsa's remaining performances at Rainbow and Stars had been canceled. There were quotes from Peter and from Elsa's physician. The doctor said that before performing Elsa became disoriented when an antihistamine she'd taken reacted strangely with a homemade tea containing rare medicinal herbs.

We were interrupted in our studies by a commanding knock on my apartment door. We froze. I suspected from the look on Gilbert's face that he was, like me, entertaining visions of Champion-hired thugs breaking down the door and going at us like deranged osteopaths. The reality proved even darker.

"It's me," said Claire, "and I know you're in there."

"The hell she does," whispered Gilbert, eyeing my fire escape.

"I still have the keys from when I watered your plants. It will be nicer for us all if you let me in."

I opened the door, emphasizing in my bearing the full-body wince of the hung over in the hopes that this would inspire pity and mercy.

"Good morning," said Claire, entering briskly. I noted joyfully that she had a *Times* under her arm.

"Claire!" said Gilbert. "I want you to know I'm *incensed* about this review! I'm writing a letter first thing—"

"Oh, stuff it, Gilbert," said Claire. "This whole nightmare I've been through is your fault to begin with."

"I fail to see—" began Gilbert, but then he saw and shut up.

I groped for words but realized there's no really adequate way to apologize to a friend who, thanks to you, has just received her second vile notice from the *Times* in a mere four months. It's harder still when you realize that lately the only time you're *not* apologizing to her is when you're doing things to apologize for. I whined a bit, saying how guilty I felt about the review. She replied coldly that it was nothing so happy as the review that had brought her here.

"What was it, then?" asked Gilbert, who wanted to know.

She pulled a sheet of notepaper from her pocket. "It may interest you to know that I passed my morning exchanging pleasantries with one Howard Winthrop. He informs me that I am a co-defendent in a ten-million-dollar suit for theft, invasion of privacy, breach of contract, and, quote, emotional terrorism, end quote. Naturally I professed sweet ignorance, saying I hadn't a clue what he was referring to. He didn't buy it, though. He said he'd just spoken to *you* and that you acknowledged *everything* and countered with threats and obscenities."

"Uh, actually," murmured Gilbert, "*I* said all that. Philip felt queasy so I took the call for him."

"What shrewd deputizing. I'm not going to go into my personal feelings toward you at this moment, Philip, because they're frankly inexpressible. Let's put all that aside for now and confine our energies to bringing this rancid episode to a close, all right?"

"Sounds good," I said, and Gilbert asked if she had any ideas.

She rose and paced slowly, as she tends to do when her brain's going on all cylinders. She stopped.

"You gave the tape to Tommy last night, but I'm sure you took the precaution of dubbing a copy. I suggest you exchange your copy for Peter's written assurance that he'll confine his lawsuits to Larkin and leave us out of it."

Gilbert asked why Peter would concede anything for a copy of the tape when Boyd would still clobber him with the original.

"Well," said Claire, "for Peter it's a matter of buying time. Larkin plans to use his ammo for an exposé in *Choice*. *Choice* is a monthly, so the piece wouldn't hit the stands for weeks. But *you* could hand yours over to Geraldo tomorrow."

"Please!" sniffed Gilbert. "Philip wouldn't *dream* of letting someone scoop Boyd after all this!"

"Yes, but Peter doesn't *know* that. Faced with exposure tomorrow or a month's reprieve, I'm sure he'll bargain."

I smiled wanly and said this seemed an excellent plan, but it was somewhat moot as I had, in the hurly-burly of events, omitted to actually make a copy.

"Oh?" said Claire, and a hell of an "oh" it was, too.

"Well," I said, *"you're* the one with the fancy dubbing deck, not me, and I could hardly ask *you* to make a copy. Besides—"

For the first time that morning I was relieved to hear the phone ring. Wagering that no one on the other end could have harsher words for me than Claire, I picked up the receiver.

"Good morning, O prince of investigators!"

"Tommy!"

"Hi, Tommy!" screamed Gilbert from the couch.

"Gilbert there, too? Splendid! I trust you both slept the sleep of the just and feel fit and restored?"

"We're fine," I said. "How are you?"

"Look out the window and see for yourself."

I dropped the phone, which Gilbert fell upon and began purring into in his phone sex voice. Raising my blinds, I lifted my window and peered out onto West Ninety-ninth. Across from my building sat a gleaming white Rolls. The rear window glided down and there was Tommy, looking crisp and marvelous as he burbled away on the car phone. I waved and he waved back.

Seeing him there on the street where I lived and all was very pleasant, but I soon saw I'd made a strategic blunder in relinquishing the phone.

"Yes," said Gilbert, "that *was* a lot of champagne we went through. I felt fine, but poor Philip threw up in his sleep."

"Give me that phone."

"When you're both through making asses of yourselves," said Claire, "I'd like a word with Mr. Parker."

"Yes," said Gilbert, "we just read them the *Times*. *Ouch*, huh?"

I reached for my glass and, after dropping a few ice cubes down Gilbert's shirt, regained control of the phone.

"Me again! So, are you going to sit down there or do you want to come up?"

"Actually, dear, I want you boys to come down. Boyd and I have arranged a little get-together and we thought you'd like to attend."

"A get-together? With who?"

"Why, with Peter and Elsa, of course," he said, then added with a droll flourish, "Let the games begin!"

Twenty-one

I don't think any of us expected a really cordial meeting. I was prepared to regard any outcome short of gunplay as a triumph of civility.

The summit, which was convened at Peter's insistence, took place aboard Boyd's yacht, the *Heigh-Ho*. The boat, built years ago by Boyd's father, reflected the elder Larkin's manly, somewhat stodgy taste. The main salon, to which we were largely confined, resembled a cramped version of some venerable London club where bloated industrialists would meet to sip port and harumph over the general decline in standards. There was lots of burnished brass and rich dark leather. The sole signs of Boyd's stewardship were the cabin boys, whose languid, saucy airs would not, I sensed, have thrilled Dad.

Claire insisted on attending, of course. I feared Tommy might balk at her inclusion, but he was gallantry itself. Yes, yes, of *course*, he said, she had every right to be kept abreast of developments. She'd gotten rather swept up in events and had, albeit through no one's specific intention, suffered the most appalling indignities.

"We empathize fully with your position, Claire, and we want to assure you that whatever unpleasantness ensues, your interests will be diligently safeguarded."

I could see Claire was uncertain what to make of Tommy. At first she regarded him with such cool mistrust you'd have thought he was wearing a soiled raincoat and proffering Hershey bars. Eventually, though, his charm thawed her reserve, and she adopted a dry, cordial manner, as though to say "I don't trust you an inch yet, but I'm enjoying you."

Luckily we reached the yacht before Peter and Elsa. Boyd greeted us effusively and showered Claire with praise and sympathy. If he was wary of a newcomer's presence at what was bound to be a delicate negotiation, he didn't let on but acted his usual giddy self, showing the boat off and screaming for cocktails.

Peter and Elsa were late, but with reason. They'd naturally preferred to depart Champion Plaza in privacy but knew that all escape routes were clogged with reporters. Elsa would sooner have faced death than the press, besides which she was purportedly languishing in bed. They would not disperse, though, without a burnt offering, so Peter had to come down and rehash the tragic history of the antihistamine and the herb tea. He then had to field many rude inquiries on Elsa's mental health and the current status of his plans to build her a nightclub. He soon declared the interview finished and fled the building, whereupon the mob, clutching its pound of footage, raced off to file their stories. This left the coast clear for Elsa to skulk through the lobby in dark glasses and a wig, then rendezvous with Peter's car.

These trials did not leave the Champions in the gayest of moods, nor was Peter's mood improved when Boyd's bodyguard greeted him on the deck, waved some sort of electric wand around him, and demanded he hand over the microphone taped to his chest. By the time they entered the yacht's main salon, they had the air of two unchained pit bulls who'd been starved at length and teased with feather dusters.

"Peter!" Boyd said convivially. "And Elsa! What *have* you done to your hair?"

"Drop dead, you fag monster!"

"Temper, temper!" Boyd said cheerfully. "You two suggested this get-together, not me, and if you can't be nice I'll have Bjorn show you out."

Boyd politely introduced Tommy to the Champions. He said he believed they already knew Gilbert, who miraculously summoned the tact to say hello and not *bonjour*. Boyd then sat behind a desk and, like a miniature Nero Wolfe, made a concise speech which Peter interrupted with frequent bursts of vitriol.

Boyd first extended his sympathies to Elsa on her unfortunate debut. He deeply regretted the entirely accidental mix-up with the cassettes but suggested Elsa reserve her anger for those who'd made the tape possible, not those who had, however ill-timedly, conveyed it to her. He admitted he'd hired Gilbert and me to investigate them for a proposed magazine article but said Claire had played no role in the investigation and they had no legitimate grievance against her.

"Lies!" cried Elsa.

She jumped up from her seat and advanced, glaring, on Claire.

"*You*, missy! I know all about you!"

"Oh?" said Claire, taken aback.

"I know about all of you! The signora told me before, but would I listen? No! I thought just because you wrote me nice songs you weren't out to destroy me! But *she* knew! She knew and she warned me, but I didn't listen! I just listened to you, and to *him*," she added, pointing to Peter, "when he was in with you all right from the start!"

Claire began to refute this, then just sighed and shook her head hopelessly. I saw her reasoning. When you considered recent events in Elsa's life, was there really any point in trying to convince her she had no grounds for conspiracy theories?

Peter rose in fury and poked a finger toward Boyd. "Look what you've done to my wife, you son of a bitch!"

"What *I've* done to her?" said Boyd, laughing incredulously. "Puh-leeze, Peter! Am *I* the one who begged his own sister-in-law to *tenderize* him?"

Peter snarled and moved toward Boyd, but Tommy stepped between them. Peter glared up at Tommy, who stood a good foot taller, and snorted contemptuously even as he took a step backward.

"You think I couldn't take you apart, you big fairy?"

"Don't let's be tiresome."

"Go ahead, Tommy!" said Gilbert, enjoying this all immensely. "Squash him like a bug!"

Boyd sniffed. "We mustn't do that. We'd only get him *excited*."

"You fat little toad! Let's step outside, okay, pal? Just you and me!"

"Shall I bring a *riiiding* crop?"

"Stop it now!" said Claire. "This isn't getting us anywhere!"

Boyd said, "Miss Simmons is absolutely right. I suggest we all calm down and have a nice cocktail. I'd love a martini. Peter, what would you like? A whiskey *smash*, perhaps? Or a planter's *punch?*"

Peter sneered and gruffly demanded Scotch. On receiving same, he downed half of it in a gulp, then angrily insisted Boyd return all copies of the Kitty tape or face a fifty-million-dollar suit for theft and invasion of privacy. Boyd yawned daintily and said he'd countersue. Peter had engaged me to plant bugs in *his* house, and, moreover, he had the tapes to prove it—Peter, you'll recall, having asked me to bug Boyd's place even as I was attempting to bug *his*.

Peter countered that he had me on tape discussing Larkin's boy-a-thons. Boyd laughed and said we'd invented those stories to deliberately mislead him and that I would happily testify to that effect. Those statements were, at any rate, pure hearsay and lacked the zing of Peter's live performance as the Saucy Shepherd.

So, concluded Boyd, as far as the legalities went, it was a draw. Each man had infiltrated the other's stronghold through various illegal means—would any court hold one party more culpable than the other? The only difference was that while Peter had come out with pretty bland pickings, Boyd had emerged with a barrel of the purest cayenne. And he meant to publish it. Peter could sue, but Boyd would win, and the trial would only widen the scandal's audience.

At this point Elsa got into the act, hysterically begging Boyd not to make public the contents of the tape. She'd been humiliated enough already; the added mortification would be more than she could bear.

"Elsa, honey," said Boyd, "the tape's about *Peter*, not you."

Elsa didn't see it this way. She'd heard the tape with her own ears and no doubt recalled the passage where she begged for sex in baby talk, then made reference to having conducted marital relations while pretending to be Sandra Day O'Connor.

I suspected, though, that Elsa's main resistance to the tape's release had little to do with her own embarrassment or even Peter's infidelity. I suspected the main reason was Kitty.

Elsa and Kitty had been vicious rivals their entire lives. Elsa had long considered herself the clear-cut winner, having snagged the billionaire husband and jet-set life while Kitty begged for crumbs from her table. But now Kitty had won an absolutely brutal victory. She'd seduced her husband away, plotting with him behind Elsa's very back to remove her from the scene. Worst of all, Kitty had used Elsa's own vanity and foolish hopes for stardom as tools to achieve her hateful end. The upshot had been bitter enough, but how much more bitter it would be if the world learned the full extent of her own pathetic blindness and of her vindictive sister's humiliating triumph.

Boyd informed Elsa that he planned to publish on schedule. Any grievance she had could be addressed to Peter.

Elsa seemed to concur with this. She turned to Peter in cold fury and informed him that he'd better do something to insure the tape never became public. If it did, she said, she would divorce him and, with the tape as evidence and no prenuptial agreement to gum up the works, bleed him penniless. Nor would she stop at such mild measures. Once divorced, she would contact the appropriate authorities and lay bare everything she knew about Peter's financial activities.

Everything.

Judging from Peter's reaction to this salvo, Boyd had been correct in assuming Peter had a few fiscal skeletons in his closet; it appeared, in fact, as though his closet was a virtual boneyard of improprieties.

Peter turned white and, stammering like Porky Pig, told Elsa she was being irrational. Elsa retorted that *he* was the irrational one if he doubted her for a minute. It was only her reluctance to let the world know what a fool she'd been that prevented her from getting a divorce and destroying him *now*. If the tape were made public this one barrier would fall, and nothing could forestall her revenge.

Gilbert and I sat in a corner, gobbling this all up like popcorn. I kept shooting nervous glances to Claire, who'd been watching in thoughtful silence. But now she rose and asked Boyd if she might offer her views on the matter.

"Sure," said Boyd. "Love to hear 'em, hon."

"I doubt it," said Claire, and requested a sherry, a signal that her brain work was finished and she felt free to unwind while airing the results.

"I think, Mr. Larkin," she began, "that you could bring this tawdry affair to its conclusion if only you'd tell the truth to Peter and the rest of us."

Boyd leaned forward on his chair and lazily plopped his chins into one cupped hand. "What truth would that be, dumpling?"

"That you haven't the least intention of publishing a transcript of that tape."

Boyd stared at her blandly. "Sorry, hon, but someone's been pulling your leg."

"I'm not acting on inside information. Just common sense. I've followed your little war with Peter, dumpling, and I'm sorry, but what you're threatening now isn't at all in character. Didn't the whole thing start when you made some cracks about how tacky Peter's buildings were?"

"Yes. He is morbidly sensitive about such things."

"And then, Peter announced *he* was going into publishing, with lots of chest thumping about how his magazine's circulation would double yours?"

"Which it damn well did within two years!" said Peter.

"So it did, Peter," said Claire. "And the last time I checked, french fries were outselling foie gras."

Boyd chortled in approval, but then Claire turned a gimlet eye on him.

"Which is exactly your problem, Boyd. You publish a stuffy, well-respected magazine with an illustrious pedigree. I've read it myself. Slow going sometimes, but generally high-quality stuff, which is why not half so many people read it as read Peter's.

"According to Philip here, you went into this investigation hoping to gather material for a weighty, Theodore Dreiser–style piece about a corrupt mogul reaping the price of his Faustian bargains. What you've come out with, though, is rank sensationalism—just the sort of thing *Peter* publishes all the time, and just what you look down on him for! Now, you may be envious of Peter's success, but would you really stoop to *emulating* him? Certainly not. If you publish this story in *Choice*, you're not beating Peter, you're joining him. Your readers will be fascinated, but appalled, and media wags all over town will have a high time writing about how the grande dame of journalism has gone in for mud wrestling.

"Now, *Peter* might not have figured this out, but you certainly have. You know the tape, however delicious, is fundamentally useless to you. All you can do with it is dangle it over Peter's head and drive him mad with anxiety—and you've had a rollicking time doing that, but enough's enough, so please stop it. *You* can't use the tape without damaging your magazine, and *he* can't sue you without exposing the whole humiliating story, so what say we call it a draw and go home?"

Well, it was Claire at her best, and I'd be a cad not to give her credit for it. Still, she did take the air out of things. We sat there a moment like children whose mother has interrupted a good pillow fight. At length Peter, deciding he'd won, broke the silence with some nyah nyahs.

"She's right! This whole thing's a fucking bluff!"

Boyd wearily massaged his temple, then turned to Claire.

"Miss Simmons, you're a very bright and insightful young woman. I don't think I like you."

"You've had your fun, Boyd, which is, I sense, your primary objective in life. By all means keep after your quarry—just don't include the rest of us in your plans."

Boyd scowled and said, if we'd excuse him a moment, he had to go see to lunch. He rose and padded out grumpily. Gilbert and I looked to Tommy, whose bland, dignified air could not conceal his disappointment. He returned our gaze, smiled wistfully, then, excusing himself politely, departed through the same door Boyd had.

Peter turned to Elsa with a sour smile, as if to claim credit. Elsa blew smoke in his face and asked him to get the fuck away from her. He crossed to where Claire sat and magnanimously extended his thanks. Claire said she did not deserve his gratitude as she hadn't spoken on his behalf.

"Well," he said, "I just want you to know I think you're one bright young gal—just the sort I'd like to have working for me. I could offer you a very attractive position at my magazine."

Claire stared at him. "No, thank you," she said, and she couldn't have done a better job if she'd been packing a lorgnette.

My own feelings were ambivalent. Part of me prayed Claire was right and the game had reached a standoff. The damage to our careers would not, of course, be soon undone, but we could at least stop fretting about rabid lawyers stalking us in perpetuity.

On the other hand, if the battle *was* over and done, what future was there for me and Tommy? Our friendship, though warm, had not advanced beyond a working relationship. As a man of the theater, I knew only too well how the bonds forged during an exhilarating project can evaporate once the work is done and it's time to move on. Tommy was a busy man. Would he really care to chum around with someone whose presence could only remind him of a campaign that had, after so promising a beginning, ended in stalemate and defeat?

With these thoughts buzzing in my brain, I began dissecting Claire's argument to see how valid it was. Something she'd said about Boyd envying Peter's success but refusing to stoop to emulation had especially impressed me. It seemed to sum up Boyd's problem very neatly.

An idea struck me.

It was a wicked idea, low, shifty, and unworthy of me. I hoped Gilbert hadn't thought of it first. I rose hastily, said I needed a bathroom, and made off in the direction Boyd had gone. I meandered down a dim hall lined with doors, praying Gilbert would not follow. I hoped to make a love offering of my little notion and didn't care to have Gilbert hovering behind me, saying, "Goodness! Great minds think alike!"

I noticed a door at the end was ajar, and I poked my head in. There stood Tommy, blessedly alone.

"Here you are! Where's Boyd?"

"On the phone, I believe, asking Mr. Vladimir if he knows any assassins who specialize in lady composers."

"Sorry about Claire. She has a good heart, but she can be sort of a killjoy."

"Well, she's right, of course," he said. "There's no way we'd ever publish a squalid story like this in *Choice*. We rather preferred it when Peter didn't know, though. Much more fun for us. We doubted it would occur to him that some people would put matters of taste ahead of vengeance and magazine sales."

"But you can have *both*," I said, leaning in close.

"Really?" he asked, eyebrows rising. "What do you propose?"

"Look," I said, "what Boyd *really* wants most is for his magazine to be more successful than Peter's, right?"

"It is his dearest wish."

"As it stands, though, he can't do it without making his magazine much tackier than it is. And Peter knows it."

"A masterful summary."

"But," I said, "he doesn't know you won't hand the tape over to someone who *will* use it. If he thinks you're ready to do *that*, you can name your price just for agreeing to sit on it."

And then, with an evil smile, I suggested to him what that price might be.

Tommy's face in the moment after I made this suggestion was among the more gratifying sights I'd ever beheld. The perfect mouth billowed into a broad grin, the nostrils twitched as though literally tickled by the idea, and the big blue eyes bulged in wonder and delight.

I began to bulge, too, though not in the eyes, when he flung his arms around me.

"Philip, you absolute treasure! What a glorious notion!"

He wondered if Peter could really be compelled to accede to so odious a demand, and I said that with Elsa determined to destroy him if the tape were released, he'd have no choice. It was Elsa who held the trump card. As the injury would be to Peter's pride, not hers, she'd certainly find acquiescence preferable to exposure. She might, in fact, enjoy seeing Peter suffer.

Tommy mussed my hair and said I was a bloody marvel. I smiled back, a tremulous smile, in which my naked adoration of him must have been writ more plainly than in neon. He laughed and, bending his face toward mine, kissed me.

I'd rehearsed this moment in my mind many a night and morning and was thrilled to find the reality beat the wet dreams hands down. It was not a gentlemanly kiss, all playful teasing and skilled modulation. It was an all-out mouth rape, complete with butt grabbing, crotch grinding, and hydraulic tongue. By the time it ended some thirty seconds later, I was more than enthralled, I was subjugated. What's more, I knew that once we'd consummated the affair—which we certainly would; Tommy, being a gentleman, knew that a kiss like this was no less than an IOU for a fuck—my slavery to the man would know no bounds. This made me very happy.

He gave me a last tender peck and instructed me to rejoin the others. He would advise Boyd of my brilliant strategy, after which they'd return and reopen negotiations.

I went back to the salon, where Gilbert noted my dopy smile with distinct alarm. I began perusing the shelves, taking care to avoid the inquisitive eye of Claire, who would, I sensed, disapprove of my plan. Soon Boyd and Tommy returned, looking very perky and followed by a pale faun of a cabin boy with a buffet table of little sandwiches and grapes. Boyd took some grapes and, lazily popping them into his mouth, spoke in his highest, most lulling tone.

"First I want to say that Miss Simmons here is absolutely right regarding my intentions. As a publisher, I've always drawn a firm line between public and private behavior, which is more than can be said for some people. Your sexual escapades, Peter, however revolting, are of no concern to my readers. If I intimated otherwise, it was because I was so annoyed at your placing those bugs in my private residence that I wanted to teach you a lesson.

"To sum up, then . . . I have no intention of publishing any article about you that would incorporate a single detail from that tape. Moreover, I will do everything in my power to make sure no *third party* obtains a copy of the tape and airs its contents publicly."

Peter, who knew a threat when he heard one, stiffened and asked what the hell Boyd meant by that. Boyd, smiling beatifically, said he'd meant just what he'd said. He would do his *absolute best* to see that his copies of the tape did not fall into the hands of those who, possessing lower journalistic standards than his own, would air its contents to a sensation-starved public.

Claire said if Boyd were so worried about his tape falling into malign hands, why not simply destroy it? Boyd sighed and said he'd much rather do so than shoulder the awful responsibility of safeguarding it, but Peter's orneriness and repeated threats of litigation compelled him to keep it as security against this. Granted, he did not *anticipate* that some unscrupulous agent of the gutter press would gain access to his personal belongings. Then again he did not, only weeks ago, anticipate that a rival publisher would stoop so low as to bug his private home. Life, he was learning, was fraught with uncertainty and disappointments.

Elsa got down to cases and asked what the hell he wanted. Boyd professed bewilderment as to her drift, and Elsa said, fuck him, he knew just what she meant, the weasel, and would he stop beating around the goddamn bush? This ungainly dance went on for some

time before Boyd finally tossed up his plump hands and said that as
Peter and Elsa were so intractably determined to show their gratitude
for his efforts to protect their privacy, there *was* one tiny favor they
could grant him.

Boyd's associate, Mr. Parker, had complained of late that he'd
wearied of his duties at *Boulevardier*, finding them an insufficient
challenge to his capabilities. Boyd wanted to offer this gifted man a
job more commensurate with his skills, but there was, alas, no such
position immediately available in the Larkin empire. Until such a
position should become available, would Peter mind offering Tommy
some suitable post at one of his own magazines? The editorship of
Estime would do nicely.

Peter was not enthused. Boyd said he understood completely and
assured him that his refusal to honor this request would in no way
lessen the vigilance with which he'd safeguard the tape from those
who'd trumpet its contents to the nation and make it a favored topic
among late-night talk show comedians.

Peter lost what remained of his temper. He began bellowing obscenities while tearing about the room in a manner that put me in
mind of those Bugs Bunny cartoons that feature the Tasmanian Devil.
It wasn't long, though, before Elsa rose and, in a tone that would
brook no refusal, asked Peter for a private word on the deck.

It was not a lengthy conference. They returned almost immediately,
Elsa looking bitterly triumphant and Peter resembling something
heated too long in a microwave. Elsa gave Boyd a quick, grim nod
and then drained her whiskey in one gulp.

Tommy, fearing, I supposed, that Peter might renege, calmly lifted
a phone by his elbow and dialed.

"Tommy Parker calling," he said, then, after a moment, "Daisy,
darling! How are you? . . . Of course I have something for you, why
else would I call? Now, this is God's own truth, love, but you mustn't
say you got it from me, all right? . . . Lovely! Guess who's the new
editor-in-chief of *Estime?*"

Twenty-two

The next morning this item appeared in Daisy Winters's column:

Get well bouquets are flooding into Champion Plaza, where courageous **Elsa Champion** lies recovering from the strain of her opening. Like the late, great **Judy Garland**, Elsa gave and gave at her sold-out concert, pushing her frail body so hard she literally collapsed after leaving the stage. Take it easy, Elsa baby, and know our prayers are flying your way!

As you've read by now, not everyone at Elsa's opening knew enough to give a lady her due. Besides the sour grapes gang at the *Times*, one of the biggest naysayers was billionaire publisher **Boyd Larkin**, who some say even did Elsa imitations at his table! Talk about no class!

But leave it to wily **Peter Champion** to get the last laugh. A very reliable source informs me that Peter has stolen the editor of Boyd's *Boulevardier*—right out from under Boyd's nose! Dapper **Tommy Parker** will take over immediately as editor of *Estime*, replacing **Joy Cudgel**, the sexy scoop-hound who built the magazine into the rip-roaring smash it is now. Peter, in a madly rushed phone interview (he's one busy guy!), said he felt *Estime* was "in a rut—a very dynamic rut, but a rut nonetheless. I thought it was time for fresh blood, and I only hire the best."

Sources close to Boyd say he's hopping mad and heartbroken, too, as this all hit him the same day lovely **Dame Lottie Haverford** gave him the heave-ho after discovering he's been step-

ping out with a mystery woman! Guess you're just havin' one of
those weeks, huh, Boyd?

Daisy did not deem it newsworthy, but Tommy's first act on com-
mandeering the editorship of *Estime* was to appoint Gilbert and me
his executive assistants. We would receive handsome salaries and
full benefits.

Peter greeted our inclusion in the bargain as warmly as you'd
expect, but it did, to our great advantage, bolster his thorough mis-
perception as to why Boyd was forcing Tommy upon him to begin
with.

Since we had initially infiltrated his ranks to ferret out evidence
of his fiscal depravity, Peter assumed this latest offensive was merely
another, albeit more brazen, try at the same goal. Running Peter's
own magazine would provide Tommy an excellent vantage point from
which to observe the inner workings of Peter's empire, hobnob with
his intimates, and lay bare the dark secrets that Peter—judging from
his reaction to Elsa's threats—certainly possessed. Peter didn't like
the arrangement one bit but seemed, on balance, hopeful that he'd
buried the evidence so deeply that no spies, even agents in place,
could exhume it.

What Peter failed to realize was that Boyd wasn't *looking* for evidence. Not any more.

The minute Tommy had relayed to Boyd my innocent suggestion,
Boyd's whole agenda changed. He no longer cared about proving to
the world that Peter had cheated on taxes or bribed officials or swin-
dled investors or whatever he'd done. Boyd now had a simpler, more
elegant, and infinitely more entertaining goal in mind.

He would improve *Estime*.

With Tommy on hand to implement his suggestions, Boyd would
make Peter's magazine smarter, more literate and less sensational,
more intellectually demanding, loftier in purpose, keener to educate,
broader in scope, more sensitive to minority and international voices,
and less willing to talk down to its audience. He would, in short, run
the damned thing into the ground.

But Peter, hastily departing the *Heigh-Ho* with the preoccupied air
of a man with documents to shred, suspected nothing of this. He

assumed Tommy would be too busy playing George Smiley to be more than a figurehead at the magazine, that he'd officiate benignly at editorial meetings and leave the real work to his capable staff, who could, Peter reasoned, interview serial killers and peer into the souls of Oscar contenders without guidance from above.

It was a shame about Joy, of course. Though no ray of sunshine, she'd been a capable editor and was largely responsible for the magazine's success. Still, if someone's head was going to wind up on a platter, Peter naturally preferred it be Joy's lying there, setting off the parsley, than his own.

I don't know whether Claire surmised what Tommy's true purpose in taking over *Estime* was. His offer of jobs to Gilbert and me followed immediately on his call to Daisy, and my acquiescence left Claire so stunned I doubt she thought about much else. I knew what a blow it would be to her—I couldn't even look at her after saying yes—but with the memory of Tommy's kiss only minutes old, my acceptance was never in doubt. Claire maintained a wounded silence for the brief remainder of the meeting and refused Tommy's offer of a ride home, saying she'd find a taxi.

I called her that night and played the tormented love zombie, but she wasn't having any of it.

"Your motives are beside the point," she said evenly, having reached a point well beyond anger. "All I know, Philip, is that after dragging me into this fiasco, you've rewarded my efforts to extricate you by digging yourself in even deeper. Well, as of now, dear, you're on your own. If it doesn't bother *you* that you're an accessory to blackmail, I'm not about to let it bother me. I've been talking to travel agents all afternoon, and I plan to take a long, soothing cruise. It's time I began peopling my life with friends a little more sane and honest than you two—which leaves me a wide field. As of Monday, dear, I'm sailing off to tropical ports, far, far away from you and Gilbert and that refined Pied Piper you've surrendered your meager wits to."

"Well, good!" I said with horribly forced heartiness. "You deserve a vacation. How will I be able to reach you?"

"You won't. That is the point of the exercise."

She hung up, and I passed a few hours shuffling around my apartment, feeling as if I'd just played Caliban for a long run. I went for a walk, hoping the night air would ease my throbbing conscience. I'd only gone about three blocks, though, when I heard a dread, familiar voice calling my name. I raised my eyes from the pavement and saw Marlowe Heppenstall, the same lyricist I'd swanked last week, bounding toward me with feral glee.

"Philip!" he sang. "I *thought* it was you! I'm so eager to hear more about your show! Did it open yet?" he asked ingenuously.

"Yes," I said, glancing up to check out the sky. "Last night, in fact." Overcast, but no real hope of lightning bolts.

"*Did* it really?" he exclaimed. "I didn't see the papers—how did it go?"

It was rather savage of him, but I supposed I had it coming. I grimaced humorously, playing the wry young pro who can laugh off disaster, and said it had gone very poorly.

"Really?" he gasped solicitously. "I'm sorry to hear that! Gosh, and here I've been telling everyone how I ran into you and how *confident* you seemed!"

As numbing as it was to think that my next weeks would be peppered with such encounters, and as guilty as I felt over Claire, there remained one powerful comfort in my life, and that was Tommy. Whenever I thought of the life, or, at least, the affair, that lay before us, all my calamities seemed piffling and inconsequential.

The night after the conference on the *Heigh-Ho* was the night on which Tommy had, weeks ago, agreed to dine at my apartment. I fretted all that day, certain the fallout from his abrupt career switch would disrupt his schedule, necessitating a last-minute cancellation. This would have left me feeling not just miserable, but foolish to boot, as I'd rather overprepared for the date. I had, in the past, purchased new clothes for an assignation, but this was the first time I'd actually refurnished my apartment.

He didn't disappoint me, though. He arrived on time, bearing flowers, and gave me a hello kiss that pretty well notarized yesterday's IOU.

"I made lobster salad," I said, rocking slightly on my heels.

"Splendid."

"Actually, I bought it."

"Better still."

"I was going to cook, but you know how things have been, and I didn't want to be stuck in the kitchen, basting or something, with you out here, staring at the walls and, you know, getting bored."

I don't believe I'd noticed till that moment just how thoroughly sexual tension can impair one's capacity for insouciance. I blathered on some more, and Tommy, always the gentleman, laughed as if I'd put Oscar Wilde to shame.

I poured wine and we settled onto the sofa Bloomingdale's had delivered that very afternoon. I'd looked forward to learning more about him, since for all my devotion to the man, I knew little about what he did or where he'd come from. I began to probe, but he grimaced self-effacingly and said it was all very dull. He sketchily described an undistinguished stint at Cambridge, which he'd departed without finishing. After that, he said, he fell into magazine work, when, young and penniless, he became the kept boy of a wealthy editor. He then steered the subject to me and kept it there straight through dinner. He asked about my family and school and how I'd met Gilbert and Claire. He asked about my work and what else I'd done and what I hoped to achieve and all that. Like many a young writer faced with such a query, I blushed, said it wasn't very interesting, then yammered away about it for ninety minutes. Eventually it dawned on me that discussion had given way entirely to monologue, and I babbled an apology.

He laughed and insisted I hadn't bored him at all as I'd reminded him of himself at my age. We retired to the couch and I served strong espresso (no fool I), as Tommy enthused about what fun we'd have at *Estime*, once we really began shaking things up.

It was late by then, and I suddenly feared he'd abruptly shoot his cuff, exclaim over the time, and lament how early a morning he had. But my fears were misplaced, and events proceeded with the timeless, inexorable rhythm of mutual seduction. Chat gave way to silence, silence to smiles, smiles to bigger smiles, and from there deliciously on to kisses, prolonged necking, and the whole megillah.

After the sighs and tender exchange of compliments, he dozed off with his head on my chest. He lay there, perfectly still, his lithe frame sprawled in a long graceful curve as though posed for a sculptor, and I thought, God, he even sleeps attractively. I stayed awake for a long time, staring at this elegant man lying improbably next to me. I'd never dreamed that I would, in my entire life, see my fantasies of sex, high style, and prosperity coalesce in a single, perfect moment, and the realization that they had was indescribably heady. I felt like a Bond girl.

The next morning, as I warmed the brioches, I couldn't resist commenting that Gilbert would not be pleased if he knew what had happened between us.

"Yes," agreed Tommy, "which is why we're not going to tell him."

"I wasn't planning to," I said, though I had, in fact, spent my entire shower trying to get the wording right.

"As I'm sure you're aware, love, Gilbert's been making wonderfully subtle overtures toward me for quite some time. I've rebuffed them as gently as possible. But now we're all about to begin a splendid project together—it won't help team spirit much if I add insult to injury by flaunting our romance in the poor boy's face."

I agreed, saying I'd never want to hurt Gilbert's feelings. Truth was, of course, that the way Gilbert had treated me lately, I'd have been perfectly delighted to jump up and down on his feelings with cleats. It would not do to let Tommy see this coarse, competitive side to my nature, so I vowed undying discretion.

Peter's handling of the brouhaha over Tommy's appointment dovetailed so neatly with Boyd's own purposes that we had to wonder whose side Peter was on. His knee-jerk defensiveness proved the greatest asset we possessed.

Media magpies all over town were so fascinated by the *Estime* story that it nearly eclipsed the Elsa Debacle as the leading topic of gossip. (Some, no doubt, assumed Peter had done it only to deflect attention from his wife's spectacular failure.) Most pundits, egged on by Boyd's coy fulminations about "poaching" and "disloyalty," agreed with Daisy Winters that it was a great coup for Peter. Boyd had trained Tommy from the ground up, they said, and was grooming him to take over *Choice*, so the theft had dealt a harsh blow to Peter's competitor.

But, the same critics wondered, had Peter made a mistake in

replacing a sharp cookie like Joy with a less experienced helmsman? Had he let his vendetta against Boyd mar his judgment? This was where Peter's defensiveness proved so valuable.

Peter, like a man shooting himself in the foot, then calling it the latest in bunion therapy, claimed that Tommy was *exactly* what *Estime* needed. Under his stewardship, the magazine would not merely maintain but *refine* its high commitment to excellence. Joy had served well and remained a valued member of his corporate family; he hoped she would accept the newly created job he'd offered her as Chief of Development for New Publications. Reports that she'd hurled a chair at him on being offered this post were scurrilous and possibly actionable.

I yearned to see Tommy that weekend, but he spent all his time at the offices of *Boulevardier,* frantically tying up the July issue and grooming his successor. I dined with Gilbert, eager to prove to Tommy I could spend hours in my rival's company without dropping a single hint about our romance. Gilbert whined about how I seemed to be teacher's pet since I'd hatched the *Estime* idea, and I quelled his implied suspicions by moaning that I didn't see why, if Tommy was so pleased with me, he couldn't return my calls. We agreed that things would be a mite ticklish with all of us working together and vowed that, for harmony's sake, we'd consider the office off-limits to flirting. Affecting jealous uncertainty, I said, "Promise?" and Gilbert shook my hand and said, "Promise."

Then, after a moment, he said, "Of course, *you'll* probably do it anyway," and I said, "Oh, like you won't."

We went in together on Monday morning. It felt a bit eerie walking into Champion Plaza with Gilbert at my side and eerier still to think we were reporting to *Estime* to work for Boyd Larkin.

We rode up in the elevator with a small flock of staffers who seemed, from their feverish whispers, fairly agog over recent developments. Joy, however skilled an editor, had not inspired much affection, at least judging from the way one young man's lively imitation of her response to getting axed had the rest of them in stitches.

"Don't laugh," said a dark-eyed young woman, who appeared to have a deep sense of life's essential sadness. "Just watch. This Parker guy will be even worse."

"What's he supposed to be like?" asked one.

"*Very* piss elegant," said the young mimic. "Stuck-up British chintz queen."

"Actually," said Gilbert, interrupting in a chillingly polite voice, "he's a very brilliant man. I'm happy to be coming on board as his executive assistant."

It was mean, but fun. The staffers all jumped as though the Red Death had crashed the party. The mimic made nervous, giggly apologies, saying he was only repeating what little he'd heard about Mr. Parker from some friends of his who were, as he'd been about to mention, really dreadful people. The doors opened, and the staffers all said welcome aboard before rushing out like the bulls at Pamplona.

"Did you see that?" marveled Gilbert. "We inspire fear! This is going to be fun!"

We gave our names to the receptionist, who buzzed a line and bade us wait. A tall, thin woman in her fifties emerged from the offices and greeted us. She had the dry, cheery air of those office career women who, eternally buffeted by strife, intrigue, and chaos, manage somehow not to lose their sense of humor about it all. Her name was Miss Preston. She led us back into the office, taking long strides that were hard to keep up with.

"You see us at our most frantic today—though even our least frantic is still pretty damn crazed. I head up personnel, though as usual no one's told me what the hell you've been hired for. Are you writers?"

"Yes," said Gilbert.

"Done a lot of magazine work?"

"Oh, yes! I've contributed to *scads*," he said, adding that he wrote under a variety of pseudonyms.

She looked to me, and I said I'd written mainly for the theater, adding shyly that I'd done the lyrics for Elsa's recent show.

"We don't talk about *that* here!" She laughed. "Except in the ladies' room."

There was little about the place to suggest the glamour or influence of the magazine that regularly issued forth from it. There was a huge, harshly lit maze of cramped cubicles in the center of the floor through which we were now navigating. On the walls ringing this were rows of doors leading into private offices, presumably larger and enjoying views. Nothing distinguished the atmosphere from a dozen other places I'd temped, except the framed enlargements of stylish page layouts and ads that adorned the perimeter wall.

It wasn't nine yet, but already the place was seething with nervous speculation as staffers gossiped over partitions like nervous villagers. I supposed their anxiety was well founded. Peter, never the gentlest of employers, had already unleashed Joy Cudgel upon them; what still darker brute had he dug up now? Even smooth transitions of power are often accompanied by random bloodletting as the new overlord seeks to flex his muscles and strike productive fear into the hearts of his underlings. Who could say, at this early juncture, how many heads might yet be carried out on spikes?

It was startling to note how much consternation even *we* provoked. As we passed each knot of staffers, they'd stop chatting and ogle us with ill-disguised mistrust and apprehension. It made me feel as though we'd just barged into some Slavic tavern at the stroke of midnight and asked which way to Castle Dracula.

"Here you go," said Miss Preston, opening the door to a private office in a corner of the floor. It was spacious and looked out onto Fifty-seventh Street and, farther to the left, Central Park. "It's a very coveted office, so we have you sharing it to mollify the ones who've had their eye on it."

We thanked her and said it looked plenty roomy to us, adding that we'd have supposed this would be Mr. Parker's office. Miss Preston laughed and said he was upstairs in one of the *really* impressive offices reserved for Peter and the senior staff. She said she'd tell Tommy we'd arrived, then left, wishing us luck.

"Nice layout," said Gilbert, rushing to the desk with the better view.

"Not bad," I agreed. "I just wish I knew more about what the hell we've been hired to do. Tommy's been pretty vague."

Gilbert said I fretted too much over details and switched on the computer at his desk, wondering aloud if there were any games.

There was a knock at the door. A young woman, nice-looking if a mite heavily made up for nine in the morning, entered and said she was our secretary, Miss Garcia. She was just asking if we needed anything when in barged Hoot Mulvaney.

"Hey, big guy! Fancy seeing you here! Corner office, too!"

He spotted Gilbert and could not conceal a certain annoyance. I recalled his frantic questions to me in the wake of Elsa's performance and surmised that Peter, not trusting the young glory hound an inch, had now cut him completely out of the loop. He clearly hoped to worm the facts out of me and feared Gilbert's presence would nix any tête-à-têtes.

"Hello, Hoot. Glad we'll be working together."

"Yeah, me too. Say—" he began, and broke off, staring quizzically at Gilbert. A sense of déjà vu stole over me, then I remembered that the three of us had stood in much the same configuration once before, only Gilbert had been proffering hors d'oeuvres with Gallic suavity. I won't say my blood froze, but it got pretty slushy.

"I know *you*," said Hoot, snapping his fingers. "I can't think from where, though. . . ."

Gilbert smiled blandly and said he believed they'd met at Elsa's opening. Gilbert had been with Tommy Parker and someone had introduced them late in the party. Perhaps Hoot didn't remember; he'd seemed a little drunk at the time. Hoot frowned and said he was sure there'd been another occasion as well. Did Gilbert ever attend book signings?

This line of questioning was mercifully interrupted by the reappearance of dear Miss Preston, who knocked and poked her head in.

"Your Mr. Parker doesn't waste time. Full staff meeting upstairs in ten minutes!"

Twenty-three

Tommy stood, smiling benignly upon the pale, expectant faces that peered up at him from both sides of the long, lacquered table.

"As you all know," he began, his beautifully accented voice soft but stirring, "our employer is a man of great vision and daring. There are, in this world, doers and dreamers; but Peter is that rare and inspiring combination, a dreamer who does, a doer who dreams."

He paused and arched an inquisitive eyebrow as though to say "Do we not agree?" The staff, who'd assumed it was so much obligatory hooey and that they'd already responded correctly by not rolling their eyes, rushed to fill the silence. There were murmured assents and little exchanges, with one staffer asking another if Tommy hadn't captured Peter's very essence and the other saying yes, he had.

Tommy peered approvingly over the glasses that lent him an earnest, poetic look. The assenting choir fell silent, and all eyes returned to him.

There were about thirty of us at the table and another ten or so standing by the door. There were senior editors and managing editors, literary editors and art directors, copy editors and photographers, critics and columnists and contributors. I would be misstating matters if I said they all looked pale and malleable. Several, Hoot among them, had the bored, cocky air of athletes in math class, a studied nonchalance that bespoke their confidence in their own genius and indifference to regimes. Most, though, for all the eager smiles, seemed decidedly tense.

"Peter," resumed Tommy, "began this magazine with a dream—a

dream of excellence. He chose as his motto, 'A Peek at the Peak,' for he wished to celebrate those who'd ascended to the very pinnacle of contemporary society and culture. I'm sure most of you in this room feel Peter unequivocally succeeded in doing this. I feel so myself. But Peter himself does not agree with us. And it is Peter's opinion that counts. . . . By the way, I offer you apologies from Peter, who wanted very much to be with us but had to accompany his wife to an appointment with a leading allergist.

"To return to my point . . . when Peter approached me, oh, many months ago to sound me out about this job, he said a number of things that astounded me. He said he'd been feeling for some time that, in shaping the tone and policy of *Estime*, he had, perhaps, been unduly timid. He worried that in his desire to win approval for his fledgling publication, he'd wound up merely *reflecting* the public's taste and perception of excellence, when he had, in fact, meant to *challenge* that taste, to mold and refine it.

"But, Peter, we know, is a leader, not a follower. When he offered me this post he looked me straight in the eye and said, 'Tommy, it's time for me to stop condescending to my readers—time to listen to my inner voice, and trust that the public, which has followed me this far, will follow me if I dare lead them on to still higher peaks.' "

Well, not even Tommy's exalted delivery could keep eyes from rolling at that one. All around the table people swiveled their heads, shooting big looks to each other. You could hardly blame them. Peter, whatever his achievements, was not noted for the keen discernment he brought to the fine arts. It was known that he shunned the ballet, attended museums only when that's where dinner was, and had been to the opera exactly once—on which memorable occasion a reporter had asked him what his favorite aria was and he'd replied the front, because he could hear better. That he should now lay claim to a sensibility so exquisitely cultivated that he'd not dared impose it upon his magazine, lest he distress the masses, was so painfully ludicrous one could only howl.

On the other hand, or so the pensive looks around me seemed to be saying, could one really dismiss it as a joke? Laugh all you like, but Peter had secretly negotiated with this refined Brit for months and had, in the end, hired him, giving Joy an ungrateful boot. Publicly questioned on the wisdom of this, he'd hotly defended Tommy, saying he was just the man to lead *Estime* into the future.

"Peter," said Tommy, raising a hand, "begged me to stress, in putting this to you, that he had no qualms about the work you've done thus far. He thinks you're all prodigiously talented. He just feels things have gotten a bit down-market. He perceives the occasional whiff of the tabloid, and insists that, starting immediately, we set our sights a little higher."

"How much higher?" asked a heavyset literary editor.

"*Considerably,*" said Tommy. "I have no elaborate manifestos to present, but I shall, beginning this afternoon, start meeting with you individually. We'll discuss your past contributions and see how we might, perhaps, improve things in the future. I shall, of course, be horribly busy, so please feel free to voice any suggestions or concerns you might have to my able executive assistants, Mr. Gilbert Selwyn and Mr. Philip Cavanaugh."

He motioned to us, and we nodded politely to one and all, receiving in exchange a variety of obsequious or poisonous smiles.

"They'll also be contributing the occasional short piece. Philip, as you know, is the dazzling writer mentioned in this month's cover profile of Elsa. Gilbert served under me at *Boulevardier*. Those of you from Massachusetts are no doubt familiar with his marvelous pieces for the *Clarion*."

With that, Tommy once more voiced his delight over meeting everyone and declared the meeting concluded.

As the last of us meandered out to the executive-floor reception area, an elevator opened and Peter emerged, bodyguards in tow, looking wary and dyspeptic.

"Ah, Peter, old man!" Tommy said ebulliently, and hastened to shake his hand. The presence of several senior editors forced Peter to feign a semblance of chumminess. He bared his teeth and asked how things were going.

"Swimmingly," said Tommy. "Just finished a marvelous meeting. Everyone gung-ho! Full of team spirit."

The sight of both publisher and editor-in-chief standing about, available for immediate buttering, prompted three senior editors to rush to the scene and start slathering away.

"You picked one hell of a leader here, Peter!" opined the features editor.

"Yes," concurred the art director. "And I've really gotta applaud your approach to the future of this publication!"

"Thank you, Marty," said Peter, who never needed to understand a compliment to accept it.

There followed a torrent of tributes, all mercifully vague, extolling Peter's vision and exacting standards. The exchange soon blossomed into an all-out love feast, Peter praising his staff and concurring modestly with their opinion that he'd displayed boldness and brilliance in appointing Tommy chief. No single word of substance was uttered, but the editors came away firmly convinced that Tommy's policies enjoyed Peter's enthusiastic backing and that the two men were perfectly in sync.

Peter oiled off to his office, and Gilbert and I, who'd hung back during Peter's appearance, accompanied Tommy to his.

"Now," he began, leading us in, "as my executive assistants, dears, your duties will be rather comprehensive."

It was a large room, and the sparse decor, all selected by the previous occupant, seemed scrupulously designed to suggest wealth and authority grimly wielded. The desk was a V-shaped, black lacquered business, angled to point threateningly at underlings called on the carpet. The sitting area had a huge coffee table that was simply one incalculably heavy square of solid glass, placed directly on the carpet. Facing this were two sleek black leather couches.

Perched now on one of these, as though to round out the general air of corporate menace, was Joy Cudgel. She swiveled to face us and quickly exhaled a thick stream of smoke, which, I was relieved to note, had originated in a cigarette.

"Ah!" Tommy said brightly. " 'Joy cometh in the morning'! And a beautiful Joy she is. How may I help you, Ms. Cudgel? Did you leave something behind?"

"Only my standing in this whole fucking industry!" said Joy, violently extinguishing her cigarette in a huge onyx ashtray.

"Don't be silly, Ms. Cudgel. Our industry has the highest respect for you. I'm sure you've been deluged with offers."

"You bet your ass I have, but that's beside the point."

She advanced on Tommy, gesticulating violently and speaking at her usual machine-gun pace. "I do not take kindly to being dismissed from a magazine I single-handedly built from the ground up. I also don't like snotty fags skulking around behind my back. Just how the hell long were you and Peter talking about this before he sprang it on me? Because five days before I was fired he was talking long-range plans, deliberately misleading me, and that's called fraud. I want answers, pal, and I want them now!"

Tommy sighed and sat at his desk. Gilbert and I remained by the door, not least because Joy had also been aboard the *Siren* during Gilbert's increasingly regrettable stint as Henri. I doubted she'd be as slow to recognize him as the substance-addled Mr. Mulvaney. I leaned in toward him and whispered in his ear.

"Scrammez-vous."

He wasn't budging, though. He obviously felt this was far too juicy a showdown to miss and that if he remained inconspicuously by the door, no harm could result.

"My dear Ms. Cudgel," said Tommy, "I sense from the drift of your remarks that you're contemplating suing Mr. Champion for damages. If you hope I'll provide you with information to assist you in such a suit, you hope in vain. Peter's my employer and I owe him a certain measure of loyalty."

"Loyalty! Sounds pretty funny coming from *you*, after the way you ran out on Boyd Larkin!"

"My relations with Mr. Larkin are of no concern to you. For your own sake, I advise strongly against any legal reprisals, as they will only backfire. You were respected here, Ms. Cudgel, but not loved. If you compel Peter to defend his dismissal of you, he need only inform the court that your overbearing nature was so great a source of misery to his staff that he felt he could no longer inflict you upon them. Any number of your former subordinates will be happy to supply corroboration. Now, if you'll excuse me, Ms. Cudgel, I have work to do."

Her back was to us, so we were spared the utterly black look that must have greeted this speech. She inhaled deeply, as though preparing to rebut at length, but then, contenting herself with base humanity's favored two-word rejoinder to eloquence, spun on her heel and made for the door. Then, abruptly, she wheeled to face Tommy again.

"I've got one more question, pal."

"Oh, goody."

She thrust a sharp lacquered nail toward where Gilbert and I lurked by the door. "Would you mind explaining why the hell you've hired Peter's French cabin boy as a fucking *executive* assistant?"

Not even silver-tongued Tommy could respond to that with anything better than a mild "Beg pardon?" accompanied by a startled blink that did not suggest probity. To make matters worse, Gilbert attempted flight, a strategy that had he employed it earlier, might have helped, but now only confirmed his guilt beyond question. To make matters *still* worse, he didn't even succeed in leaving the room. Tommy's secretary, hearing the fracas within, had discreetly closed the door without our noticing. As a result, Gilbert pivoted nimbly, hurled himself against the closed door, then stood there, muttering "Shit!" repeatedly while inspecting his nose for breakage.

We all denied, of course, that there existed more than a passing resemblance between Gilbert and Henri, but the door business did not enhance our credibility or sangfroid. If anything, our denials persuaded Joy that not only were Gilbert and the Parisian steward the same person, but that the reason behind his bizarre double life was a secret of the highest strategic significance.

Joy leered in evil triumph. Vowing that she had resources to uncover what our "little game" was, she gave us a parting laugh of contempt and swept out of the room. If she'd had a mustache, she'd have twirled it.

I must confess that my concern over this development was mitigated by my delight at seeing Gilbert make such a perfect ass of himself. Romantic rivalry again. I may have won the battle for Tommy's heart, but that didn't mean Gilbert wouldn't still be around, dogging Tommy's footsteps and vamping him like an ambitious chorine. Such blunders as this could only dim his allure.

I made much of Gilbert's mulish insistence on remaining when I'd warned him Joy might recognize him, but Tommy chivalrously dismissed the incident. What was done, he said, was done, and we'd be silly to let a noxious tick like Joy rattle us overmuch or distract us from our purpose. There was work to be done, and it was time to begin.

Time was indeed a-wasting. The next issue was due in a mere three weeks. In keeping with the normal timetable of monthly publishing, the issue was already in an advanced stage of production. Boyd, though, was an impatient man and did not care to wait seven whole weeks to see his gambit bear fruit.

Tommy had his secretary place a call to the printer. He informed the incredulous gentleman that he was making extensive changes in the June issue. The lion's share of the current version, which was all but bound, was to be scrapped and replaced by features and pictorials not yet prepared (or, for that matter, conceived). Could the printer manage to produce the new issue on schedule as long as the material was delivered within a week of the delivery date? Tommy reminded him that newsstands teemed with weekly magazines that, while slimmer in size and stapled as opposed to bound, routinely published on as demanding a schedule. After long hysterical explanations as to why this could not possibly be accomplished, the printer finally allowed that, yes, such a job was *conceivable.* The additional manpower, though, and round-the-clock labor needed would make the cost overruns astronomical. Tommy said cost was not a consideration.

This chore dispatched, he asked Gilbert and me to prepare a list of suggestions for articles. We were to look for topics and personalities whose standing in the arena of high culture was unassailable but were, at the same time, unknown to the general public or, better still, known and despised. As we left, he was settling down with the page proofs, manuscripts, and layouts that represented the current June issue.

He emerged an hour later and began his rounds of the various departments. All that morning the air sounded with the soft thud of jaws hitting industrial carpet as one contributor after another was apprised that his latest effort was not in harmony with Peter's new editorial conception and a replacement would have to be found immediately. There was, of course, much strong comment on the impossibility of changing so much so late, but Tommy calmly assured everyone that the word *impossible* was (like so many others) not in Peter's vocabulary. Fortunately, Peter himself, his visits having always tended toward the brief and ceremonial, left midmorning, so he wasn't on hand to hear the wails and grumbles that echoed through the corridors of his publication.

I got my first personal glimpse of the dissension among the troops as I passed an early lunch browsing Doubleday at Fifty-fifth Street. I rounded a corner and there was Hoot Mulvaney, crouching in the aisle and frowning up a storm as he searched the bottom of the "M" shelf.

"Hello, Hoot," I said, thrilled to have caught him at it.

"Oh, hi," he said, bolting to his feet. "I was just looking for a little, uh, Melville."

"I believe he's on a somewhat higher level."

Hoot, keen to change the subject, pumped me for dish on Peter, confirming my suspicion that Peter had, since the Elsa debacle, confided nothing to him. Peter, he conceded angrily, was barely returning his calls. Hoot's investigation of Boyd had been called off, owing, so Hoot assumed, to Peter's feeling that he'd already bested Boyd by stealing Tommy and to the unlikelihood of Tommy consenting to run a piece trashing his ex-boss.

It was all very hard on Hoot. Harder still was Tommy's cancellation of his brilliant cover profile of Farrah Fawcett, which Tommy planned to replace with a piece on the action film star Vincent Bronco.

"And get this—*he* wants to write it instead of me! *Parker!* I say to him, 'So what the fuck am *I* doing for this issue?' And, get this, he tells me he wants me to write about this twelve-year-old Chinese girl—this *violin prodigy!* I say fine, what's the angle? There a custody battle? She been molested? She on pills maybe to cope with the pressure? *What?* And he says, 'She's twelve and she plays with the Philharmonic, that's not angle enough?' I mean, Christ! And this is the guy Peter hired to *improve* the magazine? What the hell is going on?"

I said his guess was as good as mine. I was just grateful my old chum Gilbert had persuaded Tommy to hire me as an assistant. If Hoot thought Peter had exercised poor judgment in hiring Tommy, why not just call Peter and tell him so? Hoot did not find this advisable.

On my way back to the office I decided to check out some weekly magazines to see what coverage Elsa had received. As I approached the nearest newsstand I was greeted by a curious spectacle.

A small, beleaguered Hispanic woman was thrusting a hundred-dollar bill at the vendor, even as she busily stuffed copies of the May *Estime* into a large canvas bag already crammed with so many of the same she could barely squeeze the new batch in. I knew I'd seen her before but couldn't think where. Peering closer at her round, pretty face, I realized she was one of Elsa's maids. She'd always been trembling when I'd seen her before and was hard to recognize now in her active state.

"Hello," I said, sidling up. "Lovely afternoon! Sorry, but I don't know your name."

"I'm Louisa," she said. She cast a nervous glance at the magazines, all of which featured Elsa, smiling delightedly from the cover.

My first impulse was to bust a gut, but then I realized this wasn't very kind of me. It must have been torment enough for Elsa to know the whole town buzzed with the tale of her shame, without also knowing this wretched magazine praising her and confidently predicting her triumph would still be on stands for weeks to come. But, while empathizing with her distress, I wasn't sure sending her maid to buy the copies up was the cleverest way to deal with it.

Louisa received her change, then turned to me, a finger to her lips. "Please don't tell anyone you saw me! Miss Champion don't want no one to know."

"My lips are sealed. Been at it long?"

She groaned in frank exasperation. "Four trips I make already! She send me and three other girls all over the place! Wall Street, West Side—even Harlem! I tell her, 'Miss Champion, no one *buys* it up there!' "

I said her bag looked full and asked if I could carry it home for her. She graciously accepted and we strolled to Champion Plaza, Louisa filling me in on the war at home.

Elsa had evicted Peter from her bed, consigning him to a guest room. With the exception of her foray to Boyd's yacht, she hadn't once set foot outside her room and seldom even rose from bed. She claimed to be deathly ill, though this did not explain her robust temper or appetite. She'd forbidden all music in the house and, just yesterday, fired a maid for humming. She was not taking phone calls and barred all visitors, including poor Mrs. Pilchard, who phoned daily begging to speak to her. The sole exception to this ban was "that bossy old signora," who had actually *moved into the apartment.*

"*No!*"

"*Jess!* She take the room next to Miss Champion! They talk all the time, and the signora, she has trances and tells Miss Champion her future. Miss Champion says to me, 'You be nice to the signora. She has powers!' She ought to have powers, the way she eats!"

The signora's appetites, however, seemed to extend well beyond the gastronomic. She apparently desired nothing less than absolute control over her pupil and was prepared to eliminate ruthlessly anyone who impeded her in this goal. Dunbar, whose position was held by the staff to be impregnable, dared be chilly to the old girl and was shortly dismissed, following the signora's somber warning to Elsa that Dunbar had, in a previous incarnation, been Charlotte Corday.

When we reached Champion Plaza, she took her burden of magazines, thanked me, and trudged off to the service elevators. It was nearing one when I got back to my office, and Gilbert was apparently at lunch.

It saddened me to think Millie was banished, though I could see why. It was, after all, Millie who had first introduced Claire and me into the household. Whatever their past friendship, Elsa could never again resist thinking of Millie as her personal Trojan horse. I felt a twinge of guilt and sheepishly instructed my secretary to send Millie a couple of dozen roses with a card saying I was thinking of her.

This done, I settled down to peruse my list of suggestions for articles. They all seemed like good tedious stuff and I decided to go upstairs, run them by my beloved, and, perhaps, steal a lunch-hour kiss or whatever.

When I reached his office he was just stepping out, arm in arm, with none other than Daisy Winters, who was grinning and scribbling away.

"How soon do you think you might find room for this?" he asked.

"Are you kidding?" asked Daisy. "I'm writin' this up in the taxi, hon. You can have it for breakfast. I see it as my duty to get positive things about the Champions into print *fast*, to balance all this malicious crap out there. People are so jealous!"

"Sad but true."

Daisy noticed me, and the sight affected her like a mouthful of vinegar. She'd obviously not forgiven me for that touchy moment in Elsa's dressing room when I'd instructed the guards to give her the old heave-ho. She inquired as to what I was doing at the magazine— "Who let him in?" was, I believe, how she put it—and I explained that Peter had, in gratitude for my meager rhymes, offered me a job. She sniffed and said Peter had always been like that. Generous to a fault. She thanked Tommy for the interview and swaggered off without a parting glance at this unworthy recipient of the Champion largesse.

I told Tommy I'd come up with a list of classy subjects all guaranteed to induce coma within three paragraphs.

"We'll have to run over them later. I'm about to have lunch with our new cover boy. I'll call soon as I'm through, though."

At that, the elevator opened, revealing the short but godlike form of that box office titan, Vincent Bronco. He emerged, clad in a tight Armani suit and sunglasses, followed by several senior editors, who, while struggling to maintain the air of blasé journalists long inured to celebrity, could not resist gaping.

I gaped myself, involuntarily struck by that dumb wonder megastars in the flesh produce even in those who are not fans of their work. I was certainly no admirer of Bronco's films. They tended to be loud, numbing affairs full of patriotism and explosions, featuring Bronco as the proudly inarticulate hero, a man who knows nothing of fear or surrender or shirts. There were, I knew, gay men who'd sit through anything to ogle those fabulous pectorals, but my own feeling has always been, if that's what you're in the mood for, head for the all-male section. The flesh is more plentiful and the acting's better.

"Mr. Bronco!" said Tommy, rushing to greet him. "I'm Tommy Parker. Good of you to come by on such short notice."

"No problem. I have a place right here in the building—I was one of the first to buy."

"A man of discernment. I can't thank you enough for consenting to be my first profile for the magazine. I wanted to start with a bang, and thanks to you, I can."

Bronco said he was happy to help a classy guy like Peter recover from all the "embarrassment about, well, you know." Tommy introduced me as his "valued associate," then they headed off to chow down at the Russian Tea Room.

A knot of loitering staffers observed their departure with palpable relief. If Tommy was chumming around with the likes of Vinnie Bronco, then obviously any fears that he was setting too ethereal a tone for the magazine were ill founded. If he insisted on assembling a new issue from scratch at the eleventh hour, this was probably just Peter's shrewd ploy to reap publicity. Let Tommy shake the place up, let him demand overtime, let him throw in some arty features to show they could be as highbrow as the next rag. What did it matter? Peter was in control. Bronco was the cover boy. *Estime* was still *Estime*.

Tommy kept his word to call when the interview was finished, which turned out to be just after two A.M. He asked if I wanted company, I said you betcha, and he came right over.

His repertoire of consonants was somewhat diminished, but he was still fairly lucid as he described the rollicking afternoon and evening he'd spent with his celebrated subject. The star's reputation for competitive machismo had proved amply warranted. Tommy remarked over lunch that the average Englishman's tolerance for booze surpassed that of his American cousin, and Bronco refused to let this go unchallenged. They spent hours downing one vodka after another, though Tommy shrewdly paid the bartenders on their route to alternate his own vodkas with mineral waters while providing Mr. Bronco an unadulterated flow of the real thing.

The star, thus lubricated, had emerged from the interview with the conviction that Tommy planned to write a rip-roaring valentine, describing their raucous night on the town and repeating many of Vinnie's surefire anecdotes.

Tommy, however, did not plan to approach the profile in quite so fawning a fashion. He planned instead to write a dry, academic piece, suitable for inclusion in some campus cinema quarterly, analyzing the star's small, repetitive, and undistinguished body of work, while tossing in the most banal and incoherent remarks he'd made during the actual drunken interview. This, said Tommy, giddily unbuttoning his shirt, would enrage not only the star, but, more important, his agent, a supremely powerful deal-maker, renowned for the bloodthirsty zeal with which he pursued his vendettas.

"He's a fiend, you know. Dreadful l'il bully! The day after this issue hits the stands we'll be absloot pryahs! Absloot pryahs!" Tommy giggled. He had an infectious laugh, and pretty soon I was giggling helplessly, too.

"Izz'n this fun!" he cried. Then he dove under the covers and a good time was had by all.

The next morning he had a bit of a hangover, but balm arrived in the form of Daisy Winters's column.

"The way you can tell a genius," Mama used to say, "is first he makes something perfect—and then he improves it!" Mama might have been talking about that human dynamo **Peter Champion**. Three years ago he gave us that great magazine *Estime*. But for Peter, great just ain't great enough. Thumbing his nose at the play-it-safers who say, "Don't tamper with success," Peter is overhauling *Estime* to make it even better. And what's more, he's doing it fast! New editor-in-chief **Tommy Parker** took a few seconds out from his killer schedule to gab about his new boss.

"When Peter wants change," says Parker, "he doesn't want to wait around for months for it! He ordered me to scrap the issue prepared for June and start all over again! It has us hopping—but what Peter wants, Peter gets!"

Peter himself was very hush-hush about his plans, but, in fact, he's so eager to create anticipation for his new *Estime*, he's even pulling the *old* one off the stands three weeks early to create a citywide *Estime* shortage! Talk about cagey! My spies tell me newsstands all over town have had their whole stocks bought out, so my advice to you *Estime* junkies out there is, get 'em while they're hot!

Well, we laughed ourselves silly over this, rolling all over my bed, hugging each other in helpless spasms of mirth. It was a wonderful moment. Tommy was just out of the shower, all wet and scrubbed and scented, and his arms were so strong and his laughter so ringing and contagious that I felt I'd never be able to stop. And I thought as I lay there, my sides aching from laughter, God, it's all worked out so perfectly for us. To think how sure I was at Elsa's opening that everything was ruined! Doesn't it go to show, it's always darkest before the dawn!

Claire, had she been present and reading my thoughts, would surely have remarked, "Yes, dear. And it's always brightest before the dark."

Twenty-four

Now that Boyd was, effectively speaking, publishing *Estime*, it was only natural that he craved opportunities to consult personally with its staff. So lunch hour that second day found me, Tommy, and Gilbert sitting round a large, ancient table in Boyd's library, shuffling through the manuscripts and photos representing the June issue we'd snatched from the cradle while debating what to offer in the way of a changeling.

Time was not on our side. The staff had read Daisy's column that morning and were understandably apoplectic to think the world was awaiting a bold new *Estime* and they, who were to produce the damn thing in record time, had yet to be let in on the contents. A few new pieces—the violin prodigy, the Bronco profile—had been initiated and the appropriate staffers mobilized, but the remainder of the issue remained a high-intentioned enigma. Tommy assured them that by day's end all assignments would be given out and our noble enterprise could begin in earnest.

It is, as you can imagine, no simple task to assassinate a magazine without seeming blatantly to have intended to. Our position in this regard was similar to that of those psychotic nurses who like to keep life interesting by bumping off the occasional patient. Poison, they know, will do the trick nicely, but the poison had better look like medicine or else it's whispers and finger pointing and a lot of embarrassing questions to answer.

Tommy, brainy fellow that he was, had already decided to let the contributors themselves commit half the crime. He knew they'd be less likely to grouse about churning out egregiously tasteful features if they could select the topics themselves, so when he'd made his rounds, telling the disheartened scribblers their efforts were being scrapped, he asked them to suggest alternatives of their own. He encouraged them to be daring, to think of innovative, "up-market" concepts more in keeping with Peter's new vision. Were there no areas or personalities they'd long yearned to explore but feared would be out of place in the old, glitzy *Estime?*

Many, of course, had no such buried inclinations, but he did find a small cadre of repressed aesthetes. Pale young Sarah Lawrence graduates who found interviewing best-selling novelists beneath them and longed to turn the spotlight on more obscure, but far worthier, authors. Closet intellectuals, pining to talk to an articulate person who *didn't* anchor a network news show. These timid souls now dared breathe names like Sontag and Derrida.

Tommy collected their notes, and we were now studying them, along with our own lists in an effort to discern which articles would best alienate the magazine's readership while seeming least deliberately designed to do so.

"Hmm," said Boyd, munching a cold herbed prawn, "I adore this Riggs woman's notion to do an appreciation of that blind Egyptian novella writer."

"Mr. Shoukri?" said Tommy. "Fine writer. Apparently he's had something optioned for a film."

"Oh, forget it, then."

Gilbert suggested we publish the work of an ex-beau of his who wrote spectacularly tedious gay science fiction. Tommy looked hopeful and asked if he'd been reviewed positively in *The New York Times.* Gilbert said he doubted it. Tommy frowned and said we'd best confine ourselves to dull writers who'd won the praise of prominent cultural arbiters, as this would give us something to point to when people asked why on earth we'd published them. Fortunately, such authors were by no means scarce.

Our confab was interrupted by a gentle cough issuing from just behind us. We turned and saw one of Boyd's sylphlike houseboys standing in the doorway with a harried air.

"Excuse me, Boyd, but there's this Miss Driscoll here and she insists on speaking to you."

The name landed like a radio in a bathtub. We rose abruptly, and Boyd motioned for the houseboy to shut the door. We could not, of course, say for sure how much Kitty already knew, but if she saw the lot of us together—particularly Henri—she'd know plenty. Given her fabulous sense of discretion, this was not to be desired.

Boyd was telling Ganymede to haul Miss Driscoll to the upstairs parlor when the door burst open and there was Kitty, eyes blazing. Many women might have refrained from yelling "Aha!" at such a moment, but Kitty wasn't one of them.

"Ah, Miss Driscoll," said Boyd, "I'm afraid this is a bad moment."

"Well, brace yourself, sweetie, 'cause it's gonna get worse."

We eyed each other warily and settled back into our seats, Gilbert and I gathering the magazine material and stashing it in folders. Kitty, who remained standing, gave a curt hello to each of us, except Gilbert, to whom she sneered, "Bone-joor!"

"You seem disgruntled, Miss Driscoll," said Tommy, putting the matter in a nutshell.

Kitty said she was plenty disgruntled and we knew why. We had invaded her privacy. What's more, we had taped it, then delivered the goods to her sister at a highly inconvenient moment. We had disrupted her once tranquil life, alienating the affections of both her sister and brother-in-law, and had, in consequence, jeopardized her entire financial future. What, she demanded to know, did we propose to do about it?

"Really, Miss Driscoll," clucked Boyd. "It's not fair to blame us for events that couldn't have happened without *considerable* cooperation from you. If your sister's mad at you, hon, that's all very sad, but you should have thought of that before you decided to enroll her husband in Hellenic *obed*ience school! If you're seeking financial reparations, I suggest you direct your request to Peter. Now, shoo, all right?"

Well, I knew Kitty a lot better than Boyd did, and I suspected this was a dangerous way to address her. This suspicion proved correct. Kitty marched over to where Boyd was sitting, plucked several prawns from the iced serving dish, and hurled them into his face.

"How *dare* you talk to me that way, you fat old fudge packer! Who do you think you're dealing with here, the Girl Scouts? You listen to me, granny, and you listen good. I had a sweet thing going before you and these *froo-ee de mer* here waltzed in and ruined it! If Elsa could've just had her career, she might've felt happy enough with that to give Peter the divorce he wanted, and *I* coulda had myself a billionaire! Maybe you can push Peter around—take over his whole magazine and fuck it up just for fun—but if I walk outta here today without what I came in for, I'm blowing the whistle on the whole damn thing!"

Boyd glowered up at her. He didn't rise, but he did kick her smartly in the shin with his pointy little shoe.

"*Ow!*"

"I am *not* Peter Champion," he said, wiping his face with immense dignity, "and I do not enjoy being *pummeled by fish!* You throw one more thing at me, cookie, and you're leaving here in mason jars!"

"That hurt," said Kitty, sitting and rubbing her shin. "I'd sue you for strikin' a lady, but I s'pose I did it first!"

At this point Tommy intervened, calling for civility. Kitty sniffed and said she was always prepared to be civil when treated likewise. Boyd asked her if she really believed it was in her best interest to go public with the details of her family's misfortunes. Mightn't her circle think less of her if she came forward as a mercenary vixen who'd repeatedly betrayed her own sister and in so singular a fashion? Kitty said she doubted very much if her circle could think less of her than it already did. Besides, she could easily paint a very different picture, with Peter the charismatic but depraved seducer and herself his pathetic, now penitent victim.

Boyd's response to this was a scrunched-up look, followed by a heavy sigh and a strange, wispy smile.

"I have misjudged you, Miss Driscoll. You are a very formidable young lady."

"You bet your ass."

"Tell me, Kitty, do you do consulting work? Because," he said, removing a checkbook from his sport coat, "I've been looking for a consultant for my magazine. *Choice*, that is."

"What do I do?" asked Kitty, a bit densely.

Boyd gazed wearily at the ceiling. "I *send* you an issue once a month, and you *tell* me what you *think* of it, all right?"

Kitty said that this sounded swell. A fee of twenty-five thousand a month was agreed upon, and Boyd dutifully cut the check.

"Nice doin' business with you," said Kitty, and, primly tucking the check into her purse, ate two prawns and wiggled out of the room.

I hated to be the one to say it, but this latest wrinkle seemed to render our little gibe rather a dicier business than it had seemed only minutes ago. This, to my astonishment, proved a minority view.

Boyd, for one, regarded the development with the casual resignation of a man for whom silence was a perennial item on life's shopping list. To him the payment was a mere routine office expense. At any rate, he argued, getting waspish, it didn't make sense to pay someone to shut up about your plans and then not *go through* with them. That was being wasteful.

Tommy's brow had looked furrowed at first, but once Boyd made clear his resolve, Tommy sighed and said, "Ah, well, in for a penny, in for a pound." I shot him an anxious look, and he responded with a gentle smile, as though to say he'd understand if I thought it prudent to withdraw from the fray. Gilbert, who, being Gilbert, had no trouble at all with blackmail if someone else was paying it, noted my troubled air and rushed to exploit it.

"Philip, are you *trembling?* You get so nervous about these things! Next you'll be having those stomach pains. If you want to call it a day, none of us will think one bit less of you!"

That was all it took to vaporize my qualms. I said I had no serious misgivings whatsoever and was merely playing devil's advocate. Then I suggested we table the issue for now, as we had work to do.

Work we did, and not wisely but well, returning to the office at three P.M. with a full outline for the first issue of the new, improved *Estime*.

We'd shrewdly selected several staffers' ideas for features and were justified in our hope that the general alarm over the magazine's contents would be blunted by excitement over Tommy's willingness to grant more autonomy to his staff than had been dreamed of under Joy Cudgel's regime. True, thus far he'd only granted this latitude to those who'd displayed a certain bent for the abstruse, but all were encouraged to hope they, too, would soon be given their heads.

Henry Kaminsky, a bookish man who headed the research department, had shyly asserted that a magazine that claimed to "peek
at the peak" might do more to introduce its readers to the true, if
unsung, intellectual giants of the day. Asked to specify, he offered
one Dr. Paul Skendarian, an MIT astrophysicist whose theories were
the cause of much debate (at least among people who actually sat
around debating astrophysical theory). A quick romp through the
man's recent essays had shown him to be an eminently suitable can-
didate. So brilliant were his speculations on the nature of matter that
not one of us could make heads or tails of them. We doubted, in fact,
if even Stephen Hawking could have read more than a page without
weeping in confusion. Tommy summoned Monica Tremayne, a contributing editor who wrote often on the fashion world, and told her to
pack her bags, as she was going to Cambridge.

The managing editor had gingerly put forth a case for excerpting
the work of a dynamic new gay novelist, Adam Peltier, assuring
Tommy that his great respect for the young man's work had nothing
to do with the fact that they were living together. Peltier's first novel,
which told of the tortured, sadomasochistic relationship between three
impoverished gay junkies, had been praised in *The New York Review
of Books* for its poetically surreal language and unsparing bleakness
of vision. William S. Burroughs had supplied a jacket blurb. Tommy
declared himself a fan of the author and was rewarded with galleys
of his second novel. The book, set in the same gritty milieu as his
first and titled *Please Don't Be Dead, Man*, was, if anything, more
unrelievedly depressing than its predecessor. Tommy purchased the
first serial rights for a large sum.

Balancing this glimpse at life's harsher realities would be an affectionate portrait of Charlotte Croft, the beloved British septuage-
narian novelist. She was, so Tommy assured his puzzled staff, the
most skilled contemporary practitioner of the novel of village life and
possessed a small but discerning following. A warmly written account
of her serene, disciplined (and all but event-free) life would help her
to win the wider audience that had eluded her thus far.

Staffers, alarmed at this rarefied parade of marginal figures from
the literary and scientific worlds, were relieved to note that the entertainment industry, long the main wellspring of the magazine's ap-

peal, was not entirely unrepresented. Apart from the Vinnie Bronco article, there were celebs galore recruited for the regular "*À Table*" feature—which, you'll recall, was a monthly transcript of a glamorous dinner party hosted by Peter or the editor-in-chief. The hubbub over Peter's plans had created such curiosity in the show-biz community that Tommy had his virtual pick of what stars he wanted in attendance. He chose carefully, inviting two wildly popular young actresses, a young male pop star, and an aging but legendary pop singer. Balancing these were a theater composer, a painter, a feminist film scholar, and a recently emigrated Soviet economist.

Most were so pleased by the blazing celebrity of the performers on the list, they didn't stop to note that the composer and painter were both notorious alcoholics, the economist spoke broken and heavily accented English, and the feminist was on record as deploring the entire oeuvres of the young film stars, none of whom, incidentally, had won fame for their eloquence. The staff no doubt assumed Peter would, as Joy had, meticulously edit the transcripts, concocting whole witty monologues if the need arose, so that everyone came off as scintillating as possible. Such assumptions were, of course, doomed to disillusionment.

Along with these features and Hoot's piece about the violin prodigy, Tommy announced two new columns to appear in the front section, "Estimations," which featured reviews of books, fashions, and movies. A Miss Enid Smythe would now offer a monthly critique of the museum scene. The other column, to be penned by one Milo Fessendon, would focus on television. This struck some as another welcome hedge against elitism. At least it did until they met Mr. Fessendon, a drooping young poet and semiotician, apparently possessed by the ghost of Ronald Firbank. So exquisite and ethereal was his nature that one gruff staffer was moved to bluntly inquire to his face if he ever consumed actual food or if he got by all right on photosynthesis.

Gilbert and I were kept busy, our most time-consuming chore being the writing of fan letters in response to the forthcoming issue. Tommy knew the issue would, if we got it right, provoke sacks of mail from *Estime*'s outraged fans. He hoped if there were appreciative letters as well, this would calm the staff and prevent a complete mutiny. So we laboriously wrote about a hundred letters each, praising articles that had not been written and signing them with names plucked at random from the subscription list. Boyd, who had far-flung connections, would have them mailed from the appropriate cities.

I was also writing a good bit of Tommy's cover story on Mr. Bronco, as Tommy hadn't a moment for it. He not only had to supervise the frenzied staff and cope with the vast technical difficulties imposed by the schedule, he also had to prepare and devise the *next* issue, which was, of course, desperately behind schedule as well.

He also had his hands full with Peter, who, in due season, began to suspect that Boyd, in forcing Tommy upon him, had had more on his mind than the facilitation of espionage.

Peter must surely have suspected that the frantic overhaul being enacted in his name was an act of pure and deliberate sabotage. It was, however, difficult for him to voice this suspicion to anyone on staff, as they would certainly ask what could have led him to suspect so heinous and improbable a crime. At any rate, his editors, fearing for their jobs and continuing to assume all policy originated with Peter himself, heaped so much praise on Peter that he could not have helped wondering if Tommy was not, in fact, improving the magazine.

Some hard evidence of the new issue's contents might have dispelled the fog of uncertainty, but the actual manuscripts weren't written yet and probably wouldn't be finished and edited (if at all) until zero hour. And by then, of course, there'd be no hope of altering a word. In the meanwhile, all Peter could do was roam the corridors of his magazine, sick with foreboding, while frenzied editors raced by calling, "Love the piece about the scientist!"

Of course, we knew the day would soon arrive when Peter would see he'd been well and truly hornswoggled. The question was, what would he do about it? Or more accurately, what *could* he do about it?

If he fired Tommy before Boyd was ready to call a halt to his campaign, Boyd would release the tape. Peter could counter by suing us all for blackmail, but could he prove it? It wouldn't be easy, not after all his bombastic endorsements of Tommy. To claim now that he'd made these with a gun to his head would strike most as a pathetic attempt to avoid taking responsibility for his own inept judgment.

And even if he could make a blackmail charge stick, this would not diminish the horrible price of exposure. The ribald mockery of the public would follow him to the grave, even as Elsa moved heaven and earth to demolish his name, his fortune, and his very freedom. No doubt about it, Peter was in a bind, and not the sort he preferred.

I was distressed, if not surprised, to find that Tommy's chaotic schedule did not leave him much time to play the ardent swain. He did, bless him, work to keep our romance at least a going concern, but our trysts were hurried affairs, conducted either very late or very early. At times I could not subdue the feeling that after each orgasm he was mentally crossing my name off a "To Do" list.

Still, he was, however rushed and unfortunately limited in his sexual repertoire a very sweet lover. He would, even while hurriedly dressing, beg my understanding for the rigors of his schedule and vow that the minute Boyd had finished his prank, we'd have more and better time together. Did I want to go to London with him for a few weeks? Would that make me happy?

Over the next crazed days the atmosphere at *Estime* reached levels of hysteria that made staffers reflect on the comparatively tranquil reign of Joy Cudgel with the nostalgia of ex-hopheads wistfully recalling the peace of the opium den.

Tommy had the art department completely redesign the "Estimations" section. One layout after another was submitted and rejected till the art director resigned in protest. He was replaced by a twenty-four-year-old woman named Chloe who specialized in that downtown, whimsical style of typography that calls to mind drunks playing Scrabble. Her free-wheeling ways won her few admirers, and the whole department soon boiled with hostility.

The people in research were also beside themselves. Their tenure at the magazine had made them ardent archaeologists of scandal, primed to dig into personal histories until every shard of scandal had been unearthed, dusted off, and tagged for display. Now, bleak hours of overtime spent probing the backgrounds of astrophysicists and lady novelists who, as far as the record showed, did not even possess genitalia left the poor dears wilted and despondent.

The contributors labored mightily to deliver their pieces by dead-
line. Those who managed to finish with any time to spare were cheerfully asked to do extensive revisions.

Tommy reigned over the chaos with a relentlessly upbeat attitude
that verged on a sort of deranged ebullience. A tireless cheerleader,
he bounded from one department to another, praising the harried
staffers' efforts while spouting inspirational twaddle. "Excellent!" he'd
cry. "But you can do better still. Dig deeper! We are all miners,
excavating the ore of excellence buried in our own veins—the deeper
we dig, the higher we rise! (I cannot claim credit for the thought—
it's one of Peter's.)"

As crazy as he drove people, he was not widely disliked. There
were, of course, a few who simply detested him, but a lot of people
seemed to fall under his spell. He was, after all, kind and courteous
and awfully good looking. He *exhorted* them, unlike Joy, who was all
threats. He displayed unshakable faith in their ability to work miracles, and many, while resenting his pace and perfectionism, were
determined to live up to his expectations. Even Hoot Mulvaney, who
I'd thought would be no end of trouble, ultimately ceased his grousing
and approached his prodigy profile with a professional's dogged de-
termination to please.

Gilbert's and my relations with the staff were cordial but fairly
distant. They maintained a vague, mistrustful belief that we were
there primarily to spy. We hoped this would change eventually, but
for now there wasn't time to worry about it. Anyway, we had each
other, and I had Tommy besides. The knowledge of this filled me
with happiness. It also filled me with a blind insane optimism, the
sort that sees disaster looming and because it cannot bear to ask *when*
asks *if*, answers *maybe not*, and thinks about something else.

My eviction from this fool's paradise was no gradual affair, with first
and second notices and leisurely hours to pack things in cartons. No,
it was more like having the landlord burst in and stuff me down the
mail chute.

The fatal day was the Thursday before the magazine would reach
the stands. It was a glorious afternoon, and I'd elected to get some
sun by taking lunch on one of the benches that line the entrance to

Champion Plaza. I was just finishing my cottage cheese when a cab pulled up and Gilbert got out.

Gilbert has never been one to suppress his more extravagant emotions, and I could see, even at a distance, that he'd been through some shattering experience and didn't care who knew it. He stood, stricken, on the sidewalk, running his hands through his hair and looking rather the way Oedipus must have looked in the moments preceding his elective surgery. He began to advance toward the building with the staggering gait of a cat emerging from a clothes dryer, and lurched right past me without even noticing me there.

"Gilbert!" I said.

He stopped and turned. He started a bit and then fixed me with a look of infinite pathos.

"Philip!" he said woefully.

"You look awful, hon! What the hell happened?"

"Oh, *Philip!*" he repeated, shaking his head miserably.

"What *happened?*"

"Philip, Philip, *Philip!*"

It took him a while to stop Philiping, but I got him to sit down and eventually he reclaimed his vocabulary.

"You're a lucky man, Philip!"

"How do you mean?"

"I mean about Tommy."

I flinched. So, I thought, that's what all the drama's about. Tommy had decided the time had come to end our back street affair and at last walk proudly in the sun. He'd apparently started by giving the news to Gilbert.

"Oh . . . Tommy," I said with appropriate gravity. "So, he told you, did he?"

Gilbert peered at me in confusion.

"You mean, you knew about it, *too?*"

Now it was my turn to be confused.

"I'm not sure I know what you're talking about. You just said I was lucky about Tommy—"

"Yes," said Gilbert, "that he never slept with you, and seduced you into thinking he loved you, the way he did to me!"

It's not easy to stagger sitting down, but I managed, falling against the back of the bench and gripping the seat for support.

"Oh?" I said.

"Don't be angry with me, Philip! He insisted we keep it from you. For the sake of team spirit. And don't envy me, either! The man is scum! I just stopped by his place—I still have my keys, though he's always told me to call first. I heard voices in the bathroom. I popped in and there he was, standing in the shower—with Hoot *Mulvaney!*"

"Oh?"

"Hoot *Mulvaney!* He tried to be all suave about it—said, 'Oh, hello, Gilbert, I was just going over Mr. Mulvaney's piece.' I looked right at Hoot's thing and said he'd edited too much. The man is slime, Philip! He'll seduce anyone or anything to make them do what he wants! How I envy you. It must have been hard to be led on by him, but at least you didn't have your heart broken like me! He used me, Philip. He's used us both!"

"*Hoot Mulvaney?*" I repeated, still having a hard time with that part.

"Can you *believe* it! No standards at all!"

"I didn't even know Hoot was bisexual."

"Please! You've read his books," sneered Gilbert. "Anything with a pulse!"

As numb and confused and heartbroken as I was, I knew it was time to tell Gilbert of my own role in the Tommy saga, if only to prevent him from once again decrying Tommy's complete lack of standards while congratulating me on being rebuffed by him. As I began to speak, though, I became suddenly aware that the shoppers scurrying past were stopping and pointing excitedly toward something behind our bench. I turned and realized this was no longer an appropriate moment to divulge the tragic details of my love life.

A tall, heavyset man was three feet away, training a minicam directly on Gilbert and me. Beside him, microphone in hand, stood Spark Chandler.

"Excuse me, gentlemen," said Spark, entering the frame. "I was wondering if you could answer some questions?"

Twenty-five

There is, of course, no really *good* moment to be publicly accosted by an investigative reporter, but it would have been hard to imagine one more inopportune than this. I remember thinking as I stared, openmouthed, into the camera that it was probably some divine vengeance for all the times I'd sat in front of my TV, cackling in delight as Mike Wallace waylaid some alleged malefactor and made him wish he'd rehearsed more. On such occasions, as I watched the sweat fly off the poor sap's head as if he were a garden sprinkler, I'd invariably think, Boy, does *he* ever look guilty!—for they always looked very guilty indeed. What never occurred to me was how damned difficult it is *not* to look guilty when some smoothly coiffed anchorfiend leaps out of the shrubbery with a camera and starts inquiring away. You're unprepared, naturally, and so flustered it's difficult to act innocent even if you *are*. And we *weren't*, which, as you know, makes it even harder.

"Mr. Cavanaugh and Mr. Selwyn," said Spark, clarifying the cast for the home audience, "would you mind discussing some puzzling events at Champion Publishing?"

"It's a bad moment," Gilbert said stonily. I didn't imagine this would deter Spark. Reporters don't do these things at our convenience any more than owls make appointments with field mice.

"In that case," said Spark, "I'll try to be brief."

By now a crowd had gathered. Even the most jaded New Yorkers, the sort who affect airy indifference when passing location shoots, cannot resist the spectacle of a hardbitten TV journalist devouring his stunned prey.

"Mr. Selwyn," he began. "Your name *is* Gilbert Selwyn, isn't it?"

"Yes. What about it?"

"I'm just curious. Because some weeks ago I was a guest on Peter Champion's yacht, the *Siren,* and you were also on board, working as a steward. Your hair was darker, you wore a false mustache, and you said your name was Henri Foumier. I've since located the real Henri Foumier, who says he's an acquaintance of yours, and that when you last saw him, six weeks ago, his wallet mysteriously disappeared. At the same time you were working on the boat for Peter Champion, you were also working for his rival, Boyd Larkin, at *Boulevardier.* Perhaps you could tell me, Mr. Selwyn, why you went to work for Mr. Champion, using a stolen identity, and why you're now working at *Estime* in an executive position, even though your magazine experience is severely limited?"

As probing questions go, it was a little convoluted, but the crowd, catching the general theme of corporate intrigue, was hooked and not about to touch the dial. Spark smiled a cruel smile and waited, well pleased with himself.

What Spark could not see was that he'd made a serious miscalculation. He'd hoped a public ambush would produce the kind of sputtering evasions his audience lived for, and at another time, perhaps, it might have. But Spark had interrupted a man mourning the death of love, and Gilbert's anger at this superseded his fears.

"Get that thing out of my face!" he said, swatting Spark's microphone. "What are you breathing down *my* neck for, you big goon? Did the necrophiliacs cancel?"

This won a chuckle from the peanut gallery, which didn't please Spark any.

"If you'll just explain, please, why you impersonated Mr. Foumier?"

"What impersonation? Henri's an excellent waiter—it was an homage! Why, I'm surprised you *noticed* me on that cruise, the way you were knocking back the gin and tonics!"

"Mr. Selwyn," fumed Spark, "if you'll just explain why Peter Champion—"

"No! If you have a question for Peter, ask him!"

At this point, Gilbert decided to put his case before the crowd.

"Know why he's doing all this? I'll tell you why! Peter *fired* his *wife* a few weeks ago—small wonder, too, if she's half the pain in the ass he is! Now she's probably hanging around the apartment all day in her bathrobe, making his life miserable, saying, '*Spark! Spark! Peter fired me! Make him pay for it! Make him pay!*' "

"My wife," said Spark, straining to be heard above the buzz of the spectators, "is indeed part of this story! Perhaps you can tell me why Peter would replace an editor who brought circulation higher with every issue?"

"She was a *bitch*, that's why!" shouted Gilbert. "An absolute *tyrant!* Nobody could *stand* her!"

"Hey! She happens to be my *wife!*"

"Well, then you know what I'm talking about. If you could hear some of the things they say about her up there! There's this one fellow has a photo of her where he's superimposed this—"

"*All right!*" bellowed Spark. "That's enough! Interview's over!"

He gestured violently to his cameraman, who was fighting laughter with marginal success. "We'll speak again, Mr. Selwyn!" said Spark, and, striding briskly toward the curb, huffed off down the avenue, leaving the cameraman free to laugh all he pleased as he waddled to catch up with him.

A lively debate erupted among the observers over Gilbert's remarks about Joy, some claiming he'd displayed a misogynist's knee-jerk contempt for women in power and others saying they worked at the magazine and she really was a bitch. It seemed a prudent time to slip away from the crowd and find a quiet bar where we could raise a glass and sift through the ruins of our dreams.

We found a nice dive on Eighth Avenue and settled down with two Scotches. I finally had the chance to tell Gilbert that my experience with Tommy had been remarkably similar to his own. Though initially stunned and waspish, he soon saw it was a bit cheeky to rail at me for crimes he was no less guilty of himself. He switched gears then, saying he was *glad* it had turned out this way. It created a bond between us, a foundation of shared anger and sorrow on which to rebuild the friendship we'd so stupidly damaged in our pursuit of a charming cad. The Tommys of this life, he said, raising his glass, came and went, but we were friends, the best and oldest. It was terrible to think how close we'd come to losing each other forever.

"We've been fools, Philip!"

"I know," I moaned. "This hatchet job on *Estime!* How could I let them talk me into it?"

"You didn't," said Gilbert. "You talked *them* into it."

"Don't remind me!"

"Quite a stink there'll be when it all comes out," he mused. "I mean, think of it!"

"Believe me, I'm thinking of it."

"I've been trying not to myself," he confessed. "Tried it once. Didn't care for it."

I admitted that I, too, had gone out of my way not to ponder the ramifications of our prank, particularly its effect on the innocent members of *Estime*'s staff. When we'd planned it all, their fates hadn't even crossed our minds, yet here we were now, making life pure hell for them. Some had already quit, and how many more would find themselves unemployed once the circulation began plummeting?

"Oh, they'll find other jobs," said Gilbert, whose moral arithmetic makes up in swiftness what it lacks in precision.

What was most painful to contemplate was how horribly far we'd strayed from our original goal. We'd begun the enterprise full of the noblest intentions, determined to be fearless, triumphant crusaders for truth. We would infiltrate a corrupt financial empire and expose its dark secrets to the world so justice could be served.

Well, we'd infiltrated all right, and it was indeed a corrupt empire, as witness Peter's terror of Elsa spilling his beans. All *we'd* managed to dig up, however, were some tacky sexual secrets of no legitimate concern to anyone but the participants. And these we'd spitefully exploited not in the service of journalism—even *gutter* journalism— but in that of an overage delinquent who couldn't bear that his rival should sell more magazines than he did!

To think how easily we'd gone along with it all! Drunk with status, blinded by lust, we'd made the transition from defenders of truth to blackmailing lackeys so smoothly that my mind reeled at the thought of it. We'd started out to write an exposé and wound up as subjects for one!

The question was, how could we undo the damage and avoid exposure? The answer: Where's Claire when you need her? We agreed, though, that the very first thing to do was quit, and fortifying ourselves with a final Scotch, we marched off to confront our three-timing editor.

Tommy, as might have been expected, was maddeningly urbane about the whole thing.

"I feel *dreadful*, of course, to see you both so put out. But ask yourselves—is it fair to be angry with me for hurting your feelings when it's obvious my sole intention was to *spare* them? You both seemed so infatuated with me, which was incredibly flattering. I liked you both very much, too, and saw no harm in making you happy until your infatuation had run its course, which I trusted it would in due time. And I *did* make you happy. You've told me so yourselves. We've had a lovely time! I doubt we're likely to face our sunset years together, but I see no reason not to maintain our arrangement for now."

"Including Hoot?" sneered Gilbert.

"Let's not bandy a gentleman's name. Mr. Mulvaney was having some difficulty apprehending my vision for the future of *Estime*. Sometimes actions speak louder than words. Rather shameful of me, I know, but one makes sacrifices for the cause. Though I hope you don't think for a *minute* that I think of either of *you* that way. Because I don't, really."

The phone rang, which surprised me, as he'd asked to have his calls held. He answered immediately, though.

"Hello, dear, may I phone you back? . . . Yes, at the moment, in fact. . . . Tell you at dinner." He hung up.

Hearing the casual intimacy of his tone, I had a sudden and altogether horrible intuition. I knew it had been Boyd on the line, and I knew with equal certainty that Tommy served his employer in more capacities than I'd ever cared to realize.

I remembered how the first night I'd met Boyd, he kept coming on to Tommy, who primly rebuffed him; the scene had obviously been solely for my benefit. They knew I was smitten with Tommy and played brilliantly on my hopes to keep me eager and cooperative. God only knew what sort of arrangement they had—it was obviously not exclusive, but I doubted anyone lasted with Tommy much longer than they were useful to Boyd.

"Listen, darlings," said Tommy, smoothly escorting us to the door, "I will not hear of you resigning over this romantic nonsense. Your work is done on this issue—and marvelous work it's been—so why don't you both take a little time off? As much as you need. When you're both ready, hurry back, and then . . . onward and upward! I assure you, you'll have very lucrative positions with us for years to come!"

We chewed it over as we walked glumly home through the park, and the more we thought about it, the more depressingly clear it seemed. Tommy had done a great deal more for Boyd than one does for a mere boss. Any reporter might go to extremes for a good scoop—but *blackmail* people? Seduce others? Drive a magazine into the ground—thereby ruining your *own* reputation as an editor? These were things you did only for a lover—one who was old, obscenely rich, and who lacked any obvious heir to leave his staggering fortune to. There was a man whose whims you would gratify, regardless of difficulty, methods, or cost.

Boyd's whim was indeed meticulously realized. The magazine was on the late side, not appearing on stands till four P.M., but it had all the weight and glossy production values of a regular issue. Gilbert and I picked up copies and trudged back to my place to assess the damage.

The first affront to the reader's eye was the cover picture of Vincent Bronco. It was as unflattering a photo as had ever graced a major magazine. The star seemed to have been captured in some moment when the photographer said something he either didn't quite hear or else failed to comprehend. Whatever the reason, his expression was one of complete slack-jawed confusion. Nine out of ten people, asked to fill in a word balloon over the star's head, would have immediately chosen "Duh."

The caption next to this read simply, "Vincent Bronco: An Appraisal." This studied blandness was echoed in the other cover headlines, which, once geared to provoke and titillate, now strove only to sedate. Thus, a headline that might, under Joy, have read, CHARLOTTE CROFT—PROBING THE NAUGHTY UNDERSIDE OF VILLAGE LIFE! instead ran, CHARLOTTE CROFT: ANOTHER COMPTON-BURNETT? Similarly, we did not get SPACED OUT! A TOUR THROUGH THE AMAZING BRAIN OF PAUL SKENDARIAN! but, PAUL SKENDARIAN, BELEAGUERED THEORETICIAN.

These, combined with that bovine photograph, plus smaller headlines announcing "Two New Columns: Television and Museums" and "Exclusive Book Excerpt: *Please Don't Be Dead, Man*" made for a cover that throbbed with the promise of tedium.

As for the actual articles, I was already familiar with some of them. I'd written half the snidely academic Bronco piece and had personally selected the mercilessly grim passage from *Please Don't Be Dead, Man*. I glanced up at Gilbert and guessed, from the crinkling of his nose, that he was now perusing the latter.

"Reading the junkie book, huh?"

"Yes. *Eeuuuuuw!* I mean, he can't just say, 'The medics pumped my stomach'? He has to *describe* it for three pages?"

I skimmed the astrophysicist profile. The poor writer, completely unable to summarize or even paraphrase Skendarian's theories, had simply transcribed her tapes, letting him speak for himself in long, incomprehensible paragraphs. She'd interspersed these quotes with painful attempts to give the piece some of the old *Estime* oomph, but the abstruse quotes kept getting in the way, like speed bumps on a race track.

> You may have trouble making sense of this debonair man of science's groundbreaking theories (after a while my head was spinning, too!), but one thing's for sure—Dr. Skendarian is *hot!* Just mention his name in any leading observatory and watch while the Big Bang repeats itself! Says Dietmar Shickellhoff, Princeton's tousle-haired bad boy of astronomy, "It's Skendarian's ability to glimpse new postulates in bold extrapolations of fragmentary data that make his hypotheses intriguing not only to cosmologists, but to epistemologists as well."

Tommy had been correct in assuming the life of Charlotte Croft had not been fraught with drama. Married to the same village apothecary for forty-five years, she spent most of the three-thousand-word feature describing her sedate home life, while professing sweet astonishment that an American magazine should wish to interview her, as her books sold so very poorly in the States.

The museum columnist dished up a less-than-gripping appreciation of the Prado, while Mr. Fessendon offered an airy if impenetrable dissection of a popular sitcom's roots in commedia dell'arte.

Without a doubt, the issue's most embarrassing feature was "*À Table.*" Tommy had winkingly promised the participants the tapes would, as always, be "edited" but in fact the only thing he edited out were the participants' frequent pleas for assurance that everything they said would be rewritten. The results were harrowing.

None of the older guests had seen the young stars' films, except the feminist critic, who loathed them and wanted to discuss the way they perpetuated demeaning sexual stereotypes. The more well spoken of the two actresses countered that they were "just, you know, movies, *okay?*" and begged that the topic be changed. Eliminating the subject of their films, though, left the actresses little they could knowledgeably discuss, especially when the feminist witheringly dismissed the topic of hair care the moment it was introduced.

Amiability was briefly achieved as Tommy and the composer breezily discussed the current opera scene, but then the painter, who was drunk, said opera bored him, and the pop star said, yes, him too. The painter launched into some unseemly boasting, saying he'd just received two hundred thousand dollars for a canvas that had taken him half a day to paint. This interested the pop star, who'd seen the artist's work and felt he could do as well and in still less time. The painter became truculent.

The aging Vegas legend, half in his cups, commenced flirting with the actresses, making low, ribald references to their physical charms while wittily claiming to be "more endowed than Harvard." This prompted much strident comment from the feminist critic, even as the composer, now also drunk, began making coy overtures to the young male pop star. The distinguished Soviet economist maintained a confused silence throughout, speaking only to request salt and to accept the painter's apology for spilling a bottle of sauterne wine on him.

The participants, Gilbert and I agreed, must have been stunned to see their most banal and obstreperous remarks rendered with such damning fidelity, right down to parenthetical asides reading "(*inaudible; mouth full*)."

"You think they'll sue?" I asked timidly.

"They'll have to get in line behind Bronco. 'Cinema for the brain dead'! Was that yours?"

"Oh, God," I whimpered, heaving the issue aside. "I wish Claire were here!"

"Still on her cruise, is she?"

"God knows. I've been leaving messages all weekend."

Gilbert regarded me with condescension and pique. "Really, Philip!" he clucked. "To hear you go on you'd think Claire was the only one of us with half an ounce of intelligence! I'll grant you she's a bright girl, but so am I—bright, I mean—when I'm not totally blinded by love, which, I admit, I was, but I'm not anymore, so let me just *think*, all right?"

A moment passed.

"Yes?" I prodded.

"I'm thinking!"

I said I'd assumed as much from his face, which resembled the first half of a laxative commercial. He threw his magazine at me, and the phone rang.

I picked it up, hoping it might be Claire, and instead heard the last player in our drama I'd expected ever to hear from again.

"*Buon giorno, Meester* Cavanaugh!"

"Signora!" I blanched.

She cooed that she did not wish to interrupt all my clever writing, but as she'd been unable to get through to Boyd, perhaps I might deliver a message for her?

"Meester Champion says he would like very much to sue Meester Larkin. But he is afraid if he does this, Elsa, who is very angry with him, will be embarrassed and take revenge upon him and tell all his secrets! You are aware of thees?"

"Uh, yeah."

"Well, Meester Champion thinks perhaps Elsa *would* stand by him and not tell his secrets—*that she would even testify that Boyd Larkin was blackmailing him*—if only *I* would advise her to do so. You see, Elsa listens to me very much now—thanks mainly to *you*, Meester Cavanaugh! Peter will be most *grateful* to me if I tell Elsa my spirits advise her to be loyal to her husband."

"Really?" I said.

"*Sì.* I have not yet made contact with my spirits—I would like first to know what Mr. Larkin has to say."

"I see," I said. "Uh, these spirits of yours—they have kids to put through school and all that, I guess, huh?"

"Ah! I see at last we are *simpatico*, Meester Cavanaugh!"

I told her I'd duly relay her message to Boyd or Mr. Parker. She thanked me, gave me a number where she and her spirits could be reached most afternoons, and, bidding me a cheerful ciao, hung up.

I gave Gilbert the lowdown (and seldom has that word been more aptly applied), saying that, as long as he was busy masterfully solving all our problems, he might want to pause and factor the signora into his calculations.

"Actually," said Gilbert in the dry, self-assured tone of Gore Vidal on a book tour, "the signora's little call has already made me see the easiest way out."

"Oh?"

"Yes. It's quite obvious, really. Or is to *me*, anyway. Perhaps you'd care to hazard a guess as to my approach?"

"I haven't a clue, Gilbert."

"I thought not," he sniffed, and outlined his approach.

It was possible, he argued, that even if Elsa *did* agree to back up a blackmail charge, Peter would still refrain from bringing one. The embarrassment would, after all, still be hefty. Peter might just use the threat of Elsa's cooperation to force Boyd to surrender *Estime* and let the matter rest there, avoiding the humiliation of a trial.

It was, however, possible that Peter's desire to destroy Boyd might outweigh even his reluctance to go public with the story. He'd be mortified, yes, but Boyd—and we—would face the full wrath of the law. Which course Peter chose would ultimately depend on his reaction to the rape of his magazine and the ensuing embarrassment and financial loss, both of which, on the evidence of the June issue, seemed likely to be considerable.

But, concluded Gilbert, the two of us could completely neutralize Peter, seeing to it that the first scenario prevailed and the game ended in a draw.

"How?"

"You're so dense, Philip! Think about it—why hasn't Peter been able to make a move yet? Because Elsa has evidence of all his shady business deals. All we have to do is get the *same* evidence and we're home free!"

"Oh, good," I said, sinking back on the couch. "I was worried it might be hard."

"It's *perfect*, Philip! Peter holds the Elsa card over Boyd's head to make *him* withdraw, we hold the evidence over *Peter's* to keep him from suing, and the whole nightmare is over!"

"Yes, lovely, really, I can't see a single flaw. Unless you count our not having any evidence."

"I *know* that, you ass," he said with a snort of impatience. "We have to *get* the evidence. And we know just where to find it."

"Where?"

"On the *Siren*, of course. It's the most logical place for him to hide things. He wouldn't leave anything damning in the apartment with Elsa and the signora there all day, and he wouldn't keep it at the office, either—not with Tommy right across the hall. In fact, if he'd *had* anything good in his office, he probably moved it to the boat when he hired Tommy. Do you still have that burglar kit Boyd gave you?"

"Yes, but I really don't think it's a good idea to go—"

"You're such a wuss!" he cried. "Wuss, wuss, wuss! What are you afraid of? That we'll get *caught?* That Peter will *find out* we're spying on him?"

I balked some more, but he asked if I had a better plan, which, of course, I hadn't. So I called Tommy and dutifully informed him of the signora's new demands, then went to my dresser and found Boyd's rabbit's foot with its secret compartment and assortment of little keys and picks. Gilbert fingered the set, smiling fiendishly, then uttered the least prescient remark any of us had spoken since the whole sorry affair commenced.

"It's worth a try. After all—it's not as if we could make things any *worse*."

Twenty-six

Gilbert made another check on the list of the *Siren*'s stewards, then dialed the final number.

" '*Al-looo!*" he sang into the phone. "*Bonjour!* 'Ow are you, Florindo? Eet's me, Onri! . . . I meese you, too! Eet's mah birzday tomorrow and I'm having a party at a beeg restaurant! Can you come? . . . No, I pay for evvysing! Beaucoup booze! . . . I have now a vairy reech, vairy handsome young *père du sucre!* Maybe you come try steal him away from me, *non?* Ah, *bon,* I see you there!"

He gave Florindo the address, told him to be there by seven, and hung up.

"Voilà!" he said, intoxicated with his genius. "Ze boat, she will be empty!"

I pointed out that of a skeleton crew of sixteen, he'd invited a mere ten, leaving six on the boat, plus such stewards as decided Henri wasn't worth buying a gift for, beaucoup booze or not. He dismissed my concerns, saying his intimate knowledge of the boat's routines guaranteed our success. At seven o'clock those who hadn't gone to the party would be in the officer's mess, eating dinner. It would be the merest lark to steal onto the boat, plunder its secrets, then rush to the restaurant, which had been paid in advance and instructed to keep the guests lubricated until the birthday boy's arrival.

I reiterated my qualms about tagging along but was swayed again by Gilbert's assertion that he needed help and that action of any sort beat sitting around helplessly, waiting for the subpoenas to arrive.

Flurries of subpoenas were indeed seeming increasingly likely. By this point, the Wednesday after the issue's appearance, prospects were looking more sinister by the hour.

Spark had stepped up his ambush campaign, widening his net to include Tommy, Peter, Boyd, Kitty, and even Elsa, whom he caught en route to a dentist appointment. He got an outraged or hysterical "No comment" from everyone but Tommy, who laughingly dismissed Spark's elaborate conspiracy theories, saying that if there were, in fact, rumors afoot, Peter had probably started them himself to sell magazines. It was, however, getting more difficult daily to pretend that the storm over the "improved" *Estime* was remotely advantageous to anyone at the magazine, least of all its owner.

The June issue generated great gales of media comment. Opinion diverged, some saying it was a spectacular disaster, and others saying no, it was only a moderate disaster. This more forgiving, and less populated, group was made up of earnest intellectuals who felt Peter deserved credit for at least trying to give his magazine more substance, even if the results were, as one gently summarized, "uneven."

Tommy had, if anything, underestimated the responses his Bronco piece would evoke from the touchy megastar and his agent, the despotic genius of deals, Fred Caesar.

Mr. Caesar, unable to believe *Estime* had shattered Celebrity Journalism's sacred covenant with Stardom, was inspired to flights of rhetoric that made his usual bombast seem positively understated. He decried the piece as an act of "pusillanimous betrayal, unparalleled in the history of entertainment." Never again, he vowed, would one of his stars consent to "submit to the treacherous butchers of *Estime*." He also predicted the *rest* of the film community would join the boycott "through no coercion from this office, but instead, in righteous solidarity with a great and greatly maligned Star."

The younger celebs who'd been skewered "À *Table*" joined in the shrill chorus denouncing the magazine's "betrayal." Several claimed, rather stupidly, that they hadn't, in fact, said a word attributed to them. Tommy calmly replied that he had the tapes, and the feminist critic, who'd come off as pretty intelligent, if a mite cranky, swore that every word printed was a direct quote. Tommy went on to say that if the stars had leapt to the conclusion that their remarks would actually be *improved upon,* he could only weep for those who spent so much time in makeup chairs they expected even their words to be cosmetically enhanced for them.

I hoped, briefly, that the controversy would make Boyd's strategy backfire by sending sales soaring. But the more I read the issue, the less likely this seemed. While there are, of course, rabid media watchers in big cities who cherish a good industry feud, readers as a rule don't much care whose agent is up in arms over what unflattering profile. They want only to be entertained, and on that score the issue was, controversial or not, an unqualified failure. The movie star pieces, however alarming to the stars, were dull reading—and I'm sure Mr. Bronco's legion of fans did not appreciate being termed "brain dead." The rest of the issue was duller still, with one ponderous and unreadable piece after another. If the contributors' opening paragraphs were read by many, their closing remarks were studied by few indeed.

Angry letters began flooding in, though these were balanced by the ones Gilbert and I had written. Our rapturous, if rather vague, epistles of praise might have consoled the contributors but cut no ice at all with the magazine's advertisers, who didn't care for the issue one bit. These chic purveyors of expensive fashions, liquors, cars, and perfumes did not feel the new *Estime* spoke to their desired clienteles. Particularly displeased was the *chocolatier* who found his ad directly opposite the gay junkie's vivid description of having his stomach pumped. The advertisers, as one, smelled an imminent plunge in circulation, and ad page sales for the next issue suffered a steep decline.

Peter must have been a cauldron of rage over the losses. I doubt, though, if any financial blow could have galled him as much as the anonymous industry insider who, quoted in the *Times* business page, said, "Well, it's pretty obvious, isn't it? Peter Champion has tried to be Boyd Larkin. And he's failed."

With these black clouds rumbling overhead, I tended to agree with Gilbert's assessment that there was no way a little more breaking and entering could worsen our situation. And so the next evening found me lurking in the shadows near the Twenty-third Street docks, clad

in one of the ghastly green-and-gold mess jackets Gilbert had purloined during his stint as Henri.

"Ten minutes to seven," he fumed, peering at the gangplank
through opera glasses. "Can't queens be on time for *anything!*"

"Perhaps," I suggested, "Henri wasn't as popular as all that."

"Oh, shut up. I was loved. Just keep your eye peeled for Florindo—
he's the important one."

Florindo, Gilbert had explained, was the key to the whole operation.
The housekeeping schedule of the boat called for him to clean Peter's
office three times a week. The number code for the lock was changed
Thursdays, which was today. Florindo was under orders to memorize
the number, then destroy the paper it was written on.

Florindo, however, did not possess the sort of brain that delights
in memorizing nine-digit numbers. He tended, Gilbert had noted, to
hold on to the paper. Our plan was to rifle Florindo's cabin, find the
combination, and infiltrate the office.

"Well, it's about time," said Gilbert as a merry gaggle of stewards
emerged onto the deck. "They're going, en masse. Should have known
they'd do that."

They bounced down the gangplank and crossed the street half a
block uptown from us. I counted seven, including Florindo. As they
bumped along, one of them was striking exaggerated poses suggesting
pretension and vanity, while the others watched, screaming with
laughter.

"What the hell's *he* doing?" asked Gilbert.

"I think he's imitating you."

"Well, *that's* nice! *Seven* of 'em, too, you'll notice, and one gift
between them! Well, fuck 'em. Let's move!"

"My stomach suddenly hurts."

"Oh, hush. Just follow me and do what I do."

Checking the impulse to remark that it was just this tendency that
had brought me to this happy point, I rose and followed him across
the street.

Rehearsing the moment in my mind, I'd imagined a crouched,
serpentine approach with lots of mad zigzagging from one hiding spot
to the next. In reality, though, we just strode briskly up the gangplank
onto the A deck, streamed down the port side and right through a
door to the smart little foyer by the main salon.

The crew quarters and Florindo's room were on the lowest deck. We descended the circular stairs in slow, quiet steps, listening for any signs of activity. We heard nothing and, on reaching the bottom deck, peered cautiously through the little window on the door to the crew quarters. The corridor was empty. We opened the door and scampered down the hall. Gilbert led us into a cabin on the port side and swiftly closed the door behind us.

To complete such a maneuver without getting caught is a heady pleasure, and our mood as we surveyed the little room was one of elation. We giggled and did hand slaps, and we might have bumped once or twice. Then, remembering our task, we proceeded to comb the place for the precious slip that was our passport to salvation.

Our great fear, of course, was that Florindo had put it in his wallet and was even now conveying it to a party for a nonexistent Frenchman. Our joy, as such, was all the greater when Gilbert discovered the blessed slip in the pocket of a shirt on the closet floor.

"What did I tell you, hon!" he said, capering about ecstatically. "This is gonna be perfect!"

"Florindo! I thought you already left!"

We did a sort of involuntary jeté together, then grabbed each other and stared at the door.

The voice had come from just outside. Whoever it was now knocked sharply and said, "Florinnnndo! Are you coming or what?"

Gilbert, without pause or consultation, hurled me onto the bed. Then, with the grace of a man who'd speed-trained for the event, he dropped his trousers and undies, leapt on top of me, and began kissing me so hard he nearly chipped my tooth.

I was startled, naturally, but when the door opened and I heard the shriek, I saw the reasoning behind the maneuver.

"Well, *pardonnez-moi!*" said whoever. "You should've *said* something!"

Gilbert made a low growling sound.

"I'm *going*, I'm *going*! I'll just tell everyone you were *de-tained!*"

And with that, the door closed. Gilbert, sighing with relief, rose and began dressing. I inquired, in the manner of a Mormon film critic, if the nudity had really been necessary. He replied that as his resemblance to Florindo was mild at best, he'd thought it wise to give our intruder something to focus on besides the back of his head. I allowed that his logic was unassailable and suggested we make tracks; our interloper would soon reach the restaurant to find Florindo present and dressed, and who knew what the upshot of that might be?

We stole down the hall to the base of the stairs, then crept cautiously up the three flights to the wheelhouse deck. There before us once more was the massive, ornate door, its gleaming keypad as chilly and forbidding as ever. To touch it, I reflected poetically, was to point a billion-chambered gun to your head, only one chamber of which was empty. But Gilbert, unflappable, glanced once at the paper, then began tapping in the code with cavalier swiftness. I clenched my fists and held my breath. He finished. The little green light blinked exactly once. Exchanging a quick handshake, we pulled tiny flashlights from our pockets, opened the door, and entered the room.

"*Shit!*" said Gilbert.

"*Shit!*" I concurred, and we both dove to the floor.

As those New Yorkers fortunate enough to possess West Side river views can attest, there are few things more glorious than sunset over the Hudson. The low, bright sun sparkles and glints off the water, bathing everything in a golden, Technicolor glow. Such a sunset was in progress, and with the curtain of the window onto the pool deck fully open, Peter's office was bathed in nature's own klieg lights.

This annoyed us. It made the whole atmosphere seem dead wrong for our mission. We'd come to perform daring, furtive deeds in darkness and stealth. The last thing we'd expected was to feel we'd wandered into the opening scene of *Oklahoma!* and any minute Curley would come in singing about the bright golden haze on the meadow.

I rose to my knees and crawled to where Gilbert crouched behind the cover of the desk.

"I think you can put your flashlight away."

"Ho, ho. Peek up and see if there's anyone on the deck who can see us."

"If there's anyone who can see us, they'll see me."

"Just *peek*, all right?"

I did. There was no one in any of the chairs by the pool. The pool itself, however, was occupied by a bikini-clad woman, lolling on her back on an inflated raft. My angle prevented a clear view of the face, but given the general contours, this was no impediment to identification.

"Kitty's out there," I said, dropping back down.

"What—*her?*" said Gilbert in a voice of aggrieved incredulity. I felt the same way. It was not often we burgled Peter's office, and you'd have thought just once Kitty could coordinate her schedule with ours.

"What the hell's *she* doing here?"

"Just lying on a raft," I said. "I think she may be asleep."

We surfaced warily, like gophers unsure where the lawn mower's gotten to. Gilbert rose higher for a better view and peered through his opera glasses. Her eyes, he said, were indeed closed. A champagne bottle upended in a bucket by the pool lent further hope that she was, for the moment, insensible.

This was heartening, but it still seemed a good idea to close the curtains. I rose, nipped over to the window, and gave them a firm tug. This produced no results, so I tried again. No amount of force, however, could move them more than a grudging inch.

"What's wrong now?" groaned Gilbert.

"They won't move! Wait—I think I remember Peter operating them mechanically. There was a button in that console over there."

Gilbert stood and hurried to a console on the other side of the room. He flipped the lid, squinted in, and pressed a button. The long drapes began gliding smoothly from either side of the window and, within seconds, met in the middle.

When I'd first watched Peter perform this maneuver, there'd been a light on in the room. I hadn't, as such, noticed the drapes were so heavy as to block all outside light. I noticed now. The room was pitch dark and seemed all the more so for having been so bright just seconds ago.

"Great," I said. "Where's your flashlight?"

Gilbert replied with lamentable imprecision that it was somewhere. I said I knew of a light by the door and, advancing away from the curtains, collided with the desk, banging my knee and uttering heated curses.

"Just stay put, Mr. Graceful," said Gilbert. "There are tons of buttons here. Some of them *have* to be lights."

"Gilbert, please don't—"

He jabbed at random and the stereo system sprang to life, regaling us with Frank Sinatra singing "Up, Up and Away." Gilbert cursed wildly and jabbed more buttons, to no discernible effect. Suddenly the music stopped and the amber mood light over the mosaic of Romulus and Remus came on, producing a romantic glow just like the artificial moon under which Peter, when in shepherd mode, abided his flock by night.

Gilbert laughed. "Look familiar?"

"Yes—a little brighter would help, though."

He adjusted the dimmer, and maximum visibility was achieved. He pulled the rabbit's foot from his pocket and, taking a seat behind Peter's desk, began burgling away, taking out keys and trying them in each of seven drawers as I stood observing. After a bit he turned and asked if I proposed to stand there gawking, or could I make use of myself by taking the used keys and trying them on the other cabinets? I took some keys and was about to do this when I decided, on a nervous whim, to check on the status of our favorite water nymph. I found the crack in the drapes and, parting them slightly, peeked through.

I shrieked like a frightened kettle.

"Don't do that!" said Gilbert, jumping half a foot off his chair. "God! What's your problem?"

I frantically waved him to the window and pointed to the pool deck.

Kitty had vanished.

And so had the pool.

"The dance floor, Gilbert! It's closed over the pool! Did *you* do that?"

"How should I know!" he snapped. "It was dark! Where do you suppose Kitty went?"

We exchanged a fleeting gaze of absolute horror and barreled toward the console. I ran so fast I went crashing into the wall and bounced off, sprawling on my ass at the edge of the mosaic floor.

It's astonishing, really, how at moments like this the most elaborately detailed scenarios can spring full-blown into your mind. In mere seconds I saw my whole future unspool before me in a horrific montage. *Screaming headlines! Live coverage of the trial!* I scrambled to my feet. *Conviction! Appeal!* I joined Gilbert where he stood peering down at the buttons and switches. *Jail! Unimaginable daily horrors!*

"Is there one marked 'Pool'?" I pleaded.

The TV movie!

There was indeed. He pressed it now and we raced to the window. At first we saw nothing except the great peach marble slabs slowly retracting into the sides of the pool. Then a body bobbed to the surface.

"Oh, *nooo!*" I cried.

Shower stabbing in retaliation for sarcasm! Disrespectful obituary!

My despair, however, proved premature. Kitty was not dead. She was not, of course, especially happy, either.

She lunged, wild-eyed, toward the end of the pool closest to the office window, leading us to close the drapes till we had only a thin crack through which to observe the unfolding drama.

Kitty clung to the side of the pool, drawing in big sobbing gulps of air, trembling with the effort. Soon, though, she'd refilled her oxygen supply and began putting it to use.

"*Helllllllp!*" she screamed. "*Somebody fucking help me!*"

"Dear oh dear," said Gilbert.

I opened my mouth to suggest now might be a good time to be shoving along, but then I witnessed a sight so improbable the words froze on my lips and I stared, transfixed and disbelieving.

Elsa, wearing heels, a light trench coat, dark glasses, and a wig came careening around the starboard side onto the pool deck. Seeing her despised and, let us not forget, banished sister brazenly enjoying the use of her pool, Elsa whipped off her glasses and fixed the young hussy with a look of pure malevolence.

"*You!*" she said.

"*You!*" replied Kitty, her eyes bulging with horror and loathing. "I shoulda known it was you! You wanted me dead, didn't you!"

Elsa, in her present frame of mind, found little to argue with there. "I hate you!" she cried. "And I want you gone! This minute! I want you out of my life!"

"Well, then," said Kitty, leaping from the pool, "you shoulda waited longer! You never could do anything right! You couldn't hold on to Peter and you can't get rid of me!"

Elsa sobbed hoarsely and reached into her purse. She was probably just looking for a handkerchief, but the move clearly put Kitty in mind of snub-nosed revolvers.

"*Eeeeeeeeeee!*" she observed, and, lunging at her sister, seized her by an arm and threw her into the pool.

The boat's remaining occupants, hearing the dueling banshees on the wheelhouse deck, rushed to investigate. They found Elsa, her drenched wig hanging over her eyes, sobbing desperately and trying to get out of the pool, even as Kitty, screaming bloody murder, was stomping on her fingers every time she grabbed the edge.

I closed the curtain.

"Well—better get going!" said Gilbert.

I agreed that departure would not be untimely. With the whole crew now glued to the spectacle, it was not difficult to gather our tools, depart the office, tiptoe down one deck, and flee down the gangplank.

We lurked a while behind some parked cars, eyeing the boat to see what developed. Within minutes Kitty raced down the gangplank wearing nothing but a robe over her bikini. She was screaming and obviously still feared for her life. As she reached the street, she turned to glare back at the yacht and the sororicidal fiend who remained its mistress. She shook a defiant fist and screamed at the top of her lungs.

"Just you wait, Elsa! I'll fix you! I'm calling Spark Chandler! Right now!"

And with that the semi-nude Kitty jumped into one of two passing cabs vying frantically for her custom, and sped off to tell the world her story.

Twenty-seven

Elsa's appearance on the boat at that of all moments seemed to me one of those staggering coincidences that make a man think about God and wonder if He ought, perhaps, to take His job more seriously. We discovered later, though, that Elsa's arrival was not so divine a coincidence after all. Lurking behind it had been the gnarled, meddlesome hand of the Signora di Corteggiano.

The signora, determined at this key juncture to cement her grip on Elsa, had been seeking opportunities to demonstrate her cozy rapport with the spirit world. She had, toward this end, paid the dishwasher on the *Siren* one hundred dollars to alert her if the banned Miss Driscoll ever made an appearance. The honest fellow dutifully phoned the old girl when Kitty arrived, and the signora played it for all it was worth, babbling in tongues to Elsa in the middle of a whist game, then describing horrific visions of Kitty stalking her yacht, seeking ways to do her fresh harm. Elsa, thus goaded, was off like a shot to investigate.

Of course, even if we had known at the time what brought this cataclysm upon us, the knowledge would have done little to assuage our grief; the dead take no comfort in pathology. And dead is just what we were or, at any rate, would be within fifteen hours, if Kitty could not be dissuaded from appearing on "Spark Chandler" and telling her shocking story to millions.

That she intended to do so was beyond question. Spark himself phoned us each that night to gloat and offer us the chance to appear on the broadcast and respond to Kitty's charges.

Naturally, I feigned bewilderment as to what these charges could be, but Spark cheerfully ran down the list. I was relieved, if only mildly, to see that he possessed a mere broad outline of the story and few of the really ticklish details.

Kitty, he said, had called him around eight, barely able to control her hysterics. She said her sister had just tried to drown her, both in revenge and to silence her about the Champions' ever-widening scandal. As for the scandal, she sketched it in quick strokes: she'd had a kinky affair with Peter, then Elsa had found out just before her concert and fallen apart on stage. Boyd Larkin had, thanks to me and Henri, obtained tapes of her and Peter in flagrante, which Boyd and Tommy were now using to blackmail Peter into ruin. She'd offered no further details, as she was calling from her apartment and feared that any minute Elsa would drop by with an ax and some Lysol.

"My, my! Kitty said all that, did she?" I said, striving for innocence even as my strangled tone suggested a coloratura doing recitative.

"You sound shook up, Phil," chortled Spark.

"Not a bit," I squeaked. "Did, uh, she say anything else?"

"No. Hell, she was scared shitless! She wanted to find a hiding place but quick."

I clucked sadly. Kitty, I said, had obviously suffered a complete mental breakdown and would require intense psychiatric treatment, if not hospitalization; one hoped Spark would not exploit her emotional fragility by letting her air her delusions before millions, as the trauma involved would add years to her recovery. Spark thought this was pretty funny. He said Kitty had indeed asked to appear on his program tomorrow and he'd been glad to oblige.

"I told her, 'Listen, I've already got a whole panel booked for tomorrow and I can't cancel them now on just a promise from you. But if you show up, baby, it's your show.' So what do you say, Phil? You want to tell your part in all this, or do you want to let her tell it for you?"

I mumbled something about checking my book and getting back to him, then hung up.

As you can imagine, the phone calls flew thick and fast that night as each of the principals received the glad word from Spark and follow-up gloating from Joy. Gilbert and I took turns confessing to everyone about our infiltration of the *Siren* and our blunder that had made Kitty assume Elsa had attempted to drown her sorrows. It was the sort of story that made us really appreciate the miracle of call waiting; we never had to listen to too much invective before being able to say, "Oh, sorry, I've gotta get this!"

The wires got pretty congested, what with Joy interrupting panic-stricken calls from Tommy and Boyd, and the signora and Elsa cutting in on foaming tirades from Peter. After an hour of this it was agreed that a summit had to be convened and pronto. Since the greatest number of principals resided at Champion Plaza, we agreed to meet there at ten.

Gilbert and I arrived seconds ahead of Boyd's Rolls. It was the first time I'd seen Tommy since our showdown, and the pangs I felt on once more beholding that gorgeous visage were mitigated by the sight of the bloated munchkin to whom he'd auctioned both body and allegiance. As he helped Boyd from the backseat, his eye caught mine. He gave me a desolate smile and nodded. I got the sense that the glacial composure he'd maintained throughout was beginning to crack. I did not think I'd care to see what was under it.

Boyd was boiling mad, and from the look he gave us I suspected we now occupied an even lower rung in his affections than Peter.

"Oh, *look!*" he exclaimed. "It's those two *master spies!*"

"Stuff it, you tree toad!" snapped Gilbert. "You're a fine one to point fingers! None of this would have ever happened if you and Mr. Smooth here hadn't decided to—"

Lights exploded around us.

The ubiquitous Mr. Chandler, microphone in hand, zipped out from behind a truck and trotted our way. He'd known, the worm, that his round of calls would stir up some activity at Champion Plaza and felt the panicky traffic, whether coming or going, would make for first-rate family viewing.

"Gentlemen," he said with feral glee. "I'd like to talk to you about the attempted murder of Kitty Driscoll!"

There's nothing like a media skirmish to turn four cranky conspirators into a loving, tight-knit family. Screaming "No comment" with the unity of a gospel choir, we closed ranks and began making for the revolving door, Tommy, Gilbert, and I all but carrying Boyd, who was not built for speed.

Our aversion to small talk did not especially vex Spark, for he knew his was a no-lose situation. What did it matter to him if we fled or lingered to proclaim our innocence, even as we hurried to visit the alleged perpetrator? Either response looked guilty and would provide tomorrow's studio audience no end of amusement.

Spark and his entourage were stopped at the door by two burly security guards who barred them from entering, but it hardly mattered by then. The damage had been done.

My friend Louisa the maid greeted us at the door and showed us into the music room. Peter was pacing up a storm, Elsa was sitting, knocking back the whiskeys, and the signora, determined as ever to be useful, pondered a tarot deck.

I'll spare you a detailed transcript of our meeting, as it was the single most acrimonious and unproductive discussion it's ever been my misfortune to take part in. Nobody would take responsibility for a single event that had transpired from day one, but all vehemently vowed that should Kitty broadcast the story, they would unleash their full arsenals on those who'd brought this fate upon them.

Tommy, his manner growing more snappish by the minute, tried repeatedly to steer the conversation away from invective and toward practical solutions. We seemed, alas, hard put to suggest even impractical ones.

There was, obviously enough, only one hope of averting catastrophe. This was to persuade Kitty not only to shut up, but to recant what she'd already said. This could either be accomplished through force—a position the Champions keenly advocated—through bribery, or, most logically, by convincing her that her belief she'd been marked for death was, however understandable, wholly mistaken.

This last approach seemed, ironically, least apt to prove workable. What use was the truth to us when Kitty would never in a million years believe it? Her nature had, since earliest childhood, been a pragmatic and deeply suspicious one. We doubted if the experience of being compelled to hold her breath at length in pitch-dark water while pounding hopelessly on a three-ton marble lid had left her more open-minded and willing to think the best of people. The more vociferously Gilbert and I claimed responsibility, the more Kitty, terrified and mistrustful, would think Elsa had paid us to do so, silencing her today the better to eliminate her tomorrow.

Violence was morally untenable (except to her immediate family) and threats would only toughen her resolve to go public. Bribery, too, seemed a dubious proposition. Kitty was not, after all, a fool. She knew very well that if you're *already* keen to bump a girl off, being suddenly obliged to give her valises full of hush money will in no way diminish your desire to do so. And can a girl really enjoy the fruits of blackmail when she's forever checking the bed for scorpions?

The worst thing of all, of course, was that we couldn't attempt any strategy at all until Kitty emerged from hiding. She did not intend to do so until an hour before show time, so our window of opportunity was open the merest crack. Not only that, but what discussion we *could* have with her would have to take place in the very lair and pit of the man who'd devoted himself to our ruin!

Those were the facts, and no amount of pacing or screaming or pathetic what-ifs could alter them a fraction. Boyd and Elsa, Tommy, Peter, and the signora could not begin to agree on how to proceed. In fact, the only thing they *could* agree on was that Gilbert and I were the two most god-awful, bungling cretins on earth and that Satan himself must have delivered us to them.

Elsa, who'd grown increasingly drunk and maudlin, swooned onto the love seat and begged the signora to summon her spirits for guidance. This was entirely too much for Peter and Boyd, who began screaming at the signora, saying her spirits had broken every RICO law on the books. Elsa covered her ears and began to sob violently, saying they could not destroy her faith in the one person who truly had her interests at heart. Gilbert and I, sensing that no progress seemed likely beyond the further demolition of our egos, left.

As we stood on the deserted avenue trying to flag a cab, Gilbert sheepishly asked if he could spend the night at my place, as he didn't feel like being alone. I was glad he'd asked, as I yearned for sympathetic company myself.

When we reached home, the phone was ringing. I was tired and loath to weather fresh assaults from the Larkin, Champion or Chandler camps, but then I thought, Maybe it's Kitty, and I answered.

"Hello?" I said.

"Hello to you, too," said Claire. "Perhaps you'll be so kind as to explain to me why my answering machine has no fewer than seven messages from Spark Chandler?"

Well! I thought as I danced on top of my coffee table, Claire's back and Philip's got her! But after a few more How-are-you's and Welcome-home's, I noted the iciness of her tone and my euphoria began to subside. It was doubtful, after all I'd done, that she'd consent to apply her intellect to our dilemma at all. And even if she did, could anyone, even Claire, keep our runaway train from its appointment with the cliff? As much as I hoped she'd arrived in the nick of time, I had to wonder if the nick of time had not, in fact, been the day before yesterday.

Fears or not, though, we had to at least try to talk her into trying.

"Claire, my darling! You have to come over right away! I mean, no, you don't have to come *here*—we'll go there! We need you, Claire! Desperately! Things have gone terribly wrong!"

"You don't have to tell me. I read *Estime* on the plane. Are you really dispensing those without a prescription?"

I told her that we'd quit the magazine, that we were disgusted with everyone involved and thoroughly ashamed of ourselves. A most alarming crisis, however, had just arisen and demanded immediate attention. Could we please come over and sound out her views? Please? Please, please, *pleeeease?*

"Not tonight, really, Philip," she groaned. "It's late and I'm tired and in a vile mood."

"Why the mood?" I asked. "You just got back from a cruise! Wasn't it fun?"

"The first half was delightful. The last part was all tears and tormented journal entries. If you don't mind, I'd rather not go into it."

I knew that if she really hadn't wanted to go into it, she wouldn't have brought it up to begin with. I pried delicately, and she admitted she'd had a shipboard fling, and that the gentleman, though very nice looking, had not proved a model of probity.

"True to you in his fashion, huh?"

"Yes. And a lovely fashion it was, if you don't mind being the first event in some sexual triathlon."

"Oh, hon, that really stinks. I'm so sorry."

"Ah, well, I should have known. He seemed the type right off, but he was funny and straight *and* he could dance—an improbable combination, so I thought, Why not? I tried to adopt this zesty, damn-it-all, Melina Mercouri sort of attitude. And, of course, I *still* wound up miserably pissed off and depressed. I was an idiot."

"If it's idiocy you're boasting of, love, remember, you're talking to pros. Why not let us come over and tell you a story that will make you feel brilliant again?"

"All right," she sighed. "I suppose I could use the company."

As we raced the two blocks to her place, I realized how shamefully relieved I felt over the news of her messy romance. Sorry as I was for her, I couldn't help hoping the experience had left her more inclined to forgive the crimes of lovesick nincompoops.

We found her looking glum but marvelously tan and thinner than she'd been since college. We rushed to both butter and cheer her up.

"God, honey!" I said. "You're gorgeous! Doesn't she look gorgeous?"

"Va-va-va-voom!" concurred Gilbert.

"All right, all right," she said wearily. "Just give me the worst."

We did our best to summarize all that had transpired in her absence, but so jangled were our nerves that we tended to confuse the order of events. It was a lot to unload on someone fresh from her own tragedy, and by the time we'd gotten to Spark's threats, she looked a bit shell-shocked. Even her tan seemed to be fading.

"But these people have *warehouses* of cash!" she exclaimed. "Can't they just pay Kitty to shut up?"

"No. She's too scared for that. She's convinced Elsa is trying to kill her."

"*My God!*" said Claire. "*Is* she?"

"No," said Gilbert. "Oh, wait, we forgot that part."

"You see," I said, "we infiltrated the boat again, just this afternoon, and Kitty was drunk in the pool and we accidentally pushed this button that locked her under the dance floor, then Elsa came by and Kitty blamed it all on her."

Claire regarded us blankly for a long moment.

"I never know when you're kidding anymore."

It was flattering of her to think we were pulling her leg, though it did put us in the position of having to explain that, no, we really were stupid as all that. Claire, aghast, inquired if it hadn't occurred to us at the time to come forward and correct Kitty's misapprehension then, when she might have believed us. We agreed that, yes, that would in retrospect have been the thing to do, but at the moment we'd simply yearned to put it all behind us and get on with life.

"So," said Gilbert by way of conclusion, "any ideas?"

"NO!" said Claire with sudden vehemence. "*No ideas!* Do you understand me? *None!* My God, you two truly astound me! You really do! You get yourself into these completely deplorable situations that I've done my level best to steer you away from—and *then*, when you've fucked things up to the point where *God* would throw His hands up, you expect me to waltz in and set it all right! Well, I'm sorry, but I can't! I do not have the first *idea* how to pull you out of this! I don't even know that I care to try!"

It was at that point that I began to cry. It's not something I do really often, but the mix of hopelessness, fatigue, and guilt just hit me all at once, and down rolled the tears. I certainly didn't do it deliberately to gain sympathy, but it did seem to calm Claire, even as it embarrassed her. She threw a hankie at me and grumbled that I should go home and get some sleep, as the morning would not be without its challenges. She'd accompany us to the studio where Spark's show was taped. As to what she'd do or say when we got there, she hadn't the vaguest idea.

Gilbert and I trudged back to my place. Without exchanging a word, we stripped down to skivvies and crawled into the bed I'd purchased only weeks ago in anticipation of a glorious, lasting relationship. Pondering that, I sighed and consoled myself with the thought that my relationship with Gilbert, while not glorious, certainly seemed to be lasting. We nestled in together, facing the same direction, Gilbert's slim frame conforming neatly to mine. We were silent a moment, and then Gilbert asked me what Tommy liked to do in bed with me. I told him.

"Me too," said Gilbert.

"Every time?"

"Yes, every damned time."

"Same here."

"*No* imagination," murmured Gilbert.

And then we slept.

Twenty-eight

Claire, dressed in a spiffy new navy suit, emerged from the dankness of her lobby into the bright light of that callously beautiful June morning.

"*Please* don't look at me that way," she said to us.

"What way?" asked Gilbert.

"Like you're a couple of Fatima schoolgirls and I'm the Blessed Mother. I mean, sorry, but I accomplished no miracles in my sleep."

"You'll think of something in the cab!" I said. She sighed murderously and led the way to West End Avenue.

"So," she asked, "when did you boys decide to give Tommy his ring back?"

"Oh, days ago," I said. "I kept trying to call you."

"What spoiled the honeymoon?"

"*Well—*" began Gilbert, but I jumped in to shut him up. However much her own soured fling had inspired empathy, she remained a sternly ethical woman and I felt it prudent to paint our departure as more a moral reawakening than mere *jalousie d'amour.*

"You of all people should know *that*, Claire! I mean, granted, it took us a while to come to our senses, but eventually we realized what we were doing was just *wrong!*"

Gilbert caught on. "Oh, yes! *Terribly* wrong! We were *riddled* with guilt, even if it wasn't really our fault—I mean," he added, noting Claire's incredulous gaze, "to the extent that we were *seduced.*"

"Yes—*love!*" I said with a hollow laugh. "Still, smitten as we were, we had our *principles,* and in time they came to the fore and we knew we had to stop, no matter what we felt for Tommy."

"The slut," added Gilbert.

"One begins," Claire said tartly, "to glimpse the shape of your principles. Well, never mind that for now. Just tell me who you think will be there today."

I said, as far as I knew Peter, Tommy, and Boyd would be on hand. "And Elsa damn well *ought* to be there to tell Kitty she wasn't the one who closed the dance floor over the pool. I don't know about the signora."

"The signora," said Claire, "will be nowhere near the place—and a good thing for us."

"How do you know?" asked Gilbert.

"Well," she said, hailing a taxi, "according to your rundown of who Spark's ambushed, the signora's the only one he seems not to have caught on to. Don't think *she's* not aware of that. I'm sure she'd rather keep a low profile than appear publicly as a co-conspirator."

A taxi stopped and we piled into the backseat, Claire taking the middle. I gave him the address.

"Now," said Claire, settling back, "we haven't a lot of time, but I want you to tell me everything you can about Kitty."

"Hell, *you* know Kitty," I said. "You've met her yourself."

"Yes, but not nearly so often or in such vivid circumstances as you. I know you've told me before. Tell me again. In as much detail as we've time for. Maybe *something* will give me a clue how to reason with the woman."

Noting with relief that our driver did not appear to speak English, we began to rehash every encounter we'd had with la Driscoll. We did not dredge up anything I haven't included in this account, but Claire sat, taking it all in with a faraway look. I thrilled to think that somewhere inside that powerful brain of hers, the wheels of genius were grinding away.

The traffic was dense and we didn't make it to the studio until just after nine, leaving less than an hour before the taping. A young, clipboard-wielding assistant ushered us down a hall and into an elevator. He was a peppy fellow, fresh out of college.

"So," he asked, "are you all on the show?"

"That remains to be seen," said Claire.

"Must be a hell of a segment! We bumped some dynamite guests for you. We had children of father/mother murder/suicides!"

"Children of *what?*" asked Claire.

"You know, Dad killed Mom, then himself, or else the other way around, though most of 'em, Dad killed Mom. Really rough on the kids, but there's a healing process."

"Oh, good," said Gilbert, to fill in the silence.

"Yup! Had five of 'em all geared up to talk about it, and I hadda tell 'em all to go home, we'd reschedule. This is us!"

He led us out of the elevator and down a wide corridor. My stomach, already halfway to macramé, gained a few more knots when we rounded the corner to see a rabble of spectators who'd arrived early for the good seats. There was the usual preponderance of large middle-aged ladies, and they chattered away perkily. The conversation I heard as we passed centered mainly on Spark, his handsomeness, his fairness, and whether the speaker would die if he called on her.

The studio, which had seemed such a festive place on my last visit, now had the stark, forbidding air of a courtroom. It was empty at the moment, save for a few scurrying technicians. As our guide led us down toward the stage, Claire pulled us back and spoke in a tense whisper.

"I have a plan, all right?"

"*You do!*"

She winced and shook her head. "No, sorry, I *don't*—what I meant was, we should *say* I have a plan. I'll need to talk to Kitty in private, and I don't think the others will let me if they're not at least hopeful I can accomplish something."

"Right," we said, and followed our handler past the stage and through the same swinging doors through which Spark made his athletic entrance at the opening of each show. We were now in a hall of dressing and control rooms. He opened a door near the studio and bade us enter.

It was a large, bright dressing room lined with mirrors and long tables. Peter and Elsa were there, as were Tommy and Boyd, and there was not an unclenched muscle in the lot. Spark stood smirking at the rear. Next to him sat Joy, who, you had to hand it to her, could gloat silently with more galling gusto than most can manage using every taunt in the book.

"The gang's all here!" Spark said wittily.

"Not quite, Mr. Chandler," said Claire. "I don't see Kitty."

"She requested complete privacy before the taping."

"Produce her, would you?"

I had to marvel at the way Claire could swagger in and take charge. Her air of prim authority was all the more remarkable when you considered that she hadn't a clue what she was going to do.

"No can do, darling," said Spark.

"Kitty," said Claire, "is laboring under several misconceptions. We'd like a chance to correct them."

"For God's sake!" snapped Boyd. "Don't you suppose we've already been *through* this?"

"If you have something to say to Kitty," said Joy, "you can say it to her—and me—on the air. Spark, I want to go study my notes. I'll be in your office."

She crossed to the door and, with a lighthearted "You're history" to Peter, glided out.

"I'm *not* going on the air!" wailed Elsa. "Nobody can make me!"

Claire approached Spark and asked if he'd be so good as to withdraw. He grinned smugly and said he'd be glad to; he was sure we all had lots to talk about. He'd drop by in a while to see who wanted to join the show, which, he assured us, would tape with or without our participation. When he reached the door, he turned,

"By the way," he said, smiling, "Kitty asked me to invite some publishers—she's fishing for a book deal."

As he withdrew, Claire grabbed the door to keep it from closing behind him. She then turned to Gilbert and whispered, "Follow him!"

"Huh!"

"*Follow him!* He's bound to check in on Kitty and we'll find out where he's hiding her. Stay and keep an eye on her door, and when he leaves and the coast's clear, come back and tell us."

Gilbert saluted and made tracks. Then Claire, wasting no time, pulled up a chair next to Elsa.

"Elsa," she said evenly, "I know I'm not one of your favorite people, but I think I may be able to keep your sister quiet and spare everyone here untold miseries. I'll need everyone's cooperation, though, including yours. Can I count on that?"

Elsa replied in a shaky voice that she'd ignored the signora's warning about Claire once and was not so foolish as to do so again.

"Christ!" fumed Tommy. "We need a bloody deprogrammer!"

"I notice," said Claire to Elsa, "that the signora's not here today."

Elsa retorted that the signora had been violently ill that morning. "I don't wonder, either! This whole affair's been hell on her! She weeps herself to sleep!"

Claire gently laid a hand on Elsa's shoulder. "The signora, dear, is a very clever old fraud, and I'm going to try to prove it to you. Please don't be mad at me if I succeed."

She handed Elsa a phone from the dressing table. "Unscrew the mouthpiece. I'll make a call on the other phone over here, and I want you to listen."

Elsa warily did as she was instructed. Claire took another phone and dialed the signora's private line at the Champions' apartment.

"Hello, signora?" said Claire cheerfully. "It's Claire Simmons, remember me? . . . Ciao to you, too. I'm calling on behalf of Boyd Larkin. . . . That's right, I work for him, too. So many of us do. He wants you to know he's willing to pay you *triple* whatever you can get from Peter. . . . That's right, triple! If only you'll tell Elsa your spirits advise her to divorce Peter and testify against him in court."

Naturally, I couldn't hear the signora's half of the negotiation, but it wasn't hard to get the gist from Claire's end.

"You're *quite* sure Elsa will do *whatever you tell her to?* . . . Goodness! Is she really as gullible as all *that?*"

Even if I'd been unable to hear Claire's end, I could have still deduced the substance from Elsa's face, the shifting expressions on which contained a whole miniseries' worth of emotions. There was bewilderment, then shock, despair, embarrassment, and finally a look of the purest icy rage. If you'd been asked to set it to music, you'd have picked the "Carmina Burana."

"*Scusa*, signora," chirped Claire, sensing Elsa was ready, "but there's someone here who'd like to speak to you."

"GET OUT OF MY HOUSE, YOU VIPER!"

Everyone jumped, then began frantically shushing her.

"I want you out *now!* This minute! Pack your bags and go! If I get back and find you, I'll shoot you for a thief, which is just what you are! To think I ever trusted you, you . . . you cassoulet!"

It went on a bit longer, the signora apparently trying to convince Elsa it was all a misunderstanding and that Elsa still needed her mystical guidance, but to no avail. The only form of soothsaying for which Elsa would ever again desire her assistance was the sort that involved the reading of entrails. At length Elsa slammed the phone down and, turning to the rest of us, asked what the fuck we were all looking at.

At this point Gilbert returned.

His mission had been a total success. Spark led him straight to Kitty's dressing room, which was on the same floor as ours, though much farther from the studio; he'd distinctly heard Kitty say, "Who's there?" when Spark knocked. He lingered nearby, and Spark left five minutes later, entering a nearby elevator, which suggested, happily enough, that his office was on another floor.

"So what now?" Gilbert asked eagerly.

The room fell silent, and then, as if on signal, everyone, Gilbert and me, Boyd and Tommy, Peter and Elsa, turned and looked to Claire with pleading eyes.

It was a lovely moment. It touched me to see I was not alone in my faith, that these rich and powerful people, once so arrogant and blustering, had in their hour of need become humble converts to Claireism. The only thing marring the beauty of it all was Claire herself, whose eyes, under hooded lids, were darting madly back and forth like those of a magician who realizes midperformance that he's wearing the wrong damn coat.

"Well," she began, and I sensed she was stalling, "the main problem isn't convincing Kitty that Elsa didn't try to kill her—"

"It *isn't?*" said Tommy.

"No—not if she'll listen to common sense, anyway. I mean, the switch to operate the dance floor was in Peter's office, right?"

"Yes."

"Well, then—*How did Elsa get in?* Where did she get the *combination?* Not from *Peter*, certainly. With her already threatening to expose his secrets, he'd guard it with his life. She could have had

the staff open it, I suppose, though if you're planning to kill someone, that's hardly the way to cover your tracks. So how'd she get
in then? Through *espionage?* Let's be frank, shall we? Elsa hardly
has the—"

"The what?" asked Elsa, indignantly.

"Let's call it evil genius, shall we? Especially when you consider
that Kitty had only been there an hour and Elsa couldn't have known
in advance she'd be there."

Framed that way, Kitty might indeed see how silly it was to suppose
Elsa could have learned she was on the boat, run down to the dock,
cracked the code, and attempted to kill her, without being seen, all
within an hour.

"On the other hand, *these* two," said Claire, gesturing to Gilbert
and me, "have broken in there before, as Kitty remembers only too
well. No, I can convince her what really happened. But does that
even make a difference now? The real problem is what she's already
told Spark. She has to recant all that. *And* explain why she 'lied' to
begin with!"

"If she no longer feels she's in danger," said Tommy, "then surely
she'll settle for cash."

It wasn't as simple as that, said Claire. Kitty, whether she felt
threatened or not, was a very pragmatic woman, and one who enjoyed
the limelight. Having committed herself this far, might she not decide
the pleasures of fame and a lucrative book deal were safer bets than
any promises this slippery crew might make?

"What does it matter?" bleated Elsa, rising dramatically. "Even if
she shuts up today, she'll still have the story to hold over our heads!
And Boyd will have his goddamned tape! Even if he gives Peter back
his magazine, he'll still have the tape to taunt us and bully us with!
We'll never know a moment's peace, and this horrible war will go on
forever!"

"Well, yes." Claire sighed. "I'm not sure there's anything I can
do about that."

"Oh, for God's sake!" screamed Boyd, leaping up in great agitation.
"Who the fuck cares about forever! We've got half an hour before
this kamikaze bimbo goes on the air and crucifies us! Find out what
she wants and *give it to her!*"

Peter, who'd offered nothing himself, sniped that he hadn't heard Boyd contributing any brilliant solutions. Peter then reminded Boyd, for the eighth time in twelve hours, that extortion was a felony, and that if Kitty indeed told all that she knew, Boyd would go to prison and spend his declining years at the mercy of tatooed sociopaths who would trade him for cigarettes. Boyd turned rather pale and initiated yet another acrimonious debate on whose fault it had all been to begin with. But just as things were beginning to look truly bleak, I noticed that Claire was standing there, smiling a serene smile in the midst of the chaos. She proceeded calmly to the door, took Gilbert, our guide dog, by the arm, and turned to address the bickering throng.

"Follow me everyone," she said firmly, and pulled Gilbert out through the door. We stood a moment, paralyzed by hope, then scrambled after her.

Gilbert led us around a corner and down another long hall, past offices and elevators. He rounded a second corner and stopped at an unmarked door.

"Hang back," whispered Claire to us, and knocked sharply. Kitty's voice issued loud and clear from the other side.

"Hang on! I'm not decent!"

Claire did not stand on ceremony. She opened the door and slid in, closing it quickly behind her. We heard a little shriek, but nothing so piercing as to be heard in the nearby offices.

There being little else to do, we stood there, trying to appear nonchalant in front of passing staffers and secretaries, none of whom could refrain from gawking at the singular spectacle of Boyd Larkin and Peter and Elsa Champion, all loitering in the hall as though waiting to use the Xerox machine. After four minutes that seemed like eternity, Claire poked her head out and asked Gilbert and me to come in.

It wasn't a real dressing room at all, but a small office hastily equipped as one to give Kitty the distance she craved from her loved ones. There was a mirror propped up against the wall behind the desk and a few lamps doubled as makeup lights.

As tense as we were, our first impulse on seeing Kitty was to burst out laughing. She'd obviously decided that her usual garb, which looked as if she ordered it direct from the Homewrecking Bombshell

Catalog, would not go very well with her new role as the Innocent Seduced and Imperiled. She'd traded it all in for a more subdued look. Every inch of that spectacular bosom was now covered by a white silk blouse with a high lace collar and a small antique cameo at the neck. With this she wore a plain navy jacket and matching knee-length skirt. Her shoes were dark flats, and her hair was pulled back in a chaste bun. She looked like Jayne Mansfield in a Merchant Ivory film.

Raucous laughter does not, of course, set the desired note of contrition when greeting a woman you nearly drowned the preceding day, so we bit our tongues and hung our heads dolefully.

"I believe," said Claire coolly, "that you boys owe Miss Driscoll an apology."

"We know!" we said, and promptly groveled at her feet, begging her forgiveness and credulity.

"We're really sorry, Kitty!"

"It wasn't Elsa! We *swear* it, hon!"

"Okay, okay," breathed Kitty. "This one here"—she jerked her head toward Claire—"says Elsa hasn't got the brains to drown a bug in a jar, and I can't argue with that."

"We're *so* sorry, Kitty!"

"Apology accepted," said Kitty.

"Out," said Claire, with an imperial wave, "and send Elsa in, would you?"

Kitty made a sour face at this, but we did as Claire bade us. Elsa, looking no more enchanted by the prospect than her sister, stalked into the room and closed the door behind her.

From this point in the proceedings on, Gilbert and I were demoted to the role of Crowd Without. We didn't much relish this but supposed we'd learn soon enough if peace had been negotiated or if Kitty, unappeased, would emerge and head implacably for the studio with a full payload.

A nervous coordinator arrived to prep Kitty for the show. He was informed by Kitty, through the closed door, that she knew how to talk and would he kindly get out of her face? He asked the rest of us what we were doing in the hall, and we said it was a free hallway, wasn't it? He bustled off, clearly alarmed, and there was no doubt in our minds he'd go straight back to Spark. Elsa popped her head out and asked if Boyd could come in for a moment. Boyd complied as Peter and Tommy wondered petulantly when *their* turn would come. Never, as it turned out.

Spark and Joy, in tandem with the coordinator and the peppy assistant who'd shown us in, came racing around the corner with the annoyingly self-important air of cavalry riding to the rescue. Spark angrily asked if we were threatening his guest.

"Do shut up," said Tommy.

Spark pounded on the door. Claire opened it, saw who was there, and slammed it briskly in his face. He knocked again and tried the knob, which was now locked. He told an acolyte to page security, but then Kitty burst out of the dressing room in a raging snit as Claire, Elsa, and Boyd streamed out behind her, looking dazed and stricken.

"Leave me the hell alone!" she screamed. "All of you!"

My heart sank, and I gripped Gilbert's shoulder for support.

"I'm ready for my interview, Mr. Chandler," Kitty said grandly, and linked one arm through his and another through Joy's.

"So what do you say, folks?" said Spark, all but jigging in victory. "You want to come on and rebut?"

"Absolutely!" said Elsa, seizing Peter's hand in a death grip.

I was stunned. I'd assumed naturally that if Kitty decided to go ahead, Elsa would be in France by lunch. Here she was, though, firmly resolved to stand her ground and fight to the death before a national audience! Peter, not surprisingly, was of another view.

"Fine! You go right ahead! But if you think I'm so foolish as to dignify these scurrilous—*Ow!*"

He yanked his hand away from Elsa, who had apparently inserted her nails a fair depth into the palm. He furiously inspected his stigmata, even as Elsa informed him in the steeliest of tones that she would be grateful for his support. He wasn't happy, but given Elsa's nuclear capability, he had no choice but to consent.

Spark turned an inquiring gaze to Boyd, who shook his head in numb acquiescence, then gave Tommy a curt nod to say that he too could consider himself conscripted for the event.

Spark looked to the rest of us.

I quaked, of course, at the very idea of being placed on trial before a crowd that now seemed, in my fevered imagination, like so many Madame Defarges in rayon, but then I observed Elsa's cold defiance and thought, If she can do it, so can I.

"We won't be needing you three," said Spark. "I only asked you in case the rest of them refused to go on. We've got some seats for you in the house, and maybe I'll ask you some questions."

My jaw dropped and I swiveled to Gilbert, who clearly shared my sense of stunned pique. We'd had our share of insults recently, but nothing that approached this bit of brass. We were to be hanged, it seemed, but not on the VIP scaffold.

Reflecting a moment, though, I supposed it wasn't so awful to be spared the more prominent hot seats. Besides, the audience would be an easier place to bolt from if the inclination arose—and it was hard to imagine it wouldn't.

It was now just minutes to show time, and our wretched parade, led by Spark, Joy, and a tight-lipped Kitty, began its march to the studio.

"No luck, huh?" I said to Claire.

"It's still too early to say," she replied.

"Well, it sure doesn't look rosy to me," said Gilbert. "She just bit your heads off and said to leave her alone."

"That was an act," murmured Claire. "When Spark arrived I suggested we pretend we weren't getting along. To throw him off."

"Then what really happened?" I asked, hope rising from the slab.

"I only wish I knew," said Claire. "We didn't have much time. I proposed an alternative to mutual destruction—but like the song says, kids, she didn't say yes and she didn't say no."

"What alternative?" I asked.

"Right this way, please!" boomed Mr. Pep, and dragged us off to the audience even as the more glamorous culprits were shown onto the set and fitted with mikes.

At the sight of this notorious assemblage, the audience erupted into thrilled applause. Here, they must have felt, was a lineup bubbling with promise. There were *two* flamboyant billionaires—both looking fit to be tied!—the beautiful, tragic wife of one of the billionaires, *Spark's* wife, a tall debonair man, and a terribly sexy nun. Though no one in the crowd knew what particular scandal had erupted among them, they could see at a glance that the possibilities were endless.

We peons were ushered halfway up the center stairs and given three on the aisle. Gilbert, keen to be farthest from Spark's maraudings, grabbed the third seat in. I sat next to him, and Claire took the end. All around us Spark's ladies jabbered away in a happy froth of speculation about what had brought these famous people together and why they were all looking so terribly cross.

Not one of them, though, could have wondered with half the curiosity of one aging fan across the aisle and down from us, who was all but standing on her seat, waving to the stage while calling, "Elsa! Elsa, my love!"

It was Millie Pilchard.

"What's *she* doing here?" asked Gilbert. I told him Millie was devoted to Spark's policy of free live sensationalism and often attended; she'd probably attended more often than ever since Elsa had banished her, loosening her schedule while tightening her budget.

Elsa caught sight of her, shriveled, then returned the limpest of waves.

"Elsa, darling!" shrieked Millie. "What a lovely surprise! And what are you here to talk about, darling?"

Elsa, pining for a revolver, smiled vaguely and placed a finger to her lips to indicate that this, for now, remained a secret. Millie laughed and said she couldn't wait, then resumed her seat. This little display had made her an object of mild fascination among the ladies in her row. Displaying that keen sense of inquiry that so characterizes a Chandler audience, they leaned in toward Millie with quizzical stares and commenced interrogating her. This made Millie very happy.

Millie had distracted me, but I turned now again to Claire and repeated my question. What alternative had she proposed to Kitty in the hope of calming her itch for vengeance? Claire motioned me closer and whispered her suggestion into my ear.

"Jumping Jesus!" I said, rising half out of my seat. "Are you *serious?!*"

"Well," said Claire, a bit defensively, "it *did* seem to cover a number of bases."

"What what what?" inquired Gilbert.

"Gawd! What did *Kitty* say?"

"She seemed intrigued."

"*Whaaaaaaaat?!*" asked Gilbert, but our whispers were now over-whelmed by a deafening surge in the noise level as cheers and whoops and fresh applause filled the studio. Spark had arrived.

He worked his way down the front row, shaking hands and giving the occasional lady a kiss to remember evermore. Then, taking center stage, he waited patiently for his public to fall silent. He raised his mike to his face and began in a grim, pregnant tone.

"I cover a lot of stories and people on this show, but I've never before been drawn to a story because of my personal connection to it. The story you're about to hear, though, has had a major effect on my life."

He paused for effect, and the crowd, tantalized, drew forward in their seats.

"It began for me when my dear wife, Joy"—he pointed her out—"informed me that her employer and our longtime friend, Peter Champion, had fired her from her job as editor-in-chief of Peter's magazine, *Estime*. This shocked and disappointed us, because Joy was the magazine's first editor and she had built *Estime* into a stunning success.

"More shocking still was the direction the magazine took after Joy left. Joy was replaced by this man—Tommy Parker." Tommy, to his credit, gave a smile of melting suavity to the ladies up front. "Mr. Parker had long been a loyal employee of Boyd Larkin, and when he took over *Estime*, he set about 'improving' it. I want to read you some of the reviews this new, uh, '*improved*' version of the magazine received."

Pulling an index card from his pocket, he ran down a list of phrases, the most flattering of which was "soporific twaddle." He read them slowly, with a mock incredulity that won him lots of chuckles. Handing the card to an old darling down front, he went into his "regular guy" mode.

"Boy, oh, *boy!* Now, izzat any way to improve a magazine or *what?* Whadda *you* think?"

"I think it's *crazy!*" replied the old pundit.

He dropped the shtick and resumed his probing, Rod Serling voice.

"The question is this: Did Peter *willingly* drop his magazine's editor and winning formula? Or was he forced to, *blackmailed* into destroying his own magazine by . . . *this man?*"

He wheeled melodramatically and pointed to Boyd, sending a gasp through the crowd. Boyd rolled his eyes at the theatricality of it all, then flashed Peter an oddly complicitous look, as though to say "Well, don't *we* feel silly now?" Peter, by now a pretty cerise shade, just scowled and kept his eyes on Spark.

"This was my wife's suspicion, and let me tell you, she is one shrewd lady. The question was, *why* was Peter being blackmailed? I pursued the story tirelessly, trying to break through thick walls, walls whose bricks were secrecy and lies. I tried to get some answers, but here's what happened."

He gestured toward the monitors flanking the stage, and we were shown a skillfully edited montage of Spark ambushing us all. There were Peter and Boyd fleeing gruffly into limos. There was Elsa, in her wig and dark glasses, bushwacked en route to the dentist. There was our little foursome last night, doing the hundred-yard dash to Champion Plaza. And there, to my surprise, was Kitty, on Boyd's very doorstep. She had, I supposed, been on a second blackmail outing and didn't even see the camera advancing on her, so intently was she studying the check.

"But last night," said Spark when the tape ended, "the key piece of the puzzle fell into place when Kitty Driscoll, Elsa Champion's sister, came forward with a shocking tale."

Here he ticked off, briefly, the list of Kitty's charges, from her affair with Peter to the sex tapes to Boyd's ruthless blackmail. The crowd's reactions were so vocal that I glanced at the ceiling, wondering if there was not, next to the sign marked APPLAUSE, another reading GASPS. The gang on stage sat silent and tight-lipped, staring straight at Kitty, waiting in pure agony to see how she'd respond.

"The reason she came forward," concluded Spark, "was that the game had taken an even uglier twist. Kitty, who'd been paid to maintain her silence, nearly paid herself—*with her life!*"

He sat in the unoccupied chair next to Kitty's and looked into her eyes with a stern, compassionate gaze. "Kitty," he said, "it's time for you to tell your story."

"Whaddaya wanna know?" she asked.

He was taken aback by her breeziness, having set the stage for something a little more choked and haunted. He adopted a still grimmer tone, hoping to set a proper example.

"I want you to tell these people your story, Kitty—in the same words you told it to me last night."

"All right," said Kitty gravely.

She turned her face to the hushed and anxious crowd. Gilbert, Claire, and I took each other's hands, squeezing tightly as we held our breath and leaned forward.

"Before I do," Kitty said slowly, "I think it's only fair to tell you I made most of it up."

The GASPS sign went on again, and this time we joined in, exhaling with dizzy relief and slumping back on our seats. Spark did exactly the opposite, leaping forward on his chair as though someone had plugged it in.

"*What did you say?!*" he thundered as an astonished buzz filled the air.

"I said I made it up. Sure fooled you, though!"

The buzz grew still louder, until the place sounded like a lumber camp under attack by bees. Spark waved an angry hand for silence, and the crowd shut up and leaned in, gawking in wonder at this impertinent sexpot and her apoplectic interrogator.

"You're saying now . . . *what?* That you *invented* the whole story? *Including your own sister's attempt on your life?*" he added, determined to get that in.

The GASPS sign went off again, and another reading TALK AMONGST YOURSELVES.

"You got it," Kitty said feistily, adding, "I bet *you're* pretty annoyed, huh?"

Spark called for silence again, and Joy rose, quivering, from her seat. She pointed a trembling finger at her co-panelists and addressed the crowd.

"She told us this story *herself!* Every *word* of it! Then *they* went to her dressing room before the show! They bribed her! They paid her to shut her up!"

"Oh, *yeah?*" inquired Kitty. "And what'll it cost to shut *you* up?"

"Now, just wait one minute, Miss Driscoll," said Spark, struggling to regain the commanding tone he'd brought to his introduction. "I agree with my wife here. Perhaps they threatened you? Told you they'd have you killed if you spoke up? Don't be afraid of them! We can provide you with protection!"

"Protection from what? Earth to Spark, Earth to Spark! I told you, *I made it up!*"

"I don't believe you!" he shouted. "Why would you tell me a story like that if it wasn't true?"

"I'll tell you why!" shouted Kitty. She rose. Her whole attitude changed, and I could see that her careful preparations to portray the innocent victim of sinister forces would not go to waste after all. She clasped her hands together and took a deep breath, as one struggling to contain turbulent emotions.

"For the last few weeks," she said, her voice quivering with indignation, "ever since my brother-in-law fired Mr. Chandler's wife, my family and dear friends have not known one single moment of peace. Though none of us has done a single wrong thing, we have been hounded and badgered by Mr. Chandler here. Everywhere we went we were terrorized by cameras and questions, and our every waking moment was a living hell!"

"That's *bullshit!*" screamed Spark, completely beside himself.

"Is it?" brayed Elsa. She, too, rose and addressed the crowd. "You saw the tape. What did you think?"

"It was intolerable!" said Peter.

"Horrible!" Boyd agreed. "Pure *harassment!*"

"Freedom of the press is all well and good," throbbed Elsa, "but when you start hectoring innocent citizens who haven't done a *thing* to deserve it—"

"Right," said Kitty, wiping a tear from her eye. "And my poor sister here just recovering from a horrible allergic reaction that coulda *killed* her!"

"So in the end," Tommy said, suavely wrapping it up, "we all said, if Mr. Chandler's so keen to uncover a scandal, why don't we cook up the juiciest one we can, and see if he'll put the silly thing on the air . . . which is just what we did!"

Joy, crazed with anger, rose and began excoriating them all, screaming that they were cheats and liars and frauds.

She was entirely correct, of course, but her manner was even less winning than usual, which is saying some.

"*Please*, Ms. Cudgel!" said Tommy with a pained smile. "If you could try to express yourself with a shade less venom, we might have a more productive discussion of the issues." He turned and addressed the audience. "If you'll pardon a bit of ungentlemanly frankness on my part, it was Ms. Cudgels's extreme temper that prompted Mr. Champion to terminate her contract in the first place. He felt she was too cruel to the staff."

"*That is a total fabrication!*" screamed Joy, froth flying from her lips. "No one on my staff *ever* complained about my behavior!"

"Well," Boyd said dryly, "I doubt if Hitler's secretary ever told him *he* was a pain in the butt either."

At this, Spark threatened to slug Boyd, effectively bolstering his opponents' contention that where his wife was concerned, he was not always rational.

As for the spectators, their sympathies seemed divided. On the one hand, it seemed bad manners of Kitty to promise so succulent a scandal and then renege. On the other hand, pulling a stunt like this on Spark Chandler was pretty juicy in itself and made for riveting entertainment. Spark, sensing the crowd's ambivalence, took steps to capture its sympathies before they should fall to the enemy.

"If this is indeed some sick joke," he declaimed, "then it's a grievous assault against the very foundations of journalism and an *insult to my viewers,* who turn to this show to get the truth, not snide practical jokes!"

A young woman in the third row was clearly eager to speak. He raced up to her and, asking, "What do *you* think?" handed her his mike.

The woman said it was all very confusing, but she mainly wanted to know if Mr. Parker was married. There were groans from the house, indicating a general consensus that this was not the issue at hand. Tommy smiled sexily, though, and said, no, was she?

Spark, disgusted, reached for his mike, but before he could take it, Millie Pilchard, two seats away, snatched it and began a high-spirited speech.

"I want to say, first, that I'm a great fan of yours, Mr. Chandler!"

"Thanks!" said Spark, encouraged.

"I watch your show every day, and I'm constantly defending it to friends who think it's just trash. But, much as I admire you, I must say I agree completely with your guests. Not your wife, I mean, the rest of them. Just because you're a famous reporter and all doesn't give you the right to harass innocent people just because they couldn't get along with your wife, who seems a *very* difficult girl."

"Somebody else?" said Spark, lunging for his mike.

"I'm not done. If you want to say people are blackmailing each other just because one got some bad reviews, well, I could bring in some of *your* reviews—which I don't agree with; I like your show, don't think it's a bit tasteless—but some of your reviews are *quite* unkind, and no one asks who's blackmailing *you*. Elsa here has been very ill from herbs, you know, and stress, too, I shouldn't wonder, and the last thing her family needed was you accosting them. I watched you in that film, and to this old woman you seemed very rude indeed! If they decided to get back at you by playing a joke, well, it's no more or less than you deserved! Thank you!"

The laughter and applause that greeted this showed beyond question that the pendulum of favor was swinging toward the panel and away from Spark, who was looking increasingly distraught. One could understand his emotions. He had stalked his prey, killed it, trussed it up, and cooked it at length in a high oven, only to have the thing bound off the platter and kick him in the teeth. He was pink with rage, and his efforts at damage control had a manic edge that did not enhance his credibility.

"I want everyone here to know," he shouted, pointing to Millie, "that this woman here happens to be a *close personal friend* of Elsa Champion's!"

"And a good thing we *have* friends, Spark," shouted Elsa, "with people like you around! Thank you very much, Millie. We'll have lunch after the show!"

"Aren't you a dear!" cooed Millie.

Now the crowd was writhing with eagerness to contribute. Spark bounded from one lady to the next, searching frantically for one who'd echo his bitter denunciation of Kitty's high-handed mendacity. No such strong view, however, could be solicited. There was finger wagging, to be sure, from those who found the Champions' method of redressing their injuries extreme, but even these philosophers had to concede they'd been much provoked. One lady was keen to know if Peter really fired Joy because of her "cranky" disposition, and Peter responded with a chivalrous tact no one could have failed to read as a blunt "yes." In response to various spectators' assertions that the new *Estime* was pretty damned dull, Tommy cheerfully averred that transitions were bound to be bumpy and he'd certainly listen to the opinions of *Estime*'s loyal readers.

As Spark navigated madly through the house, calling, "Back me up here!" with increasingly forced humor, I kept my eye on the panel, who, in victory, took care to preserve a pose of good-natured humility. One burning question alone awaited resolution: Now that Kitty had kept her end of the dark bargain struck backstage, when would she claim her prize? I guessed she was waiting until the trend in the discussion presented a suitable springboard for her announcement. Opportunity presented itself in the form of a pert young devotee of the gossip columns.

"My question's for Mr. Champion and Mr. Larkin. How come you two got together on this? 'Cause from what I read in the papers, you guys are always out to get each other."

"Not at all," said Peter.

"We just pretend that," Boyd agreed.

"Yes," said Kitty, "Boyd would never *dream* of doing anything to hurt Peter or Elsa. I mean, God—they're practically family!"

"What?" asked the inquisitor.

"Whoops!" said Kitty, with a daffy smile. She turned two twinkling eyes on Boyd. "Guess I let the cat out of the bag, huh! Whaddaya say we tell the world?"

She took Boyd's hand in hers, leaned forward, and whispered loudly as though every woman in the crowd were her own extra-special girlfriend.

"Boyd and I are engaged!"

The ladies erupted into ahhhs and warm applause at the revelation of this sweet May-December romance. As the cheers and whistles grew, Kitty dragged her touchingly embarrassed fiancé to his feet, and they bowed in acknowledgment. The rest of the panel joined the applause, Elsa and Peter clapping away like bleacher bums after a grand slam, Tommy applauding lightly with a tepid smile, and Joy performing small involuntary hand movements. Even Spark, poor wretch, had no choice but to offer his congratulations and thanks for having sprung the news on his show.

Needless to say, there was no further discussion of scandals or ethics or grievances. Love was the only topic on the dear ladies' minds, and hand after hand shot up as they sought details of this romance kept so long and skillfully under wraps. How had they met? When would the wedding be? What, one romantic wanted to know, made Kitty more special than the many many other beautiful and celebrated women Boyd had dated over the years but who'd failed to capture his bachelor heart? Boyd, obviously shy at being revealed a lovesick old fool, said he thought *that* was clear enough, and this got a big dirty laugh from the ladies.

Kitty, resourceful girl that she was, showed a real flair for improvisation, describing their efforts to conduct their courtship away from the prying eyes of the press. Her girlish air when she spoke of her "Boydy" seemed proof positive of the sincerity of her affections, as was the tender way she teased her man for his shy inability to stop blushing.

Only one further moment of stickiness arose, and that came when Millie, after much indefatigable hand waving, was permitted to speak a second time.

"I was just thinking, you know, what a shame it was that Elsa was so terribly ill during her concert. Now that she's feeling better, perhaps she'll be so kind as to favor us all with a song!"

Elsa's eyes widened in terror, and Claire, Gilbert, and I exchanged horrified looks. The vengeful Mr. Chandler, remembering the concert only too well, endorsed the notion with cruel gusto, calling for a piano from the hall and a hand mike for the star. Elsa demurred, but Spark got the whole place stomping its feet and applauding with a fervor that would brook no refusal.

Elsa stared out, glazed with panic. But as she inspected the faces in the crowd, faces shining with uncomplicated affection and encouragement, the fear left her eyes. She waved for Claire to come down. Claire obliged and, advancing to the stage amid cheers, whispered something into Elsa's ear. Elsa smiled and nodded, and Claire proceeded to the piano. I knew she'd have picked something from Elsa's act and hoped, after all we'd been through, that we'd at least get one of our songs played on the air. But when the intro began, I saw that she'd instead chosen a Gershwin tune that, apart from being easy for Elsa to sing, aptly summarized her sentiments.

She sailed confidently through the arrangement's rubato verse, her voice smoky but steady in pitch, and attacked the refrain with buoyant charm and many a droll look to the panel.

> *You say eether,*
> *And I say eyether.*
> *You say neether*
> *And I say nyether.*
> *Eether! Eyether!*
> *Neether! Nyether!*
> Let's call the whole thing off!

The crowd ate it up. Some rocked in time to the catchy melody or even sang along under their breath. Elsa, noting their approval, grew in volume and confidence, building to a bravura finish.

> *For we know we*
> *Need each other so we*
> *Better call the calling off off!*
> Let's call the whole thing off!

The applause was tumultuous, and there were hoots and shouts of "Bravo!" Elsa received the accolades with a wide, sweet smile, bowing with becoming grace. Spark, who had died and gone to hell, came forward applauding, then informed the audience that, tragic as it was, they'd run out of time. The panel rose, Kitty linking an arm through that of her fiancé. Joy made straight for Spark and began whispering into his ear. We can only guess what endearments passed between them.

The ladies drifted into the aisles, chattering away. What a wonderful show it had been! Wasn't Elsa lovely! Wasn't Joy a pain? How much older did you suppose Boyd was than Kitty? Claire was heading up from the piano, and we pushed our way through the crowd to meet her in the middle, just as the breathless and delighted Millie emerged from her own row.

"Claire, my dear! Wasn't Elsa superb! Philip! You came, too! And who is this? Claire's boyfriend, would it be? I can always tell! You played beautifully, Claire. Now, you two promise you won't forget who it was first introduced you to Elsa!"

"We won't," said Claire.

"Thanks, Millie," I said, kissing her cheek.

"Don't thank me, dears! It's my pleasure. I never pass up a chance to do a good turn!"

As she pumped our hands in farewell, I couldn't help smiling, for I was genuinely glad for her. Banished once from her friend's affections, she had seen her chance, boldly stormed the barricades of Elsa's heart, and broken through. Her lonely exile had ended, and she was returning to the Champions' gilded circle, even as we entered our own more voluntary exile. As we turned and filed out with the rest of the hoi polloi, I could still hear Millie's shrill, primitive joy rising above the babble.

"Elsa, my angel! How marvelous you were! And Kitty and Boyd! So naughty, keeping your secret so long! If you need help with the wedding, I'm *always* here! Peter, love, and Mr. Parker, too! How commanding you all were! How proud I am to know you!"

Epilogue

As you can imagine, Spark did not treasure the thought of that segment being broadcast to an amused nation. Given the option, he'd have seized all the copies, burned them, and hired assassins to hunt down every last dame in the audience.

Spark did, in fact, attempt to suppress the program, saying that to air it would be to dignify the Champions' "gross contempt for freedom of inquiry." He could not, of course, keep secret the segment's combustible contents. His loyal staff was phoning the press before the segment was half-finished and media Furies were stalking the suspects by lunch. Everyone involved, excluding ourselves, supplied lively statements for the six o'clock news, Millie displaying particular eloquence. As news of the segment spread and the clamor to see it grew, Spark's lofty rhetoric rebounded on him. How, commentators queried, was Mr. Chandler defending "freedom of inquiry" by refusing to air what was, in effect, a debate on that very subject? Spark had no answer for this, and a few days later, amid extensive hoopla, the segment was broadcast, breaking the ratings record for its time slot.

We were not, in the weeks that followed, much disposed to contact our former employers, though I suppose our craving for distance was nothing compared to their own profound desire never to lay eyes on us again. Whatever gratitude they might have felt over Claire's bold salvage job was mitigated by their distress over its long-term repercussions and lingering rage over all that preceded it.

However relieved Peter felt to be forever spared exposure—for Boyd could hardly unmask his own sweet bride as a former paid disciplinarian—this did nothing to lessen his umbrage over the harm done both his and his magazine's reputations. Nor would Elsa, despite the warm reviews afforded her TV debut, ever forget her musical crucifixion at the Rainbow Room or who supplied the nails. Less forgiving still were Boyd, whom Claire had given a beard he couldn't shave, and Tommy, whose status as Boyd's sole heir would surely not go unchallenged by Boyd's feisty fiancée.

On the bright side, the war was, for now, at least, over. There would perhaps be future skirmishes, but it was hard to say where the battle lines would be drawn, so bizarrely had the factions become integrated. Boyd was now Elsa's brother-in-law, and Tommy, once devoted to Peter's destruction, was working diligently on Peter's (and his own) behalf as editor of *Estime.*

Uncertain of his future with Boyd and keen to undo the damage to his own reputation, Tommy denounced the June issue as a failed experiment on the road to a new *Estime.* Peter allowed him to stay and try to rebuild the magazine's shattered fortunes. This was partly because reconciliation with Joy was now improbable, but mainly, I believed, to vindicate his having "chosen" Tommy to begin with. Tommy toiled away, and soon the July issue hit the stands. But for a certain focus on newer, hungrier celebrities, and a piece praising a brilliant translator of Russian drama (who was battling suicidal tendencies), the magazine seemed uncannily like the *Estime* of old. And happily for all, Vincent Bronco's new film lost forty million, leading Mr. Caesar to decide that the ongoing boycott on his client's behalf had, perhaps, made its point.

I suppose if any of the old gang had a charitable thought for us, it was Kitty. Things had worked out just dandy for her.

The story of her romance with Boyd enthralled the public, all but eclipsing the controversies over *Estime* and Spark. The press clamored for details, which Kitty supplied as fast as she could invent them, telling Daisy Winters about Boyd's insomnia and the "positively embarrassing" amounts of jewelry he'd given her that she hadn't even had a chance to wear yet. The wedding would be in September; yes, they'd discussed children. That whole summer you could hardly open a magazine without seeing her photo, posed either with Boyd or alone, winsomely ogling her miniature glacier of an engagement ring.

The most remarkable upshot of the whole affair was the sudden change in Kitty's position in life. Boyd was as venerable and respected a son of privilege as the old guard could claim, so Kitty had, like it or lump it, Arrived. Society, in a touching display of loyalty to Boyd, stood by his choice, proclaiming Kitty "delightful." The very best ladies embraced her in their tan, scrawny arms and labored to make smooth her metamorphosis. She now lunched at Mortimer's and Le Cirque. She became active on behalf of the New York Public Library and organized parties for PEN in the Hamptons. She gardened. She was, all seemed to agree, a tad rough at the edges but possessed nonetheless the raw material to make an attractive and suitable wife and, in due season, a simply fantastic widow.

Elsa, buoyed by her reception on Spark's program, stopped living the life of a tormented mollusk and once again sought the spotlight. She played out her aborted engagement at the Rainbow and Stars cabaret, singing a breezy program of up-tempo standards (though none by the team of Cavanaugh and Simmons). The reviews ranged from tactful to rhapsodic, and the houses were booked solid.

As Kitty's new status solidified, Elsa must have felt some strongly conflicting emotions. She cannot, after Kitty's betrayals, have enjoyed watching her rise. Viewed another way, though, Kitty had gone overnight from being a social albatross to a positive asset. There was, however, a hitch: what advantage could Elsa reap from Kitty's ascendance if the two of them remained bitter enemies? Indeed—so Elsa must have conjectured—if relations did not improve swiftly, she might in time find herself playing Millie Pilchard to Kitty's Horsey Kimball, which would make for untold agonies.

And so the lifelong rift was repaired. They began lunching with each other and performing good works together. They proclaimed their mutual affection in many a touching interview. In August *New York* magazine carried a jaunty story about their hectic but happily intertwined lives. I will never forget the shock I felt on first seeing the two of them on the cover, stunningly gowned and coiffed, hand in

hand, jumping girlishly in the air together under a headline reading
SIBLING REVELRY!

The only message we received from our old chums came a week after
the Spark Chandler segment aired. Apparently fearing some leakage
on our part, they sent us each fifteen grand in hush money. When
Claire received her check, she phoned me to cheerfully list the charities to which she planned to donate her windfall. She pointedly asked
what I planned to do with mine, and I paused only briefly before
naming an array of worthy causes badly in need of funds.

It was a painful bit of expiation. I'd squandered the cash I'd already
earned, leaving me with nothing but a lot of books and records and
a closet full of clothes suitable for restaurants I could no longer afford.
Still, after what I'd put Claire through, I knew no less a gesture was
called for. I made the sacrifice willingly, earning Claire's renewed
respect—and Gilbert's lasting incredulity.

The last time we saw them all was at the marriage of Boyd and Kitty,
which was hailed as the society wedding of the decade. We were not
among the invited, but Gilbert insisted we join the gang of gawkers
who crowded the steps of Saint Patrick's Cathedral, hoping to glimpse
Boyd and Kitty Larkin as they emerged into the glow of a radiant
September afternoon. We couldn't get near the steps, so we took up
a position across the street, clambering onto the statue of Atlas to be
able to see over people's heads.

After some minutes the doors were flung open and a phalanx of
photographers and cameramen emerged, walking backward, snapping
away, just as they'd been doing the first moment we laid eyes on Elsa.
Cheers and oohs issued from the crowd as the spherical old gnome
in his morning suit and arctic smile emerged into the sunlight with
that splendid amazon in white lace clutching his little arm. Behind
them came the families, including the best man, Tommy, the bride's
teary sister, and her brother-in-law, all gorgeously attired. They waved
magnanimously to the cheering peons as they descended the steps
toward the waiting cars.

Gilbert reached into his pocket and pulled out something yellow
and lumpy in a plastic bag. He opened the bag, and our nostrils were

assaulted by what smelled like Gorgonzola, kept at length un-refrigerated.

"You can't!" said Claire, instantly gleaning his intent.

"Why not?" said Gilbert, asking if she supposed that all things considered, they'd dare press charges.

Claire thought about it a moment.

"Go for his hat," she advised.

Gilbert, using the plastic bag as a glove, leaned back and with a skill that argued weeks of practice, sent the gob of cheese sailing across the street in a graceful arc that ended at the base of Peter Champion's hat—or at any rate would have, had he not lifted the topper at that instant in a jaunty pose for the cameras. The cheese plopped onto the center of his head and did not bounce off but remained there, ensnared.

"It's all the hairspray," opined Gilbert.

The crowd gasped and began babbling in alarm while looking around for the culprits. We'd already jumped off the statue and were now walking downtown very quickly. We turned west and broke into a trot, running past Rockefeller Center and the Rainbow Room, over to Broadway, and from there, by subway, to the Upper West Side.